Kiss

OF THE
SPINDLE

Other Proper Romance Novels

Nancy Campbell Allen
My Fair Gentleman
Beauty and the Clockwork Beast
The Secret of the India Orchid

Julianne Donaldson
Edenbrooke
Blackmoore
Heir to Edenbrooke (eBook only)

Sarah M. Eden
Longing for Home
Longing for Home, vol. 2: Hope Springs
The Sheriffs of Savage Wells
Ashes on the Moor

Josi S. Kilpack
A Heart Revealed
Lord Fenton's Folly
Forever and Forever
A Lady's Favor (eBook only)
The Lady of the Lakes
The Vicar's Daughter
All That Makes Life Bright
Miss Wilton's Waltz

Becca Wilhite
Check Me Out

Julie Wright
Lies Jane Austen Told Me

Kiss
OF THE
SPINDLE

NANCY CAMPBELL ALLEN

SHADOW
MOUNTAIN

For Karin, Julie, Craig, and Syd
How wonderful it is when siblings are also the best of friends

Library of Congress Cataloging-in-Publication Data
Names: Allen, Nancy Campbell, 1969– author.
Title: Kiss of the spindle / Nancy Campbell Allen.
Description: Salt Lake City, Utah : Shadow Mountain, [2018]
Identifiers: LCCN 2017040903 | ISBN 9781629724140 (paperbound)
Subjects: LCSH: Jamaica, setting. | LCGFT: Paranormal fiction. | Fantasy fiction.
  | Novels.
Classification: LCC PS3551.L39644 K57 2018 | DDC 813/.54—dc23
LC record available at https://lccn.loc.gov/2017040903

Printed in the United States of America
PubLitho, Draper, Utah

10   9   8   7   6   5   4   3   2   1

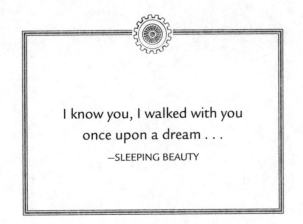

I know you, I walked with you
once upon a dream . . .
—SLEEPING BEAUTY

Chapter 1

Isla Elizabeth Cooper extended her hand toward the airship ticket agent. "If you don't have any flights leaving for the Caribbean immediately, return my passport and I'll find another way."

The young man, obviously new at the position, scrunched up his eyes. "I doubt you'll find a flight with another company. Pickett is the only line that circumnavigates consistently, and—"

"Yes, which is why I am here." Isla drummed her fingers on the tabletop, considering possible options. "Do you have flights leaving for New Orleans?"

"In the colonies?"

"In America. They are a country now. Over a century."

"Yes, yes. Messy, that one was." The agent ran his finger down the thick ledger. "New Orleans . . . Orleans . . ." He shook his head. "No, Miss Cooper. None to New Orleans for another six weeks."

Isla exhaled quietly. "Do you have flights going *anywhere* near Port Lucy in the next few days?"

His eyes widened. "Port Lucy, miss? Surely you don't mean to go there!"

Isla held his gaze.

"That is, you're a gentlewoman, and I hear tales coming out of Port Lucy that would shock and horrify you!"

Isla shifted her weight and nudged her coat open, placing a hand on the ray gun at her hip. "I shall be vigilant." Aside from that, she'd done her research. There was nothing shocking or horrifying about Port Lucy, not in the last fifteen years. Pickett Airships needed to educate their employees.

"Oh! Oh, well." He glanced down at her passport, then back up to her face. "You're a Predatory Shifter Counselor?" He further scrutinized the fine print. "You work for Cooper Counseling and Investigations?" The last came out on a squeak. "Is Dr. Cooper your father? Or husband?"

She sighed, unsurprised by his reaction. "*I* am Dr. Cooper." Isla saw the boy's disbelief in his blank stare.

"But . . . Cooper Investigations—they hunt predatory criminals!"

"Yes. We do. I do." She also offered a valuable service to shifters who needed help adjusting to the life. Her reputation as a therapist and animal empath usually preceded her.

Isla retrieved the satchel by her feet. "I am pressed for time, sir."

Still gaping, he gave the documents another long look. "What sort of name is 'Iz-luh'?"

Isla attempted counting to ten, but reached only to five. "It is pronounced 'Eye-luh.'"

His expression cleared. "Oh, yes, rather like 'island,' then."

She twitched her fingers toward her palm. "My passport?"

He returned the documentation. "Terribly sorry to have been unable to meet your needs, Miss Cooper—*Dr.* Cooper. We at Pickett Airships pride ourselves on providing the best service available when using flight to reach your destination, and—"

"Thank you." She turned away before the boy could recite Pickett's list of finer points. The lobby's soaring ceilings and gilded girders amplified conversation and made coherent thought a challenge. She pulled her telescriber from her satchel when she spied her friend, Hazel Hughes, on the far side of the crowded lobby near the exits.

Hazel was the sort of woman who turned heads and didn't realize it. She was the most kindhearted person Isla knew, and had been since childhood. Her natural beauty radiated from within and manifested itself comfortably in her pretty features and curled tresses the color of dark honey.

Pushing her way through the crowd, Isla reached Hazel, and together they exited the building. Isla breathed in the fresh, early autumn air.

"Quite stuffy in there," Hazel said. "What did you learn? Are there available flights to Port Lucy?"

Isla shook her head. "Not for another two months."

Hazel winced. "It could work, but you would be pushing it dangerously close."

Isla stepped aside as a family of seven barreled their way toward the entrance, dragging luggage and looking flushed.

Hazel bit the inside of her cheeks as the door closed behind them. "Probably late for a flight."

"Which is why I never leave pressing matters to the last

minute." Isla looked at Hazel with a mounting sense of panic. "I cannot wait two months."

Hazel looped an arm through Isla's. "I agree. While I am relatively certain you have another three months before the spell becomes permanent, suppose I am the least bit off in that prediction? The sooner you reach Malette, the better."

Isla allowed Hazel to guide her along the path that led to the airfield. "Where are we going?"

"To find Daniel Pickett." Hazel glanced at her. "I know his sister. Perhaps he can be persuaded to take you along on his personal run to Port Lucy."

Isla raised a brow. "We don't know for certain that's where he's headed."

Hazel smiled. "I may have done a discreet bit of eavesdropping in the Pickett offices while you were at the ticket desk. Not only is he headed for the Caribbean, but he has three passengers booked."

Isla felt faint stirrings of hope. She knew exactly why Mr. Pickett sometimes flew noncommercial flights, and with three passengers booked on board, she might be able to sell herself as an asset to the flight. If not, she wasn't above stooping to blackmail.

"This way." Hazel tugged on Isla's arm and pulled her around the ground crews working on docked airships and impatient passengers waiting to board. They crossed the expansive field to Pickett's fleet, which occupied as much acreage as the rest of the airship competition combined.

The air was heavy with the scent of airship fuel, and Isla wrinkled her nose. "How do you know he's already out here?"

"I might have also looked at today's schedule while I eavesdropped." Hazel glanced at her with a shrug.

Isla shook her head, a smile teasing the corner of her lips. Hazel never forgot anything she saw, read, or experienced. Her demeanor was also innocent enough that the unsuspecting would never imagine her capable of subterfuge.

"That one." Hazel pointed at the sleek dirigible docked at the far end. "The *Briar Rose*."

Isla frowned. "He uses his personal craft for trips to the Caribbean?"

"It's been docked for repairs. And from what I gather, Mr. Pickett has been rather in a mood because of it. The employees do not know why, exactly."

Isla knew why, exactly. Daniel Pickett smuggled predatory shifters from England and helped them begin anew in countries that didn't call for the registry and possible execution of their kind. If the ship he normally used to conduct his illegal activities was out of commission, he would be forced to use a contingency plan that might not be as effective. Or as safe.

Much of the Caribbean and pockets of America provided a haven for law-abiding shifters who had made enemies on the Predatory Shifter Regulations Committee. Citizens who had status or could bribe the Committee were left alone. Those who did not were harassed until they "voluntarily" added their names to a national registry and paid a "Predatory Shifter Fee." The fee was extortion, and the Committee denied all charges when questioned. But predatory shifters who wouldn't—or couldn't—pay the fee found themselves or their families harassed, threatened, or arrested on fabricated charges.

The official reason predatory shifters were prevented from leaving the country was because it didn't reflect well on Queen and Country to have British citizen shifters running amok in the world. The unofficial reason was because the Committee lined their own pockets with extortion money and favors. If all their victims left England, their coffers would diminish.

Isla knew of Mr. Pickett's enterprise because her work made her privy to quiet gossip and rumor. She also knew that the man loomed large in many minds, either as an avenging angel or a law-breaking menace. He had a reputation for being imposing, intimidating, and aloof.

As she and Hazel neared the airship, Isla spotted the man himself loading cargo into the hold with three airfield employees.

She had never been formally introduced to Mr. Pickett, having seen him only from afar or in newspaper photos. He was tall, with a thick head of coffee-brown hair. Most ladies found him more than a little alluring, and as Isla watched him move with fluid grace in a captain's greatcoat that strained against his athletic form, she understood the attraction.

"We can't load this one without a lifter, sir. It's too heavy." An employee pointed to a barrel of Stirling Engine fuel.

Isla held Hazel back when her friend continued to move forward. She wanted a moment to study the enigmatic Mr. Pickett.

"Then you should secure a lift, wouldn't you say? And why do we not have one already here at our disposal?"

Mr. Pickett eyed the employee until the man squirmed. "You must be new."

"Yes, sir."

One of the other attendants pulled on the new man's arm. "We'll locate a lifter right away, sir. The airfield is unusually busy tonight, and we weren't able to find one earlier."

Mr. Pickett nodded, and the three employees turned and ran.

Isla frowned. Convincing him to allow her passage might be more difficult than she'd hoped. She glanced at Hazel, who watched Mr. Pickett with brows drawn and her lip caught between her teeth. Her concern clearly mirrored Isla's, and Isla sighed.

She decided to approach him directly and show no fear. As she nudged Hazel forward, however, Mr. Pickett glanced quickly to his left and right, and then grasped the heavy barrel. He hefted it easily onto his shoulder and loaded it into the cargo hold.

Isla's mouth dropped open, and she heard Hazel's quiet gasp. Only automatons possessed such strength. Mr. Pickett reappeared and made quick work loading the remaining barrels and steam trunks into the ship.

He brushed his hands together, and when the three employees returned, one of them driving a lifter, he waved a hand at them. "I secured help from a passing 'ton," he called out. "We won't be needing it now. I do not expect such problems in the future, however."

The employee driving the lifter shook his head. "It will not happen again, sir."

Mr. Pickett checked his pocket watch as the employees secured the ship for departure.

Isla turned to Hazel. "My window of opportunity is closing, and I fear we have no time for proper introductions. Go, and I'll manage this on my own. I'll scribe you once we're airborne."

Hazel frowned. "You're certain?"

Isla looked at the impatient captain who was making his way around the stern of the ship with ground-eating strides. "Yes. I believe the element of surprise may serve best."

She hugged Hazel and kissed her cheek. "Wish me luck."

"Good luck! The best of luck!" Hazel pressed her lips together, her expressive golden eyes suddenly liquid. "Be safe."

Isla nodded, grasped her portmanteau, and with a pounding heart, raced after Daniel Pickett. "Captain," she called, grateful for the relative seclusion behind the ship.

She reached his side, hating that she was slightly breathless and knowing it wasn't because she was winded from the brief run. Isla Cooper faced down dangerous predators on a regular basis. She would not be intimidated by one bad-tempered man.

He turned and frowned, and her breath caught in her throat. Oh, dear. Evidently the photos she'd seen had come criminally far from doing him justice.

"Yes?" he prompted.

She exhaled. "I need to join you on this voyage. Money is no issue; I am prepared to pay twice the usual fare."

"This is not a commercial flight, miss." He turned away, and she grasped his arm. He looked at her in surprise, which turned quickly to incredulity, and then something she decided she'd rather not decipher.

Isla tightened her grip on his bicep, noting the very human feel of the very not-human limb. "I must get to Port Lucy. Immediately."

"There is a commercial flight bound for New Orleans with a connecting ship to Port Lucy in six weeks."

"I do not have six weeks, sir. Furthermore, I am a natural empath and a Doctor of Shifter Therapy and Human Relations."

He stilled. "I do not see the relevance."

"I believe you do."

"What exactly are you implying, Miss . . . ?"

"Dr. Cooper. I am implying that with this particular cargo, you might benefit from my expertise."

He pulled his arm roughly away from her with a scoff. He opened his pocket watch again. "If you'll excuse me, Dr. Cooper, I have an airship to fly."

"Or perhaps Her Majesty's Cyborg Regulations Division would be interested to know that England's most prominent airship mogul is rather more than he appears to be."

He stopped mid-stride, and she swallowed. Her heart thumped, and she wished she were facing a beast with fangs; those she could usually tame.

Mr. Pickett slowly returned. "I do not know what it is you *think* you know, lady, but you can take your threats and—"

"Your arm, likely fusing into your pectoral," Isla said quietly and pointed from his bicep up along his chest. "Most forward, rational thinkers realize such implants have no bearing on one's ability to live a healthy life, run an empire. Government agencies, though, are not always known for rational thinking, are they?"

His jaw clenched and nostrils flared. "Turn around and walk away, Dr. Cooper, and I'll do you the favor of forgetting this conversation occurred."

Isla forced her feet to remain firmly planted. "I assure you, I would not pester you were it not of dire importance. I am desperate—enough that I will resort to tactics usually deemed distasteful."

He stared at her and finally shook his head with his lips twisted in what could only loosely be termed a smile. "Pester," he repeated.

Isla was amazed he couldn't hear her heart thumping. "I must reach Port Lucy immediately, Captain, and I will stay away from your affairs. Should the need arise, I would be happy to help manage your 'cargo.' Otherwise, you needn't lay eyes on me for the voyage's entirety."

"What is it that has you so desperate, I wonder?"

Mercy, did those eyes ever smile? "My concern, none of yours."

"Nor is my business any of yours, and yet you've made it such."

"Unusual circumstances," she muttered, feeling a twinge of conscience.

He folded his arms. "One who is desperate can be coerced, used, even."

She felt her temper stir. "Name your price."

"As it happens, I have no need for a shifter empath of any sort."

"Then I shall owe you a favor. In your line of work, such services may be beneficial."

He affected surprise. "I own an air fleet. My line of work has no overlap with yours."

She smiled. "We both know that to be untrue."

He shook his head and ran a hand through his hair, and she felt the first stirrings of true hope. She may be bound for Port Lucy after all. "I have no spare accommodations other than my first mate's cabin; he is not accompanying this voyage. It is not as large as the passenger suites."

"It is of no consequence to me. If necessary, I would travel in the cargo hold." She fought a shudder.

"What are you running from? Will I find an angry spouse or relative on my heels? An enemy colleague, perhaps?"

"I am running from nothing. I am going *to* something. My actions are my own entirely, and involve nobody else."

He examined her for another long, inscrutable moment, his eye snagging on her hip. "You're holstered."

She moved her coat aside. "A Crowley triple-blast ray gun."

"You'll check that and any other weaponry in my quarters, of course. Unless you are also a certified Air Marshall and permitted to carry."

Count to ten, Isla. "Very well." She hesitated. She never parted with her weapons; her profession demanded safety. What were her options, though? "I am permitted to carry, however, and accustomed to maintaining the tools of my trade, keeping them close at hand. Perhaps after a short time—"

"You blackmail your way onto a voyage and think to

remain heavily armed? While occupying the cabin adjacent mine? I am not a fool, Dr. Cooper." He extended his hand and beckoned with his fingers. "We'll begin with that one. And once we're boarded, I'll search your belongings."

Isla fought back the anger she knew would not serve her. Forcing her hand to do her bidding, she unsnapped her holster and withdrew her ray gun, her eyes locked with his. She slapped the grip in his outstretched hand. and he wrapped his fingers around it.

"Release it."

She drew in a breath, two.

"You may threaten me all you like, Doctor, but my patience stretches only so far. Do not tempt me into dispatching you right now and leaving your body for the attendants to find."

"Threats, Captain?"

He smiled grimly. "Seems to be the order of the day."

Isla released her grip and felt immediately vulnerable. She rarely fired it outside target practice, but she had walked with a weapon at her hip since her early teens.

"After you, Dr. Cooper." Mr. Pickett swept an arm toward the ship. "With any luck, this will be an uneventful voyage."

Chapter 2

D aniel Pickett followed the woman up three flights of stairs from the hull to the main deck, fuming the entire way. He wouldn't truly have killed her, he was relatively certain of that. But his anger roiled, and he knew one wrong word from anyone would push him over the proverbial edge. An ache settled behind his eyes, and he sighed, weary before the voyage had even begun.

The automatons on the main deck readied the ship for departure. All seemed in order, and a quick glance at the glass-encased wheelhouse high on the quarterdeck showed his personal 'ton, Samson, running through the departure checklist. Daniel gestured for the good doctor to follow him. He descended a short companionway and turned left onto the narrow corridor, turning her name over in his mind and wondering why it sounded familiar.

He withdrew his keys. "This is the first mate's cabin. I trust it will suffice."

The woman nodded. She was on the smaller side, not at

all the sort of person he imagined taking down a predatory shifter.

"I am stronger than I look." She offered a half-smile.

She was also astute.

"Why is your first mate not accompanying this voyage?"

"I utilize my personal 'ton on select flights."

"Very sound. A 'ton can be programmed to keep secrets."

Daniel glanced behind them and unlocked the cabin door. He ushered the woman inside with a muttered oath and kicked the door shut. "You are aboard this flight against my wishes, Doctor. I do not want to hear another word about secrets or blackmail or whatever it is you believe you know. Am I clear?"

She studied him evenly, but a muscle worked in her throat as she swallowed. To her credit, she stood her ground. Grown men had backed away from his anger. She was either incredibly foolhardy or extremely confident in her abilities to defend herself. He glanced at her portmanteau and wondered what additional weapons she carried.

"Very clear, Mr. Pickett. My humblest apologies." She spoke softly, the pitch a fraction lower than before.

He took a breath, feeling a sense of calm, which was followed by a quick surge of anger. "I am not a shifter. Do not attempt to control me with your empath skills!"

She raised a brow. "It worked, then? Do you have shifter lineage?"

"No!" He fumed quietly, then said, "Only the one uncle."

She tipped her head. "A thin tie, but possible."

"He's just a fox," he said, dismissing the notion. Another thought struck him, and he felt cold all over. After the war, his friend Dr. Samuel MacInnes had exchanged Daniel's battered left lung for a healthy one from a donor who had died in an accident. A donor who had been a predatory shifter.

Daniel tried to dampen his fears. There was no documentation showing any contamination from a donor to a surgical recipient. Sam had been certain of it. The procedure itself had been conducted under the cover of darkness in Sam's secret lab in his London home. Transplants were legal only with approved medical devices, but Sam had insisted natural tissue was a better alternative, especially if the organ came from a donor deceased less than twelve hours. To that point, Sam had been right; Daniel's body had accepted the lung without issue.

He sought to distract himself and his unwelcome passenger by grabbing the doctor's portmanteau and thumping it down on the tidy built-in bed on the left wall, adjoining his cabin. He motioned brusquely for her to unlock the satchel, which she did with a sideways, assessing glance.

"Please do not read more than is there," Isla said, smiling. "I also am adept at understanding and perceiving human emotion. Often my skills as an animal empath also extend to the . . . human animal, if you will."

He pulled it toward him before she could take anything from it. He felt her glance but ignored it, fighting genuine panic that he may have serious complications because of the lung. As if he didn't have enough to worry about with the 'ton implants Sam had used to rebuild his shredded muscle. Dr. Cooper, curse her, had been correct. His entire left arm and shoulder, plus pectoral and lateral muscles, were genetically engineered from human tissue and metal reserved for 'ton construction. Not illegal, precisely, but socially taboo. Widespread knowledge of his situation could affect his business disastrously.

A quick but thorough examination of Dr. Cooper's portmanteau produced two knives and a smaller version of the ray gun he'd already confiscated. He held the three weapons in one hand while giving the bag a final once-over. "This would be easier if you'd simply produce any additional weapons you might have."

She shook her head, her lips tight. "Those are all. And you're leaving me utterly defenseless."

He raised a single brow. "I should think a natural empath would possess innate survival skills the rest of us do not. Remove your overcoat, if you please."

She opened her mouth but must have thought better of snapping a reply. Instead, she met his eyes while shrugging out of her formfitting greatcoat. She tossed it onto the bed and held her hands out to her sides. He took in her attire, noting the white under-corset blouse and the thin, black leather corset that might contain smaller implements sewn in but he couldn't be certain without a closer examination. Which, he silently admitted, would not be distasteful in the least.

Continued perusal showed black trousers, knee-high boots, and a holster wrapped around one thigh, which she subtly angled away from him.

He smiled and put a hand on her shoulder to pivot her around. "Clever girl." The small knife blended into her clothing—at a distance one might miss seeing it altogether. He reached down, released the small holster snap, and removed the knife. He tested the weight of it in his palm with reluctant admiration; it was small but also substantial and deadly. Much like its owner.

She glared at him; he stood close enough to note the gold flecks in her green irises. A man could lose himself in eyes like that. She radiated an intense energy he couldn't define but felt keenly.

"You've divested me of every means of defense."

He shook his head. "Somehow I doubt that, Dr. Cooper." He crossed to the door, pausing to turn the key in the connecting door between the cabins to show he intended her no ill. "We travel with the sparest of crew, so I cannot provide a personal maid or assistant for you. We do have an efficient 'ton cook, however, and two formal meals per day in the wardroom at the bow, plus tea in your cabin, if you choose."

One of the 'tons on his crew appeared in the doorway, and Daniel frowned. "What takes you away from the Stirling Engine? It's past time for departure."

"Sir, we have an additional passenger aboard."

"Yes, I am aware." He glanced at Dr. Cooper, who had begun refolding articles of clothing.

"No, sir, in addition to this guest."

Daniel's patience wore perilously thin. "We haven't the space, dismiss him."

"He says he is from the Predatory Shifter Regulations Committee and is demanding passage. Mr. Samson instructed me to bring the matter to you."

Dr. Cooper appeared at his side. "Who is it?"

"Mr. Nigel Crowe," the 'ton answered.

Daniel closed his eyes briefly. The day grew worse by the minute.

"Tell him no." Dr. Cooper looked to Daniel, then the 'ton. "You mustn't . . . You cannot . . ."

"I am aware," Daniel ground out. He didn't need his first unwelcome passenger to warn him of the dangers of the second. "Regrettably, however, Mr. Crowe has potentially more blackmail leverage than you do, Doctor."

Her eyes widened, and she visibly paled. "Offer him this cabin if you must, but please allow me a . . . a . . . a storage closet somewhere, or the galley pantry. Anything, anywhere. I must reach Port Lucy, and soon."

Daniel's headache blossomed and settled in comfortably behind his eyes. Occasionally, government officials demanded passage for emergency circumstances, and Daniel often granted those favors. He considered denying Crowe, but Daniel could not afford to make him an enemy. He turned to the 'ton. "The tiny infirmary adjacent the lounge, across from the three other cabins. Inform him that is his only option."

"Yes, sir." The 'ton nodded and left. Daniel glanced at the small arsenal he still held in his hand and turned his attention back to Dr. Cooper. "How are you acquainted with Mr. Crowe?"

Dr. Cooper flushed. "He does not approve of my efforts to distinguish the predatory criminal population from the predatory innocent. He believes in wholesale extermination." She scratched behind her ear. "I may have had an unpleasant encounter with him in the last year. Possibly three or four— dozen."

He exhaled. "Of course you have." He exited the cabin

and turned to his own door in the corridor. Two unwelcome passengers, one who communed on a deep biological level with predatory shifters and another who would like to see all shifters executed. And the *coup de grace*? Daniel smuggled predatory shifters out of England and currently had three aboard.

He locked the doctor's weapons in his office safe and decided that if he were ever granted a wish, it would be to begin this day over and depart immediately for the continent. Alone.

Chapter 3

Isla withdrew from her portmanteau two skirts, another pair of breeches, two blouses, and an additional corset. She shook them out and hung them in the small wardrobe, chewing on her lip and deciding that if she were the weepy type, now might be a good time for it. Tears were useless, however, and she'd realized as a child that when she encountered problems, finding solutions was entirely her own responsibility. She'd yet to experience a situation where crying helped.

Nigel Crowe. What on earth were the odds he would demand passage on this particular flight? She rifled through her underthings in the portmanteau to feel for the ridge of the false bottom. Underneath were two additional knives and a pack of throwing stars, a few extra rounds of Tesla chargers for the ray gun, and a packet of herbs that could stun a large opponent. She'd lied to the captain about not having more weapons, but desperate times and all that. Now that Nigel Crowe was going to be within shouting distance for the next three weeks, she wanted to be doubly certain she had access to her defenses.

She withdrew a leather-bound book and pen from the bag and sat at the small desk next to the bed. She checked off several items on the list she'd made earlier in the week and breathed a sigh of relief when she heard the engines fire up. The sooner the ship left England, the closer she would be to finding a cure for the botanical curse that had plagued her for ten long months. Captain Pickett hadn't realized the boon he was handing to Isla when he offered the use of this private cabin. The curse made her vulnerable, and if she were forced to bunk among other people . . . She'd been willing to take the chance, but hadn't realized until now how much the danger had weighed on her mind.

She turned to a fresh page in her notebook and started a new list, titled *Curing the Curse*. She could just as easily have called it *Fixing the Mess Melody Made* or *Ten Reasons Why Melody Is the World's Worst Sister*.

Thoughts of her younger sister lodged a familiar pit in her stomach, and Isla wondered how Melody would possibly avoid trouble without Isla to keep her well in hand. She amended her thinking; trying to control Melody at this point in the seventeen-year-old's life had led to nothing but trouble. Trouble that even now found her aboard an airship bound for the Caribbean with a hostile captain, an enemy from the PSRC, and a trio of predatory shifters. Of the three dangers, she feared the shifters the least.

1. Obtain passage to Port Lucy.

She began with this item so she would have something already accomplished she could cross off.

2. Locate Malette.

3. Bribe Malette for a cure. Blackmail, if necessary.

This did Isla little good because she had nothing to hold over the Dark Magick witch's head. She frowned at her list.

4. Threaten Malette with bodily harm if she refuses to help.

5. Avoid Nigel Crowe like the plague. Which he probably has.

She smirked.

6. Enact the cure.

She didn't know how long this step would take, or even what the cure would entail. She would have to content herself with leaving item number six open-ended in terms of a deadline.

7. Return to England before the Autumn Festival, where Melody will surely wreak havoc upon all and sundry, most especially upon herself.

Some things would not change. She would always feel responsible for Melody, and Melody would always resent it. Isla set down her pen and closed her eyes, rubbing her temples. She considered telescribing their mother with the reasons for her sudden departure to the tropics, but quickly dismissed it. Bella Castle Cooper and her sister, Hester Castle O'Shea, had a successful dress shop in Mayfair that consumed their every waking thought. Isla had grown too accustomed to the situation to begrudge it.

Bella and Hester had put their skills to good use when Bella's husband had left her a widow with two young daughters, and she and her sister had not only survived, but flourished. Everybody who was *anybody* shopped at Castles' Boutique, and some even dressed their 'tons in Castles' creations.

The boutique had provided a comfortable living for Isla and Melody, and also Hester's children, cousins whom Isla had found informally under her charge while the women created a small empire. It wasn't old money, but it was substantial money, and it had provided every educational opportunity Isla had desired. Her mother had even fronted the money for Cooper Counseling and Investigations, a business Isla had been unable to begin on her own for lack of capital. Bella was an unconventional mother, emotionally flighty perhaps, but she loved her daughters in her way. Regrettably, when Melody had run amok this past year, Isla found herself parenting a teenager who most definitely did not desire parenting.

Isla reviewed her list and wished she had a more detailed, useful plan to follow. There were too many variables and that made her uneasy. Perhaps she wouldn't mind so much if her entire future—professional and personal—wasn't at stake.

Daniel stood in the wheelhouse with Samson, relieved that all seemed in working order, but he still felt edgy. Smuggling missions were never carefree, but he usually had use of the bigger ship, which had been specifically designed for the purpose. With this voyage, he had been forced to improvise and it didn't sit well.

"You are uneasy, Captain." Samson glanced at Daniel. "Your body temperature has risen, and your heart rate is substantially elevated."

"You sound like a grandmother, Samson. Remind me to reprogram you at the earliest possible convenience." Daniel glanced at the control panel at the helm and checked the figures the 'ton had logged once the ship had reached altitude. "No problems with the instrumentation, then?"

"None thus far, sir, other than the wall clock I recalibrated to Greenwich Mean before liftoff. And please dispense with further thoughts of reprogramming me."

Daniel smiled. He had personally seen to Samson's design and functionality. The 'ton could easily pass for a handsome human male in his early thirties, distinguishable only by the fact that he never blinked. His design was the finest and most progressive the programming community had to offer. Samson was adept at countless tasks and calculations, his brain held volumes of information on a stunning array of subjects, and his personality was pleasant and comfortable; he was even adept at subtle humor. Daniel had mused on more than one occasion that these days his best friend was a machine. It spoke volumes about the complicated stage of his life.

"I am uneasy, Samson," Daniel admitted. "I do not like unexpected events on runs such as these."

Samson nodded and flipped a switch that set the Stirling Engine heating mechanism into motion. That, in turn, engaged the mechanism that drove power to the airship's two enormous propellers. The huge black balloon above the ship was sleek and expertly constructed, and proudly bore the large *P* and *A* of the Pickett Airship logo that had become Daniel's easily recognizable brand.

His fleet was head and shoulders above the competition in both style and function, sophistication and comfort. Daniel made it his business to stay abreast of modern discoveries in the scientific community that could be applied to his air-bound empire. He had been the first to convert to exclusive use of Stirling Engines, which required only oil as a heat source; many of his competitors were still obliged to carry enormous amounts of coal and water. His adaptation of the Stirling freed up much needed space, not to mention lightened the entire load.

The airship's body resembled a sailing ship, exquisitely and tastefully appointed in dark woods and full sails, which were largely ornamental but utilized at high altitudes as wind shields. The *Briar Rose* was Daniel's personal craft, and he supposed some of the disquiet he felt stemmed from that fact. Its purpose was pleasure, which Daniel rarely mixed with business.

"Have you spoken with Mr. Crowe, Captain?" Samson glanced at Daniel, eyebrows raised in question, vocal inflections so effective that Daniel had to remind himself the 'ton wasn't actually human.

"No." He rubbed the back of his neck. "I'm avoiding it as long as I can."

"Better to be proactive, sir, is it not?"

"Definitely in need of reprogramming. You're entirely too helpful."

"And what of Dr. Cooper? Do you anticipate a pleasant voyage where she is concerned?"

Daniel sighed. "I do not know. What can you tell me about her?"

Samson paused, and Daniel heard the subtle whir of well-oiled cogs and gears in the 'ton's brain unit.

"Dr. Isla Elizabeth Cooper, eldest of two children. Father, Edmund Cooper, died when she was ten years. Mother is Bella Castle Cooper, founder of Castles' Boutique with her sister, Hester Castle O'Shea. Shall I continue?"

"Please. I could have gleaned that much on my own."

Samson shot him a sidelong glance, but resumed his recitation. "Dr. Cooper finished her primary degree in Shifter Studies in two years rather than the customary four, aided by her natural abilities as an empath. She then earned an advanced degree in Shifter Behavior and Physiology and became a Doctor of Shifter Therapy, Rehabilitation, and Human Relations."

Daniel blinked. "How old is the woman?"

"Twenty-five." Samson tipped his head in afterthought. "Twenty-six in two weeks, coincidentally. She founded Cooper Counseling and Investigations two years ago and acts as a government consultant on Shifter Affairs."

Ah. That was why her name was familiar. Cooper Counseling and Investigations had an excellent reputation. It was also the only organization of its kind. To define Dr. Cooper as "busy" was an understatement. What on earth would take the woman so far away from home and under such desperate circumstances? He couldn't deny a lingering sense of irritation at the way she'd secured her passage but had to admit reluctant admiration for her resourcefulness.

Samson engaged the propellers, and the ship glided through the early evening sky. A single horn sounded throughout the ship's communication system, signaling the dinner hour.

"I suppose you have no choice now but to speak with Mr. Crowe." Samson smiled at Daniel in sympathy. "Do remember to keep your temper, Captain. I know how little patience you have for anyone on the Predatory Shifter Regulations Committee."

"Very sage advice, my friend. Alert me at once to any concerns. Your charge is still adequate?"

Samson nodded. "I will need to connect at one a.m."

"Very good. I'll relieve you then." Daniel clapped Samson on the shoulder and exited the wheelhouse.

Chapter 4

Daniel changed into a fresh shirt for dinner, dreading having to break bread with Nigel Crowe. He couldn't imagine a more inconvenient complication for this flight than that man's presence. Daniel rolled his shoulders, which were stiff with tension.

He had always defended those who were unable to defend themselves. As a child, it had been simple; children were often cruel to one another, and he was always the biggest of the lot. He had naively assumed people would learn how to be decent by adulthood. Disillusionment had found him swiftly, enhanced by his military time in India. He was more jaded now than he cared to admit.

He shrugged into a jacket and left his cabin just as Dr. Cooper was locking her door. She had freshened up as well, he noted involuntarily with a masculine nod of approval. She wore a crisp blouse with short sleeves that showed the muscle definition in her arms, a trait not necessarily considered attractive by polite society but it held appeal for him. It meant she worked hard, didn't wait to be served or pampered.

Atop the blouse was a tight-fitting corset, and she'd changed from breeches to a long, burgundy-hued skirt. She held a light jacket over her arm, and her hair was arranged in curls, twisted and fastened at her crown and ornamented with combs edged in small white pearls that stood out against her dark hair. Her eyes seemed a deeper green in the dim light of the passageway, and he swallowed, fighting the urge to loosen his necktie.

"You'll want the coat," he said, motioning to her arm. "It gets cold, even with the sails unfurled as windbreaks."

Dr. Cooper nodded and threaded one arm through the sleeve as she walked down the narrow corridor. He fell into step beside her, wondering if he should have offered to hold the coat for her but she hadn't given him time to. He settled for holding the other sleeve when she fumbled twice to get her hand through it. His mother had raised a gentleman, after all.

"Thank you." She lifted a curl from beneath her collar and gave him a guarded smile. He couldn't blame her reticence. He'd completely disarmed her and stored her weapons in his cabin after impressing upon her his displeasure at her presence on the voyage. But who could blame him? His passengers' safety was paramount, and this was not a typical commercial flight. It would be a sad state of affairs indeed if the men under his care came to harm before he delivered them to Port Lucy, where they at least stood a chance of building a future free from harassment.

Daniel guided Isla up the companionway leading to the main deck and across to the wardroom at the bow. As they reached the doors, she said, "Captain Pickett, thank you again for accommodating me. I do not customarily resort to distasteful tactics to further my own needs. I hope you can forgive the insult."

"I can." He managed a half-smile, which was a far cry from the charm and genuine levity he'd possessed before the war. It was better than nothing, he supposed.

"Thank you. So you'll return my weapons?"

"No." His lips twitched at her angry, indrawn breath. "I still know little to nothing of your character, Dr. Cooper, and the cabin you're using is the only one in proximity to my own."

Her nostrils flared.

He lifted a brow. "Do you retract your apology?"

"I'm considering it."

He opened the door and gallantly gestured for her to enter first. Her lips tightened, but she refrained from further comment, and he followed her into the dining salon.

"Captain." Nigel Crowe stood near the entrance, and Daniel fought to keep his smile in place. Crowe was as tall as Daniel, clean-cut, with short black hair and dark brown eyes. His strong features were striking, but he was cold. He was rumored to be of Romanian descent, but nobody knew much of his origins before he'd arrived in London and found a place on the Committee.

"And Miss Cooper." Crowe's dark eyes narrowed slightly. "What brings you on this flight, I wonder?"

Daniel tensed, cursing inwardly. Of course Crowe would assume the doctor flew with them in her professional capacity as a Shifter Empath. If the man were trying to catch Daniel in the act of smuggling, her presence would only add fuel to his suspicions. Daniel considered retracting his acceptance of her apology.

"Mr. Crowe." Dr. Cooper nodded once but did not smile. "How wonderful to see you again, and how unsurprising, considering the frequency with which our paths have crossed in recent months."

"Mmm. I was just introducing myself to our fellow passengers." Crowe motioned to the three other men in the room, all of whom eyed Crowe with expressions that varied from wariness to fear.

Daniel angled toward Isla. "Dr. Cooper, as you are clearly acquainted with Mr. Crowe, allow me to introduce Mr. Arnold Quince, Mr. Jacob Bonadea, and Mr. Adam Lewis."

Dr. Cooper extended her hand to each of the three gentlemen, a genuine smile crossing her face. "A pleasure."

The gentlemen expressed a measure of surprise and said that they recognized her name. The doctor's good reputation preceded her, it seemed, and though Daniel prided himself on being aware of all players in town, he realized that perhaps he was ridiculously out of touch. He was the only man aboard who hadn't known she was the power behind Cooper Investigations.

"Now, then." Daniel rubbed his hands together. "As there are so few of us on this trip, our mealtimes will be scheduled but otherwise we do not observe convention as closely. Please, take a seat at the table as you will."

He hadn't expected anyone to take the seat at the table's head, and he'd been correct. It was typically the captain's chair, and not only was he most comfortable there, but it also provided him with a good perspective to observe his passengers as they interacted.

Dr. Cooper skirted around Nigel Crowe, who observed her with an unreadable expression. She sat at Daniel's right, and he imagined she probably couldn't decide whom she was angriest with—Daniel, for refusing to return her weapons, or Crowe, for being underfoot. She glanced at Daniel, and a muscle worked in her jaw. She snapped her napkin open on her lap as Mr. Lewis claimed the seat next to her while Mr. Quince and Mr. Bonadea settled across the table.

Crowe took the seat at the foot of the table in Daniel's direct line of sight, a visual reminder that the voyage was certain to be hell. If Crowe were a bumbling fool, as was Bryce Randolph, Crowe's superior, he would be manageable. But Crowe was, if anything, too observant. He missed nothing.

Daniel signaled the two 'ton attendants to serve the first course and breathed a sigh of relief when Arnold Quince struck up conversation with the doctor.

"I find myself a mite awestruck, Dr. Cooper. I've heard of your accomplishments, and it is an honor to meet you."

"Oh, Mr. Quince, how kind of you to say." Her face softened with a smile.

Quince beamed in return, and Daniel was glad. Whatever he might think of the doctor's underhandedness, she was gracious to those who needed it, and as an empath, she certainly would have sensed it in Mr. Quince.

Quince was a widowed father of five and grandfather of twelve. He had spent a career in the study of obscure botanicals and on occasion consulted for the Botanical Aid Society of which Daniel's sister, Lucy, was a part. She'd spoken of the mature gentleman in glowing terms, and when she learned the PSRC had targeted Quince for closer study, she'd mentioned it to her husband, Miles Blake, Earl of Blackwell. Miles was one of three people in Daniel's close circle of friends who knew of his subversive activities. He'd told Daniel about Quince's predicament and arranged for them to meet.

If Miles hadn't told him, Daniel would never have believed Quince was a predatory wolf at night when the moon was full.

"How is it you have heard of Miss Cooper, Mr. Quince?" Crowe asked the question innocently enough, but Daniel felt a fissure of unease and no small amount of anger. "I wonder why she would be known to a botanist." Crowe smiled, but it came nowhere near his eyes.

Quince looked at Nigel Crowe as might a deer caught in a snare. He opened his mouth but closed it again, and to Daniel's relief, Jacob Bonadea filled the awkward silence.

"Who *hasn't* heard of Dr. Cooper? She is something of a legend. A *doctor* at such a young age, and doing wonderful work for a populace often misunderstood. I have four young daughters, and they will be delighted to hear I've met you in person. I have hopes they might follow in your footsteps."

She tilted her head and a light flush stained her cheeks. "My thanks for the compliment, sir. I enjoy what I do—why, it rarely feels like 'work.' To find respect among colleagues and peers, well, I am honored."

"'Doctor' is misleading, however, is it not?" Crowe speared a piece of salmon with his fork. "After all, you are not an actual doctor."

The silence was uncomfortably heavy.

Adam Lewis, a medic Daniel and his friends had known during their time spent at war in India, was the only one of the three shifter passengers who actually looked as though he might be predatory. He was broad through the arms and shoulders, fit, muscled, and handsome as well. His size alone intimidated on occasion, but he also possessed piercing blue eyes that were the one physical constant when he shifted into a wolf. They were intense, and he now turned their full attention to Crowe.

"I fear I do not understand, Mr. Crowe."

Crowe raised a single brow. "A doctor works in a hospital, or in battlefield surgery. With medicine. What Miss Cooper does involves calming wild animals and helping them express their feelings. Any mother worth her salt ought to be able to accomplish that."

Lewis smiled. "It happens that I do work in a hospital, Mr. Crowe, and with professionals like Dr. Cooper daily. I'm certain I must have misunderstood any implied slight on your part, especially as I've witnessed firsthand the work of a trained empath. I do not know your mother, sir, but my own is not at all effective in soothing an agitated toddler let alone a predatory shifter in need of help."

Daniel watched the scene play out before him, resigned. Perhaps they might experience bloodshed before the New Moon Phase after all. It seemed the good doctor had her champions. How surprised might they be if they knew the arsenal she usually carried.

"Of course." Crowe smiled, eyes narrowed. "Certainly no slight intended. I do wonder, though, how it is you all seem to know a person whose occupation is devoted solely to the care, rehabilitation, or in extreme cases, capture of predatory shifters."

Lewis quirked a brow and returned to his meal. "Everyone of import in London's professional circles knows of Dr. Cooper's expertise and successes. I confess I find it rather a surprise *you* seem to know her, Mr. Crowe."

Daniel silently applauded his friend. He'd forgotten Lewis's smooth approach. He was a master of the subtle insult, and if that should fail in silencing a foe, a well-placed throat punch proved effective.

Crowe smiled. "Oh, Miss Cooper and I have been acquainted for some time. I fear we have found ourselves on opposite sides of a recurring issue over the last several months." He took another bite of his salmon. "But I do enjoy a healthy debate."

Mr. Quince cleared his throat and nodded to Dr. Cooper. "At any rate, dear lady, it is an honor to make your acquaintance. If I might be so bold, what is the purpose for your visit to the islands?"

"Research. I hope to study the habits of shifters in differing environs."

Daniel highly doubted that. What kind of research project would have her in mortal fear of missing an immediate flight? Still, she was hardly the only person at the table with secrets. The one soul among them who seemed transparent was the man at the foot of the table who worked for the government and delighted in seeing predatory shifters arrested, tried, and executed, usually for the flimsiest of reasons or under fabricated charges. Crowe made no excuses for his career. Everybody else had something to hide.

Daniel's appetite was sparse, and he noted that Dr. Cooper was doing little more than cleverly cutting her food and moving it around on her plate. In fact, the only two people at the table who seemed to have appetites were Nigel Crowe and Adam Lewis, the former oblivious to—or perhaps reveling in—the discomfort he'd caused and the latter confident enough in his ability to beat an adversary to a pulp that little seemed to bother him.

"Might I assume you gentlemen also travel to the islands for research purposes?" The doctor kept her tone light, but Daniel spied her clutching the napkin in her lap.

Bonadea nodded. "Mr. Quince and I are working on a project for the Botanical Aid Society. My specialty is indigenous fauna on the outskirts of London, and Arnold and I have had occasion to work together before on various projects. Mr. Lewis was telling us before dinner that he intends to work at Port Lucy's new hospital."

"Excellent! A new hospital will surely benefit from your experience, Mr. Lewis." Dr. Cooper smiled at Lewis, and Daniel smirked, turning his attention to his plate rather than give into the temptation to wink at his friend. Lewis turned heads wherever he went, and while Dr. Cooper's enthusiasm was probably nothing more than professional, Daniel would wager that Dr. Cooper would find herself smitten with Adam Lewis by the time they reached Port Lucy.

Daniel's only goal was to actually *reach* Port Lucy without harm coming to his passengers, either of their own unintended actions or because of the man who sat at the table examining them with unconcealed speculation. Crowe probably knew—or strongly suspected—that Quince, Bonadea, and

Lewis were predatory shifters, just as he probably knew—or strongly suspected—that Daniel had been smuggling undocumented shifters out of the country. That Dr. Cooper, an obviously well-known predatory shifter empath and counselor, was also aboard suggested her purpose was to act as support if the need should arise.

Discovery meant professional ruin at best, imprisonment at worst.

Of all the flights for Dr. Isla Cooper to bully her way onto, why this one?

Chapter 5

Isla had never wanted to inflict bodily harm upon a person as much as she wished she could on Nigel Crowe. In her current state, she figured she could comfortably flick a throwing star dead center in his forehead without batting an eye. He was underhanded and insulting. Isla had never met a man with such a handsome exterior who possessed such an icy interior. Worse, he was nearly impossible for her to read, which was unusual.

She had battled him on multiple occasions right in his very offices where he worked under Bryce Randolph, an odious and self-serving man. Her most contentious confrontation to date with Crowe had occurred six months previously when he had ordered the immediate arrest of a man she'd been counseling. Her client was a good man with a wife and seven children, but he had been caught too late in the city after midnight on a full moon and was responsible for some minor destruction of property. Isla had used every ounce of reasoning, knowledge, charm, and finesse she possessed, but to no avail. She had never forgiven Nigel Crowe, the force behind the arrest, and she'd vowed to find the chink in his armor, some bit of evidence that would overturn the harsh sentence placed on a man with poor judgment but no intended violence or destruction.

Mr. Lewis, on the other hand, was quite a dashing hero, and she appreciated his defense of her at the meal's beginning, when Crowe had wasted little time in finding his way to his personal store of familiar insults. A woman could certainly do worse than spend a dinner being defended by a handsome medic.

Her protective instincts had surged immediately to the surface upon meeting the three men and realizing that Nigel Crowe's presence aboard the flight was no coincidence. The man didn't need to visit Port Lucy; he sought to catch one or all three of the shifters in the act. Mr. Quince, especially, engendered a soft spot in Isla's heart. He was a gentle grandfather, for heaven's sake, forced from his home because threats had been leveled against either him or his family.

The meal wound to a close, mercifully, and although Mr. Bonadea politely invited her to join them for port and cigars, she cited fatigue and made her excuses for the evening. She also politely declined Captain Pickett's offer of escort back to her quarters, insisting he remain with the other passengers. "I've asked enough of you already," she told him. "I'll not be responsible for your dereliction of duty."

He bowed lightly and replied, "Your wish, madam. We shall see you in the morning then at breakfast. It is prepared by half past five, however the 'tons keep it warmed for those who sleep later."

Isla bid the gentlemen good evening and crossed the

outer top deck, drawing her jacket tight, and muttering. "Wish I could be up at half past five." Thanks to Melody, Isla, who usually awoke refreshed and energetic at five every morning was no longer able to do so. Six was now the earliest she could manage, and she arose feeling like death.

She ventured close to the side and peeked around the sail windscreens, holding her breath at the stiff gust of wind that caught her face as she squinted to see the world below. They were well away from England, and the ocean stretched out eternally, dark and mysterious. She'd never been on the other side of the Atlantic, and now that she had time to think, she found it intimidating. She'd been so worried about finding passage to get to Malette that she hadn't really considered how far from home, from everything and everyone familiar, she was going to be.

The huge propeller on the ship's side sliced through the air with a comforting, if loud, rhythm, and she looked overhead at the enormous balloon attached to the ship with cables as thick as her arm. She grew dizzy and steadied herself against the bulwark. The airship was a scientific marvel, truly magnificent, and although she'd flown plenty of times in her life, she'd never taken time to be still and appreciate the sheer size and power of the vessel.

She sighed and rotated her head, stretching her neck and massaging her knotted muscles with fingertips that were numb with cold. Had it only been forty-eight hours since Hazel had told her Malette's curse might become permanent? Since then, her sole purpose had been to find the witch. And when she'd learned that Malette was in the Caribbean, she'd felt a panic like no other. All things considered, she was better off on this flight than a larger, commercial one. Other than Nigel Crowe's insidious presence, there were far fewer people to interfere, to ask questions. She would be safer at night while she slept.

Isla made her way to the first mate's cabin and switched on a small Tesla lamp before shutting the door and locking it. She readied for bed, but felt restless. She withdrew her diary and pen and sat at the small table near the bed.

>*Captain Pickett: irascible, impatient, arrogant*
>*Adam Lewis: pleasant, well-mannered, charming*
>*Arnold Quince: gentle, kindhearted, patient*
>*Jacob Bonadea: intelligent, professional, genial*
>*Nigel Crowe: spawn of the underworld*

She supposed that last bit was unfair, but she'd never met anyone with such a strong dislike for shifters. She suspected some of his vitriol stemmed from fear, from not understanding that the majority of predatory shifters were no danger to the human population. Scientific studies showed clearly and repeatedly that the temperament of the animal reflected that of the human. If a man were not a murderer as a human, he would not be so as a wolf, either. Instinct remained when a person shifted, however, so proper containment or arrangements were necessities for those who lived with families or in densely populated areas.

Unfortunately, many shifters had limited options, so unintentional destruction of property or general mayhem were often incidental consequences of their poverty and lack of resources. Some shifters self-medicated with illegal botanical aids, but that often led to painful addictions or even death.

Isla sighed and snapped shut her diary. She tossed it inside her portmanteau and pulled out a book she'd bought the day before. A colleague had developed a new treatment, a hypnosis that could affect the shifter's behavior even while in animal form during the full moon. The implications were tremendous. If a shifter's human brain could exert control over the animal's instincts, many of the population's current problems could be mitigated.

She secured the lamp into a docking station on the nightstand next to the bed and settled under the covers.

This will be the night. I will read and lose myself in the book, and it will keep me awake half the night. I'll be tired tomorrow, but happy, because I will have stayed awake . . .

If only . . .

Every night she hoped for the same thing, and every morning she realized the curse was still in place. With a sigh, she cracked open her new book and burrowed down, intending to read the whole night through. After a few fits and starts, and rereading the same two paragraphs repeatedly, she finally quieted her mind enough to focus. Time slipped by, and she was nearly halfway through the book when she yawned and rubbed her eyes.

She retrieved her pocket watch from under her pillow where she kept it next to a small dagger. Five minutes until midnight. She swallowed her disappointment. She'd hoped more time had passed. In five minutes, she would lose consciousness, her heartrate and breathing would slow dramatically, and she would remain in that state, entirely un-revivable, until six in the morning.

She was going to have to accept that Hazel's research had been sound, that the spell would not reverse on its own. Isla would never be free of it without a cure from the witch who had cast it, no matter how much she willed it. Night after night, for ten long months, she'd tried to keep her eyes open past the stroke of twelve, but to no avail.

She huffed out a frustrated breath and closed the book. She replaced the pocket watch and turned down the lamp, but not entirely. The remaining minutes ticked by, and she felt herself slipping into that deep, dark place of nothingness. A place that was void of *anything*. A place where even night-mares might have been a comfort.

Her limbs grew heavy, her chest rising and falling in its own rhythm that she was powerless to control, and she fell noiselessly into the abyss, her last conscious thought a sound-less protest of frustration and fear.

Chapter 6

L ight pierced like a blade through Isla's still-closed eyes all the way to the back of her skull. She groaned and turned her face into the bed, the familiar lethargy clinging to her as she clawed her way to the surface. This was perhaps the most disconcerting part of it all. Morning had always been her favorite, her most productive, time of day. As her career had demanded it, she'd adjusted to staying alert throughout the night, but her natural biological rhythms favored the sunrise. How she missed the feeling!

She cursed Melody with the same long litany of muttered insults that she did every morning; it had somehow become her routine, and she didn't feel complete without it. "Die a thousand hideous deaths . . . I should stretch you out on a rack . . . Marry you off to a doddering old man . . ." She thrust the covers aside and rolled out of bed. The ship pitching beneath her feet made her more disoriented than usual. They must be flying through turbulent air, and she decided the blame for that could also be laid at Melody's feet.

Isla closed her eyes and took several deep breaths,

blowing out slowly as her heart picked up speed, and she felt the tingling of increased blood flow in her extremities. She shook out her hands and looked to be sure they'd regained their proper color. To her dismay initially, atop every other indignity that accompanied the curse, her skin was tinged a light blue when she awoke each morning. She'd sworn to kill Melody if word spread—even among family—that Dr. Isla Cooper was nearly dead every night, so she'd had a bear of a time explaining her appearance when her cousin Emmeline stopped by early one morning.

Emme routinely organized marches against the PSRC in protest of the registry and their harassment of the shifter community, and that morning, she had a handful of advertisements for Isla and Melody to distribute.

"You're blue," she had stated.

"I'm cold," had been Isla's response, and Emme had studied her, brows drawn. Isla was rarely cold.

She stomped her feet now, and, as the ship lifted in altitude, she stumbled against the bulkhead with a loud thud and winced. She added a bruised shoulder to her list of complaints against her sister. "Definitely marrying you off to a doddering old man, who has no teeth and foul breath." She yanked open the wardrobe and was pulling out fresh clothing when a knock sounded on the connecting door.

"Wonderful," she muttered. "Yes?" she called and looked down at her hands. She frowned and shook them again.

"I heard a noise—did you fall?" Captain Pickett's deep voice sounded through the door.

"I am fine."

There was a pause. "Not much of a morning person, then?"

She sighed silently. "No. Never have been."

"I did mention breakfast is kept on warmers, so you needn't be up so soon."

There was no way in blazes Isla would sleep one moment longer than necessary. "I hate to waste the day."

Another pause. "We are aboard a ship, and you're a paying passenger." She thought she heard a smirk in his voice. "You could lay abed all day if you chose."

She closed her eyes and lightly thumped her head against the wardrobe. "Oh, you know, make hay while the sun shines and all that."

The next pause was significantly longer. "Yes. Well, I shall be in the wheelhouse most of the morning. I trust you can entertain yourself."

She ground her teeth together. "I can indeed. Thank you."

"You're welcome."

This time she definitely heard the smirk.

"Honestly," she muttered and quickly readied herself for the day. The light pouring through the bank of angled windows was still painful to her, but she preferred it to the dark. She had come to hate the dark.

The wardroom had only one passenger for breakfast—Mr. Quince, who smiled warmly. "The oatmeal is delightful, as is the toast and jam."

The thought of food turned Isla's stomach, yet another side effect of the spell. She wouldn't be hungry for at least another hour, but tea was a welcome start to the day. She poured herself a cup of Earl Grey and sat next to Mr. Quince.

"Did you sleep well, Dr. Cooper?"

She blew softly across the rim of her teacup. "Like the dead." She took a sip and smiled. "And you?"

"Quite well, thank you." Mr. Quince ate in silence and glanced at Isla a few times. She sensed he wanted to say something but was clearly reticent.

"Did you have a question for me, Mr. Quince? People are often curious about my work, but do not always know what to ask." She felt her energy returning by degrees and breathed a quiet sigh of relief. She smiled at the older man, seeking to put him at ease.

He nodded and relaxed the death grip he held on his spoon. "Do you know a shifter on sight? That is, can you differentiate someone who shifts from the normal population?"

"Ah, Mr. Quince, but what is normal, really? We all have differences, and every one of us has issues, challenges, traits." She shrugged. "I see nothing abnormal about the shifter population at all. A shifter is a person. A human."

He nodded, his eyes suspiciously bright.

"But yes, I can recognize full shifters on sight—not always, but usually." She paused. "I would hope that any shifter who knows of my work also knows I never stand in judgment, that my first concern is always the well-being of that person and his or her family." She lowered her voice. "It is certainly no secret that I have issues with current rules and regulations in play by certain committees. I believe some laws are meant to be broken."

He cleared his throat, his eyes teary, and he blinked. "I imagine a shifter of any sort would be nervous to be on a flight, a long flight, with a member of the government who wielded certain power."

"And *I* would imagine that such a person need not fear with an experienced shifter professional aboard. One skilled not only in hunting but also in defensive arts." She smiled gently. "I shall protect you, Mr. Quince," she whispered.

His expression tightened. "Although I am leaving the country without permission or having registered my name with the committee?" He paused. "It is illegal."

"It is necessary." She placed her hand on his arm and leaned close. "The committee is heinous and discriminatory. Positive changes are coming, but in the meantime, we must keep people—families—safe." She sighed. "The queen is aging, and I fear there are elements in certain circles that have escaped her notice. But I firmly believe that there are more enlightened people than not, that there is more good in the world than bad."

She gave his arm a light squeeze, and he patted her hand while blinking rapidly. Motion at the doorway drew her attention as Mr. Lewis and Nigel Crowe entered and perused the sideboard. Her nostrils flared of their own accord, and she had barely smoothed her face into a polite mask when Crowe gave her what he probably thought was a pleasant smile.

"Ah, Miss Cooper. You grace this meal with your feminine charm."

She glanced at Mr. Quince with a smile. "And with that, I am off." She stood and took a perverse satisfaction at Crowe's clear distaste of her ensemble. She wore breeches and custom Hessian boots. She knew her blouse and corset emphasized her "feminine charm" to perfection, but she would also wager

Nigel Crowe was a man who disapproved of any woman in breeches.

"I leave you in the capable company of Mr. Lewis," she murmured to Mr. Quince, who smiled tightly at the newcomers. "Perhaps later you will meet me in the library? I would love to discuss your work. I imagine it is fascinating."

"Dr. Cooper." Mr. Lewis tipped his head as he made his way to the table with a plate of food. "A beautiful morning, is it not? We seem to have moved above much of the stormy air. Captain believes we'll see smooth sailing for the rest of the day."

"Excellent." She returned his smile, wondering how many hearts he had broken with his.

"I am not certain I trust these modern scientific instruments." Mr. Quince frowned. "The older materials seemed more accurate."

Lewis placed a napkin in his lap and turned his attention to his food as he answered. "The world has come to accept the aneroid barometer as a legitimate tool." He added under his breath, "For nearly fifty years, now."

"But there's no liquid in it. In my day, barometers used mercury. And they were stationary. Very reliable."

"These are portable. Therein lies the benefit . . ."

Nigel Crowe watched the exchange with a smirk, and Isla made her exit, blaming Melody for the fact that she was obliged to spend three weeks with him. Isla had heaped so many sins at her sister's feet that absolution was a guaranteed impossibility.

She made her way onto the deck and shielded her eyes as she looked up at the wheelhouse situated at the stern, atop the quarterdeck. It was large, entirely enclosed in iron-framed glass that gave it the look of an ornate greenhouse or solarium. She imagined the view from inside would be spectacular.

There were two men in the wheelhouse; one was the captain, but she'd not met the other. She just turned away when she heard the door to the wheelhouse open.

"Dr. Cooper." The captain stood at the top of the stairs and motioned her forward.

She raised a brow and slowly climbed the steps. "I'm neither a senior officer nor quartermaster, Captain. I should not be climbing these hallowed stairs."

"You imply an awe for shipboard protocol—then this shall be a treat. We do not stand on ceremony on my personal flights, especially with so few passengers aboard."

She wouldn't label it "awe," precisely, but she wasn't about to argue, so she merely nodded.

He bowed lightly. "You seem much refreshed."

She smiled, determined to show her gratitude for allowing her aboard. "I am, and I wish to truly express my thanks to you for so graciously—"

"—capitulating to your threats of blackmail and ruination?"

She cleared her throat. He would not make it easy. And why should he, really? He was correct. She had extorted his weakness to gain something she needed. Did he need to forgive her? Was it unreasonable of her to ask it of him? If she possessed any remaining decency, she would make herself scarce and keep out of his way for the rest of the trip. "I am—Captain, I am genuinely sorry. I was . . ." She glanced away. His scrutiny was overpowering. "I was desperate. I am desperate."

He studied her for a moment. "Come in here."

She entered the wheelhouse, feeling awkward. What must the other man think of her? Surely the captain would have explained her presence to him. The gentleman nodded to her and returned his attention to a large instrument panel.

She couldn't quite put her finger on it, but there was something about him that felt slightly off. Not negatively so, but different.

Captain Pickett motioned with his head, and she joined him at the instrument panel. "Samson, our esteemed passenger, Dr. Cooper."

She extended her hand, and the gentleman smiled at her. When she looked at his eyes, she caught her breath. "A pleasure, Mr. Samson," she said, stunned. He was the most lifelike 'ton she'd ever seen.

"Just Samson, Dr. Cooper. And the pleasure is mine. Are you enjoying the voyage thus far?"

She glanced at Captain Pickett, who quirked a half smile. "I . . . Yes. Very much, thank you."

"Samson is my valet and personal assistant whenever we operate commercial flights. He's my right-hand man and virtually half of my brain. Don't know how to function without him."

"You are too modest, sir." He turned to Isla. "He gives me far too much credit."

"Check the coordinates in ten minutes." Pickett looked at a large chart near the control panel. "I'd also like a forecast for the next twelve hours."

"Very good, sir."

Captain Pickett took Isla's elbow and guided her to a row of cushioned benches at the other end of the room.

"How on earth?" She tried to keep her voice down. "How did you come upon that kind of programming? I've never seen the likes of it anywhere!"

He smiled. "I know some talented people. And it also doesn't hurt to donate large sums of money to the brightest minds in science and technological advancement industries."

She tried to keep her mouth from dropping open, but as she watched Samson, she was flabbergasted. "I have seen lifelike 'tons before, but there is usually something, some movement that gives them away." She looked at the captain, eyes wide.

"He was two years in the making, and he's very much a companion." He lifted a shoulder. "Helpful when one doesn't have much time for the human variety. Now, then, Dr. Isla Cooper. Suppose you tell me why you bullied your way onto my ship."

Chapter 7

Daniel sat beside Dr. Cooper and waited for her to regain her composure after the shock of meeting Samson. She certainly wasn't the first person to react in such surprise, and he doubted she'd be the last.

"I knew there was something about him." She watched the 'ton, her brow wrinkled.

Her pronouncement surprised him. "You sensed he wasn't human?"

She shook her head. "I sensed something different." She laughed. "I was trying to determine what manner of shifter he was."

He'd seen little levity from her, and her laugh caused his heart to skip a beat. She really was a beautiful woman. A beautiful woman who was in desperate straits, by her own admission, and he remained uncertain how it would affect him and his "cargo."

"Why are you here?" he asked quietly.

She sobered, turning her attention to the stunning view

of clouds and endless sky outside the windows. "I must find someone in Port Lucy, and time is of the essence."

"Who is this someone? Perhaps I know him." He'd been instrumental in establishing the port city, after all. Even named it after his sister.

She shook her head. "She is not native to the Caribbean, and in fact only left England a few months ago. I am not certain how long she plans to remain away, or if she will ever return."

"Have you an address?"

She shook her head and turned her green eyes to his. "My reasons are my own, and I ask that you not press me. Just know that this trip is extraordinarily important to me."

"Is it a matter of life or death?"

She exhaled quietly. "I hope not."

"You *hope* not?"

She pressed a hand to her forehead. "My friend, Hazel Hughes, is a brilliant woman who has been helping me learn some . . . things, but even with all the resources at her disposal, she has been unable to ascertain the exact nature of the . . . situation's potential outcome."

He knit his brow. "Hazel Hughes. Why do I know that name?"

"She is acquainted with your sister, Lucy. Perhaps she has mentioned her?"

"You know Lucy?"

She shook her head. "I personally do not."

Hazel . . . Ah, yes. Miss Hughes was a medium who had been hired to help with some issues at Blackwell Manor though the results of her efforts had led to a violent attack on both her and Lucy. "I'm afraid what little I know of Miss Hughes does not speak well of her expertise."

She flushed. "Her expertise as a medium, no. A practitioner of Light Magick, yes. And as a mind that can store facts, retain them like a steel trap, unparalleled. Her mother seems to think . . ." The doctor waved her hand. "It matters not. Suffice it to say that Hazel is the best person I know to locate obscure facts and resources. And her best information has directed me here. I'm afraid nobody knows the solution to my problem except the person I must find in Port Lucy."

"How long do you anticipate it will take? What are your plans for returning home?"

She lifted a shoulder and looked out the window. "That is a bridge I will cross when I reach it."

"You could find yourself stuck in Port Lucy for weeks—a month, two months."

She snapped her attention back to him. "It doesn't matter! I'll figure out how to get home after I've taken care of everything else."

He studied her. She was flushed, agitated, her foot wiggled as though she had a difficult time remaining stationary. The woman was a doctor, a well-known professional in London, and she had handily secured passage on a flight he would never have ordinarily allowed. Given her accomplishments and her clear talents, the circumstances prompting her mad flight to Port Lucy must be severe.

It wasn't his concern, and he couldn't fathom why he cared one way or the other about her intentions. He had troubles enough of his own to manage. Thinking of that brought to mind something she'd said when she had tried to convince him she could be an asset.

"You're an empath, and you deal with predatory shifters both in animal and human form, yes?"

She blinked at the change of subject. "Yes. I offer therapy for clients who need help adjusting to relationships or family life. Many people don't begin shifting until adulthood. I also hunt criminal shifters when necessary, help bring them to justice." She wrinkled her nose. "Which is part of my contention with Nigel Crowe. I refuse to turn over to the Committee people whose crimes are minor. Most local constabulary agree with me and don't force people onto the registry unless the crimes are severe. Harmful."

"It occurs to me that you may be able to help, should the need arise."

"How so?"

"You'll note, I'm sure, that Full Moon Phase is a scant three weeks out. A little less."

She nodded.

"I never undertake flights with certain passengers aboard that span that three-day window. This trip marches uncomfortably close to that deadline."

"I did wonder."

"Our three friends who travel with us now were supposed to have departed last week on an entirely different airship. One with different accommodations in case of emergency. Last week, a component in that ship's engine room malfunctioned and caused systemic failure. We're still working to fix it, but there was no time. Quince, Bonadea, and Lewis were being pressured from the PSRC's security control. It wouldn't be long before false charges were drummed up and filed, harassment of the families increased—it wasn't safe."

He rubbed the knot at the base of his neck. "I scraped this trip together last minute, but the extra accommodations—large, secure, caged rooms—are unavailable."

"So if we experience the slightest delay and one or all of the men shift, there is no containment."

"Exactly."

She paled and swallowed. "Yes, I see." She exhaled. "And shifting hours for predators are from midnight to six."

"Indeed." He frowned, confused. "Are you afraid? I agree the circumstances are not optimal, but in the worst case, we could at least get out of the sky, spend a few hours on the water . . ."

"No, I'm not afraid." She laughed a little, almost to herself. "That is the problem at home, too. Those shifting hours—when I most need to be available."

"I'm afraid I don't follow."

She smiled at him. "Another bridge we shall cross when we arrive there."

"Dr. Cooper, are you suggesting you will be unable to help if we have an emergency?"

She sighed. "No, I shall be fine. Everything is fine."

"Everything does not sound 'fine.'" His frustration mounted. "Enough of the cryptic comments and nonsense. If there is an issue that would have an adverse effect on me or the souls in my care, I must know what it is."

She closed her eyes and leaned her head against the window. "I fall asleep at midnight and do not awaken for six hours. No exceptions."

He stared. "No exceptions? It seems to me you chose the wrong profession if you refuse to work those critical hours for three scant days per month!"

"No, it's not that I refuse!" She made an exasperated sound and stood, her hand on her forehead. She walked a few steps and faced him, leaning against the windows at her back. "I have been cursed. With a spell. I lose consciousness at midnight, and I cannot awaken until six. I sleep as though dead. *That* is my problem. *That* is what I must fix. And if I cannot be awake, *I cannot do my job.* It's my company, I founded it, I train students, I tutor them in the field—there are aspects of the business that I cannot entrust to anyone else, and I must be out among the people in order to know exactly how to approach each individual situation, to be helpful to my clients, to hunt murderous shifters that others are unable to track. And what of the rest of my life? Suppose I should ever actually have a family?"

Her voice broke, and she looked down, her cheeks flushed. She'd not wanted to admit any of it to him, that was certain. It took him a moment to gather his thoughts.

"The person in Port Lucy is the one who cast the spell?"

She nodded.

"What was the reason?"

"I'd rather not say," she mumbled.

"And what does the cure involve?"

"That is why I cannot make plans for my return home. I don't know what the cure will entail. I don't know how long it will take, what I shall have to do, where it needs to be done. I don't know if she can say a few words of magick and throw some rat bones at me and I will be cured, or if I shall have to walk the entirety of the Great Wall of China backwards while fasting." She spread her hands wide. "I don't know! And not knowing is making me mad as a hatter."

"How much time do you have?"

She shrugged listlessly. "If I do not obtain and enact the cure within the next eight weeks, it becomes permanent."

Her pronouncement hung heavy in the air between them, and he understood her need to blackmail her way onto his ship. His lips quirked, and she narrowed her eyes.

"My predicament amuses you, Captain Pickett?"

"I understand now the reason for your subterfuge." He cleared his throat. "I suppose as we are compatriots of a sort, you needn't call me 'Captain Pickett.'"

She nodded, surprised. "Very well."

"Pickett is fine."

Her mouth hung slack and then she closed it. "Well then, you should call me 'Cooper.'" She lifted the corner of her mouth into a half-smile. "Does this mean you'll return my weapons?"

Chapter 8

I sla left the captain, feeling lighter. She'd not realized how heavy her burden had been, how much Hazel had been a support for her, a place to express her fears. Even though the captain hadn't found a magical solution to her dilemma, it was immeasurably reassuring to have confided in him. She fought a grin. "Pickett," indeed. It was as though she were now one of the men.

Pickett may not be entirely approachable or warm at first glance, but she trusted him. And he'd promised to return her weapons. She missed her throwing knife and the thigh holster she always had settled in place.

With the day to herself, she decided to explore the ship. As she wandered the common areas, she saw the captain's personality reflected in the deep, rich tones of the timber, the masculine, solid craftsmanship that combined strength with form. The smallest details—trim around doors and along the hallways, new Tesla lamps fastened to the walls—none of it was fussy or ornate. It suited him, she decided as she descended to the middle deck, which was bisected lengthwise by a narrow hallway. To the right were passenger cabins; to the left, a library, a lounge, and the infirmary.

The door to the lounge was open, and she spied Mr. Quince and Mr. Bonadea comparing notes. She wondered if they were truly working together on a project in Port Lucy or if it had been a story concocted for her sake and Nigel Crowe's.

Thoughts of her nemesis soured her mood, and she frowned as she passed the library and descended another level to the engine rooms and cargo hold. It was loud, but the genius of the Stirling Engine cut the noise of a regular airship by three-quarters. She stepped inside the large room, keeping to the perimeter and away from the six 'tons who operated the engine.

Two of the 'tons maintained a steady level of the oil necessary for the engine's heating component, and she stood aside and watched the process, impressed by their efficiency and with the sheer size of the engine. And this was a small ship!

She observed a moment longer, then returned to the dark hallway. The doors to the cargo hold were locked for safety purposes, which she didn't mind in the least. She'd told Pickett that she'd been prepared to stay in there if that was her only option, but she had to admit an irrational fear of the place. Cargo holds were loud, cold, and typically dark.

The hair on the back of her neck stood up, and she suddenly felt uneasy. She turned away from the cargo hold door to find Nigel Crowe standing behind her, quietly watching. Her heart jumped into her throat, and she put her hand on her waist atop her extra knife.

He took a long drag on a cheroot, smiled, and released a plume of smoke.

"What are you doing, Mr. Crowe?" Her voice was steady, pitched low and soft as she reverted to years' worth of training and practice.

"Taking a tour of the ship, much as you are, I assume."

She kept her fingers relaxed. "But what are you *doing*, Mr. Crowe? Why are you here?"

"It's not safe for a woman to be wandering alone on a ship filled with men and automatons."

"No." She shook her head. "Why are you aboard this ship? What in Port Lucy takes you away from London right this minute?"

His eyes narrowed, and his smile faded. "Important business."

"I would love to hear about it."

"Undoubtedly."

Her heart thumped. She suspected he truly meant harm to the three shifters aboard, but she wasn't certain how or when because he was so frustratingly impossible to read.

"Perhaps I can lend a hand. I understand your responsibilities on the Committee better than most."

He chuckled. "You thwart my responsibilities at every turn, Miss Cooper."

"Not at all. I am more than willing, as you are aware, to apprehend violent criminal shifters and turn them over for trial. You also know I willingly testify against those who deserve it; I have seen you at more than one tribunal."

He studied her for a long, unnerving moment. "Your refusal to notify the Committee of *every* predatory shifter you encounter has led to destruction of property and life."

"Please return to the upper decks, Mr. Crowe. I prefer my passengers to stay away from the lower level."

Nigel glanced at Isla. "All of your passengers? Or do you allow privileges to the prettier ones? Perhaps you hope to give Miss Cooper a personal tour?"

"My activities are none of your concern, and if you give voice to that insinuation again, you'll find my fist in your face."

Crowe smirked, but rather than belabor the point, he turned and left.

Isla breathed a sigh of relief and wondered if the entire voyage would be charged with tension because of the government agent.

The captain's attention turned to her, and she suddenly felt like a misbehaving child who had been caught fighting with a sibling. She lifted her chin, defensive before he even uttered a word.

"Did he hurt you?" The question was gruff, but still caught her by surprise.

She shook her head, disarmed. "There wasn't time. And I was nigh unto ending the conversation."

"Perhaps consider avoiding dark and isolated places for the remainder of our voyage."

Her irritation returned, and she reminded herself that Pickett did not know her well. "I should not have to do that," she said evenly.

He waved a hand. "We can discuss social philosophy later. Of course you should not *have* to, but the fact is, you do."

"I am not foolish. I am aware of whom I can and cannot best. I am not concerned about that one. And I thank you for your defense of me, but I did have the situation in hand."

"You are assuming you have control over who may corner you in a dark hallway, Cooper." His gaze flicked to her waist. "I presume you did not enter my locked cabin to retrieve your weapons."

"Of course not!"

"Then you lied to me." He held out his hand.

Her temper frayed. "Would you not have done the same? Favor or not, I have no way of knowing what your intentions are, or anyone else's aboard. When you searched my belongings I had yet to meet the other passengers; I had no idea what I might face."

She snatched her knife from her waistband and flipped it quickly in the air, catching the blade and handing it to him handle-first. "Here, then." She used her other hand to pluck two throwing stars from her corset and brandished them as well. "May as well confiscate these also! I might throw them through the wall from my cabin to yours, kill you in your sleep, then stage a mutiny."

He endured her angry tirade. Holding her gaze, he took the weapons from her and held them up for closer inspection. He raised a brow at the throwing stars, as though reluctantly impressed. "Japanese shuriken." He glanced at her. "Are you any good?"

Suddenly she was figuratively disarmed again. She frowned and cleared her throat. "Absolutely."

He studied her for a moment. "Come here, Cooper." He handed the knife and stars back to her and unlocked the cargo door. A rush of cold air invaded the hallway, and Isla shivered. When she hesitated, he looked at her over his shoulder. "Come."

"It's dark," she muttered.

"I'm sorry?"

She shook her head. "Nothing." She followed him into the cargo hold, where he flicked on a wall-mounted Tesla lamp and closed the door.

The hold was neatly organized, a combination of the passengers' personal belongings and oil barrels used for operating the engine. There were also crates marked PORT LUCY against the far wall. She'd forgotten that Pickett conducted legitimate trade with other countries and governments.

He pulled her elbow when she hovered near the door and motioned with his head toward the far wall, which was stacked waist-high with crates. "Show me your star-throwing skills."

She looked at him in surprise. "It will scratch the wall."

He shrugged. "It's a cargo hold. I have no issue with a few nicks and scratches on the walls. But perhaps you brandish your weapons more for deterrent than actual use, which I can certainly understand—"

She whipped her knife from its sheath and lodged it in the target wall before he finished his sentence.

"Well, well. So the good doctor is more than just talk."

She rolled her eyes, and he motioned at her other hand. "Now those."

With a quick flick of her wrist, she stuck the stars fast in the wall on either side of the knife. She smiled, satisfied.

"Impressive."

"I ought to be able to hit anything moving or stationary, considering how much time I devote to it."

He looked at her askance. "When do you have time to practice knife throwing?"

"Between clients. After dinner. Early morning before work." She winced. "Used to be early morning. Not so much now."

He eyed her, and then moved to the far wall and retrieved the stars and knife. "Who taught you to use these?"

"A gentleman from Japan owned a sword and knife shop near my home. Taught my friend, Will, and me. He was tickled a little British girl had such an interest in katana and shuriken." She smiled. "He was a good man. Very patient."

Pickett extended the stars, and she took them. "They typically aren't used for the final blow like a knife would be, but are often tipped with poison. The star scratches the skin, the poison seeps in . . ." She drew a thumb across her neck.

He raised a brow and handed back her knife. "And you wonder why I confiscated your arsenal."

She smiled in spite of herself and shook her head. "I can count on one hand the times I've actually used these things in an altercation. The ray gun is usually deterrent enough."

"I suppose you're equally precise and deadly with the gun."

"Mais bien sûr." She grinned. "Perhaps you should be grateful I'm here and can act as *your* protection, Pickett."

"If I return your gun, what guarantee do I have that you won't accidentally blast a hole in the side of my ship?"

"You do not know me well, so I will forgive you for asking that."

His lips turned up at the corners, and he nodded toward the door. "We should return before Crowe spreads rumors and ruins your good name."

Chapter 9

D aniel stood in the wheelhouse, pretending to read an instruction manual on Tesla lamp repair. One moment he had been ready to kill Nigel Crowe— who had clearly been harassing the good doctor—and the next, he'd had that same doctor in the cargo hold, showing off her skills and impressing him to no end. *Intriguing* him to no end.

He was as baffled as he'd ever been in his life.

He found her beautiful, surely, but she was so unlike any other women of his acquaintance that he was riveted, fascinated. She hunted large, deadly animals. She operated a thriving business. She commanded the respect of experts in her field. She was half his size and Crowe's, yet between the two, he'd put his money behind her in a fight.

And when he'd come upon her and Crowe in the dark corridor, realized he was up to no good and that she had a hand at her side, likely ready to bury a knife in Crowe's chest if he assaulted her, Daniel found he couldn't even be angry that she'd lied to him about not having any more weapons.

He'd seen her wearing her ray gun and knife the first time they'd met, but today was different. Was that the reason he'd lost his head? Because the woman hadn't only been wearing the accoutrements but also knew how to defend herself with them? He tipped his head, considering. Yes. Yes, that would be the cause. He didn't know a man in the world who wouldn't find that alluring. Unconventional? Absolutely. But the world was on the brink of a new century, and society evolved along with technology.

"Samson, do you know of many women who brandish weapons? Employ them with skill? It would be an attractive habit, I should think."

His 'ton kept his attention on the weather pattern charts he had spread on a counter. "Your sister has a ray gun, sir."

Daniel grimaced. "Never mind."

Samson smiled. "Are you thinking of one woman in particular?"

"No. . . . Perhaps."

"And you seem to be searching for validation of your attraction to women who are armed?"

"Not just any woman, I suppose," he mumbled and wished he'd never broached the subject with a 'ton who comprehended entirely too much about human emotion and motivation.

"If I were a human, I presume I would find Dr. Cooper an attractive woman. Her features are symmetrical, her hair is a rich shade of brown that appears deep red in the sunlight, and she controls her physical body smoothly. She doesn't stumble about even when the ship catches a good breeze."

"Symmetrical features, nice hair, doesn't stumble." Daniel

flipped another page in the manual, which, now that he looked closer, he realized was written in a series of numbers and characters he couldn't decipher.

"I sense you are flummoxed, sir."

"My life is extremely complicated these days. I do not need the distraction."

"Therefore you expect to be impervious to attraction?"

"It would help." He sighed and tossed the manual on the counter. "If we are caught, Crowe could see me imprisoned and tried. There is no room for mistakes on this trip, and yet it is chaos personified." He frowned. "I haven't time for . . . anything, really."

"Perhaps you ought to have courted the woman from Bath your mother chose for you years ago. You would have hearth and home settled by now. No surprises, no complications."

Daniel scowled at the 'ton. "I do not recall programming you to sound like my mother, and yet that was a remarkable imitation."

"I promised to look after you."

Daniel stared. "When? When did you promise my mother anything?"

"More specifically, I promised your grandmother when they visited the offices in London. I believe she might have mistaken me for a human friend."

"Mmm. Her eyesight is fading."

"Yes. I told her of a shop in London that specializes in a wide variety of vision issues and solutions. The right pair of spectacles may make all the difference for her."

Daniel shook his head and crossed to the door, unsure

of exactly when he'd fallen down the rabbit hole. He was inconveniently attracted to a woman he'd just met—a woman who had threatened him with exposure if he didn't allow her passage on a restricted flight—and his 'ton had become his grandmother's confidant. "I will be in the library should you need me."

"Very good, sir. Shall I translate this manual you were attempting to read?"

"No, I don't need it. All the Tesla lamps seem to be in working order. Trying to busy myself, I suppose."

As Daniel left the wheelhouse, he heard Samson say, "I did wonder why you were attempting to read computation code."

Nothing in the library caught Daniel's interest, and for once he regretted having such a proficient 'ton. He supposed he should be grateful for the lack of drama, especially since having a government agent aboard determined to catch them all breaking the law was enough of a powder keg on its own. He had general business paperwork to tend to, but he couldn't summon the interest to do it. He considered doing inventory checks on their food stores, but he'd done that before departure. All the 'tons were working properly, each working piece of the engine and the enormous propellers functioned beautifully. The small party enjoyed quite literal smooth sailing throughout the afternoon, and Daniel found himself pacing with no real destination in mind.

He made his way down to his cabin as the dinner hour approached, and freshened up. He heard the doctor moving around in the cabin next door. When he was ready, he knocked on the outer door of her cabin.

She opened the door and looked like the self-assured Dr. Cooper he'd first met. She was calm, no traces of her earlier irritation present. She'd dressed for dinner in a blouse, corset, and skirt, shoulders back, smile in place, and as she turned to lock the door, he noted the slight bump of her sheathed knife at her side.

He swallowed.

"Ready?" She started down the hallway but turned back when she reached the stairs. "Aren't you coming to dinner?"

"Yes." He stood rooted to the spot.

She paused with a foot on the bottom stair. "Is something amiss?"

He shook his head. "I realized I still haven't returned your arsenal."

She smiled and shrugged. "It can wait until after dinner."

He nodded and covered the distance to her in a few strides. He placed a hand at her back, noting the stark contrast in their sizes. How on earth did a woman so small take down dangerous shifters and defend herself against real physical danger? An image of her knife sailing through the air in the cargo hold flashed through his mind, and he reasoned that was probably how she managed her profession. Skill, practice, study, and wits. Preparation, effective tools, and probably a bit of luck. His hand spanned her waist, and his thumb brushed against the sheathed knife at her side.

He gestured with his free hand. "After you, Dr. Cooper."

She climbed the steps but said over her shoulder, "Watch the knife, Captain. I'd hate to have to pull it on you."

He certainly hoped she wouldn't. She'd likely find herself pushed up against the nearest wall and kissed senseless. At which point, she might slip the knife between his ribs, which, he reasoned, might not be such a bad way to end a life well-lived.

They crossed the upper deck, and when they neared the wardroom, she stopped him with a touch on his arm. "Captain Pickett, I apologize for my impatience earlier. I was rude when you were merely expressing concern for my safety." She paused. "I am certainly not infallible, quite the contrary. I am, however, unconventional, and I realize it. I suppose . . ." She locked onto his eyes, her own a sea of green. "I work hard in a field largely populated by men, and not only must I be as good as they are, I must be better. If I fall short, make a mistake any of my contemporaries might make, I risk seeming incompetent." She spread her hands. "So I find myself adept at throwing sharp weaponry and soothing agitated predators but sometimes lacking skill in conventional exchanges."

Blast, but the woman was breathtaking. Hers was an unconventional beauty that grew more stunning, more interesting, with each conversation.

He realized he should probably say something. "These circumstances are unusual, Cooper," he said in a clumsy attempt at comfort. "I imagine if I were facing your challenges, I might be short-tempered as well."

"Captain! Dr. Cooper!" Alfred Quince's balding head appeared as he climbed the stairs from the passenger cabins.

"Mr. Quince." Daniel smiled. "I trust you enjoyed your day?"

"Indeed! Mr. Bonadea and I have created the framework with which to begin our study of Port Lucy. I have a renewed sense of hope that this next phase of my life will find its share of joys."

Cooper's features softened. "You've been apprehensive, Mr. Quince?" She took his arm and walked slowly with him into dinner.

Daniel looked after her, strangely irritated he'd been summarily dismissed when he should have been glad to have another person aboard who understood the danger his passengers faced. He was usually alone, utterly and completely, bearing the emotional burden of ferrying people to safety whose lives were at stake.

Bonadea and Lewis emerged next from the stairs, deep in discussion about advanced medical care for animals. Daniel followed them into the wardroom, and, as the clock struck the hour, he signaled the 'tons to begin serving. They were absent only one guest, and with any luck, Crowe's appetite was sparse and he would stay away for the evening.

The passengers claimed their prior seats, something Daniel noticed each voyage. People were creatures of habit, of consistency. He wasn't going to complain in the least this time since Cooper sat to his right. Quince and Bonadea had taken up an animated discussion on his left, and Lewis sat next to Isla with a murmured comment. Isla laughed and leaned toward the handsome medic and said something that must have been equally witty, because he chuckled and gifted her with a smile that showed his perfect, white teeth.

Daniel's lips tightened. Samson would probably tell him that Adam Lewis was a visually appealing human, what with his even, symmetrical features, his head of thick blond hair, and his physical grace that Daniel had seen both in battle and once when the man had shifted during a full moon in India. Why such perfection bothered him now, he couldn't imagine, especially as Lewis had always been a friend, someone whose company he enjoyed.

A 'ton served his food, and Daniel picked up his silverware, his attention still on the couple to his right who seemed content to laugh themselves into oblivion.

"Very well, then! We should say grace." His loud pronouncement drew four pairs of eyes, and had he not been so irritated, he'd have laughed at the variety of expressions that ranged from surprise to bafflement.

Isla cleared her throat. "Of course. We must have forgotten last evening. And this morning."

"And during teatime," Quince offered.

Daniel knew a moment's panic when he realized he would have to now pronounce a blessing on the meal, something he hadn't done since childhood. "Would anyone care to do the honors?"

Four blank faces stared back at him, mute.

"I believe we should be most grateful for our captain to do so," Bonadea said.

"Very well," Daniel muttered.

They each bowed their heads, glancing around at both him and each other. He opened his mouth to begin when Quince sat up straight in his chair. "We ought to join hands!"

The others looked at him, and after a lengthy pause, Dr. Cooper nodded. "Of course we should." She smiled at Quince and extended her arms to either side.

Daniel supposed he should be grateful he had an excuse to touch her, but Lewis clasped her right hand, and Daniel felt his nostrils flare. He grabbed her left hand and reached for Quince's, knowing he had only himself to blame for the extreme awkwardness that enveloped the room.

The situation was made more bizarre as Lewis had to stretch across the table to reach Bonadea, who was forced to rise up in his seat to join hands. Dr. Cooper bowed her head, signaling the others, and Daniel stared at the tableau, wondering what had possessed him.

Cooper gave him a side-glance, eyes wide and one brow lifted. She deliberately squeezed her eyes shut and bowed her head again.

He took a deep breath. "Thank you for the food we eat, thank you for the world so sweet, thank you for the birds that sing, thank you, God, for everything."

They each looked up, mouths slack, still clasping hands.

"Amen," he said firmly.

"Amen!" Cooper and Quince echoed. The other two mumbled their endorsement, and they all released hands.

"What a heartwarming scene." Crowe stood at the door, smiling. "I am sorry to have missed it." He took his place at the foot of the table, and a 'ton bustled to serve his plate.

Daniel thought he might have heard Quince whisper something about Satan, but it was drowned out by the clinking of silverware and renewed conversation, which started up again like a Victrola that had had its power cut abruptly with the needle still in the middle of the vinyl disc.

"I must say, Captain, I find your sudden show of spiritualism surprising," Quince said.

"As do I," Lewis drawled.

"Oh, but refreshing," Quince hastened to add. "The world could use more of it, I say."

"Indeed." Crowe snapped his napkin into place. "Heathens are quite overrunning it."

"Agreed," Bonadea said flatly and glanced at Crowe before turning his attention to Cooper. "Now, then, Dr. Cooper, suppose you tell us about your family. I've not heard much, other than your mother is the proprietress of Castles'."

"Is she?" Lewis looked at her in surprise. "It seems you come from a well-accomplished family."

Cooper smiled. "Thank you, and yes, Mr. Bonadea. My father passed when I was ten years old, leaving my mother, my younger sister, and me alone. He had not been a man of means, so my mother and aunt, who was also widowed, established Castles' Boutique out of necessity. It has flourished, and we are grateful."

"Oh my, I should say!" Quince beamed at her. "My daughters and granddaughters are always in fits of ecstasy after returning from an excursion to Castles'. Your mother is to be commended."

"Thank you, Mr. Quince. She has indeed put all of herself into the boutique. Very determined from the start."

"I imagine such a venture must have consumed all of her time." Crowe watched her as he took another bite.

She glanced at him, and Daniel noted her fingers tightening on her fork.

"Who cared for you and your sister, then, I wonder?" Crowe continued.

Cooper took her time cutting a small piece of beef into smaller squares, and Daniel wondered what kind of damage she could do to the meat with her throwing stars. "I did—but we were part of a close neighborhood." She looked at Crowe, her expression hard, even in profile.

Daniel wondered how deeply the man would dig a hole for himself.

"A pity she never remarried." Crowe affected an expression of sympathy. "Set a rather odd example for you, no? Certainly explains your own unique choices."

Cooper smiled. "I suppose when my father died, she could have stood outside the house with a large placard, advertising the vacant position."

Crowe smiled, and Lewis raised a brow, glancing at Daniel as if he, too, realized Crowe was venturing into dangerous waters. The man was not obtuse—anything but. He baited the doctor deliberately.

Bonadea cleared his throat. "Your mother must be a remarkable person. And her sister, as well."

"Thank you, Mr. Bonadea. And Mr. Crowe, you'll be pleased to hear that my aunt did remarry. A man with five daughters, each more delightful than the last. Mr. O'Shea has been a boon to our family."

There was an edge to her voice, and Daniel guessed Mr. O'Shea had been anything but a boon to the family.

"And have you any other relatives in London?" Lewis asked.

Isla nodded, this time her smile was genuine, less forced. "Emmeline, my aunt's daughter. Two years my junior, and I quite adore her."

Crowe's knife clattered against his plate, and he hastily retrieved it. "Emmeline O'Shea is your *cousin*?"

Chapter 10

D r. Cooper raised her brows, her expression innocent. "Are you acquainted with Emme?"

Crowe looked at Isla for a moment, and then twitched the side of his mouth. "Emmeline O'Shea has caused more mayhem to the Predatory Shifter Regulations Committee than anyone in the entire United Kingdom."

"Mmm." Cooper nodded and continued her meal. "It does stand to reason you would know of her. She's quite spirited."

"She is—"

The doctor looked at Crowe, directly and without flinching. "Yes?"

"She is . . . indeed spirited."

"I'm delighted you agree."

"Makes so much sense," Crowe muttered to his plate. "So much sense."

"Mr. Bonadea," Cooper said, "you mentioned studying fauna in London's outskirts. Have you by any chance come across a flying squirrel? I was so surprised to hear of such a thing!"

With the conversation smoothly diverted from discussions of Cooper's family and into neutral territory, the remainder of the meal was pleasant and relatively comfortable despite the glowering presence of Nigel Crowe, who was a veritable thundercloud.

When the meal ended, Daniel declined offers to join the group in the lounge for after-dinner drinks and whist; Crowe also declined, stating he had paperwork to attend to.

Daniel stopped by the galley to see that all was functioning with Robert, the 'ton who served as chef, and then he made his way to the wheelhouse to relieve Samson so the 'ton could power down and recharge.

"Samson," he asked before the 'ton left, "what do you know of Emmeline O'Shea?"

"Emmeline O'Shea. Known as 'Emme' to close friends and family, twenty-four years old, writes newspaper columns and educational leaflets. Daughter of Hester O'Shea and adoptive father, Ronald O'Shea. She made headlines six months ago by chaining herself to the wheel of the prime minister's carriage to bring attention to the injustices of the Shifter Committee."

Daniel smiled. Little wonder Crowe didn't care for her. "I remember the news about the prime minister's carriage wheel, just never paid attention to the name. In fact, Oliver Reed was obliged to leave Lucy and Miles's wedding celebration early to deal with a 'do-gooder' who raised enough ruckus to require the Yard's interference." He smiled. "I had forgotten that."

Samson nodded. "You are focused on your work, sir, both with your 'cargo transfers' and the entire Pickett Airship empire. Little wonder details escape your limited human brain."

"Go charge, Samson."

"Very good, sir. I shall relieve you in six hours." Samson left the wheelhouse, closing the door quietly behind him.

"Limited human brain," he muttered. Having an extremely advanced 'ton as a best friend was an exercise in self-flagellation.

He went about his routines, checking status reports and running diagnostic tests on some of the navigation equipment. He then reached for the paperwork he'd avoided earlier. The documents his solicitor had prepared gave him updates on the state of his entire fleet, issues with individual ships, required repairs, expansion plans, budgetary projections—all things that ordinarily held his interest. He enjoyed everything about his business empire, even the mundane details, but for the first time in a while, he was distracted and concerned. Nigel Crowe had come aboard clearly prejudiced against Isla Cooper because of their past confrontations. Now he'd learned that the doctor was related to a woman he seemed to despise with as much, if not more, intensity.

Daniel was mulling over the details, wondering what the new revelation would bring to the strained dynamic among the passengers, when he saw Cooper cross the deck and climb the steps to the wheelhouse. She knocked on the glass door with a smile, and he beckoned her in.

"Captain, I am headed to my cabin but wanted to tell you how much your efforts are appreciated by your three passengers. They speak of you in glowing terms, almost emotionally grateful. Mr. Quince told me about his grand-children being harassed. Mr. Bonadea said he was released from his job because of pressure put on his employers to do so, and that you helped him secure employment in Port Lucy and plan to transport his family in the next few months." She took a breath and smiled. "I want you to know, especially as one who has fondness for people and families like these, that I am so glad you are doing this. I'm grateful. And to be honest, I would never have given you over to the authorities had you refused to bring me on this voyage."

Daniel leaned against a countertop and folded his arms. "Is that so?"

She laughed softly. "You know very well that it is."

"I did not know then."

"And I was wagering on that."

He tipped his head. "As I recall, you threatened me not only with that, but also with exposure of what you assumed to be cyborg implants on my person."

"Are you telling me it isn't true?" She pursed her lips, seemingly fighting a smirk.

"I don't know what would have given you such an idea."

"I saw you hefting oil drums aboard with one arm."

"I am quite strong."

She nodded. "Because of cyborg implants. Tell me I'm wrong."

He sighed. "You're not wrong. You know much about me that could lead to my ruin, Cooper."

"Then you should consider yourself fortunate that I like you, Pickett." She smiled again. "I believe we could be good friends."

He lifted a brow. "Good friends."

"Well, yes. We both work to help predatory shifters who are being unjustly persecuted. We also have a mutual disdain for the PSRC."

"A solid foundation for friendship."

"Pickett, sarcasm does not . . . well, actually sarcasm *does* become you, but you are being difficult, and I am going to retire. Good night."

"Cooper," he said, halting her mid-exit. "I appreciate your offer of friendship." He approached her slowly, putting his hands in his pockets so he wouldn't be tempted to do something foolish, like touch her. "I am glad you stopped by before retiring. I wanted to tell you to be twice as vigilant around Crowe now."

Her brows knit.

"He was belligerent to you even before realizing who your cousin is. I have no proof, but I sense he is one who cannot always keep his temper in check. Cannot or does not—either way, watch your back."

She smiled at him as a parent would to a child. "We've discussed this at some length. I can defend myself against him; you needn't worry."

"I am serious." His tone was sharp. "Even the best among us can be caught unaware. Just because you've taken down a shifter or two does not mean you're invincible."

She narrowed her eyes. "I do not for a moment believe I am invincible, but I can handle the likes of that odious man."

"Oh, I've no doubt you could get away from him, even kill him if necessary. But think of the consequences, and the political suspicion it would cast on you and your cousin, the

negative impact it would have on your mother's business."
He shook his head, frustrated. "Even if you acted in self-defense, it would not paint you in a good light, especially with so many people aware of your antagonistic relationship with him. I personally do not trust him, and his superior, Bryce Randolph, is twice the menace. I detest that man, and still I must tread carefully around him because of the trouble he could cause for not only the people I sneak out of England but also for some of my friends still there—friends in positions of power who have much to lose."

She nodded once. "Very well. Consider me warned."

"Cooper." He rubbed the back of his neck. "I can think of only two reasons Crowe would have insisted on accompanying this flight. We both know he doesn't have business awaiting him in Port Lucy. He and the Committee have either been alerted to my activities and they sent him to investigate, or he followed you."

She frowned, shaking her head. "Why on earth would he be following me?"

He shrugged. "It is only a theory. I initially assumed the first scenario when he joined us at the last minute, but that was before I knew of the bad blood between the two of you." He lowered his voice although they were alone. "If he is here because of you, he now has twice the motivation to dislike you."

"Because of Emme."

He nodded.

"If he wishes me dead, he has had multitudinous opportunities in London when he might have done it, or had it carried out."

"Perhaps that isn't his aim. We do not yet know his plans, so again I would tell you to proceed with caution."

She took a breath and released it slowly. "I will. I really quite dislike him."

He smiled. "You are not alone. I imagine only his mother bears him true affection, and even that is likely strained."

She laughed, and he swayed closer. She smelled good. It wasn't even anything he could define. Soap? Scented oil at her wrists and throat?

She stepped through the door and grabbed the handrail leading down the stairs. "Good night then," she said with a breezy smile. "I really must be settled before—well, before."

Ah, yes. Midnight, when she slept as though dead. The thought made him uneasy. For all her tactics and training, she was completely vulnerable for those six hours, and he hoped her enemies never discovered that. His heart thumped as he thought of Nigel Crowe, in a cabin only a deck away from her and with plenty of reasons to keep her from returning home. Did he know about her curse? Or where had it come from?

Daniel hadn't asked and Cooper hadn't offered, and as he watched her turn the corner at the bottom of the stairs and disappear beneath the wheelhouse, he determined to question her thoroughly. Forewarned was forearmed, and he was now even more bothered by the flight's odd assortment of people as he'd been when they embarked.

Chapter 11

Isla dragged herself out of bed the next morning feeling her usual combination of exhaustion and death. The fresh water she'd requested from the galley 'ton the night before went a long way to helping her awaken. She sponge-bathed, managed to wash her hair, and looked with satisfaction at the set of clothing she'd washed the night before, still drying over the back of the chair and the wardrobe door.

She combed her hair and braided it, leaving it to hang down her back in a thick rope rather than pin it up. She remembered braiding Melody's wet hair as a young girl, and how they would laugh the next day when they released the braids to reveal unruly, wavy curls.

She absently shook out her hands to remove the last tinges of blue from her skin, although she knew logically it didn't speed the process. She needed to check in with her mother and Melody, but they were too far out of range. She and the other passengers could telescribe each other on the ship due to the portable, scaled-down Tesla Room near the engine room and cargo hold, and a few more days should see them within scribing distance of the Caribbean.

She had writing sheets in her journal, and even though handwritten letters couldn't be sent home until they landed in Port Lucy, she'd left so hastily and in such a short temper with Melody that she felt an urge to express her affection.

She sat at the table and drafted a quick letter to her mother, explaining her "research holiday" in greater detail, creating a plausible scenario and enumerating several benefits to the excursion. Bella was busier with Castle's than ever; the last thing she needed was to know that one daughter had cursed the other with a sleeping spell.

When she moved to Melody's letter, she wasn't certain where to begin. *I love you, although you've ruined my life* hardly seemed warm. *I know we have been strained with each other lately, and I am sorry. It's just that . . . you've ruined my life . . .*

Isla sighed and sat back in her chair, tossing her fountain pen on the desk. This shouldn't be so difficult. The fact was she was still angry, and beneath that, hurt. Melody had been innocent enough, her motives immature but not malignant, but the consequences had altered Isla's life so drastically that her stifling fear occasionally took her breath away. If she was unable to find Malette, if she was unable to convince her to supply a cure . . .

Isla shook her head, sat up again, and retrieved the pen.

Melody, I had memories today of when you were small, and they made me smile. You meant the world to me then, and you do now. I've not said it much of late, but I do love you. You are my sister and my friend, and I miss you.

Isla's eyes burned, which surprised her. She never cried.

Feelings that produced tears were complicated, and she avoided them at all costs. She scowled.

As she finished drafting the letter, she noted the usually light sway of the airship giving way to broader and wider swings. Daniel had mentioned yesterday about flying into a storm but not to be concerned—the ship's propellers were the most powerful available, and if they couldn't fly above the storm safely, the propellers would still see them through.

She examined her hands, satisfied her skin had regained its normal hue, and left the cabin, locking the door. The sun usually shone brightly into the corridor from the stairs, and the absence of light bore testament of the coming storm. She climbed to the main deck, swaying and gripping the handrail, and looked up to see a sky that roiled and tumbled with dark clouds.

It was unsettling but strangely beautiful, and she stood at the top of the stairs, transfixed by the movement overhead. A shout from the bow drew her attention, and she spied Mr. Lewis, who had his hands cupped around his mouth. Having caught her attention, he jogged the length of the deck, admirably keeping his balance, and reached her side.

"Are you headed to the wardroom, then?" He bent close both to make himself heard and shield her from the wind.

"I had thought to, but perhaps I won't have much of an appetite for long."

"Captain Pickett suggested we take our meal in the library as it is situated near the center of the ship—although in this wind, that may not make much of a difference."

She nodded.

"Crossing the deck is faster, or we can go down and around. Whichever you prefer."

"I believe we should run across the deck, don't you?"

He grinned, and she took his proffered arm, laughing as they ran from stern to bow, slipping and nearly falling twice. She had never been gladder to be wearing snug breeches instead of a skirt. When they reached the other side, she looked back at the wheelhouse to see Samson speaking to Daniel, who was examining something at the control panel.

She turned with Mr. Lewis and descended the stairs, wondering why she suddenly felt that something was different. Wrong. She couldn't put her finger on it, and she slowed her steps, brows knit in thought. What was it? Something *sounded* different.

"Do you hear that, Mr. Lewis?"

He tilted his head. "Hear what?"

"Something odd. The propeller cadence?"

They paused at the bottom of the stairs and remained still. She wondered if she was wrong. "Maybe it's the wind. I could be hearing things that aren't there."

He frowned. "No, I believe you're right." They stayed still a moment longer when, alarmingly, the noise of the propeller ceased altogether.

They stared at each other, mute, and suddenly the ship pivoted sharply, careening in a circle. She fell against the wall, cracking her head. Mr. Lewis held tight to the railing and lunged for her, pulling her upward by the arm when she would have fallen to the floor. The haphazard movement of the ship slowed, but Isla still felt as though she stood in a spinning top.

"The propeller stopped," she murmured and put a hand to her aching head.

"Are you hurt?" He turned her face toward him and studied her eyes. "You hit your head."

"A bit, but it will pass." She managed a smile. "I do believe I've quite lost my appetite, though."

He didn't return her smile, but continued to look from one eye to the other. "I'd like to see your eyes in better light," he said. It was then she realized that both Tesla lamps in the corridor had gone dark.

Multiple footsteps sounded in the hall, and the other three passengers joined them, wide-eyed.

"Everybody in one piece?" Mr. Lewis asked.

"What on earth has happened?" Mr. Quince stammered. "The storm?"

Mr. Lewis frowned. "I'll speak with Captain Pickett. He's in the wheelhouse."

"I'll come with you," Isla said.

"We'll all go," Nigel Crowe added.

The entire group trooped back up the stairs and stepped out onto the main deck, crossing in fits and starts. Isla could only imagine how comical they might have appeared from the helm, like terrified mice scurrying together after a lightning strike.

Samson opened the wheelhouse door, and they filed in. Isla crossed the room to Pickett, where he made quick notations on a chart and checked the instrument panel.

"Well, Pickett? I thought you said this ship could handle any storm." Nigel Crowe didn't shout, but somehow his quiet anger was worse.

Daniel clenched his jaw. "There has been a problem with the port side propeller. I am going down to the engine room now to assess."

"But that shouldn't have caused such a violent spin," Mr. Bonadea noted.

Pickett grimaced. The ship rocked with a stiff burst of wind, and Isla realized that with one propeller stopped, they were less likely to pass through the storm with ease. The balloon held them aloft, but they were at the mercy of the airstream. The ship dipped and danced again, and Isla envisioned a feather blowing willy-nilly without direction.

"Your 'ton has no idea how to handle the wheel, Pickett!" Crowe glared at Samson, who stood at the ship's double wheel, but his efforts seemed ineffectual. There was no purpose in the ship's direction.

"Crowe, I have yet to ascertain the extent of the damage. It might possibly go beyond the propeller." Pickett's delivery was even and measured, but Isla noted a clenched fist and wondered if he would maintain hold on his temper.

Mr. Lewis moved close to Isla's side. "Let me see your pupils," he murmured. He placed both hands on her face, tipped her chin, and looked at her eyes again.

She heard Pickett approach, and he appeared in her periphery. "What happened?" he barked.

"She cracked her head against the wall when we spun. Her pupils are larger than I'd like. Does it hurt, Dr. Cooper?"

"Not at all," she lied.

Pickett's expression matched the thunderclouds outside, and she didn't know if it was a result of anger or concern.

Mr. Lewis ran a hand along the side of her head, and

she winced involuntarily when he probed what she assumed would be a rather large goose egg before long.

"You are hurt," Pickett accused.

"Truly, I am fine." She moved back, and Mr. Lewis dropped his hands. "What can we do to help you?"

"Indeed," Mr. Quince added, although he looked decidedly pale. "We are at your service, sir."

Pickett regarded Isla for a moment longer and then turned his attention to the rest of the group. "Samson and I will determine the nature of the problem and have it fixed straightaway. He is working on diagnostics."

Crowe refrained from comment but went to the lookout windows at the back of the room.

Mr. Bonadea watched him and rolled his eyes. "Shall we retire to our cabins, then?" he asked the captain.

"That would be fine, or you may want to pass the time together in the lounge or library."

"Can we climb above the storm?" Mr. Lewis asked Daniel.

Pickett shook his head. "I was reviewing the chart. It's too high."

Silence met his pronouncement, and he held up his hand. "Rest assured, we will weather the storm, as it were, and repair the faulty propeller. Breakfast has been prepared, and the 'ton, Robert, can deliver it wherever you prefer. As I mentioned earlier, you may be more comfortable in one of the rooms on the middle deck."

The ship's continual bobbing and sudden, harsh movements combined with the bump on Isla's head left her feeling nauseated. She rarely suffered from motion sickness, but often found that if she had a clear view of the terrain ahead, such as atop a carriage or in the front seat of an automated Traveler, the illness abated.

She stumbled to the bank of windows at the front of the helm and looked out over the length of the ship, taking long, deep breaths. She had no fixed point of reference, however, and wondered if she would lose whatever remained in her stomach from last night's dinner. She registered Pickett shooing the others from the wheelhouse, and Mr. Lewis appeared at her side.

"Where would you like to go, Dr. Cooper? Can I accompany you somewhere?"

She didn't dare look at him to express thanks for his concern, as she figured any additional movement might push her over the proverbial edge.

"She can stay here," Pickett said, and she heard him approach from behind. "Are you sick?" He put a hand on her shoulder, and she nodded, regretting the movement, and still looking out the window at sails that bobbed up and down. The thick, gray fog grew darker with each passing moment. They were flying into an abyss.

"The others have gone now," Mr. Lewis said, and Isla saw them crossing the deck below, Mr. Bonadea helping Mr. Quince. Crowe paused to look out into the storm before glancing up at the wheelhouse and leaving the deck. "This is more than the propeller, Pickett."

Pickett exhaled quietly. "It appears the cable attached to the rudder has snapped, and coding instructions from the Stirling Engine to the port side propeller are incorrect. Most likely an aged programming tin." He closed his eyes. "I had ordered repairs to this ship a month ago, and I've inspected it since, but there were a few items still outstanding that I had deemed low on the list of potential problems."

"The cable to the rudder?" Lewis's eyebrows went up. "Very high on a prioritized list of improvements, I should think."

"I checked the cable myself! I cannot imagine where it has severed."

Isla chanced a look at Pickett. "Could it have been deliberate?"

He shook his head. "I suppose anything is possible, but I fear these problems stem from the usual ship being out of commission. I was forced to make alternate plans with limited options and time." He sighed. "The rest of the fleet is unavailable—out on flights or leaving soon for other destinations. There were not many choices."

The ship dipped again, crazily, throwing them all off-balance. Isla fell against the window, her hands smacking the glass. Daniel and Mr. Lewis both fought to remain upright, and both cursed quite fluently.

"Sir," Samson called from the wheel, "preliminary reports on each 'ton aboard show no malfunction, no unusual or rogue activity."

"Good."

Mr. Lewis nodded. "We do not need to concern ourselves with 'ton reprogramming at this point. It can be tedious to search for one coding error."

"And I did not sabotage anything, technical or otherwise." Isla tried for a playful tone but sounded sickly, even to her own ears.

Mr. Lewis chuckled. "You were my first suspect. Assumed you were the most likely among us to commit nefarious deeds."

"You have no idea," Pickett muttered close to Isla's ear, and she scowled. "Come." He braced a hand under her elbow and put his arm around her shoulders. "At least sit back here on the window seat. You can still see outside but won't fall over. I know nausea when I see it, and you're better off up here than below deck." He then made his way to Samson, who still examined the ship's big wheel.

Mr. Lewis bent at the waist and studied Isla's eyes, this time looking back and forth repeatedly. "One pupil is dilating more than the other." His mouth tightened fractionally. "Try to remain alert, Dr. Cooper. You knocked your head quite impressively."

Isla had seen enough injury and medical emergency in her work that she understood the problem her dilated pupil suggested. "I'll not nap." She managed a smile. "I shall stay in this spot, perfectly awake."

"Lewis," Pickett called. "Have you maintained your programming skills?"

"Of course."

Pickett returned from the wheel, running his hand absently through his hair. "Samson will remain here while I check the cable. I believe I know where it snapped. It's the only place I didn't inspect beyond the cursory." He shook his head, grim. "And this is diagnostic data from the engine room. These codes here, and here"—he pointed on the page, and Mr. Lewis nodded—"are missing a couple digits."

Mr. Lewis nodded. "I've seen it happen before. Some tins are thinner than regulation dictates."

The captain fumed silently. "I pay for the best quality materials. Someone will hear of this."

Isla decided she would not like to be on the receiving end of that conversation, but losing power mid-flight because of cheap coding materials could result in death. She sighed, thinking of the delay they might now be facing, and wondered how long the repairs would take. She felt cold, suddenly, and closed her eyes as a horrifying thought struck. "This could postpone our arrival in Port Lucy."

She opened her eyes and met Pickett's gaze.

"If we are delayed and somewhere over the Atlantic when the full moon is upon us, we will have three predatory shifters aboard this ship with no containment cages."

Chapter 12

"Well, then, Dr. Cooper, I am glad you are aboard. Your skills will be extremely convenient and helpful, I should think." Lewis's face was pale, and Daniel's heart was racing.

Cooper's gaze flickered to Daniel and then back to Lewis. "I . . . Yes, under ordinary circumstances. There are complications of late, and—"

Daniel waved a hand. "We can discuss everything later. Let us focus on one problem at a time." There was no sense in anyone else knowing of Cooper's vulnerability. The fewer who knew, the safer she would be. "Wait here with Samson."

"Tyrant," she muttered, extremely pale, with a light green cast that spoke to her nausea.

"Please," he added. "I'll return shortly. Lewis, take those pages to the engine room. You'll see the control panels labeled along the interior wall. The last page there contains correct codes. New tins are next to the coding machine; pull the faulty ones and reprogram new."

Lewis nodded and paused by Isla. "Doctor, can I bring you anything when I return?"

"Please, call me Isla. And no, thank you."

He smiled, and Daniel ground his teeth together. Why was she telling him to use her given name? And why had Lewis cradled her face in his hands as though he had the right? Daniel knew he was being petty and irrational—Lewis was only seeing to her care—but it didn't halt his irritation. Her left pupil covered more of that bright green iris than the right one, and he was grateful they were hours away from midnight. She needed to remain awake.

"I would invite you to call me 'Adam,' but only my mother does that. My friends simply refer to me as 'Lewis.'"

She smiled, but then the ship dipped again, and she blew out a shallow breath. "Very well, Lewis. I should hate to usurp your mother's privilege."

He laughed. "It isn't much of a privilege, truly, it's only that she—"

"Right then, Lewis," Daniel interrupted. "To the engine room with you. Meet back here in thirty minutes."

Lewis eyed him askance but sketched Cooper a brief bow and left the wheelhouse.

Daniel wanted to take his time examining the bump on Isla's head—she occasionally touched it and winced when she thought he wasn't looking—but he had to content himself with giving her a quick once-over, moving her hair gently this way and that with his fingertips.

She brushed his hands away. "Go, then, or I'll find the severed cable for you. It is not in my nature to sit idly by when there are problems to solve."

"This is not your problem to solve. I am sorrier than I can say that you were injured." He grabbed a satchel that contained a few basic tools.

"Do not be ridiculous, Captain. This was not your doing, and furthermore, you didn't want me here in the first place. The fault lies with me."

"Pickett," he reminded her gruffly as he shoved an additional tool into the bag. "Only my mother calls me 'Captain.'"

She laughed and then winced, but her smile remained. "I should hate to usurp her privilege then, Pickett."

Daniel frowned, remembering that she had said something similar to Lewis.

Samson approached and handed him the most recent weather prediction the onboard processors had generated. Daniel scanned it, disappointed to see that the storm still stretched for miles in every possible direction, including up. He folded the paper and stashed it in his tool bag while watching Cooper try to not be ill.

"Besides, I thought we were friends," he said. "You are reverting to the formal."

"Trying to give all the respect due your position."

He fastened the bag shut and gave her his full regard. "Now that would be a first."

Her smile weakened, and she pulled her knees up to her chest, hugging her legs close. The defensive posture, combined with the long braid that hung over her shoulder had her suddenly looking very young. Vulnerable.

"You are ill indeed, if you can't manage a snappy reply."

"I shall not be ill forever, Pickett, and you've seen me

wield sharp instruments. I should proceed with caution, if I were you."

He lifted a brow. If she knew he quite enjoyed images of her throwing weapons around, she'd probably not use it as a threat. The ship lurched again, bringing him back to the moment, and he slung the tool bag over his shoulder, the heavy fabric of his formal jacket thick and cumbersome.

"Stay here," he ordered again, and left the wheelhouse.

The day passed into evening before Daniel admitted it wouldn't be as simple as he'd hoped to unravel the strange events that had quite literally blown them off course. He and Samson had toiled for hours fixing the cable—it had been severed at an awkward angle between decks—and he held himself responsible. He had inspected each repair made to the *Briar Rose* in the days before departure, but he had been desperately pressed for time and decided the cable was new enough to weather at least three more flights.

The ship had continued to sail erratically in the storm, and he had known a tense moment when a barrel in the cargo hold crashed against the hull behind him. He'd sucked in his breath and spun around in blind panic, familiar sensations from battle settling into his limbs. His rapid movement, combined with the ship's lurch, threw him to the floor, where he knelt, taking several huge breaths.

Unexpected, loud noises—especially behind his back—had prompted similar reactions a handful of times since his return from battle in India. He'd been home less than a month and was attending the garden party of a former classmate when a child had set off a round of firecrackers. Daniel had dropped to the ground, covering his head with his hands.

Blessedly few people had seen, but his mortification had been complete. He avoided events with the potential for sudden, loud noises as much as possible.

Once the cable had been repaired, he met Lewis in the engine room to review the faulty propeller programming codes. It was one more thing that should have been caught ahead of time, even with the ship having been readied hastily. It wasn't necessary to automate the equipment for the entirety of a voyage; it could all be manually overridden or programmed in increments, if desired. He preferred all preparation done beforehand, though, and perhaps this time his efficiency had not been to his benefit.

His conversation with Isla about the possibility of his passengers shifting while still aboard rang in his ears as he returned to the wheelhouse. It certainly was something he'd worried about from the moment they departed, but now it seemed entirely plausible. According to Samson, Isla had left the wheelhouse with Lewis, who had offered to escort her to her quarters. Daniel had checked on her briefly to be sure she was well, relieved to find her eyes normal and her complexion less intensely green.

He worked through the dinner hour and beyond with Samson, and when the skies cleared and they had access to the stars again, they made the grim realization that they had lost at least two, possibly three days' travel time.

Samson took the wheel and gently maneuvered the ship's rudder to be certain all was in working order. The propellers were at full speed, the rudder was functional, and even with delays, they would not run out of fuel. Unfortunately, he had exchanged one set of problems for another.

He leaned against the counter, his shirtsleeves rolled up, his coat and vest having long since been thrown off. He pinched the bridge of his nose and rotated his aching shoulders and neck. His 'ton showed no signs of fatigue, and for a moment, Daniel was envious.

"Samson, I need you to make specific note of all islands between here and Port Lucy. We must determine which are inhabited, which have diplomatic ties to the Crown, and which are independent. I suspect we may need to stop before we reach the port. An uninhabited space would be ideal."

Samson nodded. "Yes, sir. And how do you plan to explain such a detour to Mr. Crowe?"

Daniel sighed. "I shall manufacture a good story—tell him we are heading into another patch of bad weather. Or perhaps stage another malfunction. Crowe can hardly question it if he believes we've been forced to land."

"I understand the preference for finding an uninhabited space." Samson nodded, then paused. "Sir, I believe the extra exertion today may have caused me to run low prematurely. I should charge soon."

"Excellent. Your cyborg-exhaustion makes me feel marginally better about my own limitations. Go—charge for a few hours. Relieve me at seven bells."

"Very good, sir."

"Thank you for your brilliance today, Samson. Although my gratitude means nothing to you."

"On the contrary, Captain. I am intellectually aware that if I possessed emotions, your expressions of gratitude and appreciation would be of great benefit to me." Samson smiled. "So, you are welcome."

Daniel chuckled, and the 'ton left him alone. He withdrew his telescriber and typed in Cooper's scribe code. He'd seen her cross the deck earlier, with Lewis's solicitous help, which had made him scowl enough to bring on a headache. He knew from his quick visit to her quarters earlier that Cooper was recovering remarkably well. When the storm abated and the ship was calm, she had sat out on the deck for a long time before the cold drove her to the lounge. She still hadn't had much of an appetite, but neither had Quince, Bonadea, or Crowe, so he heard dinner had been a subdued affair.

With your permission, I will unlock the connecting door between the cabins tonight. I shall leave you in peace, of course, but I will rest easier knowing that, should something happen, I would be able to assist you.

He sent the message, uncertain of how it would be received, but his motives were entirely pure; if anything, the open door would be a favor she granted to allay *his* concerns. The thought of her trapped in an unnatural sleep made him uneasy. The worst part was knowing that nothing he or anyone else did would awaken her. If she had a mortal enemy—Nigel Crowe came to mind—her life was forfeit without a fight.

His telescriber dinged in response.

If it will put your mind at ease, then I do not mind. Know that it is not necessary for me, however.

He smiled. Fiercely independent, as always. And although her response was true and he readily acknowledged it, it was telling that she felt the need to express it.

He busied himself over the next two hours documenting the day's events. By the time Samson appeared at the door, Daniel was nearly asleep on his feet. He had hoped to return to his cabin before midnight, but by the time he and Samson discussed forecasts and plans for the next day, the time had come and gone.

Daniel left the wheelhouse. He checked Isla's hallway door to be certain it was locked, and then entered his own quarters. Using the dry sink Robert had filled with fresh water, he cleaned away the day's grime and scrubbed his hair. He donned a fresh shirt and trousers since he planned to open the connecting door and glanced at his bed with a ridiculous sense of anticipation. He hadn't been so tired in a long while.

There were two locks on the connecting door, one on either side. He used his key to unlock his side, and was prepared to pick the lock on hers, but when he tried the handle, it opened.

As he stood on the threshold of Isla Cooper's cabin, his heart beat ridiculously fast, and he realized he was well and truly nervous. He'd struggled through the grueling tasks of creating his business, had served time in a bloody war, had lost limbs and organs and experienced excruciating surgeries and treatments—only to hesitate now? He rolled his eyes at his reluctance and took a deep breath.

She's just sleeping, he told himself, and because she'd left a lamp on low, he saw her form in the bed. He moved quietly into the room and crept to her side. He bent down to see her better, and his heart lodged in his throat. He stumbled back and came up against the table or he would have fallen completely flat.

Isla Cooper was dead.

Chapter 13

She was blue. She wasn't breathing.

He scrambled back to her side and grabbed her shoulders. "Cooper! *Cooper*!" What had happened? Short of breath and light-headed, he sank onto the bed and shook her again. "Isla!"

Her head lolled back, and in a panic, unable to think, he lifted her against his chest, cradling her head close. Her arms hung limp and heavy; her body was cold. He rocked slowly back and forth, an ache spreading in his chest. It made no sense. She was vibrant, strong. Full of energy and life. He could not equate the woman he had seen in action over the last few days with the one who now exhibited less animation than a 'ton.

He released her, his throat raw, and set her gently back down on the pillow. He returned to his room for his telescriber and sent a quick message to Lewis, then waited by his door, his eyes burning and his stomach hurting so much he thought he might be ill.

In moments, a soft knock sounded and he opened the door.

Lewis's expression was exhausted disbelief. "What happened to her?"

Daniel simply gestured for Lewis to follow him into the first mate's cabin. He was numb. "I don't know the details, but it is why she is going to Port Lucy," he stammered. "A curse, a spell—she cannot awaken from midnight until six in the morning, but she never . . ." His voice broke, and he swallowed back bile. "She said she sleeps! That is not sleep!"

Lewis frowned and sat on the bed. He picked up her wrist and laid two fingers on the inside pulse point, then shook his head and put his hand at her throat. He repositioned his fingertips several times until he relaxed and straightened.

"She's alive."

Daniel stared at him, hardly believing it. He shoved Lewis's arm aside and put his ear to her heart. Faintly, as light as a bird, he heard it beat. He tried to stand but his legs buckled, and he dropped to his knees.

"Daniel, look. A breath."

Daniel looked up at Lewis, who watched Isla closely. They waited for what seemed an eternity, and then Daniel, too, saw the subtle rise and fall of her chest.

Lewis's brows drew down in confusion. "She breathes every thirty seconds." He looked at Daniel. "What is this?"

Daniel shook his head, his eyes gritty. "She hasn't shared details, only that it involves her sister and a witch who was in London nearly a year ago before leaving for Port Lucy."

Lewis nodded grimly. "And she needs the cure from the witch who cast it."

"How do you know that?"

Lewis lifted a shoulder. "My mother is a Light Magick witch. She says I have some of her traits." He smiled. "Why do you think I'm such a good medic?"

Daniel shoved himself upright and pulled the desk chair to her bedside. "I do not know if this is normal for her or if it's gotten worse."

"And she's had it a year?"

"Nearly a year, she said." He shook his head. "Her friend tracked the dark witch's movements and discovered enough details about the curse to determine that Isla must have the cure immediately or it may become irreversible. She will be in this state every night."

Lewis frowned. "Not only irreversible, I'm afraid. If it is at all similar to other curses with a deadline, she may not survive it at all."

"It will kill her outright?"

"More likely she would be like this day and night—not dead, not quite alive—forever."

Daniel stared at him. "What can we do?"

Lewis lifted his mouth in a small smile. "We are going to help the good doctor find her cure. And then I suppose I'll watch you try to court her."

Daniel scowled. "Don't be ridiculous."

Lewis looked pointedly at Daniel's hand, which clutched the sleeve of her nightdress.

He forced his fingers loose. "I hardly know her."

Lewis raised a brow. "Are you this concerned about all the people you hardly know?"

Daniel's chest began to loosen by degrees, as though

his mind and body finally accepted Isla wasn't dead. He shrugged, exhausted. "I don't know what it is. Perhaps I'm tired. Perhaps I've been too long without the company of a woman of society."

Lewis grinned. "My mother believes in soul mates. Two halves of the same whole and all that rot." He clapped Daniel's shoulder and stood. "I am hoping I possess my own soul in its entirety. So much simpler." He walked to the door and turned, sobering. "Awaken me at once if anything changes. Tomorrow I suggest we have her tell us all the details. We need to know what we're up against. She may not be thrilled about the suggestion, but Quince and Bonadea are both a wealth of information, and the more people she has aiding her cause, the better her chances of success." He shook his head. "Entirely too independent for her own good, that one. Needs to learn to allow others to help."

"Thank you for coming so quickly. I didn't know what to do." The admission cost him dearly, because he was a man who always knew what to do.

"Get some sleep, my friend."

He nodded. "I will." Daniel's throat was raw, and his exhaustion had reached new heights.

Lewis quietly exited through Daniel's cabin, and the room was still again.

Daniel reviewed the events of the last thirty minutes or so, from the time he'd left the wheelhouse. He'd known it from the first moment that first day when she'd stood before him and threatened her way onto his ship. He'd known then somehow that she would upend his life, and it had already begun.

He didn't believe in supernatural foresight, or fate, or anything that flew in the face of his well-honed senses of logic and pragmatism. When he'd thought she was dead, however, he'd felt as though his heart had been pulled from his chest. He tried to tell himself he would have been just as horrified to walk into Quince's cabin and find him lifeless. It was a useless endeavor to convince himself *that* was true. Somehow he couldn't envision himself being so far gone in grief that he would clutch the old man's nightshirt.

He straightened and stood, stretching his cramped legs. "I need to sleep," he muttered and looked down at her still form. "Isla Cooper, we have much to discuss tomorrow." First on his list of complaints would be that she neglected to tell him that when she said she "slept as though dead" that she *slept as though dead.*

He reached down, brushing her hair away from her face and settling her blankets. He looked at her face, peaceful but still appearing so lifeless that his heart thumped hard, and he waited interminably to see her chest rise and fall with a breath.

With a heavy sigh, he returned to his cabin. As exhausted as he was, he ought to have been able to drift immediately into oblivion, but Lewis's words tumbled around in his brain until he thought he'd go mad. If she couldn't find a cure in time, she may sleep forever. The thought of her lying alone in the next room, barely breathing and having lived her life believing she could depend on only herself made him feel ill. He muttered a curse and yanked his blankets off the bed. He crossed his cabin to the window seat and lifted the long cushion, dragging it with him into the other room.

He settled the cushion on the deck next to her bunk and tried to make himself comfortable on it, although it was a foot too short. It wasn't any worse than the sleep he wasn't getting in his bed, though. His breathing deepened, his exhausted muscles grew heavy, and for the first time since the eternally long day had begun, he relaxed.

Chapter 14

Isla awoke the next morning and noted immediately that the chair usually situated at the table had been moved. She frowned, wondering if they'd passed through another storm in the night. If so, she was grateful she'd slept through it. She stretched and stood, pulling against the lethargy and cold. She'd found that moving helped her warm up more quickly. She glanced at the door that connected her cabin to Pickett's and noted it was still closed. Had he not opened it, then?

She shrugged and went through her routine, shaking her hands, preparing for the day, donning the fresh clothing she'd laundered, and shaking her hands some more. She twisted and pinned her hair up, feeling the lump on her head and wincing. It would be tender for a while.

Yesterday's events had been unsettling, and she wondered if the others felt the same sense of weariness. She left the cabin, hoping to find Daniel in the wheelhouse, and spied him with Samson as soon as she stepped onto the deck. She moved to the stairs leading to the upper deck, and sunlight slipped through the cracks between the sails, glinting off the enormous wheelhouse windows.

For the first time in ages, she couldn't be irritated with the bright sunlight. It was such a welcome relief from the storms that she didn't even mind having to squint. The ship moved forward at its customary pace, the propellers' thrum steady and consistent, and a stream of bright blue sky was like a comforting dome above.

She spied Samson on the other side of the wheelhouse door, and he nodded at her as he opened it.

"Good morning, Dr. Cooper."

"Good morning, Samson, and thankfully it is!" She looked across the wheelhouse at Pickett, who held papers and a spyglass in his hands and glanced at her with a quick smile.

"Did you rest well, Captain?"

"Oh, indeed. Like the dead."

"Good." There was something off about his demeanor, and she wondered if another problem with the airship had cropped up. "Everything repaired and in good working condition?" She lifted her brows and smiled brightly, hoping he appreciated the effort it took to do so. Her head was stuffy, and her hands and feet were still cold and tingly.

He set down the spyglass and gave the charts another quick glance before tossing them on the countertop. "Yes. Everything seems to be working perfectly. We are off course, though."

"Oh, dear. I feared as much. How far off course?"

"Four hundred miles north."

"Four . . ." Her eyes opened wide. "Four *hundred*?" How much extra time would it take to reach Port Lucy, then?

He must have read her thoughts. "It has added several days to the journey."

She chewed absently on her lip and nodded. "Well, then, several days it is."

"I've been thinking of your comment yesterday—that the delays could prove troublesome for the other passengers. Samson and I are mapping appropriate island sites to stop at for the three days over full moon, should it become necessary."

She exhaled slowly. "And we all know it will most assuredly be necessary." She looked out the windows at the blue sky, which had seemed so glorious the moment before. "Three days over the full moon," she murmured. "It's not so horribly bad. Three days is not much in the grander scheme of things." Except adding the four days from being blown off course meant Isla had a week less to locate Malette and find the cure.

Pickett crossed the room to stand next to her, and she couldn't meet his eyes. She was the last person who had a right to complain; she was not even a welcome passenger.

"Isla." He stood close, hands in his pockets, warmth radiating from him, and she wasn't sure if the source was physical or emotional. For someone who had spent the bulk of her life feeling as though the weight of her world was a burden she must carry alone, the unspoken support was overwhelming.

Her eyes pricked with tears that must have been due to the bright sunlight. "You're a good man, Daniel Pickett, with a kind heart. Please know I shall do my best, and the very worst-case scenario awaiting me means I receive six good solid hours of rest each night. Not such a bad fate, is it?"

"Not a bad fate at all." But he didn't smile with her, or laugh. The moment was not as light-hearted as she would have liked. "Go and have some tea and a morning biscuit, and I will join everyone momentarily."

She nodded and fidgeted, tapping her fingertips together. Something hung in the air between them, and she didn't know what it was. "Very good. I will do just that." She hesitated, but eventually turned for the door.

"Try not to fret," he said behind her. "We will find your solutions. I'll help you."

She looked over her shoulder with another false, bright smile. "I will be fine; please don't concern yourself. You have an extremely busy life yourself, a dangerous one. My issues pale in comparison. I shall see you later in the morning, then."

She descended the stairs with a heavy heart but was determined to put on a brave face. She straightened her shoulders and glanced at the wheelhouse as she crossed the deck. Daniel stood at the windows, watching her, and she offered a smile that he didn't return, merely nodded.

She smelled breakfast and heard the pleasant rumble of voices before reaching the wardroom. Everybody on board dealt with hard things. As much as she wished life would be simple, just for once, she realized it never was for anyone.

The day passed uneventfully, which stood in stark contrast to the chaos of yesterday. Isla spent her time with the other passengers; even Nigel Crowe, who kept mostly to himself, made random appearances in the library or lounge. He observed in silence, as was his habit, and the other passengers were left wondering what he was about. A sense of unease played in the back of her mind whenever he was with the three passengers. She tensed when they spoke, wondering if that might be the time they gave themselves away.

She played chess with Mr. Quince and compared interesting animal anecdotes with Mr. Bonadea. He missed his wife and children, and Isla hurt for him. She determined to aid Emme's cause more actively when she returned home. There must be government officials who could be swayed to see reason. Most predatory shifters were law-abiding citizens who never ran afoul of the law or caused harm.

Lewis was especially solicitous and checked the wound on her head. He told her about some of the war experiences he had had with the captain, stories both amusing and horrifying. He was handsome and charming, but guarded, consistently keeping parts of himself separate. Hidden. She sensed if people pried too much, asked too many questions, he withdrew completely. Still, they were becoming comfortable friends.

There was a notable difference, however, in the pull she felt toward the captain. Pickett was something else altogether, and she was at a loss to understand it.

She didn't see much of Daniel during the day—he was occupied in the wheelhouse—though she occasionally spied him returning from the engine room or inspecting the heavy rope coils that connected the ship to the huge balloon that kept them aloft. He had informed them all about the delay caused by the storm and the ship malfunctions, and she assumed he would notify the shifters separately about his plans to stop over the Full Moon Phase. He couldn't very well discuss it with Crowe present. She suspected Crowe was merely waiting for the right crumb to fall from the table and then he would pounce.

As evening became night, she stopped by the wheelhouse to bid Pickett good night, but he wasn't there. Samson told her he would pass along her message, so she retired to her chambers, not bothering to pretend she wasn't disappointed she hadn't seen more of him during the day.

She was settled for the evening in her nightgown and reading a book Mr. Bonadea had loaned to her when she heard a low, quiet rumble of voices in the captain's cabin, followed by a knock on the connecting door. She sat up in bed and pulled her blankets close, surprised.

"Come in?"

The door opened, and Daniel poked his head inside. "We must speak with you. Is that all right?"

She stared. "Who is we?"

He had the grace to look sheepish. "Everyone but Crowe. And the 'tons. Will you join us in here?"

"I . . . Very well, give me a moment to dress . . ." She trailed off when he shook his head.

"Do you have a housecoat or nightgown covering? We don't have much time before midnight."

She nodded.

He closed the door, and she got out of bed and hastily shrugged her arms into her robe, tying the ribbons.

Why on earth did they want to speak with her now? She assumed it dealt with the upcoming moon phase, and she hoped she could put their minds at ease. She knocked on the door, then entered to find Pickett, along with Lewis, Mr. Bonadea, and Mr. Quince. Their collective presence loomed large in the cabin, and, dressed in her nightclothes, she felt awkward.

She shook herself mentally as Pickett pulled out one of the two chairs at the table for her; Mr. Bonadea gave Mr. Quince the other. She was a seasoned hunter and counselor. She had seen and handled more things in her lifetime than most. She could have a discussion with four adults, even if she was dressed in her nightclothes and—she glanced at the clock on the wall—less than half an hour from succumbing to involuntary oblivion.

She met Pickett's eye after checking the time, and he nodded. He moved to the edge of his bed near her chair, and she looked around at the group. "Shall I steal a snack from the kitchen, and we can comb each other's hair? Perhaps discuss the upcoming Season and who will likely court whom?"

Lewis laughed, and Pickett bit the inside of his cheek. He tipped his head in acknowledgment of her teasing and spoke quietly. "We are all here because you require assistance but will never ask for it."

She stared at him and then at each of the others, who looked at her with kind expressions. Mr. Quince's eyes held the sheen of tears. Warmth enveloped the room, and she caught her breath.

"I don't know what—"

Pickett held up a hand and cut her short. "You do know what I mean. You must find a cure for this curse, and time is of the essence." He glanced around the room. "Five heads are better than one, and we must discuss this now so that Crowe is unaware. For obvious reasons."

She cleared her throat, uncomfortable, and wished she could crawl out of the room unnoticed.

Lewis leaned comfortably against the hull. "Suppose you share details—all of them—from the beginning of the curse. We must know what we are facing."

She frowned. "I could never, would never, ask this of *any* of you. We each have our own challenges, and I can solve—"

Mr. Quince waved his hand in her direction. "The details, please, my dear."

It was the first time he had referred to her as anything other than "doctor," and she imagined him to be a grandfather she'd always wanted but never had. Rather than blubber sentimentality, she nodded.

"Very well." She rubbed her forehead, swallowing past the uncomfortable lump in her throat. "My younger sister, Melody, is seventeen years old. She is the life of every party, and she attracts her share of male suitors, although my mother and I both feel she is emotionally immature." Isla paused. "She is so young, despite being of marriageable age, and impulsive, and impetuous, and the absolute bane of my existence.

"Last year, Mr. Brixton, a young man new to the area, nearly twenty years old, took an avid interest in her. He was a shifter, newly coming into it."

The men exchanged glances.

"She began spending time with him more frequently and less with other friends. The more she devoted her attention exclusively to him, the more irritated I became with her. I had no worries about the fact he was a shifter. It's what he did with his time during the rest of the month." She paused. "I could never get a satisfactory feel for who he was at his core, and he left me uneasy for Melody's sake."

She drew a breath and shook her head. "I learned through an associate that he was heavily in debt, he gambled incessantly, and he had broken two engagements to young women in the countryside. Ruined them completely."

Mr. Bonadea's eyes narrowed. "One of my fears for my own daughters—the cad!"

Isla nodded. "Melody and I are close. My mother was so busy establishing the boutique that it fell to me to raise my sister. When I took this issue to our mother for support, she tried to speak to Melody, but the girl is so stubborn that she wouldn't hear a word.

"So, I sat her down one evening just over a year ago and told her that I forbade her association with this man and that I would cut short her pin money and other social activities if she did not end the relationship. It was the week before the nearby village's autumn celebration, which is quite a big event in the area—dancing, merriment, bonfires, chaperones turning a blind eye with a wink, that sort of event. You understand."

They nodded.

"She was quiet for that week leading up to the celebration. I thought she might have listened to me, taken me at my word. I was overjoyed. I was convinced she finally believed me and trusted my judgment about this wretched man she'd insisted she loved.

"Festival day approached, and I attended with Melody

and our cousins, but we had to leave at ten o'clock that night. I'd received word that a shifter who had intentionally committed several murders as a wolf was seen near Whitechapel, and it might be our only chance to apprehend him."

Isla drew in a breath, irritated that it shook. "I went home to scribe my employees and another hunter from the area. We made plans to meet at midnight. Melody said she wanted to fix a snack for me before I left, and when I told her I needed to leave, she looked so hurt. I decided I could spare ten minutes and then leave."

Her lip trembled, and she bit it. She shoved her hair back from her face. "She fixed us tea and gave me a scone she'd made earlier. She made a point of serving my tea in my favorite pink teacup—the one that belonged to my mother when she was a child."

Isla shook her head. "She'd slipped a powdered concoction into the drink along with a large spoonful of sugar when I wasn't looking. She sipped her tea, and I sipped mine, and I choked it down because she'd seemed so delighted with herself and with us . . ."

Mr. Quince sniffed.

"I was about to gather my things to leave when I felt heavy, exhausted. I thought I might fall to the floor, and my vision clouded. Melody helped me to the parlor, where I collapsed on the sofa. That is the last I remember until morning. When I awoke, I was sluggish, felt as though my head had been used as a drum. The first thing I saw was Melody. She was sitting next to me, her face splotchy and tearstained, and when I looked at her, she sobbed and threw her arms around me. She admitted she'd put a 'sleeping aid' in my tea so she could sneak back to the festival and meet her beau. But when she returned home hours later and couldn't awaken me, she became frantic.

"She said she'd been introduced to a Dark Magick witch in the sorcery quarter and paid six months' worth of pin money and an emerald bracelet belonging to my paternal grandmother for a spell that would put someone into a deep sleep for a night."

Isla frowned and looked at her hands. "My skin had a blue tinge that faded fairly quickly, but I was so cold, so frightened. It was nothing compared to Melody's panic, though, so I assured her all was forgiven, that I would discuss the matter with Mother to determine a consequence for her behavior. I was more concerned that she'd venture into the sorcery quarter again.

"I went about my day, and before long, felt my customary self. My colleagues had missed the man we were to arrest, so we determined to gather more information and try again. We apprehended him at eleven o'clock that night. I went to my offices downtown, sent my employees home, and worked on the case notes for the Yard. I finished late, intending to hail a 'ton-operated hansom, but I never made it that far. I collapsed in the alley behind the building and awoke the next morning, exactly as I had the morning before. Groggy, limbs heavy and cold, a blue, translucent tinge to my skin."

The men stared at her, silent. A muscle in Pickett's jaw flexed, and he rubbed the back of his neck. "You were fortunate you were left alone in that alley."

Isla nodded. "Most assuredly. The crime rate around the offices is not exorbitant, but we have the occasional attack for money or jewelry." She shook her head with a small, bitter laugh. "I made my way home and cornered Melody, demanding full details about what she'd given me and the woman who had provided it. She knew nothing about the contents of the spell; she had ordered it from a witch named Malette, who told her it would take a week to prepare and instructed her to return then."

Lewis whistled, low. "It's no wonder the spell continues. Preparation that involved is usually reserved for large-scale curses." He frowned. "Is this Malette known to you?"

Isla shook her head. "My friend Hazel is from a Light Magick family, but she is not a witch in the traditional sense. She has studied the art and history of it, and she recalls details like a well-programmed 'ton. I took the problem to her, and she immediately went to work researching the spell. We went to the sorcery quarter to find Malette, but she had disappeared. Her trail was completely nonexistent." Isla smiled. "And I am a very good tracker."

She continued. "Hazel dug and dug. She told me early on that we would need to find Malette, that any cure must be generated by her or come directly from her notes. Night after night, the spell continued. Melody was beside herself—it was supposed to have worked for only the one night." Isla sighed. "And I was correct about that beau of hers. He left. Broke her heart."

Pickett had been silent throughout her tale, mostly studying the floor, feet crossed at the ankles and arms folded across his chest. He looked at her now, his expression giving nothing away. "How did you learn Malette is in Port Lucy?"

Isla nodded. "Hazel finally bribed the right person. We

learned that Malette had disappeared almost immediately after selling Melody the spell. Hazel told me she had feared from the beginning that the spell may contain a deadline. A 'point of no return' after which any cure would be useless. She calculated the duration of the time needed to form and prepare it, noted my symptoms, studied the bag that had contained the powder, and questioned Melody about anything she could tell her about the smell of the stuff, sensory observances, that sort of thing. Hazel's best guess is one year from administration to No-Return."

The silence again hung thick in the small room.

"And you'd never met this witch? Are you certain?" Daniel knit his brow. "I might think she had made a mistake in her measurements or combination, but it took a week to prepare. Seems awfully extreme for someone she didn't know."

Isla shrugged. "I've wracked my brain, dug for answers about her without making anyone suspicious, but I cannot remember ever knowing her." She paused, attempting levity. "Perhaps I have already passed No-Return, and this whole voyage is for naught. Perhaps the curse is permanent already, and I'll just sleep well each night."

Lewis shook his head, his expression something close to pained. "I do not believe you have passed it yet. You're still waking up every morning."

Isla registered Daniel's swift glance at his friend. "We don't know that," Pickett murmured.

Isla blinked. "Are you suggesting after No-Return, the spell will kill me?"

He shook his head, regret clear in his eyes. "Not kill you. But perhaps leave you in that state indefinitely. There were two instances I knew of as a child that resulted in permanence of this sort."

"We don't know that will happen here," Pickett repeated, his voice rising.

"Perhaps there are other options," Mr. Quince interjected, leaning forward in the chair. "I know much about plant life, dear lady, and we will find a viable alternative. I cannot reverse the curse, but I can instruct you on exact procedures if we can retrieve her spell book. Spells are temperamental, and a good knowledge of the herbs and ingredients will make a world of difference. Sometimes it is a matter of combining them in the most optimal order."

Isla's throat felt tight. "Even though you're not a witch?"

He nodded, sympathy pouring from him in waves. He reached across the table for her hand, clasping her fingers with his elderly ones. "There is always hope. And we do have a witch among us." He nodded toward Lewis, whose blush was visible even in the room's low light.

"Half-witch," he muttered and shrugged. "My mother."

"My point is we will find a way together." Mr. Quince squeezed her fingers again and released her.

"And none of this 'I can do it by myself' business." Mr. Bonadea looked at her directly and held her gaze. "I am far from my own children, and as a father, I would like to help. I would want someone to help my daughters."

"Oh, drat, then," Isla said, her eyes burning. "I welcome the help, and if I can, I shall return it tenfold."

"Right," Pickett said. "We'll all ruminate for the next few days and formulate a plan for Port Lucy." He checked his pocket watch. "Time for bed."

She nodded, feeling the faint tendrils of lethargy approaching. "Thank you all."

They each murmured their good-byes and left, and Pickett gently tugged her up from the chair.

"I hardly know what to say," she told him, her head feeling heavy as he walked her back to her cabin. "You do not owe me anything. Quite the contrary."

He situated her pillow as she crawled into bed and lay down on her side.

She yawned. "Do not feel obligated to stay. I'll not be going anywhere."

He smiled.

"Does it look so very awful? When I sleep?" She blinked slowly, each lift of her eyelids a chore.

"Not at all." He cradled her hand between his. "You look very peaceful."

She smiled. "I did not take you for a liar, Captain Pickett. My skin turns blue."

"Blue is my favorite color."

Her eyes refused to open again, and as she sank into the nothing, his grip on her hand tightened. For the first time since the curse began, she didn't feel alone.

Chapter 15

The next several days settled into a comfortable routine. Isla found her time compartmentalized into
simple categories: mealtime, library or lounge time
with Quince, Bonadea, Lewis, occasionally the silent Mr.
Crowe, and sometimes Pickett, and wheelhouse time chatting
with Samson and the captain. The more she learned about
her fellow passengers, the more she admired them, enjoyed
their company. Nigel Crowe had reined in the bulk of his
insults, and she even found herself tolerating his presence.

And whenever Daniel Pickett entered a room, the harder
her heart thumped.

Since the evening nearly a week before when her concerned new friends had insisted on knowing the exact nature
of her troubles, they had each come to her with suggestions
or possible scenarios that could lead to a cure. Anecdotes
aplenty circulated: "My grandfather once cured a bout of
insomnia with some ground albermile and charred frog leg.
Perhaps a concoction with opposite components might slow
the progression . . ." And as much as her nerves were still

strung taut, the pressure she'd carried for so many months began to ease. It was as though the elephant on her chest was suddenly lighter.

Pickett continued to open the door connecting their cabins each night just before midnight. Even if he was in the wheelhouse until after midnight, she knew he still opened the door when he finally retired because the next morning when she tried the handle, the connecting door was always unlocked.

She'd not looked at her reflection directly after awakening for some time. Seeing her skin blue was disturbing, unsettling. She imagined it must have been horrifying for Pickett to see her that way—Melody had been nearly insensate with fear—so if it brought him comfort to know the door was open, the last thing she would do was forbid it. She didn't lie to herself and try to suggest it wasn't also a comfort for her.

Late one afternoon, two days away from Full Moon Phase, as the airship neared a tiny island chain not far from Port Lucy, Isla looked in the wheelhouse for Pickett. She'd not broached the topic with the entire group—they never knew when Crowe was lurking—but she desperately wanted details about the tentative plans. Although she would be useless during the late-night hours when the three men would shift, she still wanted to know where they would be, what Pickett intended, and exactly how he planned to handle Crowe.

She spied Samson in the wheelhouse and stuck her head inside the door. "Do you know where I might find the captain?"

The 'ton nodded. "He is in the engine room, reviewing programming codes."

"Very good." Pickett had obsessively checked and re-checked every possible programming and hardware element of the ship's functions daily since the malfunction. "Thank you." She smiled at Samson and descended the stairs to the bottom deck.

The hallway was dimly lit and reminded her of her encounter with Nigel Crowe. He always seemed so cold, yet stress rolled off him in waves.

She looked inside the engine room but didn't see the captain. She made her way to the cargo door and noted it was open. She pushed it with two fingers and saw Pickett hefting a barrel of oil fuel onto his shoulder, and when he spied her in the doorway, he tensed and then relaxed.

He grinned at her, and she caught her breath. His demeanor around her was easier by tenfold than when they'd first met. Perhaps it was because of her empathic nature connecting with his distant shifter lineage, although that was unlikely, or perhaps it was the ease of familiarity that came from enforced confinement with few people for days on end. Either way, she found herself drawn to Captain Pickett more with each passing day.

When he wasn't in the lounge with her and the others, she wondered what he was doing. When he was pensive, she wondered what was on his mind, whether he was worried about something she might be able to solve. She was curious about his travels, his family, his tenure in India. She was concerned that somewhere in the quiet places of her mind that she pretended didn't exist, she'd fashioned him into a hero because he'd taken on the unofficial role of "protector" while she slept.

She was grateful, surely that was the extent of it.

"Coming down to practice knife throwing?" He winked as he passed her, the barrel resting easily against his shoulder and arm. He motioned with his hand, and she moved aside as he locked the door.

"Wait here," he said and carried the barrel into the engine room.

She was so much more aware of him, more attuned to his presence, than she'd ever been to a man. She was close to her childhood friend, Will, but that was different. Will was more of a brother, a best friend. She'd never had the urge to watch him walk away when he left a room or wanted to seek him out just to speak with him about anything at all, even inconsequential matters.

She heard the murmur of Pickett's voice in the engine room as he spoke with the 'tons, and he returned shortly, pulling the door closed. "So, if you're not here to practice martial arts, what is it that has you looking so serious?"

She blinked, trying for a light expression. "Nothing pressing, just wondered if you can share any details about your plans for our unexpected detour."

He nodded and moved into the narrow corridor. She caught a brief scent of his shaving lotion—subtle, not cloying, more like soap than cologne. It suited him. He tilted his head slightly, and she hoped he couldn't suddenly read thoughts. "Are you concerned about it?"

"Concerned?"

"The full moon. Our unscheduled stop."

"Not so much, but I would like to know what to expect.

Forewarned is forearmed and all that." Why was she suddenly so unsettled?

He studied her face. "You're nervous."

"Why would you think so?"

"You're tapping your fingers together."

Isla looked down at her hands. Curses! She knew people, knew body language, knew emotions and how the tiniest details in a person's demeanor spoke to their inner dialogue. That she didn't see it in herself was galling. She puffed out a breath and rolled her eyes. She deliberately clasped her hands together and looked back up at him. "There is much on my mind, I suppose."

He rested his shoulder against the wall close to her. "Understandable."

There was a glint in his eye she didn't particularly care for. "You don't believe me."

"I believe you have much on your mind, without question."

"However?"

His lips twitched. "I wonder if you have more on your mind than you realize. Or care to acknowledge."

"I am fairly certain I know my own brain, Pickett."

"Daniel."

She blinked. "I'm sorry?"

"We've become better friends, wouldn't you say? That warrants a different level of familiarity."

Her brain was fuzzy. She admitted to herself that in recent days she'd become rather distracted when he was in the room. If only she didn't have so many pieces of chaos vying for her attention then she might be able to sort out her own thoughts. The curse, three passengers ready to shift, an elusive dark witch, a nasty government agent, delay after delay . . . It was little wonder she couldn't discern between up and down.

She leaned her back against the wall with a quiet sigh and rubbed her temples. "Some days I think I'd like to cut off my own head."

He smiled. "You would be infinitely less lovely without a head."

She tipped her head back. "But infinitely less stressed."

He laughed, and she relaxed by degrees. A smile twitched at the corners of her mouth, and she turned her head toward him. He was so close, so very *there.* Her life had been full of challenges, and she'd never abdicated her responsibility for them. But just once, how wonderful would it be to burrow close to someone, allow him to hold her and all the complicated pieces of her life. Support while she carried the load was a luxury she'd never had.

She swayed toward him without meaning to.

His smile faded, and his gaze sharpened. His intake of breath brought him closer to her, and she suddenly felt very warm.

"It is comfortable, now, isn't it," he murmured. "And yet not at all relaxing."

She nodded.

"Are you working your empath magic? Weaving a spell?" He brought his hand to her face, tracing her cheek with his thumb.

"I'm not doing anything," she whispered.

"I don't believe you."

She closed her eyes at the feather-light sensation of his fingertip.

"Who waits at home for you? This 'Will' you've mentioned?"

She opened her eyes and bravely met his even as her mind told her to protect herself and run. "Nobody waits for me, Pickett."

"Daniel." He traced her ear with his finger, barely touching her skin. "I find that hard to believe."

"I haven't the time. Daniel."

He smiled. "A pity, Dr. Cooper."

"Isla." She fought the instinct to curl into his hand like a cat.

"How many Seasons ago did you come out?" He continued his slow exploration of her skin, drawing his knuckles along her jawline.

She sighed. "Too many to count."

His eyes held hers. A smile flirted at the corner of his mouth. "Something tells me your focus was elsewhere. I cannot see you pining away, Season after Season, next to the refreshment table and a stern-faced chaperone."

She laughed softly. "You're very astute." She felt shy, which was an emotion Isla Cooper had never experienced. She was—what was the phrase? Punching above her weight. At an utter loss. At sea. Which was literally true, she supposed, and her wry smile remained despite the blush she felt spreading across her face. As much as she'd come to dislike the dark, she found she didn't mind the dim light of the corridor.

His hand lightly slipped around her neck to cup the back

of it, his thumb working in small circles behind her ear. A sigh escaped her lips, and she leaned fractionally closer. *His* magic was much more potent than anything she possessed.

She lifted her fingers and traced his jacket lapels as he slowly moved into her space, pulling her close with a hand on her hip, the other still massaging the tension from her neck. She drowned in subtle sensations as he wound his arm around her waist. He blew softly at a curl of her hair, a stubborn one that never remained in place, and she felt his lips moving on her temple, whispering something she couldn't discern.

Her hands tightened on his lapels, and she pulled herself closer, tipping her head upward as his lips trailed from her temple to her cheek.

One of the engine room doors swung open with a bang, and footsteps sounded in the hall. Isla sprung back, stunned and convinced a bucket of ice water would have been no more effective at snapping her to attention.

" . . . retrieve it from the cargo hold . . ." one of the 'tons said back into the engine room and then moved toward them.

Isla scratched her ear and looked away, grateful to have been caught by an automaton and not one of the other passengers. Her breathing was rapid, as was Daniel's, she noted. He rubbed the back of his neck and caught her eye with a self-deprecating half-grin.

The 'ton moved around them wordlessly and unlocked the cargo hold door, disappearing inside. The door remained open, and Daniel held his hand out and motioned to her. He cupped her elbow and walked with her to the stairs, where he followed her without comment to the upper decks.

What did one say in such circumstances? For the first

time in a lifetime spent soothing others with her voice, her cadence, her vocabulary, she was at a complete loss. She wished Melody had given her a tip or two from her vast flirtation repertoire. Before long, she found herself in front of her cabin, awkwardly facing Daniel and tapping her fingertips against her leg.

"Cooper—Isla, I . . ." He met her eyes, again rubbing the back of his neck and searching for the right words. He drew his brows in apparent confusion and shook his head. "I'm sorry?"

"You are?" she managed. She didn't want him to be sorry.

"I . . . no. Not especially." He pinched the bridge of his nose and then ran a hand through his hair, the other shoved into his pocket as though forcing himself to keep it there. "You . . . I . . ." He finally settled his full gaze on her face. "I am not sorry. And for *that*, I apologize."

She bit her lip, focusing on breathing in and then breathing out.

His brow wrinkled. "Are you well, then?"

She nodded. "Yes. Yes, quite." She forced levity into her tone. "I . . . um, have some correspondence I need to attend to," she said, motioning toward the cabin with her thumb.

"Yes, of course. I'm relatively certain Samson needs me in the wheelhouse." He inched back toward the stairs. "I shall see you later, for supper. But do tell Robert to bring tea to you before then. You can reach him by telescribe, of course."

"Of course."

He paused, one hand on the railing, one booted foot on the stair. He studied her until she felt herself blush, and his lips turned up again in that smile. Her breath caught in her throat, and she fumbled for the door handle, forgetting the door was still locked. She bumped her shoulder into it and closed her eyes, mortified. She was a *doctor*. She had more years of education and experience than most people she knew. She had taken down murderous, predatory wolves twice her size. She had a dagger sheathed on her thigh and throwing stars hidden in her corset. And she now blushed as though she was twelve years old and meeting a boy behind the wood-shed.

She dug into her pocket for the key and looked over at Daniel, who remained poised on the steps, watching her. His smile suddenly looked suspiciously smug. Satisfied. She narrowed her eyes at him, and he chuckled, climbing up the steps and out of sight.

Chapter 16

Daniel stood in the wheelhouse after dinner, looking into the dark night, a smile twitching when
he thought of Isla's response to him. She had been
flustered, entranced, and decidedly off-balance. He couldn't
help but be satisfied that he'd been the one to bring it about.
Isla Cooper was a force. Competent, intelligent, independent,
nearly fearless. A few moments in a dark corridor with him had
her blushing and trying to shove her way into a locked door.

"Sir," Samson said. "We will fly over one of the best island options tomorrow at noon. It's uninhabited, and part of
a small chain held by the Crown. We will not need accommodations, as we are self-sufficient with the ship's stores."

Daniel nodded. "Set our heading. I will spread word in
the morning that the propeller is likely to malfunction again.
I also need weather charts as of tonight at—"

He broke off when he saw Lewis tearing his way across
the deck and up the stairs to the wheelhouse. He crossed to
the door and yanked it open as Lewis reached the top. "What
is it?"

"It's happening again." Lewis's face was flushed, his eyes watering and pupils dilating.

"No, no . . ." Daniel stared at the man. "Are you certain? Has it happened since India?"

Lewis shook his head and pulled at the collar of his shirt. "I thought India was an anomaly because I was young."

Daniel drew in a breath. "Where am I going to put you?"

Lewis's eyes widened, and he tore at the tie. Daniel cursed himself up one side and down the other. Lewis needed to remain calm, not feed off Daniel's distress.

He took Lewis's arm and called to Samson. "Do you know if Dr. Cooper is in her cabin?"

Samson nodded. "I believe she is."

Daniel ushered Lewis down the stairs. "She can help. She's very good." He hoped it was true. They reached his quarters where he pushed Lewis inside and locked the door.

"Dan. I'm sorry. I am so sorry—you'll have to put me in the cargo hold, but I might destroy it."

Daniel shook his head. "Relax, my friend. You are not going to shift. We have the best shifter empath aboard, and you will be fine."

Lewis's eyes were bleak. "She falls asleep at midnight."

Daniel tugged Lewis's tie loose and tossed it on his table. He unfastened the top two buttons of his friend's shirt, helped him remove his jacket and then his vest. If Lewis was going to shift, he needed to undress. "Should worse come to worst, I'll move the fuel barrels out of the cargo hold. It'll be fine." He managed a tight smile.

"If the doctor is going to help, you cannot strip me to my

smallclothes." Lewis closed his eyes tightly as Daniel removed his cuff links and rolled up his sleeves.

"I won't. Just loosening everything should you need it. No sense in ruining your fine clothing." Daniel tried not to flinch as Lewis's skin rippled along the arm.

"You should tranquilize me. You must have a gun on board somewhere."

Daniel shook his head. "That's a death sentence, and you know it. There's a reason people like Isla have a job. If we could tranquilize every shifter and have them sleep it off, the problem would be solved." Ninety-nine percent of shifters who were tranquilized died. A shifter, while human, could be safely put to sleep with medicine for surgical purposes any day of the week. The result was deadly, however, in shifted form or during Full Moon Phase.

A soft knock sounded at the connecting door, and Daniel opened it to see Isla, brows drawn in worry. He pulled her into the room with little finesse. His hands were shaking.

She focused immediately on Lewis. She moved quickly and took his arm, pulling out a chair with one hand and easing him into it. "Talk to me, Lewis. What is happening?"

Lewis gulped in deep breaths. "I once shifted *before* Full Moon Phase. It was in India."

Daniel watched as Isla pulled the second chair close to Lewis and sat next to him, reaching for his hand. Her focus on the man was total, her demeanor assured, calm. He felt his own chest ease slowly, taking comfort in her complete control.

"You were young then? Not unusual for a novice."

He nodded.

"Breathe deeply with me." Isla began a slow, even pattern

of breathing and nodded when Lewis followed. She smiled. "We'll do this together. No cause at all for alarm."

He glanced down at his arms. "It's happening!"

She rubbed his forearm. "Look at me. Lewis, at me." She nodded again. "I can help you, but you must focus."

Daniel turned on an additional Tesla lamp and quietly retrieved the chair from Isla's cabin. He sat on the other side of the table and exhaled slowly.

Lewis gripped her hands. "I respect you, Isla, you know I do. But this is a physical problem, and I will endanger everybody on this ship—"

She breathed in deeply and indicated for him to join her. After reestablishing an even rhythm with him, she said quietly, "This has not occurred since the one time in India, then?"

He shook his head, shoulders sagging.

"Sometimes an early shift is brought about because of undue stress." She smiled. "Very rarely does it happen biologically with no external, social trigger. In all my experience, I've never seen it occur due to anything other than worry or emotional duress. Now here we are, flying to a new home you've never seen, with an enemy in our midst, and aboard a vessel not ideally equipped. Your worry has likely piled, step upon step, and eventually that stress will find a way to surface."

She ducked her head when he looked away, pulling his attention back to her. "It's not physiological, which means we can work to reverse the process."

Lewis sniffed and exhaled, slowly relaxing his white-knuckled grip on Isla's hands. "This is mortifying," he said, the skin on his arm still rippling, but not as aggressively as before. "Quince is an old man, and he's fine."

Isla laughed softly. "Exactly. He's an old man. He has been living this process for decades."

"Bonadea is fine," Lewis grumbled, and Daniel suppressed a smile.

"But we do not know if he has ever faced this before, do we? It is not uncommon. It is why some shifters extend their shifting time away from family with an extra two days before and after the customary three-day-phase." She gave his hands a little shake. "Because some people have issues exactly like this. Many would be quite cross with you for complaining, when this marks only the second time in your life you've had symptoms a day or two before the shifting phase."

Lewis nodded, sweat beading on his brow. Daniel reached for his handkerchief, but Isla produced one from her pocket first. She wiped his forehead as one would an ill child, the lace-edged square of white fabric in stark contrast to Lewis's masculine features.

There was something about her, and if Daniel had harbored doubts about the legitimacy of an empath's abilities, they'd have been put to quick rest. The skills, the words, the methods—all those things could be taught, but there was something about her presence, her *soul*, that evened out the chaos. Where his quarters had been awash in panic before her arrival, the air was now filled with quiet confidence. Daniel was still concerned, but he felt now that the problem wasn't insurmountable. Little wonder she was valued in her field.

"Forgive my lack of faith, but you will be asleep in a few short hours, Dr. Cooper." Lewis's voice was strained, but he tried to smile. "I wonder what I shall do then when the full shifting hour arrives."

"Daniel, do you have a pitcher of water?" Isla asked, still looking at Lewis.

He filled a glass from the pitcher at the dry sink and set it before Lewis, who let go of one of Isla's hands to take a drink of water.

She shifted subtly, and Daniel saw her slowly flex her fingers with a barely perceptible wince. She then switched to holding Lewis's other hand while still slowly rubbing her free hand along his forearm, where the ripples continued to subside.

Lewis set his glass down but kept turning it slowly on the tabletop.

"Sorry, old man," Lewis said to Daniel, his voice raw. "I've put us all at risk. I wouldn't blame you if you wanted to put down on the ocean."

Daniel raised a brow. "And throw you overboard? Wait for a giant fish to swallow you whole?" He grimaced. "I'd throw Crowe overboard before you."

"Perfect." Isla smiled. "All problems solved."

Lewis managed a half-smile. "All except the havoc I'll wreak on this vessel." He winced. "I do not function well . . . enclosed."

"You alpha lot are such a trial." Isla winked. "You make life so difficult for the rest of us. You'll be surprised to learn the such behavior is not singular to males. I've encountered many females who react in the same manner."

"Alpha females." Daniel smiled. "What I wouldn't give to see you explain that to Crowe."

Isla shook her head with a humorless laugh. "That one does not need another reason to dislike women."

"That one doesn't like anyone," Lewis muttered.

"Has he bothered you more than usual?" Isla asked.

Lewis continued turning the glass in circles by degrees on the table. "His implied suspicions are becoming less veiled."

"Toward all three of you?"

"Yes, but he seems especially antagonistic to me." Lewis released the glass and rubbed the heel of his hand into his eye. "If I have allowed that man to drive me to this . . ." He shook his head, disgust clear. "I am pathetic."

"No, you are human." Isla gave his hand a squeeze.

Lewis laughed, his eyes bleary, and he glanced at her. "After a fashion."

"Certainly you're a shifter. But you're human. I wonder if you aren't allowing some of Crowe's poisonous rhetoric to seep in here." She tapped his temple lightly. "I do not know the reason for Crowe's prejudice, but I do know that it is toxic, and it poisons his soul even as he spreads it around. Do not let it affect you."

He nodded.

Isla drummed her fingers on the table and glanced around the room. Her eyes stopped on Daniel's vest, and she nodded toward it. "May I borrow your pocket watch?"

He unfastened the end of the chain from his vest and handed the watch to her, curious.

She placed it on the table by her elbow. "Lewis, I believe I can help you achieve a state of awareness that may allow you to retain more control over your human brain, even when you shift and instinct plays a greater role in behavior."

Lewis's brow wrinkled. "I've never heard of such a thing. How is it done?"

"A colleague has pioneered a therapy method that could make a wonderful difference for shifters. However, his research is only preliminary. His sample pool is not extensive, so results are not conclusive."

"What does it entail?"

"I would place you into a deeply meditative state and then suggest to your brain that it remain forefront during and after shifting. Having never shifted personally, I cannot tell you exactly how it will affect you once you are in wolf form. I understand there ordinarily is a vague awareness of your personality, your life?"

He nodded. "I know who I am, but it is as if there are two sides that are tied together as one, but are somehow separate." He brushed a hand through his hair and sat back in the chair, releasing his grip on her fingers. "I don't know how to explain it."

"That is exactly the description I get from most shifters. The nature of the person is consistent, including the brain, but when shifted, instinct rises to a position of dominance. That is the reason for most shifters' extreme duress if contained in tight spaces or treated aggressively." She paused, again tapping her fingertips on the table. "What I am uncertain of, and what research does not yet show, is if there is any mental distress or discomfort when retaining a greater portion of human awareness while in shifted form."

Lewis considered her. "I could feel like a human trapped in a wolf's body."

She lifted a shoulder. "Early feedback from those who

have experienced it suggests no negative reactions, simply a lessening of animal instinct and a greater human awareness. If you're interested, I can plant the suggestion."

Lewis nodded. "Do it. If I don't shift, that's wonderful. If I do, perhaps I'll do less damage overall."

Daniel's head spun. An untried, experimental treatment for a shifter changing too early, miles above the earth with unstable passengers, a cursed empath, and a possible saboteur aboard. Of course it would stand to reason that another insane element should be added to the mix. He removed his jacket and vest, and untied his cravat.

Isla looked at him, her mouth lifted in a smirk. "Concerned, Captain?"

"Not in the least, Doctor."

"It is not invasive surgery. I require no scalpels or sutures."

Lewis smiled, a glint of hope in his eyes. "At this point, I believe I'd allow it."

Isla laughed and stood, looking around the room. "Somewhere for you to be comfortably seated . . ." She tapped her finger against her lip.

It wasn't until Daniel moved closer to her, scrutinized her, that he noticed her face was pale. Her lips were set tighter than usual, her eyes squinted at the corners. Daniel decided not to ask after her welfare at that moment, since Lewis was calm and appeared to have control of his shifting symptoms.

Unless Lewis isn't the one fully in control.

Chapter 17

As Daniel moved closer to Isla, he sensed a subtle energy that radiated from her and stretched to Lewis. He thought he saw a heat wave in the air connecting the two, but blinked and decided he'd been imagining things.

Isla led Lewis to the window seat, which offered an unobstructed view of both the sky and the ocean, but Daniel had yet to spend any leisure time there in quiet repose. The only thing he'd used the cushions for, in fact, was for sleeping on the floor by Isla's bed every night, a fact of which she was still blissfully unaware.

When Isla passed Daniel, there was a ripple in the air, another surge of heat. Isla somehow aided Lewis's mental stability with her own energy stores. He'd never heard of such an ability, and Isla certainly hadn't mentioned it to him when he'd asked about her work.

Lewis settled down in the seat, moving to accommodate Isla, who sat at his hip.

"Very well, Lewis." Isla held up Daniel's pocket watch a comfortable distance from Lewis's face, allowing him to focus.

She remained still, catching the watch when it moved with the gentle rhythm of the flying ship. "We are simply going to look at the beautiful watch and relax. Are you comfortable?"

Lewis nodded and focused on the timepiece. At her suggestion, he visibly relaxed his shoulders and arms, then comfortably stretched his neck and lay against the cushions.

Now that Daniel was aware Isla was using something of herself to aid Lewis, he watched her carefully, noting the deepening lines of tension in her forehead. Perhaps the strain was building. He listened as she suggested to Lewis that he was heavily relaxed and yet light as a cloud. The longer she spoke, the softer her voice grew, yet the air fairly pulsed with intensity. She told Lewis he would control his instincts when he shifted, that he would use his logic and rationale to master the wolf's behavior. That he would feel his own sense of self in either form, and be confident in his abilities to regulate his activities according to his own will.

She continued speaking, and Daniel found himself swaying slightly, woven in a cocoon of comfort and calm. He lost track of her words, but he couldn't have torn his attention from her if he'd tried. He vaguely heard her say that Lewis would awaken to a sense of his surroundings when she counted backward from three . . . two . . . one . . .

Daniel blinked, and Lewis rubbed his head, smiling uncertainly.

"You are feeling well?" Isla asked, brows raised.

"Yes, I do, actually. I feel quite calm. Rested, almost. That's odd, isn't it?"

"Not at all." Isla patted his knee and stood. "Now, if you require aid later in the night when I am . . . indisposed"—she spread her hands helplessly—"I have no objections if you believe it would help you to sit in my cabin. I don't know that proximity to me would matter, but stranger things have happened. You certainly won't bother me."

Lewis frowned. "You're tired."

Isla waved a hand in the air. "The magic hour is nearly upon me." Her laugh sounded strained. She handed Daniel the pocket watch with a tight smile. "I'll retire for bed, if you don't mind. And Lewis, my offer is sincere."

Lewis nodded and sat up. "Thank you. It is a comfort to know it's extended."

Daniel had been patient, but was now quite ready to tell Lewis to get off the cushion because he would need it later that night to camp on Isla's floor. Isla surely had the best intentions, but Daniel couldn't possibly sleep if he thought Lewis was going to turn into a wolf in her room, successful hypnosis or no.

Isla disappeared into her cabin and closed the door with a soft click.

Daniel looked at Lewis. "Are you tired enough to sleep now? You may use my bed; I don't mind."

Lewis shook his head and stood. "I can't sleep here knowing I might awaken and think you're a threat or a predator." He gathered his discarded clothing and paused at the door. "I cannot thank you enough. For everything. For getting me out of London, for helping me find a new life across the world, for caring for me in my hour of need." He gestured with his clothing-draped arms. "I am more grateful than I can express."

Daniel waved a hand in dismissal. "Telescribe if you need

me, or simply run up here and bang on the door. I know you would do the same for me, were the roles reversed."

Lewis nodded. "Until tomorrow, my friend."

"Sleep well."

Daniel locked the door behind Lewis and then went to the connecting door. He knocked quietly, whispering, "Isla?"

"Yes?"

He wasn't certain if he'd heard the response or imagined it. He cracked open the door. "May I enter?"

"Yes."

He found Isla sitting cross-legged atop her bed still dressed in her daytime clothes. She buried her head in her hands, fingers tunneled through her hair.

"I knew it was taking a toll on you," he muttered and put his hand atop hers. "Does this happen every time you work with a shifter?"

"Only those in extreme emotional crisis. My interactions are not usually so urgent or intense."

"What can I do to help?"

"Tea. Last time I 'fell asleep' with a headache this severe, I was nearly blind with it when I awoke the next morning." She closed her eyes. "It would also help tremendously if you could remove my hairpins."

Daniel wrinkled his brow, wondering how to proceed. The pins were the same shade as her hair color; how was a person to find and remove them? He patted his fingertips along her upswept hair, which she was loosening ineffectually with her fingers as she massaged her scalp. She winced, and he nudged her hands away.

"You're pulling your own hair. Be patient for a moment."

She dropped her hands to her lap and closed her eyes as he gingerly felt for pins and hoped to high heaven he wasn't adding to her headache.

"Cannot imagine why this is something women insist upon," he muttered as he pulled the small implements from thick sections of hair. He placed the pins in her open palm and frowned at the ridiculous number her coiffure required.

"We must wear our hair up to maintain propriety for the menfolk."

He raised a brow. "Is that bitterness in your voice, Dr. Cooper?" He pulled out two pins at once and several long strands came with them. She sucked in a breath, and he whispered an apology.

"I am never bitter."

"Mmm. I do not think I believe you. However, you need not stand on ceremony for my sake. You wore it down in a long braid last week—the day of the storm. For the love of heaven, how many pins are in here?"

"You noticed my hair that day? How observant of you, Captain."

He scowled, glad she couldn't see the flush he felt creeping up his neck. "No. Well, I suppose only because it was different than every day before it."

He glanced at her profile. She squeezed her eyes shut and furrowed her brows.

He smoothed his fingertip along her eyebrows. "Here, now. Do not pull everything so tight. It will be worse."

She exhaled slowly and relaxed her face. He saw a tear seeping from the corner of her eye but didn't draw attention to it. "Let us hope Lewis will be well enough on his own from this point. You cannot do that again," he said quietly. "Not tonight."

"I will be all right by morning."

He'd never removed pins from a woman's hair—not even his sister's. Piece by piece, sections of curls fell and rippled across her shoulders and down her back. A long, silky curl lay across his arm, and it was quite the most intimate thing he'd ever seen.

"Next time you blackmail your way onto an airship, consider bringing along a maid." He ran his fingers gently along her head, satisfied he'd removed every last infernal pin. "There."

"I shall bear it in mind." She smiled. "Thank you, Daniel. What is the time?"

He glanced at the clock on the wall. "One quarter 'til twelve. You need your tea," he remembered. "I have some in my cabin, I believe, but it's long since gone cold. I won't have time to heat it before . . ." He swallowed, suddenly hating that curse. He hated that it took someone so vibrant and rendered her vulnerable and helpless.

"Cold tea is fine." She began fumbling with her boots. "I'll not bother changing my clothing tonight."

Daniel quickly secured a teacup from his room and poured the cold tea through a strainer, grimacing. He carried it to her, hoping the fact that it was strong might prove serendipitously more effective since there was no time for a fresh pot to steep.

She had wrestled off one boot, and he made quick work of the other boot, dropping it to the floor with a *thunk*. She sipped the tea, shuddering involuntarily, and he winced in sympathy. She closed her eyes, and then tossed back the contents in a gulp worthy of a sailor on shore leave.

She handed him the empty cup and wiped her hand across her mouth.

He blinked, impressed.

"Curses," she whispered and shook her hands absently. "It's coming."

"The sleep?"

She bit her lip. "The dark." She wrinkled her brow again, and her eyes narrowed in pain.

His heart turned over. "I will be here." His throat felt suddenly raw. "I'll stay with you."

She shook her head and straightened her spine, clawing at the fastenings on her corset. "You need your sleep. I find comfort in the open door." Her fumbling fingers were ineffectual at releasing the securely-tied knots.

For the second time that night, he nudged her hands away and helped her with something that was for her a simple task. He wished more than anything he could ease her sense of embarrassment. "It is a good thing I have a sister, or I would have no idea how to do this." He deftly untied the knot at the base of her corset.

"That sounds wrong." Her voice grew drowsy. "You've never helped your sister remove a corset."

"True enough," he admitted. He frowned and loosened the corset with a few firm yanks. "Arms up." She raised her arms, but weakly. He hurriedly tugged the contraption up and over her head, maneuvering clumsily around her arms, leaving the blouse beneath it in place but significantly less tight around her torso. "There." He breathed a sigh of relief with her and slowly lowered her head to the pillow.

He hooked a foot around the nearby chair and slid it under him as her eyes began to drift closed.

"Go to bed," she mumbled. "I'll be fine . . ." Even as she put on a brave face, a tear escaped her closed eyes and trickled along her nose.

He thumbed it away, swallowing, his own eyes burning. "You're safe," he whispered. "I shall keep you safe." He clasped her hand and rested his lips against her knuckles.

" . . . hate the dark . . ." Her whispered words shuddered out on a sigh, and she was still.

Even having witnessed it before, Daniel hated it. She didn't breathe again for thirty seconds, and within a few minutes, as he sat holding her hand, her skin began to cool.

Chapter 18

T he first thing Isla noticed when she awoke the next morning was that her head hurt, but not nearly as badly as when she'd drifted off into oblivion.

She sat up carefully, noting the window covering had been secured at some point in the night and muted the morning light, which helped. She exhaled carefully, slowly, and took stock.

Tingling, blue limbs? Yes.

Fuzzy head? Yes.

Sensation akin to being underwater? Yes.

Normal morning, then.

She was grateful she'd managed to get Daniel's tea into her system before she'd fallen asleep, or her head would be hurting so violently she'd have pleaded for death. The one other time such a thing had happened, she'd been in bed for two days. She spied her corset on the table and her boots on the floor. Humiliating, really, that she'd needed help like a child. Another offense she laid at Melody's feet. Her lips tightened as she eased from the bed and stretched, shaking her hands and feet, and noting she was wobblier on her feet than normal.

She made her way to the dry sink, bracing herself for the splash of cold water, but as she lifted it, was surprised to find the ceramic was warm. Daniel must have filled it with heated water, and she poured it gratefully into the matching ceramic basin.

Her morning routine was pleasant, and she wasn't certain if the reason was due to the warm water or the kindness behind the gesture. Daniel had gone beyond anything she'd expected last night, caring for her and watching over her. She blushed as she changed into fresh clothes, torn between wanting to find him immediately to thank him and staying in her cabin to avoid him altogether. As she folded her shirt, she noticed a smear of red on the shoulder and frowned. Had she cut herself yesterday and not realized it? She examined her shoulder and saw nothing. She decided it must not have been too heinous of an incident if there wasn't much blood and she'd not been hurt.

She set the shirt aside. She was comfortable in clean breeches with her hair braided loosely over her shoulder. She smiled, remembering the conversation about her hair, of all things, and now that she examined their exchange with a clearer head, she realized how well Daniel had tried to distract her from her painful headache. She waited for the blue tinge to fade from her skin and then left her cabin. She wanted to see how Lewis had fared overnight.

She smelled coffee and cinnamon scones as she neared the wardroom and was pleased to see Lewis seated with Mr. Bonadea and Daniel. They stood when she entered, and she waved her hellos, stopping at the sideboard for a bracing cup of tea before selecting the vacant chair next to Lewis.

"How are you this morning?" She left the question deliberately vague as she didn't know how much Lewis had told Mr. Bonadea. "You mentioned feeling under the weather last night."

He cracked a half-smile. "He knows. I also told Quince. And I am feeling well—very well, in fact." He glanced at the doorway. "I awoke in the early morning hours aware that I was beginning to shift again. The most amazing thing happened, however—I was able to reverse the situation on my own. My symptoms stopped, and my head was perfectly clear."

"That is wonderful news!" She smiled in delight and tried to keep her voice down. "I wish I could confer with my friend right now. He'll be so pleased to hear of your success. The implications could be staggering."

Daniel nodded, albeit slowly. "What you did was truly remarkable."

She frowned. "But?"

"I am concerned that you will believe you ought to be able to do it all the time, now."

She glanced at the doorway and lowered her voice. "There's every possibility we could use this technique on all three of our guests"—she nodded toward Mr. Bonadea—"and need not stop before reaching Port Lucy." Even as she said the words, she realized the naiveté of the thought.

"Except we do not know if the method would work on a shifter in the actual Full Moon Phase." Mr. Bonadea spoke quietly and with regret, as though he didn't want to dampen her optimism. "Lewis's condition was atypical."

"You're right. Of course." She bit her lip, thinking. "To halt the process when it shouldn't be happening is one thing, but preventing the natural course of things may prove harmful."

Lewis rested his forearms on the table. "That said, what you were able to do for me was nothing short of miraculous. I am eternally in your debt. The repercussions for all of us could have been disastrous if I'd been unable to prevent the transformation."

Isla smiled. "We can repeat the process again, if necessary. But we land today, yes?"

Daniel nodded. "In five hours."

The unscheduled stop was not ideal for her, but safer for the whole. She would simply redouble her efforts to locate Malette once they reached Port Lucy.

The small group finished breakfast, and Bonadea and Lewis left the wardroom. Daniel and Isla remained at the table, and she eyed him over her teacup. His expression was inscrutable.

He sat back in his chair, one arm resting on the table and fingers spinning a fountain pen in place. "You cannot do that again."

She didn't bother feigning innocence. "I am fully recovered, as you can see. And thank you for the hot water, incidentally." She smiled, but he didn't return it.

"Isla, you seem to suffer under the delusion that it is your job to save the world. The personal cost will one day catch you, and . . ." He held her attention. "You did not see yourself last night. Keeping Lewis from shifting drained everything you had."

"We didn't have much choice, short of tranquilizing him, and we know the dangers of that."

His eyes narrowed. "I am glad you sacrificed for the greater good, but I believe I'm coming to understand the workings of your brain. You believe you can repeat the action at will."

She couldn't remember the last time someone had shown her such solicitous concern, and she wasn't sure what to do with it. Her life followed a predictable pattern of locating a problem then finding a solution, and those in her realm expecting nothing less. Never mind that the load was a heavy one—it defined her, and she had grown accustomed to it. It was one thing to imagine trusting someone to help carry the load. It was another altogether for someone to be so concerned for her that it meant preventing her from helping people because it caused her discomfort.

"You are a good man, Daniel Pickett. I'm glad for your concern, but—"

He stood so swiftly she blinked, and he placed both hands flat on the table, looming close to her. "You're not hearing me. You are deliberately not listening." His deep voice rumbled through her. "Isla, your body was under such stress after your session with Lewis that your nose bled while you slept." His jaw was taut.

"I readied for bed, checked on you once more, and your face was covered in blood." He shook his head. "I'll throw you in the cargo hold before I see that happen again. It's bad enough that I see it every time I close my eyes."

Her mouth dropped open. "But when I awoke, I didn't

see anything on myself or—" The blood on her shoulder. Of course.

"I cleaned you up, changed the bedding. I had covered you up before, so not much dripped onto your shirt." He pushed himself away and turned, running an agitated hand through his hair. He looked as frustrated as she'd ever seen him, and the entire conversation threw her off balance.

She'd never bled in her sleep. Never bled while awake, for that matter. She was predictably, boringly healthy. A sliver of fear snaked its way up her spine. Was the curse placing such a strain on her body that she was becoming ill? Or perhaps she'd used more energy than she'd thought with Lewis.

Daniel faced her, and she exhaled slowly. "I will employ that intensive hypnotherapy again only if it means life or death for someone." She paused uncomfortably. "Thank you for cleaning me. These circumstances are highly unusual for me—"

"And for me!" He threw his arms wide. "Have you any idea how terrified I was to find you like that? Isla, I thought you were dead!"

She stood. "I did not knowingly put myself in harm's way. My actions were not an intentional affront directed at you! And where might we all be right now if I hadn't tried *something*?"

He took a step closer, his eyes blazing. "I would rather this entire ship fall out of the sky than find you dead in that cabin," he bit out.

Silence stretched between them, and Isla stared. She swallowed and was the first to find her voice. "Let us hope neither one of those things comes to pass."

He shoved the wardroom door closed and moved toward her before she could blink. He put a hand around her waist and grasped her head, his fingers spanning the back of her neck and his thumb along her jawline. He moved her back up against the wall and lowered his mouth to hers.

She lost all sense of space and time. The onslaught of sensation was overwhelming, heightened by the intense emotion pouring off Daniel in waves. She tasted his fear, his frustration and urgency, as his lips moved over hers in a long, deep kiss. He pulled back and locked eyes with her. Just when she thought he might speak, he kissed her again, pulling her tightly against him and exploring her lips as though he would learn the taste of her by heart. She felt him relax, felt some of the tension ease from his shoulders as she wound her arms around his neck, losing herself in the beautiful oblivion of the moment. For that one moment, the world outside melted away, and there were only the two of them.

She buried her hands in his hair, the soft strands slipping between her fingers, returning his affection and knowing that if she lived to be a million years, she would never experience another kiss like this one. He lifted his head and looked at her, winded. While she tried to catch her breath, he touched his forehead to hers and closed his eyes. His arms remained tightly wound around her, and trapped as she was between him and the wall, she decided she could have remained there for an eternity and been perfectly content.

"I am not sorry," he said, eyes still closed. "Not even a bit."

She laughed, still breathing as though she'd run a mile. "I would be offended if you were."

He lifted his head, eyes heavy-lidded and lips quirked in a wry smile. "I have been wanting to do that for a long time. I would like to continue doing it for a very long time."

"Why have you waited?"

"I am navigating a different path with you. You're unlike anyone I've ever known."

She lifted a brow. "I don't know if that is a compliment."

He kissed her again. "Very much a compliment."

"I've been wanting the same thing. Since that day near the engine room."

He nuzzled her neck, the spot behind her ear. "For the love of heaven, why did you not act on it?"

She slipped her fingers into his hair again. "I am not a woman of vast experience in that field, and my talents are not at all traditional. What ought I to have done? Held a knife to your throat in the wheelhouse and demanded a moment of your time?"

He groaned against her skin and lifted his head, meeting her eyes, brows raised. "Dr. Cooper, you have no idea how well that would have been received."

She laughed. "I'll remember that for future reference."

"Please do." He released a long sigh and shifted his hold, loosening his grip and stepping back. His hands lingered at her waist, pulling her fractionally forward. He brushed at the back of her hair and cleared his throat. "Apologies for . . . for shoving you up against the wall."

"Accepted." She felt strangely, smugly satisfied. She straightened her clothing, wondering how on earth she was supposed to go about her day after that.

He moved closer, as though he couldn't stay away, and

traced his thumb along her cheek. "So good to see color in your face," he murmured.

"Daniel, I'm sorry. I'm so sorry you have to see—"

"Shh." He shook his head and rested his palm against her cheek. "I'm not. I just . . ." His brows drew together. "I do not want you to be in a position that causes you more harm. You're a grown woman, and you'll do whatever you wish. But I'll not stand by and simply watch. It may be your life, your choices, but you do not have the luxury of believing it doesn't affect anyone else."

She turned her lips to his palm, placing a kiss on it. "Thank you for taking care of me. It is completely foreign to me."

"I know." He kissed her softly and ran his thumb across her lower lip. "I was terrified. It was an experience I'd rather not repeat." He took a deep breath and quietly exhaled. "We land soon, our three friends can find themselves some seclusion on the island away from prying eyes, and you do not need to pour your soul into someone else."

"Aye, Captain."

He rolled his eyes. "If I thought you'd listen, I *would* pull rank."

"Where would be the fun in that? I am unique, is that not what you said?"

He grabbed her hand and walked to the door. "Uniquely guaranteed to drive a man mad," he muttered and put his hand on the door handle.

She smiled up at him and bravely leaned in close. "One more."

He grinned. "One more." He dipped his head and kissed

her before finally breaking it off with a muttered curse. He opened the door, still holding her hand. "And duty remains. Do you have immediate plans for the morning?"

She walked onto the deck with him, shielding her eyes against the sun. "I had thought to visit with Lewis, take notes of his experience for my colleague."

He frowned. "Lewis can wait. I need you in the wheel-house."

She knit her brow. "For what purpose?"

He continued his long-legged stride across the deck. "I need to know you're still here."

Chapter 19

D aniel touched down onto the ocean's surface near the small island with a sense of satisfaction. Perfect landing, every time, even in bad weather. The balloon remained aloft, hovering rather than lifting and using a fraction of the fuel required to fly. Sitting in salt water wasn't ideal, and it meant utilizing a gangplank, but he had to confess there was something nostalgic about using a ship for its traditional purpose.

"Take us into the bay, Samson. We'll drop anchor, and our passengers can come and go as they please." Daniel checked depth gauges and maps, confident he'd taken his passengers to the best possible place for their circumstances. The island was idyllic: deep blue sky arched overhead, lush vegetation spread over the bulk of the land, and white sandy beaches led to water that was clear, then aqua, then a deep, mesmerizing blue that glittered with reflected sunlight as it stretched to the horizon.

"Very good, sir," Samson said. "You'll be pleased to know there are three waterfalls and pools within one mile of the shore, and no evidence of large, predatory animal life, although you will, of course, be vigilant for snakes and certain insects. I've printed a list for your perusal."

"Thank you, Samson. You would do well writing travel guides for Cook's." Daniel rotated his head on stiff shoulders, tired, but cautiously optimistic that the three days spent on the island would be uneventful.

As Samson maneuvered the craft into the small harbor, Daniel looked down from the wheelhouse at the deck where the passengers had gathered to catch a glimpse of the island. Isla laughed, chatting with Quince as though he were the only person on earth. She had that way about her, and he worried at some point her exceptional skills with people may mean her destruction. Daniel's gut clenched into a tight knot.

She had so little thought for her own safety when compared to the well-being of others. It wasn't as though she were a charming little girl with a perpetual smile on her face, looking to make the world happy. He would never have described her as "sweet"—the thought was ridiculous. She was driven, focused, responsible, and aware of her ability to make a difference in a life.

He fought back a shudder. He knew he'd never forget the moment he'd entered Isla's cabin, ready to settle his cushion on the floor, and had spied the sea of blood that streamed from her nose. He hadn't dared call for Lewis, of course, so he'd staunched the blood on his own, terrified of smothering her by accident since she breathed only twice a minute anyway.

When the bleeding had finally stopped, he'd moved her onto his makeshift bed and changed all the bedding on hers.

Then he'd lifted her to place her back in her bed, but held her a moment, rocking back and forth, trying to banish the gruesome image from his memory. In that moment, he'd felt fury at her sister, a girl he'd never even met, because the vibrant, strong woman in his arms was as cold as death.

He'd covered her with blankets, telling himself she would warm up if he tucked them close about her even while knowing nothing would warm her in that state, and then had awoken intermittently through the night to get up from the floor and make sure she wasn't bleeding again. He'd called himself a fool every time he settled on her floor for the night over the last few weeks, but now a chill chased down his spine when he considered what might have happened if he hadn't returned to her cabin last night. Would she have bled to death? It had taken substantial, persistent pressure with a cloth to staunch the flow.

And now that he knew what it felt like to kiss Isla Cooper he would never know a moment's peace. One moment he had been lecturing her and angry at his vulnerability and fear, and the next he had fastened her to him like a clamp. Rather than take umbrage at his aggression, she'd met him halfway.

He watched as she pointed at something on shore and leaned close to Bonadea in conversation. Bonadea nodded and gestured, most likely going on about Caribbean island fauna, and finding a welcome audience in the good doctor. When Lewis placed a hand on her shoulder, Daniel's nostrils flared. He wasn't angry with his friend for his near-disaster last night, but of all the men on board, Lewis was the most likely to be his rival for her affection.

Daniel felt strangely proprietary concerning Isla and

wondered if that blasted shifter lung was turning him into an aggressive animal with primitive instincts. He wanted to call her up to the wheelhouse and snarl at everyone who dared get too close.

He shook his head. Ridiculous. He turned his attention to Nigel Crowe, who held himself apart from the rest. He occasionally looked at the small group that conversed without him, and Daniel wished he knew that one's thoughts. Who did he resent the most—the shifters whom he hated, or the person who fought ardently for their cause?

"Samson, if I ask you to find a way to accidentally leave someone behind when we go, you will know I'm funning you, yes?"

"Now that you've told me as much, I'll be prepared."

"Very good."

"Might I hazard a guess as to whom that might be?"

"You might."

"I believe it may be a draw between Mr. Crowe and Mr. Lewis."

Daniel looked at his 'ton in surprise. "Why Lewis?"

"Your aggression levels as evidenced in sterone readings rise substantially when Mr. Lewis is near the doctor, while your aggression levels with Mr. Crowe are consistently high regardless of other present company."

Daniel hoped he wasn't as transparent to everyone aboard the ship. "I bear Lewis no ill will. He and I are friends, have been for some time."

"There is no shame in the resentment, sir. History has shown that when two virile males are in proximity to an eligible female, they—"

"Oh, look, Samson, it is time to drop anchor." Daniel glared at the 'ton and checked the ship's readings from the control panel.

"I can simultaneously drop anchor and discuss biology, sir," Samson said.

Daniel gritted his teeth. "And I can simultaneously pull your programming tin and replace it with another."

"Oh, look. The anchor is down."

Daniel cast Samson a side-glance. "Good man."

The afternoon followed pleasantly, and Crowe seemed to believe Daniel when he told him they were headed for another patch of bad weather and would be better served to wait it out. He planned to use another malfunction as an excuse if the need arose.

While the others went ashore to explore the island, Daniel and Samson used the time to examine every inch of the ship and her equipment, performing routine checks and testing components of the Stirling Engine. He studied the engine's programming codes and ran each 'ton's programming tin through the reader in the Tesla Room to be certain all was in order. By dinnertime he was satisfied that, as of that moment, nothing on the ship was amiss. The situation around him may be constantly evolving and there were many things outside his control, but everything within it was sound. He forced himself to find comfort in that.

The following day, Samson posed a question to Daniel. "Sir, I wonder if you remember tomorrow is the doctor's birthday? Perhaps you would like to mention it to the other passengers? I believe a celebration of some sort would be appropriate."

Daniel stared at Samson, dumbstruck. He'd never planned a birthday celebration for anyone in his life. "We are on an uninhabited island."

Samson eyed Daniel with what, for a human, would have been patient good-humor. "We have resources aboard the ship, sir."

"What sort of resources?"

"We have a relatively well-stocked larder; you could make a cake. Also ask what her favorite meal is and duplicate it with the supplies on hand as closely as possible."

Daniel still looked at his 'ton, unblinking.

"We have a Victrola in the lounge. You could take it ashore and have an impromptu ball on the beach."

"An impromptu ball," Daniel repeated. "But there is only one woman present."

"Well then, perhaps she shall enjoy multiple dance partners for the evening."

Daniel rubbed his forehead, slogging his way out of the stupor. "I do not know the first thing about . . . any of that."

Samson shrugged and turned his attention to the instrument panel. "Only suggestions, of course. From what I understand, humans are resilient. The absence of a celebration honoring her entry into this life will not impact her future irreversibly." He glanced at Daniel. "I am certain she will be fine."

Daniel gritted his teeth. "Robert's repertoire is limited. I am relatively certain he is not programmed to make a cake."

"A pity there isn't a human aboard who might read a recipe and combine ingredients accordingly."

"Just because I can read a recipe doesn't mean a cake would result from it," Daniel snapped. "I've never baked a thing in my life."

"There are passengers who might combine their talents with yours, isn't that true?" Samson paused. "Though I suppose a person insecure in his masculinity might find it disconcerting to take on such a task."

Daniel narrowed his eyes. "I am not insecure in my masculinity!"

Samson looked up from his perusal of the weather report, activity which suspiciously involved little more than shuffling papers around. "I would never suggest it, sir."

"You just did!"

"I mentioned 'a person' in the most general of terms."

"Why don't *you* make a cake?"

"I would readily aid the process, Captain, however my knowledge is academic only. Having never been programmed to perform the task, I would be limited concerning human sensory reactions."

"Such as?"

"If the ship's galley caught fire. You would likely smell it before my sensors could detect it."

Daniel felt mild panic settling on his shoulders. "We shall arrive at Port Lucy the day after tomorrow. We can celebrate then."

Samson regarded him with his unblinking eyes and then turned his attention back to the papers in his hands. "Of course."

Daniel's mouth fell open. "Curse you, Samson, I did not program you to be disappointed in me!"

"I certainly do not understand the emotion of disappointment. Perhaps what you see in my expression reflects your own feelings."

"For the love . . ." Daniel stalked out of the wheelhouse. A cake? Dancing on the beach? He would have been happier steering into a hurricane. He made quick work of the stairs leading to the main deck and stopped short when Isla came around the corner.

"Oh!" She looked up in surprise and only just stopped herself from plowing headlong into him. "Well, hello, Captain!" She laughed, her eyes bright and her expression carefree. Her face showed evidence of time spent in the sun, which only enhanced her appeal. Her hair was wet and pulled back into a long braid, and she hugged two large, folded blankets to her chest.

"I do hope you will join us ashore today. I washed my entire wardrobe by the waterfall closest to the beach, and then we spent the morning in the nearby pool." Her eyes twinkled. "I am quite a proficient swimmer, you see, and I'm proud to say I beat Mr. Bonadea in two races. Lewis beat us both, however. I can comfortably admit when I am outmatched."

Daniel's traitorous mind's eye envisioned his strong friend's prowess on full display. "He is a healthy one, to be certain."

"Having captained both air and sea, I would imagine you to be comfortable in the water as well. Therefore, I hereby challenge you to a race and will not relent until you leave this ship in Samson's capable hands for at least an hour or two. If not now, then perhaps later."

Her smile was infectious, and he wished he dared take her into his arms right there. "I will certainly do so. Where are you headed now?"

"Back to the beach. I'm taking a few blankets to spread beneath the trees near the shoreline. I'm afraid Mr. Quince and I have seen our fair share of the sun and must remain in the shade for a few hours. I thought to stop by Mr. Crowe's cabin. He's locked himself in there since our arrival, showing his face only for dinner." She lifted her shoulder. "I wonder if it would do him some good to spend time outside."

Daniel eyed her. "I do believe your heart is outpacing your brain."

She scowled. "He is arrogant and mean"—she leaned closer—"but perhaps he has his reasons. If I can engage him in civilized conversation in a pleasant setting, I may better understand his motivation."

"I stand corrected. Your heart has *obliterated* your brain."

She held up a hand and tilted her head. "I have been remiss in my refusal to attempt even the pleasantest of exchanges with the man. It is inexcusable for an empath; I ought to have known better."

"He's not a shifter, Isla, so your professional talents will not make a difference. He is selfish and seeks power. Not only will he refuse a 'connection' with you, but I fear he would take advantage of your attempts. Use your own kindness to lull you into a false sense of security."

"And when I have been properly lulled, he will attack?"

Daniel shifted his stance, frustrated. "When we first

embarked on this voyage, I caught the two of you by the engine room ready to come to blows. Are you telling me you truly believe you can convince him to be . . . What are you hoping for? Friendship?"

She narrowed her eyes. "I do not expect we shall become the best of friends, but there is something deeply raw beneath his surface, and I would have him at least enjoy the beauty of an unscheduled stop on a Caribbean island before we all return to civilization and plot each other's downfall."

"I forbid it."

Her mouth dropped open in surprise, and then she laughed.

His lips twitched, and he wished he could maintain the ruse. "I thought it worth a try. I don't suppose anyone forbids Dr. Isla Cooper anything."

"Fortunate, isn't it, that I don't demand much?"

He rolled his eyes. "That is debatable. I pity the man you marry."

She stilled, slowly sobering. "You do?"

"No," he said quietly. "I envy the man you marry."

She blew out a slow breath. "You do?"

He shoved his hands into his pockets. "Go. I'll join you momentarily."

She blushed beneath her sun-kissed skin and ducked her head. It was a gesture so unlike her, so uncertain. He would have given anything to know her thoughts. The only time he ever saw her behave with anything other than complete confidence were occasional moments alone with him when he sensed she felt out of her depth. That she hadn't received masculine attention in droves astounded him. Perhaps men of her acquaintance were intimidated by her achievements and skill.

She lifted her shoulder, and her smile was halfhearted, at best. "I do not know if I will ever marry."

"Whyever not? I hear the institution does have its merits."

Her smile grew. "I do not know how a man would fit into my life, and I know I certainly cannot mold mine into something most husbands would want. My work is part of who I am."

"You do not have to give up your work."

She shot him a flat look. "You are not so naïve, Captain. A man seeks a suitable wife and mother for his children, not a shifter empath who frequently participates in midnight hunts and testifies at criminals' tribunals."

He wasn't certain how to answer that, and his pause was telling.

She raised a brow at him and smiled. "At any rate, daylight is wasting, and the island calls. Do change your clothing— at least shed the jacket and prepare to lose your boots once your feet hit the water. I am going to invite our recalcitrant friend to join in the fun and expect to see you as well."

She crossed the deck to the stairs leading down one level, and he noted she wore her white blouse without the outer corset and a light-blue skirt that was probably comfortable in the heat of the day. He didn't see any weapons on her, but couldn't imagine she wouldn't have one secreted away some- where. The thought brought a half-smile to his face until he realized she was about to talk to Crowe, alone, and might not be armed.

He snuck down the stairs after her, maintaining his distance as she walked the narrow corridor between rooms. She knocked on a door and waited, biting her lip with a frown at the protracted delay. She knocked once again, and Daniel prepared to sprint away if she gave up her quest, but the door opened and he heard Crowe's voice.

Chapter 20

"What do you want?" Nigel Crowe didn't bother with pleasantries, but then Isla hadn't expected he would.

"Mr. Crowe." She smiled. "We have not got on well, you and I, and I should like to make amends. I wonder if you would join me and the others out on the island?"

He stared at her, openmouthed. "What are you playing at, Miss Cooper?"

She shook her head. "Nothing nefarious, I assure you. I suppose I . . ." She paused. What did she want? She wasn't certain she understood her motivation herself. "This island is as close to paradise as anything I have ever seen, and the thought of anyone sitting here on the ship and missing it is positively criminal."

He smirked and braced a hand on the doorframe. "So the do-gooder is out to rescue the lonely?"

"Are you lonely?"

He flushed. "No, I am not lonely." He drew in a deep

breath. "Miss Cooper, I have much on my mind and am extremely busy. I haven't time for your philanthropy."

"What are you doing, exactly, Mr. Crowe? Why are you here?"

"I have business in Port Lucy."

"Government business?" She kept her voice as light and nonthreatening as she knew how.

"None-of-your-concern business," he snapped.

"Nigel—may I call you Nigel?"

"No, you may not."

"You may call me Isla. That we are adversaries is ridiculous." Well, that was a stretch, and she readily admitted it. He worked for a government body aimed at severely restricting the lives of the very people she sought to help. "Although our professional lives may put us at odds, perhaps we can meet on common ground." She smiled. "And might I suggest the ground outside right now? Truly, it is lovely, breathtaking, and to my knowledge, you've only viewed it from the deck. You've yet to go ashore."

He studied her with narrowed eyes.

"I have no ulterior motive, nothing to hide, and I am only minimally armed."

"Where?" He glanced at her waist as if looking for her ray gun.

She smiled. "That is a trade secret I am not at liberty to disclose."

He raised a brow, and while she hadn't meant to be suggestive, she couldn't regret it because he seemed almost amused.

"You can see I have tossed aside convention and am

casually dressed. The other gentlemen are in shirtsleeves and rolled-up trousers only, and much to our collective amazement, we are managing to behave with perfect civility and decorum." She leaned forward as though sharing a secret. "We have even divested ourselves of footwear."

He examined her as though she'd sprouted an extra head.

"I am planning to convince the captain and the cook to arrange for a picnic dinner we might enjoy outside. I do hope you'll join us. It would be a pity to miss such beauty unhampered by noisy crowds."

When he remained silent, she offered him a smile and a nod, and left his door. She didn't hear it close, and she imagined him staring after her like a gaping fish. Heaven knew she'd have done the same thing had their roles been reversed.

When she reached the end of the corridor, she thought she saw a flash of something—a boot?—quickly climbing the stairs. She narrowed her eyes and quickened her step, running up the stairs and catching Daniel halfway across the upper deck.

"What were you doing?" As though she couldn't divine the reason. He'd been worried Crowe would stab her or something equally horrific right there in the corridor.

Daniel stopped mid-stride and spun to face her. "Nothing."

"You were spying on me."

He exhaled. "Yes. Yes, I was."

"And what did you discover?"

"That I must sharpen my reconnaissance skills. If you wait a moment for me, I'll join you ashore."

She laughed, unable to be irritated when she was flattered that he cared for her safety.

He disappeared down the stairs and reappeared in a few minutes in shirtsleeves and breeches. She swallowed. No jacket, no vest, certainly no cravat. She'd seen him dressed casually the night she'd helped Lewis, but she hadn't had her wits about her enough to appreciate it. He looked carefree. Uninhibited. So ridiculously handsome. He'd also discarded his cuff links and rolled his sleeves up as he walked.

"Is the gangplank sufficient? We can always make use of the dinghy in the cargo hold."

"Sufficient," she echoed as he came to a stop at her side.

He glanced at her, a brow quirked. "Something amiss?"

She cleared her throat. "Nothing."

He focused on her face. "Do you need a drink? Some water from the galley?"

Her eyes flicked against her will to the hollow of his throat, beautifully exposed without a starched cravat. She resisted the urge to fan herself. "Just a warm day. And we have canteens ashore."

He studied her, and then a corner of his mouth lifted. "Something on your mind, Dr. Cooper? You suddenly seem out of sorts."

He looked smug, curse the man. She swallowed and shook her head. "No, nothing in particular." She walked toward the gangplank and felt flushed. Was she blushing? She rolled her eyes, chagrined.

Men and their egos—he wanted her to say something, to admit the sight of him had struck her dumb. "Hold these blankets." She thrust them at him. "Since you're here, you may as well be of use. Hand them to me when I'm on the gangplank."

"I'll carry them for you. It's my pleasure."

Isla held her skirt in one hand and stepped onto the large wooden extension, unwittingly flashing her leg. Daniel's expression sharpened.

She paused, a smile stealing across her face. When she neared the bottom of the makeshift bridge, she turned and held Daniel's arm as she slowly removed first one boot and then the other. Holding both boots in one hand, she straightened and again gathered her skirt into a bunch.

"Do remove your boots, Captain, unless you want the salt water ruining the leather. Here, I'll carry the blankets."

He glanced down at her legs again. The world saw them clearly when she wore breeches, but with a skirt on, it felt somehow scandalous, and she fought back a smug smile of her own. She took the blankets from him and stepped into the water, which hit her at the knee and splashed the ends of her skirt.

"Wait," he said, and stripped off his boots, which he threw one at a time back up onto the deck. He pulled his trousers up to his knees, maintaining eye contact with a smile.

Drat. And just when she'd been feeling the upper hand. Before she realized his intentions, he'd stepped off the gangplank and swooped her out of the water. He held her against his chest and raised his eyebrows in innocence when she gaped at him.

She glanced at the shore, relieved to find it still unoccupied. "I am much too heavy," she gasped on a horrified laugh.

"You forget," he said easily as he walked through the water to the beach, "I am part-cyborg."

"You are not 'part-cyborg,'" she said, laughing in earnest.

"If I recall, Dr. Cooper, it was one of the arguments you used to bully your way onto my ship. 'Captain Pickett, not only are you an illegal smuggler, you are half 'ton.'"

"I did not say any such thing!" She laughed so hard that she slipped, and he hefted her higher to maintain his hold.

"Be still, troublesome woman. This is how a smuggling pirate would behave, no? Carry you off under duress? I should act the part if I am thusly accused." He grinned and made his way up onto dry sand, and she kissed the tip of his nose.

The action surprised him, and she was rather stunned, herself. His face was so close to hers, and with her arm slung comfortably around his shoulders, she felt a joy she didn't think she'd ever had. An unfettered, excited, tumultuous feeling. "Adorable," she whispered, amazed at how his carefree smile transformed his entire person.

He looked at her quietly. "That is something I have never been called in my entire life."

"Impossible. Surely your mother—"

"I don't remember," he murmured.

He is going to kiss me again, and it will be lovely, here in the bright sun on this beautiful island with nobody but the two of us—

"Captain!" Mr. Quince hallooed from far away.

Isla closed her eyes.

Daniel sighed. "Wonderful." He lowered Isla to the ground and met her gaze.

She swallowed her disappointment and turned to wave

at Mr. Quince. "Have you been at the waterfall again?" she called as he neared.

"Yes, yes! It is so refreshing, that pond."

"You, sir, were to stay out of the sun," she scolded and took the blankets to a grove of trees, where she laid them out in the shade. "You are quite burned!"

"Is it not incredible? I vow I have never seen sunlight like this in my life. My grandchildren would so enjoy it!" Mr. Quince had two canteens and held one out to Isla. "Fresh from the waterfall."

She took it, then pointed to the blankets. "Sit," she ordered. "You are redder than a lobster, Mr. Quince. I hope we can locate the herbs you mentioned to make a poultice."

"Yes, of course." He took a drink from his canteen and motioned at her. "I cannot sit while you remain standing, my lady."

"Mercy," she muttered and sank down onto the blanket. "Very gallant, I suppose, but what a silly rule." She patted the spot next to her, and the older gentleman sat down with a small grunt.

"Ah, you younger generation. When I was your age, life was different."

Isla smiled. "I have heard that before, and yet were there not times when you were willful, perhaps? Got yourself into a spot of trouble?"

His eyes twinkled. "A gentleman does not tell tales out of school. Is that not right, Captain?"

"Absolutely." Daniel answered Mr. Quince, but his attention was on Isla, and his mouth held the ghost of a smile, as though they shared a secret.

The moment stretched.

"My, but it is warm." She fanned herself with her hand. She found a small, smooth stick under one edge of the blanket. She dusted it off and held it in her teeth while shaking loose her braid and twisting her mass of hair atop her head. She maneuvered the stick into the knot to hold it in place and relished the breeze that blew against her neck.

She breathed a sigh of contentment and turned her face into the wind, closing her eyes and wishing she could live in the moment forever. No worries, no curse, no ill intent toward innocent people, only warmth and a breeze and the salty smell of ocean air.

She blinked her eyes open and looked at Daniel, who still stood, and motioned to a spot on the blanket. "Will you not sit?"

"I believe I'll cool myself in the waterfall everyone seems so enamored with. I'm assuming Lewis and Bonadea are there?"

"Mmm, they are now." Mr. Quince said, resting against the tree trunk with his eyes closed. "They went exploring earlier, wanted to get the lay of the land for this evening."

"Was there a problem last night?" Daniel asked.

Mr. Quince opened his eyes. "I made certain to give myself the space I knew I would need. Lewis and Bonadea had a minor clash."

Isla straightened. "They didn't mention it."

"They didn't feel it worth mentioning, I suppose. Lewis remembers the encounter with more clarity. He was apparently the first to retreat, keep the peace. Says he had more of his wits about him."

Isla looked at Daniel, her brain spinning.

He shook his head. "No."

"You've no idea what I'm even thinking."

"No, you are not putting anyone else under deep hypnosis."

"I'll not do anything to endanger myself or anyone else. Do you not find it interesting that Lewis still has a semblance of control over his actions all these days later?"

"Interesting, yes. In the manner of 'Hmm, what an odd thing.' Not, 'Hmm, I'll try it again when Daniel is nowhere around.'"

Isla opened her mouth, but Mr. Quince interrupted. "He is quite right, dear. You are of no service to anyone if you come to harm."

Drat. Quince had the right of it. If she were hurt, and somehow worse than the last time, she couldn't help the other shifters at all.

She released a frustrated sigh and stretched out on the blanket, her knees bent comfortably, and the breeze wafting across her skin. "I believe I shall rest and contemplate the meaning of life."

"Ha," Daniel said. "You're not fooling anyone. Quince, watch her. She is conniving and resourceful."

She closed her eyes. "What on earth could I possibly do here in broad daylight?"

"Quince, if she tells you to relax, to imagine each bone, muscle, and sinew growing heavy and yet weightless, plug your ears and run for the waterfall." Daniel's voice retreated as he walked toward the interior of the island.

"Mercy," she muttered. "High-handed and interfering."

"I am inclined to follow his advice, my dear. You'll forgive me for saying it, but the morning after you aided Lewis, the captain was white as a ghost. And when I saw you later, you seemed much weaker than your usual healthy self."

Her heart sank. She didn't want to be ill. She didn't want to be a victim of anything, least of all a curse. She didn't want weaknesses, and she didn't want to be brought low by something that could be a life-changing benefit for shifters. And she didn't want Daniel Pickett to be afraid for her. She didn't want him to worry or truly believe she might die while on his watch—a watch she had bullied her way onto.

Why was he so concerned? Because he was attracted to her? Because he was innately a good person? She supposed those were good enough reasons. *She* certainly didn't want to see anyone die—just that afternoon she'd invited her nemesis to frolic in the sand because she worried he was lonely and sad. Daniel was duty-bound, and despite her initial impression of him, he was kind. Concerned for others. He put his own reputation and his business at stake to help the persecuted.

She cracked open one eye, turned her head, and found the spot on the sand where he'd held her like a child not thirty minutes prior, yet looked at her very much *not* like a child. She sighed and turned onto her side.

She liked him. She liked him very much. The worst part of that new awareness was that it was a lost cause. His life experiences were vastly different from hers, and he was adept at maneuvering in a social sphere that was foreign to her. She was the only woman on the entire ship. Who was to say he would have even spared her a second glance if she were one of dozens? Men did not seek romantic affection from

Isla Cooper. They sought her expertise with knives, throwing stars, and learning how to function in society as a person who turned into a ferocious animal every few weeks.

Daniel had kissed her, and it had been wonderful—the sun and the moon and exploding stars—and there was undeniable tension between the two of them. She must be realistic, however, and not indulge any girlish expectations. He was a mature adult, as was she. She could enjoy a kiss or two and then continue on her way with fond memories and no hurt feelings. Perhaps she would see him in the future at a function in London, and they would chat and smile and remember that time when she'd needed a flight to Port Lucy and wasn't it so funny how that had come about? Yes, yes, she'd certainly been a stubborn one! But my, how time has flown, and is this your beautiful wife? Oh, and children!

Isla stifled a groan and turned her face into the blanket. Daniel Pickett was the first man who had ever truly caught her eye. She worked all day, every day, with men of all shapes, sizes, and social statuses. She'd come to know many, some quite well, and yet there had never been this same pull she'd felt toward Daniel, nearly from the start.

What would become of this infatuation with the captain when they reached Port Lucy? Nothing. Their association would end, and she might never see him again. She didn't know how long it would take her to find Malette—he and the others had insisted on helping her—but it could take more time than any of them had to spare. Daniel would eventually need to return to London, and the other three had new lives to begin.

It was good that the whole bizarre event was nearly

finished. Daniel hadn't asked for the burden of responsibility for her—had tried hard to prevent it—but he had cared for her admirably. He deserved to be relieved of that burden, and it was fortunate they wouldn't spend much more time together. It would be easier for her to dismiss whatever it was she thought she felt for him.

"I say," Quince murmured, and Isla heard him rustle on the blanket.

She glanced up to see he'd straightened from the tree trunk and was looking intently over the water. She followed his gaze and saw Nigel Crowe making his way down the gangplank and into the water.

"Oh, dear. Does he not know to remove his boots?"

Isla winced. "I don't suppose I gave him explicit enough instructions."

"Did you invite him to join us?"

She nodded. "I aim to make a friend of him, Mr. Quince, for all of our sakes." She looked at the older gentleman. "I shall give nothing away, so please do not worry. You and the others are my first concern, of course." She looked at the man who was slogging his way through the water to the shore. "Perhaps I am hoping for miracles, but everybody has a story, and something tells me that man is fighting some demons."

Chapter 21

Isla supposed the situation could have been worse. Drawing Nigel Crowe from his cabin might have been a good idea, if awkward silences and palpable mistrust were just the thing to have at a gathering.

She had greeted Crowe warmly and suggested he would be ever so much more comfortable without his boots and heavy jacket, and when she'd taken him to the waterfall where Daniel, Bonadea, and Lewis were swimming—bare-chested, to her eternal embarrassment—they had not thrown rocks or held his head under the water.

As it was her idea to invite him, she took it upon herself to point out the items of interest she'd discovered—"These flowers are the brightest orange I have ever seen, and Mr. Bonadea tells me there are monkeys in the trees!"—and for his part, he did respond, albeit monosyllabically, with an almost pleasant expression.

With the sun sinking toward the horizon, Lewis and Daniel dragged three large logs onto the beach. Quince and Isla gathered twigs and branches for firewood, while Crowe lingered, clearly uncomfortable. He seemed relieved when Quince handed him a kit and asked him to start a fire.

Isla spied the dinghy approaching with Robert and Samson to deliver dinner. "I am quite famished," she said and sat on one of the large logs. "I haven't been swimming in an age, and I forget how much energy it requires." She smiled at Crowe and Quince, who shuffled their feet in the sand and conspicuously did not look at each other.

"Please, gentlemen, sit with me. You are obliged to provide a lady with conversation at a social event, yes?"

Mr. Quince smiled and slowly lowered himself to the log, and Mr. Crowe eventually did the same on her other side. The 'tons neared the beach and rowed up as far as they could onto the sand, at which point they began arguing about who should perform which task.

Mr. Quince rose and approached the two assistants. "Let us see if we can't sort out this tangle, my friends."

Beside her, Crowe muttered, "He is aware they're not human?"

Isla was determined to maintain her good humor. "He treats everyone and everything the same. One of his more admirable qualities." She stretched her hands toward the fire. "Now that the sun is setting, I am quite chilled."

"You'd have been better off staying aboard the ship."

She glanced at him. "Come now, Mr. Crowe. You cannot deny the beauty of this place. If you do, I shall not believe you."

He cleared his throat. "Passable, I suppose."

Coming from him, she figured it was high praise. "Very passable indeed. Have you traveled much?"

He shrugged. "To Port Lucy. All of the rest of my time has been in England."

"I have been all over our British Isles and a few times to Paris, but I have never traveled this far."

He met her eyes. "And you are going to Port Lucy for research."

She nodded. "I have questions that need answers. I was given to understand they could be found in Port Lucy."

"I can't imagine what questions the mighty Dr. Cooper might not be able to answer."

She smiled at him despite realizing he'd not meant his comment as a compliment. "So, you *do* acknowledge I am a doctor!"

He scowled, and she winked at him. "I am teasing you, Mr. Crowe. I regret that I have never taken the time to understand your moral and political leanings. I would very much like to."

"Why? So you can use everything I say to defeat me?"

"No. So I can use everything you say to better understand you—perhaps with an aim toward a smoother working relationship when we return home."

He rubbed his forehead and leaned forward, resting his arms on his knees. "One conversation before a campfire will not an alliance make. Especially one with opposing goals."

"It is a good beginning." She mirrored his stance. Quince and the 'tons faded into the background, and Daniel and the other two men had disappeared into the interior for larger firewood. "Why do you dislike shifters so much?" She kept her voice low, unobtrusive.

His smile lacked warmth. "A shifter ruined my life. Took everything from me."

She nodded. "Will you tell me about it?"

He looked at her. "No."

"And you dislike me because I offer therapy and help to shifters, when your belief is that harsher preventive measures, such as incarceration, is for the greater good."

"Something like that."

"Perhaps we can agree that there are many people who are predatory shifters who are not violent in the least, even in shifted form? Even the instinct is governed by the human's moral principles."

"You are naïve."

She shook her head. "I have seen it myself, more times than I can count. I wish you knew others besides just the one who ruined your life."

He remained silent, examining something under his fingernail.

"You must agree, you *must*, that in the time we have known each other I have brought to justice several shifters who have intentionally waited until shifting to commit their crimes. Why, I believe the first time I saw you was at the tribunal for a man who was particularly heinous." She wrinkled her brow. "His name was Glad . . . Gladworth . . ."

"Gladstone."

She looked at him in surprise. "Yes! You remember. He was not a nice person, shifter or no. He had run afoul of the law repeatedly, abused a woman and her daughter as a man and, as a wolf, went on a killing spree." She shook her head. "So you see, I fully admit that there are times when rehabilitation is not a viable option. It was a pleasure to see him stopped. To have a hand in it."

"Your testimony sealed the prosecutor's arguments." His tone was flat. Quiet. "Gladstone was executed."

She nodded slowly, confused. "You disapproved?"

He gazed into the fire. "He was my brother."

She felt as though the breath had been punched from her lungs. "Your brother . . ."

He raised a brow at her, his hands hanging between his knees. "Do not tell me you're sorry, that if you had but known . . ."

She shook her head, drawing in a desperately needed breath. "I am so sorry you had to share blood with such a cruel and tormented man."

He chuckled hollowly. "Not very understanding of you, Dr. Cooper. For all you know, I loved him and hate you for driving the final nail into his coffin."

"If you felt your brother was unjustly served, you would be marching with my cousin Emme, not remaining on the PSRC as one of its most extreme proponents of incarceration and execution." She paused, understanding dawning. "Gladstone was the shifter who ruined your life."

He met her gaze but was quiet.

"Why do you stay? Why remain on the committee? It can hold nothing positive for you. You would take vengeance against a whole populace for the actions of one?"

A muscle worked in his jaw. "If the committee doesn't remain vigilant, people like you will ensure that criminals run amok."

She shook her head. "You arrived on the committee last

year just before Gladstone was put on trial. What did you do before that? I know nearly everyone in our line of work, and you came from—well, not London. Not another government agency."

He rubbed his eyes. "I am an artist. Commissioned portraits, some architecture. Now then, are we sufficiently informed about the other? Will we work together splendidly?" His familiar sneer was back.

"Perhaps not, but at least I understand your point of reference." She tipped her head. "Answer one more question for me."

He rolled his eyes briefly. "It's no wonder shifters talk so much in your offices—your questions never stop."

"Gladstone ruined your life, took everything from you, and I was the one to brought him to an end." She paused, suddenly feeling vulnerable. "I understand frustration with a sibling—all too well, in fact. But ought we not to share some small moment of communion? A mutual respect if nothing else?"

His jaw worked, but then he said, "I believe I'll return to the ship."

Suddenly she was aware of Quince working with Samson and Robert to set up dinner, and Daniel, Bonadea, and Lewis talking as they emerged from the island's interior. Crowe stood and turned to leave, but Isla called after him.

"Nigel. Wait." She shivered despite the heat from the fire. "We need not be friends, or even pleasant colleagues. But do not return to the ship. Stay here and have dinner, at least. I will leave you in peace."

"I do not recall giving you permission to use my given name, Miss Cooper."

She raised a brow. "And I specifically recall instructing you to use mine." She motioned toward Quince and the 'tons. "Get something to eat and enjoy the fire before we all return to the ship for the evening."

"You mean before we all make a pretense of returning to the ship and retiring for the evening?"

She deliberately ignored his insinuation about the three shifters. "Oh, I will retire, I assure you. I am out like the proverbial light at midnight, no questions."

He paused before shaking his head almost imperceptibly. She wasn't certain, but she thought the corner of his mouth may have twitched slightly, and when he turned away from her, he went to the makeshift buffet table, not immediately back to the ship. Perhaps it wasn't a lost cause, perhaps she might be able to breathe easier for Quince, Bonadea, and Lewis. Maybe Crowe would begin to see them as people rather than animals. And perhaps, when she returned to London, Crowe might make an effort to pull the reins on his combative approach to her profession. It wasn't much, but it was certainly more than she'd had upon awakening that morning.

Chapter 22

Late the next night, the group gathered on the island, and Daniel's patience was stretched thin. "We shall need more twine for that string of lights," Samson said to Daniel and pointed to a long strand attached to one of the trees. "The knot you tied isn't holding."

Daniel looked at his 'ton and counted to ten. And then fifteen. "I am searching for the birthday candles," he muttered, "which somebody supposedly dropped into this basket. Do you suppose you might manage the twine?"

"It requires the work of two. I'll find Lewis. He's adept. And patient."

Daniel briefly closed his eyes as Samson walked off to find Lewis the Paragon and dug into the basket again, shoving aside linen napkins and flatware. He knew he should have kept the small candles in his pocket and vowed for the hundredth time that day that he would never again doubt his own judgment.

How could he have built an airship empire but still be stymied by a simple recipe?

That was what happened when a man who had no business being in a galley attempted to bake, which he'd known instinctively was the worst idea in the history of bad ideas. He had left a cloth under the pan while putting it into the oven and had nearly set fire to his own blasted ship.

Bonadea, bless his practical soul, had helped remix the batter while Lewis added instructions to an auxiliary programming tin for Robert. Once that had been accomplished, they had baked a three-tiered cake, added blue icing despite Quince's insistence that Isla would prefer pink, and prepared for what promised to be a scrumptious dinner of halibut, roasted potatoes, and asparagus, all things Isla said she loved and that were, blessedly, preserved in the galley's icebox.

Isla had spent the day ashore on the island, and the others had joined her in the afternoon while Robert and Samson had stayed aboard to cook the meal. Bonadea and Quince had taken Isla to the waterfall so the rest of the group could string the portable Tesla lights Lewis had found in the cargo hold and set up dinner. The cake was safely tucked under a large dome and covered with a towel to keep it hidden, and Robert set up the ship's small Victrola at the end of a second table.

Daniel looked over the scene as the sun set, ticking off items in his head. Dinner, done. Cake, done—miraculously. Decorations, done. Plates, glasses, silverware, napkins— all present. Water pitchers filled from the waterfall, done. Whiskey in a small flask secreted in Daniel's pocket for later, done.

Bonadea, Quince, and Lewis said they each had gifts for Isla, and even Crowe mumbled something about it. Daniel had thought long and hard about how to acquire an appropriate gift for an unconventional woman, especially as they were on an uninhabited island, and had been quite stumped until he thought of the one thing he could give her. And she was literally the only woman of his acquaintance who would recognize its value. He'd felt strangely reluctant to give it to her in public, and decided to wait until they returned to the ship and he could steal a few moments with her alone. There was nothing about it the others couldn't see, but he didn't want to be just another of the group lining up to give her a gift.

It was a cozy scene, he admitted. The lights were a perfect touch, logs were in place for sitting by the fire, and dinner was ready. He whistled for the others to return with Isla, and while he waited, he turned the crank on the Victrola. The music blared out, and he hastily muted the horn so they could talk without shouting, and made his way across the warm sand to Lewis and Crowe.

"Everything set?" Lewis asked.

Daniel exhaled. "Everything but the small candles for the cake. I couldn't find them."

"Oh!" Lewis reached into his pocket. "I figured they'd get lost in that basket."

Daniel's nostrils flared as he took the candles from Lewis, supposing he should be grateful they'd turned up.

"All right now, watch your step." Quince and Bonadea led Isla onto the beach with her eyes closed.

Daniel's frustration melted away. She was lovely in her loose skirt and white blouse, no shoes, sun-kissed skin, and a light shawl. Her hair hung in tangled curls, free of pins, dark in the waning light but shimmering a deep red where the firelight shone on it.

He knew he wasn't the only one affected; Lewis stilled, and even Crowe exhaled quietly. There was something arresting about the utter lack of convention in her appearance, and Daniel felt it would be a crime to truss her up again in anything confining.

"May I open my eyes?" Her smile was wry, and he knew Quince must have been the one to insist she be surprised.

"Yes," Bonadea told her with an exasperated glance at Quince.

She opened her eyes and took everything in, and her eyes grew bigger, and her mouth slackened as the seconds ticked by. She put a hand over her mouth, and to Daniel's horror, her eyes filled with tears.

"Oh, no," he muttered and hurried across the sand.

She held out her palm to stop him. The tears gathered and then spilled over, and she finally dropped her hand from her mouth. "This is the most beautiful thing I have ever seen," she whispered.

She smiled at Quince through her tears. "Thank you so much!" She wrapped her arms around the elderly man, who patted her head affectionately, his own eyes suspiciously bright.

Daniel pursed his lips together, trying and failing to not feel ridiculously immature. Quince saved him from saying something stupid by murmuring to Isla, "This was all the captain's doing, truly. He is the one to thank."

Daniel nearly scuffed his toe in the sand. "We all did it,"

he said, and at the subtle *ahem* behind him, added, "It was Samson's idea, originally."

She wiped her eyes, shaking her head. "I am not the crying sort, but this is truly lovely, and you are all so gracious and kind. This has been the most wonderful birthday of my life, and I've enjoyed every moment."

"The celebration continues," Bonadea said and gestured to the table. "Robert has outdone himself with the meal, and we even have dessert for afterward, followed by dancing, and perhaps a firework or two that I may have found in the cargo hold."

A fissure of unease snaked up Daniel's spine, and he swallowed, forcing himself to smile and gesture for the group to help themselves to the food. He wasn't aware there had been fireworks in his cargo hold. He glanced at Lewis, who met his eye with a shrug. His friend didn't smile, though, and Daniel wondered if Lewis also struggled with the strange aftereffects of battle. He took a deep breath and tried to shove his feelings aside. Tonight's celebration was for Isla, and she was thrilled with it. He was going to enjoy it with her if it killed him.

The group filled their plates, sat around the fire, chatted, and laughed. Even Crowe managed a smile or two, but mostly remained silent. Since Isla's conversation with him the night before, he'd refrained from his usual cutting remarks to the others, especially the three shifters. And while he'd not appeared for a few hours after Daniel's invitation that morning, Crowe had joined them around noon to help with Isla's birthday cake. He'd arrived in time for the oven fire, and the fact that he hadn't turned around and gone immediately back to his cabin or mocked Daniel mercilessly was to his credit.

He had helped throughout the day when asked and had replied when directly engaged in conversation.

Daniel retrieved one of the water pitchers and refilled glasses as Isla complimented everyone repeatedly on the dinner and the cozy setting. He looked at Samson, who regarded him with one raised brow as if to say, "You see? Was I not correct?" Daniel reluctantly smiled and gave his assistant a small salute.

Daniel ate absently, his attention focused on Isla. She was joy personified, and she held court with the odd assortment of gentlemen as would an accomplished queen. Yet unlike royalty, Isla was one of them. She understood them, knew them, especially Quince, Bonadea, and Lewis. Had he not seen the results of her work personally, Daniel might not have believed it. They were calmer when they were with her. More relaxed. She even affected him, Daniel realized. As he listened to her voice, her light laugh, he felt some of his anxiety diminish.

It was replaced with a different sort of stress, however, as his heart beat faster. He wanted to truly be the pirate who could throw her over his shoulder and take her to the waterfall and kiss her senseless. Knowing she would respond in kind had him wondering if perhaps he was sitting too close to the fire. The night was suddenly quite warm, and he would have tugged on his cravat, but he wasn't wearing one. She must have known he was staring at her like a besotted fool. She smiled at Lewis for offering to take her empty plate and met Daniel's eyes, her expression softening.

"Thank you," she mouthed, and he nodded, his mouth dry.

"Cake!" Quince, who seemed possessed of energy belonging to a man half his age, stood and motioned to the group. "It is time for the birthday wishes! I do hope somebody remembered the candles."

Isla laughed and took Quince's arm, and they all made their way to the table where Quince removed the towel with a flourish. The cake, praise be to heaven, stood gloriously unharmed beneath the dome, and Isla's eyes rounded with delight.

"This took some doing, my dear, I do not mind telling you. We worried for a moment we wouldn't have a cake at all."

"We worried for a moment we wouldn't have a ship at all," Crowe muttered to Daniel's left, and when Daniel glanced at the man, he saw a reluctant smile twitch.

Lewis removed the dome, and Daniel stepped around the table to place the small candles on the top tier. "Mr. Quince, you have birthday candle history to share?" He took a box of matches from Lewis and began lighting the three candles.

Quince cleared his throat. "Yes. A tradition believed to have started with the ancient Romans but brought into the current day by eighteenth-century Germany, the candles represent the glowing moon, and the smoke represents your wishes and prayers ascending to the gods." He patted Isla's hand. "If anyone deserves wishes and prayers to be answered, it is you."

"Oh, mercy, you are going to have me crying again." Isla closed her eyes. "Making a wish," she whispered, and then opened her eyes.

Daniel held her gaze as she softly blew out the candles. The others clapped and cheered, and he winked at her.

"Presents!" Quince shouted. "And then we can eat the cake. Bonadea's present is becoming especially restless."

Daniel looked at Bonadea, who was near the tree line, whispering to someone. Or something. "What does he have over there?" Daniel muttered to Lewis, who shrugged. "Blast it all, Lewis, he is supposed to be the practical one."

Lewis glanced at him. "I thought I was the practical one."

"No, wait," Bonadea called out as something darted toward the group.

Isla turned and gasped. She dropped down to the sand and extended her arms, and a small monkey jumped into them as would a child. "Who are you?" she crooned to the little creature. "Mr. Bonadea, where did he come from?"

Her delight was clear, and the monkey seemed equally besotted. He patted her cheeks and kept turning her face toward his. She palmed his head and held him close as she stood, swaying and stroking his little back.

Bonadea, looking abashed, joined the group, shaking his head. "He found me earlier this afternoon when I hiked to the third waterfall. He is the only of his species I've noticed, although he shares the same genus as many of the others. His kind is often adopted as exotic pets; perhaps you've seen some in street shows with organ grinders."

She laughed when the monkey rubbed his cheek along hers. "I have indeed. Quite smart, are they not?"

Bonadea nodded. "Smartest of the lot, near as science can tell."

"He must have been quite taken with you to have followed you all day," she observed, turning the monkey's face this way and that, examining its markings.

"Indeed. I've studied the species; I speak his language, if you will. I hoped he would linger so that I might gift him to you as a charming, albeit temporary, gift."

She leaned toward him. "Thank you ever so much. He is lovely, and I shall enjoy his company as long as possible. No family that you noticed? No mother?"

"No, which leads me to believe that either whatever family he did have here was killed by a rival group or perhaps another ship passed this way and this little one was left behind."

She frowned and tickled the monkey's chin. "Little fellow, left behind without so much as a by-your-leave."

"Why do women always do that?" Lewis said in an undertone to Daniel. "Show them a small furry animal and they ogle all over it like a child."

Daniel glanced at him, brow raised. "I don't know what kind of women keep your company. Most I know would have run screeching for the ship if something had darted at them like that."

"I think I like my women better than yours."

"The bulk of my social circle would never be seen in anything less than perfection. Not a hair out of place, not an outfit older than a Season. Plenty of money in the family bank account." He looked at Isla, the monkey in her arms and his head on her shoulder. "And definitely no affection for small, wild animals."

Lewis looked at him. "Well, then, it seems that this woman fits much more into my social circle than yours."

"Are you baiting me?" Daniel tried to smile.

"Mmm, testing the waters, perhaps. I may have been

mistaken in my earlier observations about soul mates and all that. May I inquire as to your intentions?"

He looked at Lewis. "My intentions are to marry her and buy her an island."

Lewis smiled. "All I needed to know."

Daniel looked back at Isla and realized every word was true. He wanted to marry her, wanted to be with her always, to have her in his bed at night and know she was safe by his side. He wanted to know her world, to see her at work, to learn how her brain worked, how she'd formed her business and how she managed it. He wanted all of her so much it spread like an ache in his chest.

She'd said she wasn't interested in marriage, that a husband had no place in her life. He'd grown to love her in a matter of weeks, something his cynical self scoffed at, yet it was true. But he did not know if she returned that deep affection. She was *attracted* to him—but then many women were; he could admit it practically and without guile—but he did not know if she *loved* him. According to Samson, she didn't need his money. What she didn't have in her mother's empire she'd earned on her own. There was nothing unique he could offer her but himself, and he didn't know if she wanted him.

She laughed at something Bonadea said and made her way to Daniel's side, still holding the monkey. When the monkey reached up with his hand, she held his wrist, and he wrapped his little fingers around her thumb. "I should name him, don't you think?"

Daniel smiled, but narrowed his eyes, trying to be stern so he wouldn't fall on his knees and beg her to marry him right then. "That thing is not boarding my ship."

"No, that's much too long. He needs a shorter name." She grinned. "Of course he isn't coming back to the ship. He's staying here with his other monkey friends."

"According to Bonadea, he doesn't have any other monkey friends."

"I shall introduce him to some."

"More presents!" Quince called from the fire ring.

She glanced at Quince. "He is the party king, is he not? His grandchildren must have the most splendid celebrations with him." Her smile faltered. "Will he ever see them again, do you suppose?"

"I hope so. Bonadea's wife and children have a flight booked eight weeks from now to Port Lucy."

She nodded, her brow creased. "I know." She motioned with her head, and he walked slowly with her toward the others. "But that's different than a man's grandchildren, isn't it? They won't move here, as their parents have lives in England. Will you bring them to visit him?"

Isla and the monkey looked up at him, and he would have promised her the moon. He nodded, his heart in his throat. "Of course I will."

Something roared and split the night behind him, a shell shooting into the sky and setting his pulse racing along with it. Without thought, he wrapped both arms around Isla and took her to the ground, monkey and all, and shielded them with his body.

Chaos sounded around him, concerned voices, cursing, muttered questions. The monkey screeched, and he felt something scratch at his face. The noise and confusion sounded far away, as though he were in a bubble, and all he could hear clearly was the furious beating of his own heart and his harsh breathing. He gulped for air that wouldn't fill his lungs quickly enough. They would die. He would see Isla shredded and lifeless before his eyes.

"Daniel." Her soft voice penetrated the bubble. "Daniel, look at me."

One side of his face was on fire, the other cradled in her palm.

"Look at me, Daniel. Shh, monkey, stop."

He felt her thumb smooth his brow, and mercifully, the sharp pain on his other cheek subsided. "Breathe with me. In, and out. Good, slow down. Inhale, and exhale." She kept pace with him at first, slowing by degrees until he breathed with her. He thought of nothing but pulling air in and letting it back out.

The tunnel of muted noise receded in a rush, and he was suddenly present again. He became aware of people crowding around them, of his arms wrapped tightly around Isla and buried in the sand, of an angry little primate who had stopped clawing his face only because of the influence of a strong empath.

He shuddered, and a low sob escaped, eclipsing his humiliation. He registered the rawness of his throat, the taut ache of every muscle, the ghost pain in a shredded shoulder he no longer had. How could he live his life this way? He couldn't control himself. What if he hurt someone? What if he hurt her? He touched his forehead to hers. His eyes burned, and he felt the hot sting of tears that escaped his lashes and fell onto hers.

Isla's hand curled around the back of his neck and nestled in his hair. "You're safe," she whispered. "We are safe."

He swallowed. "I am so sorry," he managed on a shuddering breath. "Isla, I am so sorry."

"Shh. We are fine, Daniel. You've no need to apologize. You reacted to what you remember as danger, and you saved me."

He pried his eyes open enough to see tears on her face. He didn't know which of them they belonged to.

"So, thank you." She rubbed her thumb along his cheek. "Thank you for saving me."

He shook his head and told himself to open his arms, but they wouldn't move. "I didn't save you. I nearly crushed you. What if we had been near the waterfall? All those rocks . . . you might have hit your head."

"No. Look at where your hand is."

He realized his right hand cradled her head, his fingers burrowed deeply into her hair.

"See?" She smiled, and this time he knew the sheen of tears was hers. "Rocks or no rocks, I was safe."

He closed his eyes briefly and released a long, slow breath. "Was it one of the fireworks?"

She nodded and bit her lip. "I believe so."

The monkey squawked, and he realized Isla's empathic hold on the creature would probably expire soon. "Sorry," he muttered to the hissing bundle of fur and slowly lifted himself, helping Isla sit up.

"Apologies," he said to the group and rubbed his forehead with the back of his hand.

"An accident, sir," Samson said. The 'ton hovered nearby,

the whirring of his gears evident as he was likely sorting through the combined biorhythms, seeking out Daniel's first, as he'd been programmed to do. "I sense your alarm. Robert was cleaning the dinner remains and placing items into the crates. The fireworks were on the bottom of one, and I believe the matches must have slipped, made contact. I've yet to gather all the information."

"I understand, Samson." He cleared his throat. "Was anyone harmed?"

"Only Robert, sir."

Daniel looked across the sand at his chef. Robert's head was missing, wires protruding garishly from his neck. He grimaced, grateful it was wires and not blood. Bonadea and Quince hovered nearby, and Lewis sat on one of the logs at the fire, his head in his hands, elbows braced on his knees. His friend's trembling was visible from where Daniel sat.

Nigel sat near Lewis, his brow drawn in concern, but he didn't seem to know what to say.

"Oh, monkey," Isla murmured. She fumbled in her pocket, pulled out a handkerchief, and held it to Daniel's face. "I'm afraid he scratched you quite fiercely."

Bonadea inched closer to examine Daniel's face. "Luckily this species doesn't have claws."

"There's looking at the bright side," Lewis remarked, his head still down. "I hear there always is one."

Isla laughed, and some of the tension eased. Daniel stood and helped her to her feet. The monkey glared at him and put his head back on her shoulder. She dusted off her skirt and blouse and smiled gently at him.

"I'm sorry," he repeated, embarrassed beyond words.

She shook her head. "We all have something we battle. Nobody escapes this life unscathed."

He ran a hand through his hair. "I should clean up, take things back to the ship."

She took his hand. "We will clean up soon. Please sit with me. I have more presents to receive, after all." Without waiting for a response, she pulled on his hand and led him over to the fire circle. She and the monkey sat beside Lewis, and she pulled Daniel down next to her.

She threaded her arm through Lewis's. "Doing better?"

He sat up straight and offered her a half smile. "I'll be well soon enough. Just takes some time."

Daniel nodded.

"Has this happened to you often? Perhaps since your return from India?"

Lewis lifted a shoulder. "A handful of times. Mostly around family. I never know what to say, and nobody wants to discuss it, which is fine with me."

"Perhaps finding someone to discuss it with would help. I know you don't want to air all of the details with friends and family, but keeping it all locked inside isn't good." She shrugged. "My own opinion, of course. Many would disagree with me."

Lewis rubbed his eyes. "I'll consider it. I would rather just forget it."

Daniel completely understood. What he wouldn't give to forget.

Chapter 23

Isla was proud of the fact that she controlled her tremors. She sat between Daniel and Lewis, occasionally shifting the monkey around to hide the fact that she was still shaking after nearly thirty minutes. Daniel's distress rolled off him in waves, and Lewis was almost as intense, but he fought harder to tamp it down. He laughed and joked with the others, even traded a couple of comments with Nigel, who seemed as rattled as everyone else at the reaction the rogue firework had caused.

She ached for Daniel. Her feelings eclipsed her professional concern for Lewis by a landslide. She wanted to protect him from the terror that clearly still lurked beneath the surface. She'd heard of soldiers experiencing mirror reactions to their time spent in battle, often triggered by a sound or a smell. Most hid it, for fear they would be locked away, fit for only Bedlam. They were not lunatics, though, and Isla had just seen her theory proven firsthand by two men who were the antithesis of lunacy. She doubted there were two more practical, lucid men on earth than Daniel or Lewis.

It would bear further study, and she added it to her mental list of things to pursue when she returned home. How ironic that she'd told her mother she was leaving England for research purposes, and she was experiencing far more work-related issues than she'd imagined.

She oohed and aahed over the large bouquet of exotic flowers Mr. Quince handed her when they returned their attention to the birthday party. She realized he must have gone inland a fair way to find some of them. "It's absolutely beautiful. I wish I could keep them alive forever."

He nodded. "Put them in water for now, and then hang them upside down in a dark, cool place. They will not be nearly as vibrant when dried, but even dried flowers are beautiful."

"I love them." She set them across her knees.

To her surprise, Nigel extended a folded parchment to her. She leaned over Daniel to take it, but when she moved to open it, Nigel stopped her. "It is only a small birthday wish. You can save it for later."

"That's kind of you, Nigel, thank you." She smiled, and it was genuine. The man had made an effort, even with his complex feelings toward her, and that meant something.

A quiet settled over the group, accompanied by the Victrola which played in the background.

Isla worried that Daniel would feel he'd spoiled the evening. "I thought someone mentioned dancing?" She was exhausted and feared she could do little more than sway back and forth.

Nigel withdrew his pocket watch and clicked it open. "It will be midnight in fifteen minutes," he quietly observed. He looked at her, his expression unreadable, and then at Lewis and the others.

Bonadea looked stunned, and Lewis cursed under his breath.

"Right!" Quince stood and moved toward the tables. "We should, we must—"

"Leave everything," Daniel ordered. "We'll clean it in the morning before we depart for Port Lucy."

"The bad weather has cleared, I take it?" Nigel asked him.

Again, Isla tried to read his expression and failed. His body language gave nothing away, other than tension.

Daniel nodded. "Smooth sailing, as it were."

"That's a relief."

"Quite."

Isla had assumed her exhaustion had been because she'd been swimming, and then her sunburn had left her feeling rather ill. She'd not realized it was so close to midnight. She fought a stab of alarm as she looked from where she sat to the ship. It wasn't far, but it was dark. Sitting by the fire had enveloped her in a cocoon of safety. The inky, black void stretched outward, and she took in a deep, shaky breath.

"Samson, leave it for now," Daniel called and stood, making his way across the sand.

"Miss Cooper," Nigel said, and cleared his throat. "Isla, you seem quite tired."

Lewis placed a hand on her elbow, but his attention was on Nigel. "He's right, Isla. You should return to the ship immediately."

"I imagine you will want to wait with the others, help

them do . . . whatever . . . needs to be done," Nigel said to Lewis. "Isla, I can take you to the ship in the dinghy."

Isla nodded. He knew the others were shifters, of course he knew, but he didn't seem inclined to catch them in the act. If anything, he was making every effort to get her away from them, whether for her safety or theirs, she didn't know.

Daniel barked another order at Samson, who grabbed the stern of the dinghy, and Daniel jogged back to the fire circle. "Come." He extended his hand to Isla, but she apparently wasn't moving quickly enough to satisfy him. He picked her up, monkey and all, and quickly made his way through the sand to the water.

Isla looked back at the group. "Nigel!"

He joined them as Daniel lowered her into the boat with Samson. Nigel and Daniel pushed the boat into the water, and Isla breathed a sigh of relief when they both climbed in. Samson rowed them swiftly into the deepening water and Isla looked back at the beach in time to see the three men disappear into the island's interior. She hoped they had enough time to put some distance between themselves before midnight hit.

"They'll be along presently," she mumbled and leaned against Daniel's arm.

Nigel shook his head. "Please do not insult me."

"They have hurt no one. Ever. Have never broken even one law." Daniel's voice was even, calm, and he wrapped his arm around Isla when she sagged forward.

"I am aware of that."

Isla fought to keep her eyes open. "Been such a long day . . ." She hoped desperately that if she went under before

Daniel could get her away from Nigel, that it would take some time before she turned blue or looked dead.

Daniel cursed under his breath and pulled Isla across his lap. The monkey squawked in protest, and she realized belatedly that she'd meant to leave him on the island. "Take you back in the morning, then . . ." she said and held the warm little body close.

Daniel murmured something to Nigel about being glad he'd realized it was so late in the evening, and the last thing Isla saw as her eyes fluttered closed was Nigel's nod to Daniel, his face grim.

Chapter 24

D aniel stood with Samson in the wheelhouse, preparing for flight. It was nearly six in the morning,
and he was eager to leave for Port Lucy. They were
past the three-day Full Moon Phase, but time was running
out for Isla. Their forced holiday had come to an end, but he
was loath to fire up the balloon and ascend before Isla had a
last look at her beloved island.

Daniel had sent Samson back to the beach after they'd
returned from the celebration to pack up the remains of the
party. He was the only being who could safely see to the task,
as shifters in animal form had never attacked a 'ton. To date,
at least. Daniel had stood on deck and watched anyway, just
to be certain.

When the morning skies filled with clouds and a light
rain began to fall, he shook his head from the irony. He'd told
Crowe they had detoured specifically to avoid the weather.
The storm would be small, however, and Daniel had checked
and then rechecked multiple operating systems in the engine

room to be certain that even in a heavy storm, the powerful ship would sail through it without problems.

It seemed fitting that the weather was gloomy the day they left the little island paradise. Daniel checked his watch for the third time in five minutes and decided to wait in his cabin for Isla to awaken.

He tidied his belongings and then paced quietly for a few minutes, wanting to give her a moment to compose herself. Yesterday had been one of the most disorganized days of his life, but seeing Isla's reaction to her celebration and the fuss they'd caused made all the chaos worth it.

He sighed. And then he had ruined it spectacularly. If anything had shown him how unfit he was to be married to anyone, that was it. Isla deserved more than another person who would need her care as an empath, more than someone who might imagine she was the enemy and choke her in her sleep. Or take her to the ground with more force than he realized, should he have another spell.

He heard a soft screech and rolled his eyes at That Thing Will Never Board My Ship. The little monkey had stayed by Isla's side long after Daniel had placed her in bed, patting her face and smoothing her hair. It appeared the little fellow wondered as much as the rest of them if she were still alive at night. Daniel had tried to lure the monkey away to leave her in peace, but the primate had stubbornly remained seated next to her head the entire night, restlessly patting her face and smoothing her hair.

"Good morning, monkey," he heard Isla groan.

He'd watched her awaken the day before, his heart in his throat, and it seemed as if she pulled herself up from the dregs of something heavy and dark. Her eyes had been ringed with shadows, frightened, as she'd blinked herself awake, clawing for the surface.

The monkey began chattering, and Daniel couldn't say he blamed the little thing. The first time he'd realized Isla did indeed awaken from that dreadful sleep, he'd nearly chattered himself.

"No, ow . . . You're sitting on my hair . . ."

Daniel knocked on the open connecting door and peeked around the corner. "Good morning." He swallowed and entered when she pushed herself upright. Veins showed beneath her light-blue skin, and lines of discomfort bracketed her mouth. He would never get used to the sight of it and knew that, try as he might, he would never forget it.

She shook her hands. "Ugh." She smiled, but it was weak.

He moved to her side and took her hands, rubbing first one and then the other.

She closed her eyes and sighed. "Warmth—the loveliest sensation ever."

"I thought you might want a final look at the island before we ascend."

Her shoulders sagged, and she smiled sadly. "I shall miss it." She glanced at the monkey in some alarm. "We need to take him back!"

"The others should be here shortly, and we can see if the little menace will go back with Bonadea. I didn't figure you would want to go tromping through the salt water yourself."

She looked at the monkey with a sigh. "No, I suppose not. I never did think of a suitable name for him."

"I think 'Monkey' suits him quite well."

She laughed. "Very true. 'Monkey' it is." She looked up at him. "What happened last night with Nigel after I fell asleep?"

"He knows about the others, of course, but we didn't discuss it. When I carried you onto the ship, you were so far unconscious you didn't move a muscle or sigh. I told him you must be a deep sleeper. He didn't ask questions."

She chewed on her lip. "He hasn't insinuated anything about me being in this cabin since the beginning of the voyage when he made snide comments about everyone all the time. I hope he doesn't think that I . . . that we . . ." She winced.

"He doesn't. None of them do. They all know you, your character."

She nodded. "It's only that I have worked so hard to build a good, respectable, and professional reputation for the sake of my career, especially as a woman, and I certainly mean no offense to you . . ."

He laughed and motioned for her other hand, which he rubbed briskly. "Offended because you don't want people to believe we are having an illicit affair. Hmm. I am *grossly* offended, Dr. Cooper."

She blushed, and he was glad it was visible. The sickly blue tinge was fading.

"My ego suffers from the truth, but persevere I must," he said.

"I am certain your ego will reclaim its former health as soon as we arrive in port. Any port, probably." She pursed her lips. "Your reputation precedes you, Captain Pickett. I would wager you have many friends in many places."

He smiled softly. "Not so many as you might imagine, Dr. Cooper." He paused, still holding her hand which was warming in his. "Isla, I must apologize for what happened—"

"No, truly, you—"

"Please. Please let me do this. I am mortified. This condition . . ." He lifted his shoulder in a shrug. "Whatever is wrong inside my head, I thought the one time it had happened before was just that—one time. Apparently not, and I am concerned for those around me, those close to me. It sickens me that I may have put you in harm's way, may have hurt you. I know you will say it is fine, that you are well, but to my mind, it is not fine, and I can never make amends." His throat felt thick, and he forced himself to stay put and not run from the room like a coward.

"Now may I speak?" She raised a brow, and the corner of his mouth twitched in a smile. "Both you and Lewis believe that there is something inherently wrong in your minds, but I have long suspected, as have others in parallel fields, that your behavior is a result of your prior experiences. It seems clear enough, would you agree? It certainly never happened to you before you fought in a war."

He nodded.

"Because there was an inciting incident that set the precedent for subsequent behavior to follow when reminded of it, there will be methods to employ, therapies to try, to modify future behavior. To be prepared for situations like last night."

"That was a lot of words."

She shook her head. "We can fix this, Daniel. Perhaps you may always carry some level of anxiety when faced with sudden noises, or loud bursts of fireworks and the like, but you can pare it back to an acceptable level for yourself." She squeezed his hand. "Do you believe me?"

"I suppose. I do not know where to begin."

She smiled. "That, my friend, is where you are in luck. I do." She sighed. "As soon as I'm freed from this blasted curse."

Blasted curse indeed. What he wouldn't give to cure it for her. That thought recalled another issue, however. "I still have a gift for you. Would you like it now?"

Her eyes lit up and she nodded. He quickly retrieved the simply-wrapped parcel from his cabin and handed it to her, suddenly feeling awkward.

She tucked her hair behind her ear and untied the string. When she unfolded the paper, she gasped. "It's a ceremonial Brandonian-Linsolofil dagger!" She traced the sturdy pewter handle, examining it from all angles. "These are so rare! Where did you get it?"

He wasn't about to tell her he'd received it from a queen's emissary for his loyal service to the Crown. She'd never accept it. "A friend, recognition for time in India." He smiled. "You are one of the few people to recognize its value, and with it I wish you the happiest of birthdays."

She looked at him, eyes huge. "I don't know if I can accept this, Daniel. It's worth a fortune, and there are perhaps three of them in the world!" Her brow wrinkled. "Why is it not locked up at home in a large vault?"

"My service in India was . . ." He shrugged, wishing he could put into words what he barely understood himself. "The things I saw were horrific. The aftermath of battle, the havoc wreaked on locals, the loss of friends—I find it difficult to celebrate the accomplishment of surviving it. And that dagger is tied to it. Under other circumstances, I would have placed it under lock and key, but as it is, immediately after receiving it, I boarded the *Briar Rose* for Port Lucy and put it in my cabin. It's been there ever since." He gave her a half-smile, feeling ridiculous.

She nodded with a gentle smile. "I do understand. It must be odd to equate a 'prize' with something that looms negatively in the memory." She inhaled and looked down at the dagger. "I am in awe. I shall cherish this gift from you always. Monkey, no." She brushed away the animal's hand when he tried to touch the dagger. "It is sharp and valuable, two things you are not allowed to touch."

He laughed.

"And heavy!" She lifted the dagger and, blocking Monkey with her left arm, flipped the blade with blinding speed, catching the hilt again. "One could do substantial damage with this weapon. Unfortunate that it will never be one I wear at my waist."

He lifted a brow. "If ever there was a woman who would do it justice, it is you, Isla Cooper."

She sighed. "And reality must now intrude. You have passengers to settle into new lives, and I have a witch to find. Onward, yes?"

"Yes, but remember you are not alone." He brought her hand to his lips and kissed it, closing his eyes briefly in relief that it was no longer stone-cold. "Would you like to blow a kiss to the island as we leave?"

She affected a pout that was so unlike her he couldn't

help but laugh. "I suppose, if we must. But may the record reflect that I leave this place under great duress."

"I'll note it in my log." He winked. "Get dressed. But leave your hair down."

She placed a hand to her chest. "Why, Captain, you are positively wicked."

"And that is why you love me."

Chapter 25

He'd been teasing, of course, but she feared it was true. Isla did love Daniel Pickett, and she didn't know what to do with that knowledge, so she shoved it aside for later perusal. When she'd embarked on her journey she'd no idea what lay ahead, and drawing nearer to Port Lucy made her nervous.

She was cautiously optimistic that Nigel Crowe might be a sympathetic colleague in the future; the letter he'd given her for her birthday was a simple one—he'd wished her well and promised that despite his knowledge of the other passengers' secrets, he would do nothing to harm them. As birthday gifts went, it was the best she could ever have expected from him.

The airship descended slowly over Port Lucy, and Isla stood on deck with her friends, and held Monkey while they all looked over the side. The world below was a vibrant carpet of green, trees and flowers in a thick array. Vegetation was dense, as was the air, and beads of sweat trickled between Isla's shoulder blades. It had been much more pleasant on the little island where she'd not been obliged to wear her formal corset, breeches, and boots. And her top hat, complete with goggles and feathers. In partial conciliation to Daniel's request about her hair, she braided it loosely in the French style and draped it forward over her left shoulder. Monkey played with the long rope, tickling his nose with the curly ends of it.

The port city was large—much larger than she'd imagined—and bustled with life. Shouts and laughter and arguments mingled in the air with the smell of food and spices that made Isla's mouth water. They flew over several winding streets that contained an odd assortment of shops, taverns, and businesses, as well as some houses.

Daniel had told her that most shop owners and families lived above the stores for easy access to their businesses. Most residences were in the town proper, although small pockets had begun to pop up along the outskirts.

The airship moved toward a large, clear field, and Daniel slowly brought the craft to the ground where 'tons ran to secure it in place. Isla's heart thumped as she realized the time was at hand. If she failed to convince Malette to give her a cure, she might sleep forever.

She quietly exhaled and tried not to let her anxiety show. Nigel stood with the others at the railing, his expression grim. His hair had grown out from its usual closely-cropped style, and a couple days' worth of stubble gave him a rougher edge. Unpredictable, not as tightly controlled.

"You do not truly want to be here, do you?" she asked him.

He looked at her for so long she figured he would either refuse to converse or was searching for something to say. He shook his head briefly. "My memories here are not the pleasant sort."

"Why did you come?" she murmured. "I have asked you that for three weeks now."

He sighed. "I saw little choice. The decision was an impulsive one." He shrugged. "No matter, Miss Cooper—Dr. Cooper."

She smiled. "Isla."

"Isla. Thank you for your overture of friendship. I do hope we shall work amicably together in the future." The words were stiff and reluctantly offered, but she appreciated them all the same.

"As do I, Mr. Crowe."

He lifted the corner of his mouth. "Nigel."

"Nigel." She grinned. "When do you return to London?"

He looked at the swarm of activity below them. "I don't know. There are things beyond my control that may impact my departure."

"Now that is certainly cryptic. Is there anyone who can help? Perhaps Dan—Captain Pickett has resources that might be useful?"

He chuckled, and she realized that, although the tone still carried a jaded air about it, he seemed genuinely amused. Not cutting. "You would solve the world's problems."

"Isn't that what we are to do, all of us? Nobody solves everything alone."

"Except you."

She frowned. "I don't know what you mean."

"Your life at home, your family, your business. Single-handed, all of it."

"That isn't true," she murmured, uncomfortable.

"Well, at any rate." He gave her a head nod and left the railing.

She watched him cross the deck, presumably to gather his belongings from his cabin. What had he implied? Had he researched her life because of her connection to the predatory shifter world?

Monkey batted her in the face with the end of her braid, and she scowled at him. "You behave, or I shall leave you locked in the cabin." She and Bonadea had discussed searching the environs of Port Lucy for Monkey's species. It was possible a group might adopt him since he was still so young. "I would miss you, though," she admitted and tapped his nose. "You are quite funny, and you make me smile."

Daniel descended the wheelhouse steps, and Lewis crossed the deck to speak with him. Bonadea turned to Isla and held out his arms for the little primate. After some hesitation, and to Isla's surprise, Monkey went to him.

"Oh, I am relieved," she murmured to him as Quince smiled at the animal. "I do not know how long I'll be here, and I was feeling rather wretched about abandoning him."

Bonadea shook his head. "Had I realized he would latch himself to you like a barnacle, I might never have encouraged him."

"I haven't minded in the least." She patted Monkey's head.

Monkey took advantage of her proximity and wrapped all four limbs around her arm.

Bonadea shook his head. "That was short-lived."

Daniel and Lewis approached, and Isla decided she could

easily watch the captain walk around all day. She didn't want to be caught staring, but she sensed her time with him was drawing to a close. Better to take in as much as possible while she could, she reasoned. He was dressed formally but in lightweight fabrics more appropriate for the current climate.

"Allow me to show you to the inn," he said when he reached them. "There is a formal restaurant attached and two taverns across the street. We shall see you settled in, and I'll locate my contacts for introductions. Employment for each of you begins as soon as you would like."

"Captain, again, I cannot thank you enough." Bonadea extended his hand to Daniel. "I and my family are forever in your debt."

"Agreed," Quince echoed and sniffled. "My family is safe from their association with me, and spending the rest of my days doing horticulture research is a boon I never expected."

"The pleasure is mine, truly." Daniel nodded. "I am in town at least four times per year, and I hope you will contact me if you have need of anything. Now, if you would gather your belongings, we shall be on our way."

Quince and Bonadea walked to the stairs and disappeared, and Lewis extended his hand to Daniel. "Goes without saying, my friend, but I owe you my life."

Daniel clasped his hand. "As you once saved mine." A muscle worked in his jaw. "I've never forgotten it. Will never forget it."

Isla's ears perked up. She was curious but couldn't very well say, "What's this? When did he save your life?"

Monkey pulled the fastening cord that held her braid, and Isla scowled. "Give me that," she muttered. "No, no."

She used both hands to refasten the cord but needn't have worried Monkey would fall; he clung to her like a vine. "We shall have a tangled mess on our hands if I lose this."

He chattered at her, a mix of chagrin and irritation.

"I shall find you something else to play with, but you leave this alone."

Lewis had left the deck, and Daniel turned his attention to her. "We shall need a nanny for that thing, I suppose."

Isla laughed. "Can you imagine? Wanted: a nanny for one very furry toddler. Has tendency to swing from trees."

He smiled, but it seemed rather halfhearted. "Will you allow me to reserve a suite of rooms for you next to mine at the inn? I customarily stay ashore when I'm in town. I've become so accustomed to your presence as my neighbor I don't know how I'll sleep otherwise."

She smiled. "Or could it be you're worried something untoward will happen to me at night? I would be happy for your assistance in finding a room, but truly, though, you needn't worry. I have lived with this for nearly a year. I am very careful." She grimaced. "Well, apart from losing track of time on my birthday."

"Which was my fault." He took her elbow. "Come, let's get your things."

Despite her insistence that she could manage her portmanteau, Daniel carried it for her from the ship and to a large 'ton-driven auto-carriage. They all climbed into it, even Nigel. When Daniel settled onto the seat next to Isla, Monkey glared at him.

"Stop that," she whispered and bounced the creature on

her knees. "If you cannot behave, you'll go to bed without dessert."

Quince laughed, and Bonadea eyed Monkey with resignation.

"Does the inn allow wildlife?" Nigel looked at Monkey with distaste, and Monkey scowled.

Daniel sighed. "I have some influence. He is a menace, though. Bonadea, I hold you responsible."

"I hold myself responsible," Bonadea said. "At least he doesn't chatter incessantly."

Daniel snorted. "You didn't hear him last night."

Isla shook her head. "Wonderful. He will bother the other guests, and if I set him loose outside, who's to say he won't camp outside my window and be even more of a nuisance?"

"Chloroform." Nigel's voice was flat.

Bonadea raised a brow with a reluctant nod. "I suppose that is an option. Too much would kill him, though."

"I'm certain Mr. Crowe was only teasing," Isla said, narrowing her eyes at Nigel. "Weren't you."

"Absolutely."

"Oh, look!" Quince gazed out the window at a cluster of red and orange blossoms that climbed a thick vine into a towering tree. Isla leaned closer to Daniel to see the vibrant colors splashed amidst the green scenery. It was a floral feast, and Quince was clearly in heaven. "I have much to research."

"It's stunning," Isla murmured. "So beautiful."

"I would have to agree," Daniel whispered in Isla's ear, and she felt herself blush to the roots of her hair. With any luck, her sunburn would hide it.

She straightened in her seat, trying to decide if she wanted to look at him with reproach or crawl into his lap. The man could tempt a saint.

The next ten minutes passed with comments on scenery that was almost too vivid to be real, and a debate between Quince and Bonadea about which was more fascinating—the flora or fauna. Lewis was quiet, gazing out of his window, and Isla wondered what he was thinking. He occasionally lifted his mouth in a partial smile at something one of the other passengers said.

"I do believe I shall miss this," he murmured. "They've quite grown on me."

"Do you have family who will visit?" Isla asked him. She'd attempted to draw details from him during the voyage, but he'd remained vague, a closed book.

He shrugged. "One never knows."

"One certainly doesn't," she said, curious and fairly frustrated.

He smirked at her without malice, more as though he recognized her gentle prying and the myriad approaches she'd used to engage him in conversation about his life.

"Here we are." Daniel looked out his window as the vehicle came to a stop. The driver climbed down from his perch and opened the door, and Isla gaped in surprise at the inn.

"This is an inn?" It was enormous, three stories high with wrap-around porches and balconies on each level. It was constructed of white stone, and the path leading to the front steps was lined with tall palm trees and orchids twice the size

Isla had ever seen. A placard at the base of the steps indicated that this was, indeed, the Port Lucy Inn.

Daniel appeared to be fighting a smile as he directed three 'tons who emerged from the lobby to unload the carriage and await his instructions regarding delivery.

Lewis shot a flat look at Daniel. "This rivals Shepheard's in Cairo."

Daniel shrugged. "And?"

"You've been holding out, friend."

"Nonsense."

Isla looked at Lewis in surprise. "You've been to Cairo?"

"I thought I'd mentioned it."

She scowled. "No. No, you did not. To think of all the time we spent in the lounge discussing everything under the sun and not once did you mention Cairo."

He laughed. "We still have time. I'll tell you all about it over dinner."

Daniel grasped her elbow. "Let's get you settled."

Isla thought she caught Lewis smirking at Daniel, but he turned and walked with the others to the wide front steps. Daniel muttered something that sounded like "trying to force my hand," and shook his head slightly with a ghost of a smile.

Isla hesitated at the door. "Should I wait out here with Monkey until you do whatever it is you think will entice the managers of this beautiful establishment to let me bring in a wild animal?"

He must have heard the doubt in her voice, because he winked at her and put his hand at her back. "It will be fine, fret not." He ushered her inside, and she forgot about Monkey as she took in the soaring ceilings, marble floors, and a vast array of colorful plants and flowers so bright and heavily scented she was nearly dizzy.

A woman in a tailored, light-colored linen ensemble approached them, a smile on her face. Her clothing seemed so much more suited to the climate that Isla felt a true pang of envy and decided to move "find a local boutique" to the top of her priority list.

The woman herself was lovely; she appeared to be a native to Port Lucy, tall with beautiful skin, a wealth of black curls atop her head, large brown eyes and thickly fringed black lashes, and possessed of a beautiful smile and perfect white teeth. She walked with a purpose, and Isla wondered if she were the proprietress. Perhaps she wouldn't be upset about Monkey.

"Daniel," the woman said with a honey-smooth, lyrical accent. She extended her hands and clasped his, moving in close with that beautiful smile. Her body language spoke of comfort and ease of familiarity. "We were expecting you days ago, of course, but received your message about the delay. Your suite is ready, as always, and at your request, the adjoining one is available."

"Thank you, Lia. Efficient and organized as always. The inn is pristine—I see the whitewash on the porch has been finished." Daniel smiled at the woman and gave her hands a squeeze.

Isla's eyes narrowed.

"It looks lovely, does it not?" Lia agreed. "Would you like to speak with the staff right away? I'll gather them whenever you're ready."

Isla's brow knit. Gather the staff?

"Later in the afternoon will be fine. And this evening I'll review the books with Shelton. He will be in later?"

"Yes. Wife and baby are doing well, and Mrs. Shelton's mother finally arrived. Shelton has been here in the evenings, but now that she's in town, he will resume his regular schedule. 'Tis good to see you, Daniel." She turned her attention to Isla, who made an effort to smooth over her expression.

"We've not met." Her smile really was stunning, and her warmth seemed genuine. She extended her hand, and Isla shook it, noting the firm grip. Isla wanted very much to hate her.

Daniel rested his hand again on Isla's back. "Lia, this is Dr. Isla Cooper. She's in Port Lucy on business. Isla, Malia Francisco manages the Port Lucy Inn and keeps the whole of it operating like a well-oiled machine."

Lia waved a hand in dismissal. "'Tis easily enough accomplished when the owner supplies everything I request."

"I can imagine," Isla said.

"And who is this little one?" Lia asked, holding her hand unthreateningly toward Monkey, who examined it and then grasped her finger. The traitor.

Daniel smiled. "This is Monkey. He is fond of the good doctor and cannot be enticed to leave her side, so we are temporarily accommodating him."

Lia scratched Monkey under the chin. Monkey leaned into the caress as though he'd never felt anything better. "I shall have the chef send up a special plate of plantains and berries."

"He will be euphoric, I'm certain," Daniel said drily.

"Too much of that treatment, and he'll be unbearable. Best include a stack of nappies with the food."

Daniel and Lia looked at Isla, and she knew they expected her to fill the conversational gap, but her head was spinning. All she could manage was a nod. Not only did Daniel apparently know and have fondness for the beautiful island goddess, it seemed he *owned the entire hotel.*

"We'll take the lift up," Daniel said. "I'll show Dr. Cooper to her suite."

"Wonderful." Lia beamed at Isla. "Welcome to Port Lucy."

Chapter 26

Isla was silent until they exited the lift on the third floor and were out of earshot of the lift operator. When they were alone, she looked up and down the hallway and then stopped. "You *own* this?"

"Yes," he admitted slowly. "You are angry."

"I am not angry." Her nostrils flared. "I am . . . irritated. You might have told me, rather than let me stew about whether the management would throw Monkey out into the street."

He squinted, puzzled. "I thought I implied it wouldn't be an issue."

"Yes, because you own the place!" She threw her arms wide, which looked amusing because Monkey clung to her without support. "I do not . . ." She broke off again. "I do not like *not* knowing things. I do not expect to be privy to the details of your life, but we are friends, and this seems like something a friend might mention."

He studied her and then motioned down the hall. "Allow me to show you to your suite, and we can talk. I wouldn't

235

have you think that I have been keeping anything from you intentionally." It seemed an odd thing for her to be so irritated about, and he wondered if the stress of her upcoming task was finally affecting her.

He unlocked the door to her suite and opened it wide. She stepped forward and looked around silently. The interior was bright, with whitewashed walls, lush area carpeting over stunning dark hardwood, and handcrafted dark-wood furniture adorned by bright cushions, seats, and pillows. The adjoining door to the bedroom was open, and she slowly wandered to it to peer inside. He knew it was decorated in similar fashion to the sitting room, with a large bed, sumptuous bedding, and a diaphanous white canopy that doubled as mosquito netting draped over it. There was an adjoining washroom with hot running water for the bath and a personal toilet.

He had built the inn from the ground up, and it was somehow important that she approve. He waited in silence until she had walked around, looking out windows and running a hand along the smooth finish of a finely-made end table. He could stand it no longer, and said, "Well?"

"This is beautiful. Stunning. Absolutely incredible, and I cannot believe you didn't tell me you had real estate here, that you had a connection other than the fact that your fleet provides England's only air transportation here."

He scratched his ear and motioned to the seating area. "Please?"

She acquiesced, and surprisingly, Monkey released his hold on her and hopped down to explore on his own.

Daniel removed his jacket and laid it over the back of a

chair. "May I take your hat?" he inquired solicitously. He set it atop his jacket and watched in envy as she ran her hands along her hair, tousling and smoothing and performing a task he would very much have liked to perform for her.

He sat next to her on the sofa, unsure of the cause of her mood, for the first time since meeting her. She was a straight-forward woman, not usually prone to veiled conversation or hidden meanings. She'd blackmailed him for a flight out of the country, for heaven's sake, and admitted to him soon thereafter the reason for it. She had never prevaricated in communicating with him from the moment they'd first met. Why was she so upset with him now?

"I don't suppose it occurred to me you might be interested in knowing I owned this inn," he said and faced her sideways, his arm along the back of the couch.

"Why would I not?" She looked at him as though he were mad. "When did this happen? How long have you had influence in Port Lucy? I mean, it makes sense now that you would have so many good contacts for those you smuggle from England—you own the grandest hotel this side of Cairo, apparently." She frowned. "There's another one keeping secrets."

"Isla, I am not keeping secrets. I don't know how it would have come up in conversation. 'Are you aware I own Port Lucy's largest hotel?' You can see how that might sound awkward, at best."

"You could have mentioned it on the way over when I was worried about Monkey. Instead you were cryptic. 'Don't worry about it,'" she mimicked in a low tone that sounded nothing like his voice.

"Nobody knew, and I didn't want to explain it to everyone in the carriage." He spread his hands wide. "I do not see the issue."

"Friends tell each other things. What else do you own here?"

"In the hotel?"

She narrowed her eyes. "Do not be obtuse. In Port Lucy."

He sighed. "Ten years ago, this place was little more than a swamp. I had just begun the airship venture and was touring to gain an understanding of the routes between countries and over oceans. I realized the potential of this locale and purchased large pieces of land for a steal. I continued to grow the air fleet and, over time, began building here. The municipality was organized at the time only in the loosest sense of the word, so I researched notable talent here and in neighboring islands and worked with a few key individuals to establish a stable port, one that could grow and thrive. The Crown was supportive once they realized my intentions and made available moneys, resources. The beauty of it was it's far enough away that I could establish the vision I'd created with my partners here without much interference from the government." He smiled. "I named the port city for my sister, Lucy.

"I served my military time in India, and kept in contact with my partners as best as I could. When I finished there, I was thrilled to see the progress they'd made, and it's only improved since then. Some of the capital I saw from my investments here went into the air fleet and allowed me to branch into more advanced technology and provide finer craftsmanship, so Pickett Airships flourished as well."

He rubbed the side of his nose, not certain why her

opinion mattered so much to him. "My father died when I was young, but left us with a fair amount of capital from his own investments in the early days of the railroad. I used much of my inheritance on the land here and in my first few airships. My success here has everything to do with timing and finding the right people."

She shook her head, her expression softening. "You minimize what was exceptional business acumen at a young age. You were twenty-four, twenty-five? And you recognized the value of this place. You infused it with cash, utilized the knowledge of people who lived here, and benefitted not only yourself but many hundreds, maybe thousands, of others."

Daniel didn't think he had anything left of himself that would feel self-conscious or bashful, yet he felt a blush heat his cheeks at her praise. "I don't say anything in casual conversation or in front of passengers about any of this because it presents itself as boastful. I also have learned to be cautious. The world is full of unscrupulous people who suddenly come out of the woodwork to claim a relationship."

She nodded and looked pensively at Monkey, who continued to examine every inch of the room. There was something about her disquiet that seemed elusive. "Is there something else on your mind? You're irritated, and I have yet to reason it out."

She shrugged and straightened. "I am not irritated anymore. Overwhelmed, perhaps. You've built an empire. It's wonderful, truly. And apparently, you climbed Mount Olympus and found the perfect goddess to manage the hotel for you. It's all amazing, and . . . wonderful. I've had your exclusive attention to myself for nearly a month, and I suppose

I was feeling proprietary." She flashed a glance in his direction. "My mistake, not yours."

He stared at her, mouth slack. *Ah. So* that *was it.* He slowly started to laugh. She whipped her gaze back to him with a frown, and he didn't imagine he'd ever seen anything more wonderful. Still laughing, he reached for her hand and yanked her toward him, catching her up close, her legs sprawled atop his. She was clearly still out of sorts, and he made an effort to rein in his humor. His smile lingered, and he rubbed his nose against hers.

"A goddess from Mount Olympus," he mused. "Why did I not see it?"

"I find it hard to believe you didn't realize you'd employed a goddess from Mount Olympus."

"No, I didn't realize you were experiencing the same infuriating emotion I've battled for the last month."

Her mouth dropped open in surprise.

"Mmm-hmm. Let us reflect on our voyage wherein I had to watch you become acquainted with other handsome gentlemen, watch you charm other handsome gentlemen, watch other gentlemen fall all over themselves to gain your attention and approval, fight back the urge to become violent with certain other gentlemen whom even Samson identified as potential rivals for my affection . . . shall I continue?"

"What on *earth*?"

"Why do you think I insisted we say grace that one night? Because Lewis had you eating from the palm of his hand and I wanted to throw him overboard. I wanted to shut him up, and it was the only thing I could think of. And then before I knew it, you had turned Crowe around—although that was to the benefit of everyone, so I cannot complain too much about it."

A smile played at the corners of her mouth. "You said grace . . ."

"Yes!" He was disgruntled at the memory. "And that was after knowing you for a day! Can you imagine what the rest has been like for me?"

She laughed softly and touched her forehead to his. "I am so sorry for being petty. This place—it is incredible."

"I find myself craving your approval."

"I feel anxious taking the time to enjoy it. I ought to be out gathering information on Malette."

"I can help with that. I'll ask some contacts, see what we can overturn."

She met his eyes. This close, he could see the flecks of yellow and blue in the green of hers. Her gaze flicked to his lips, and it was the signal he'd been waiting for. He ran his hand along the nape of her neck and pulled her to him, meeting her lips with his and reveling in her sigh of contentment. He kissed her with every pent-up emotion that had consumed him from the moment he'd demanded her ray gun and she'd refused to relinquish it. All the attraction, frustration, jealousy, fear, and longing of the past weeks poured from him, and he never wanted to come up for air. If he kissed her for an eternity it wouldn't be long enough.

She wound her arms around his neck and buried her fingers in his hair. He crushed her to him, unable to get close enough. He trailed his lips along the line of her jaw to the softness of her neck, to the sensitive spot behind her ear.

I love you, he thought. *I love you and want to be by your side every day for the rest of my life. I want to grow old with you. I want to see you carrying a child and feel the satisfaction of knowing it's mine. I want to love you with everything I am until the end of time . . .*

If he didn't tell her soon, he would explode. He needed to say the words, needed for her to know.

"Isla . . ."

She sighed, and it was nearly his undoing.

"I . . ."

A knock sounded at the door, and he froze. She breathed as though winded, her hands tangled in his hair as his face rested against her neck.

The knock repeated, and he bit back a curse.

"I'll get it," she whispered.

"I'm going to kill someone," he muttered.

She pulled back, then looked at him, her smile wicked. "One more."

He nearly groaned. "One more." He kissed her again and held her tight when she moved to stand. He let her wrestle free, and she stood with a breathless laugh and straightened her clothing. He grabbed her wrist and yanked her down again, planting a quick kiss on her before she squirmed away.

Her cheeks were flushed beyond her sunburn, and she threw him a recriminating look with widening eyes as she made her way to the door. She paused, tucking strands of hair behind her ears and smoothing her braid, and then opened the door.

"A treat for Monkey, compliments of the Port Lucy Inn." The steward's voice sounded in the hallway, and Daniel couldn't decide whether to throttle Lia or thank her. The timing was a combination of rotten and fortunate. There was much at stake, and as Daniel had told himself numerous times over the past several days, Isla needed to find the cure, and quickly.

Isla accepted the tray from the steward with a smile, and his stomach clenched. He had no business tying her to someone who flinched at the sound of firecrackers and still had nightmares like a child, but he couldn't let her go.

"Monkey, look!" She held the tray down as Monkey raced to her side from the bedroom. Daniel feared he'd find the mosquito netting in shreds or the tissue paper in the bathroom strung from the chandeliers.

"Dr. Cooper!" Quince's voice sounded in the hallway and Daniel shook his head, rueful. He clearly wasn't about to get Isla back on the couch anytime soon. Between the plantain-snarfing primate and Isla's entourage of shape-shifting fans, the moment had passed. He would express his feelings to her later, perhaps after they'd located Malette. She needed to remain focused; they both did.

There was a bright spot in the day, if nothing else. The mighty, accomplished, brilliant Dr. Isla Cooper had been jealous of Lia. A smug, satisfied smile crossed his face, and he didn't bother to hide it. Isla hadn't said she loved him, but for now, it was enough. Until she was out of the proverbial woods, he'd take whatever he could get.

Chapter 27

Port Lucy's bustling activity slowed that night as the hour approached eleven. Daniel stifled a yawn as he exited his offices on the hotel's main level. He would meet in the morning with one of his partners, Montez Azacca, who was Port Lucy's lieutenant governor and one of the finest people Daniel knew. The city experienced its share of growing pains, but with steady governance and respectable law enforcement, the problems remained manageable and the people safe. Port Lucy's populace was as varied as the flowers that lined her streets and grew wild in the tangled underbrush and swamps. Daniel not only appreciated the diversity but felt it was necessary to the success of the area.

The diverse community was what Daniel hoped would aid in the search for Malette. The other gentlemen had accompanied Isla when she had gone out not long after those few stolen moments he'd had with her on the sofa, and she'd made multiple purchases under the guise of gathering information. Lewis had told Daniel later he was impressed with her approach. She was subtle, read people well, and more often than not, she pulled information from even the least talkative of individuals.

Regrettably, however, they learned nothing specific about Malette. They would need an inside source, someone with access to secret information. Thinking about that, Daniel checked his pocket watch and went in search of Lia. Odds were she had already left for the day, but she did stay late sometimes, and he was rewarded for his efforts when he found her in the restaurant kitchens, speaking with the chef and his two assistants.

"We'll finish in the morning," she told the chef, and turned to Daniel with a notebook in hand. Lia outworked most people Daniel knew, and he considered himself fortunate to have her in his employ.

Lia had been a young teen when Daniel had first met her, the daughter of a prostitute who lived on the streets. Lieutenant Governor Azacca's wife had a soft spot for those others saw as "lost causes" and had taken on Lia as a maid. She'd discovered the girl's quick mind for numbers and organizational thinking, and by the time Daniel had returned from India and construction was well underway on the Port Lucy Inn, Lia had matured and learned enough to become one of the most well-respected business managers in the community.

"You should know Dr. Cooper compared you to a goddess," Daniel told her as they left the kitchens and made their way to the front lobby.

Lia's laugh filled the foyer. "Bless her, that is just what I needed to hear."

"Life is treating you well, I hope?"

She smiled. "It is."

"I wonder if you can help me find someone. Or perhaps you know someone who could point me in the right direction."

"I'll certainly try. Who are you looking for?"

They reached the front desk and Daniel leaned on the counter. "I do not know much, unfortunately. She is a witch, I believe a practitioner of Dark Magick, and apparently has ties to the area, perhaps family. Her name is Malette."

Lia raised a single brow. "I do not know her personally, but I recognize the name. Or the reputation behind the name."

"And what is that?"

"Not good." Lia paused. "I wonder . . . Do you remember Tante Sabine?"

"She looked after you before Mrs. Azacca hired you?"

Lia nodded. "We all called her 'tante' despite the lack of relation. She knows everything about everyone who has ever lived here." She smiled. "She is a witch herself, but Light Magick only."

"Have you kept in contact with her?"

"Yes. I take her food and supplies, visit with her weekly. She still operates a small voodoo shop down the street. How soon do you need this information about Malette?"

He rubbed the back of his neck. "As soon as possible. Time is not in our favor."

She frowned. "Are you in trouble? What is this about?"

"I'm not at liberty to say. But I must know as much as I can learn of her, and most importantly, where to find her."

"Then we should talk to Tante Sabine immediately. We can see her now, if you wish."

"Now?"

Lia nodded. "She is an insomniac, always has been. She opens the doors to her shop for afternoon teatime and is up all night. In fact, we are better off speaking to her now rather than trying to rouse her in the morning. She will be so happy. She loves to hear herself speak, so asking her questions will make her feel important."

Daniel paused, thinking. If the old woman loved to talk, it may take some time to get the information he needed from her. Which meant he couldn't invite Isla to attend as she would be out past midnight. "I need to invite one other person, if you don't mind."

"Of course not. Let me put these notes away and retrieve my reticule. I'll return straightaway."

While Lia left, Daniel telescribed Lewis. *Have potential information on M. Are you able to join me?*

Lewis agreed, and within minutes emerged from the lift. "Why the late hour?" he asked, shrugging into his jacket.

Daniel explained the situation as Lia returned with a hat, shawl, and reticule. Daniel made the introductions, and Lia led them out of the hotel and into the balmy night.

"She is old, but still as lucid as the day I first met her." Lia led them down the street, past a tavern, a boutique, and a bakery. She crossed the street, and they passed the theater, which was still crowded despite the late hour, then the post office and a printing shop. The next building bore a small sign that read TANTE SABINE'S VOODOO EMPORIUM and featured a hand pointing at the front door.

"I telescribed to be sure she's available," Lia said and un-locked the front door with a key from her reticule.

"She has a busy schedule, then?" Lewis asked, and Lia shot him a look as if trying to assess his level of sincerity.

"He is sarcastic by nature," Daniel told her. "He cannot help himself."

She gave Lewis a wry smile. "Do not judge by the cover—or age, in this case. She does readings and meets with clients all hours of the night."

They followed her into the darkened store and walked past shelves of scented oils and gris-gris bags. They reached a flight of stairs that led to the second-floor apartment. Lia knocked on the door, and at a response from within, opened it to reveal a cozy sitting room and a small woman seated at a table that overlooked the street.

"I saw you comin'," the old woman said. "You have ques-tions for Tante Sabine."

Lia closed the door and took coats and hats. She crossed the room and kissed the woman on the cheek with an affec-tionate smile. "Tante, this is Daniel Pickett and his friend, Adam Lewis. They have questions about Malette, and I didn't know enough to tell them much of anything."

Tante Sabine raised a brow that disappeared into her wrinkled forehead. Her skin was the color of deep roasted coffee, and her hair was as white as snow. Daniel had met her once before years earlier, and she hadn't aged a day. Either that, he reasoned, or she'd been ancient then.

She invited them to sit at the table with her. "But get tea from the kitchen," she told Lia. "Our guests need tea."

Her aged voice was strong, her lyrical island accent rising and falling in a familiar cadence.

Daniel nodded, figuring any protestation would fall on deaf ears. "Tea would be lovely."

"Malette," Tante Sabine said, shuffling a deck of cards in hands arthritic with age. "Why on earth would you be wantin' to know about that one?"

"She cast a spell on a friend," Daniel said, wasting no time, "and we are looking for the cure. We understand it must come from either her or her notes and supplies."

Tante Sabine nodded and eyed Lewis as she continued to shuffle the cards. "You have witch blood."

Lewis blinked in surprise, but nodded. "My mother."

"I can smell it on you."

"Well, that's lovely."

Daniel considered kicking him under the table but figured the old woman could probably see through solid objects.

Tante Sabine sighed. "Malette's mother was from the islands, her father French. The mother practiced the Light Magick, but Malette was impatient, wanted power right away. She turn quickly, not even a teen." Tante Sabine's brow wrinkled. "Broke her mama's heart."

Lia entered, carrying a tea tray, and she poured while Tante Sabine continued.

"Malette travel the world and fall in love with Paris and with a Frenchman whose father was English. They had a child together, a son. She doted on him, thought he was the most precious thing." She shook her head. "But created a monster, she did. And then her lover died, so Malette come home with the boy."

Tante Sabine sipped her tea. "By now, Malette's mother had died, so Malette and the boy moved into the family estate." She waved a gnarled hand. "Huge crumbling monstrosity of a house deep in the swamp on the peninsula. We saw her in town often, showin' off the boy. She take a man as a husband sometime later and had another son, but the husband disappeared, and she never explained where he had got to." She lifted a single brow again, a telling, ageless expression.

"As the older boy neared twenty, he fancied himself a lothario—seduces more girls than you could count! And then shifter attacks start to occur during the Full Moon Phase when we hadn't seen any for years. Shifters who come here to live are fleeing violence, not causing it." Again, the eyebrow lifted.

"Townsfolk begin to notice that the girls Malette's boy paid attention to would disappear or turn up dead, throats ripped out during the full moon. So Malette packed up the boys, boarded up the house, and moved them to England. Said she wanted to reconnect her son with his father's English family. Younger boy must have been a teen. Quiet as a mouse, that one. Always watching, always in his brother's shadow. Malette had little use for him, but she kept him as the spare, I guess.

"They were gone ten years, maybe twelve, and then Malette returned. Just last year, it was. Alone. They say the older son kills one too many people and was finally caught. He was arrested, and Malette puts the younger son on a board to influence the outcome of his brother's trial. Government something."

Daniel heard Lewis's sudden indrawn breath, and he sat forward in his chair, his heart thudding. "A government committee? Was it the Predatory Shifter Regulation Committee?"

Tante Sabine nodded. "Yes, that was it. But the younger boy fails, he does. Malette's special boy was hanged, and she flies into a rage. Malette vowed revenge on the one who brought him down."

Daniel felt sick as he remembered Isla's retelling of her conversation with Nigel on the beach. Daniel had shared the news with Lewis. "What was the older son's name?"

"Gladstone." The name hung heavy in the air.

Lewis paled. "And the younger son—is his name Crowe?"

Tante Sabine started in surprise. "You know him, then? Yes, Crowe. His father was Romany. Black hair and eyes, had the look of a crow about him. His son was a mirror image."

Daniel swore under his breath and stood. "Malette resides in her family home on the peninsula, you say?"

She nodded.

"I apologize for my rudeness, but I'm afraid we must go."

Lia followed them to the door. "What is it?"

"I'll explain later. Thank you, and I'll return with a gift for Tante Sabine."

"Tante Sabine, she adore chocolate, young Mr. Pickett," the woman called from the table.

He flashed a tense smile. "Chocolate it shall be." He jogged down the stairs, Lewis on his heels, and checked his pocket watch. It was past midnight. He had every reason to believe Isla was safe in her bed, but a cold chill snaked up his spine and settled in deep.

"He was following *her*, not us," Lewis said grimly and kept pace with Daniel. "Why? What was his purpose? And if he meant her ill, he had plenty of chances during the voyage, on the island."

Daniel shook his head, his thoughts spinning. "Isla said Crowe told her Malette wanted revenge on the one who brought Gladstone down. She obviously wanted Isla to live with the curse forever. Her intention never was to kill her; that wouldn't make her suffer."

"Isn't it awfully coincidental that Isla's sister happened to approach Malette for the one thing that would exact the witch's revenge perfectly?"

"Unless it wasn't a coincidence."

"How did she do it, then?"

"We are going to ask Crowe. Tonight."

Daniel couldn't return to the inn quickly enough. He tore up the stairs, two at a time, and called over his shoulder to Lewis, "You find Crowe and keep him with you. I'll check on Isla."

The third-floor corridor stretched out like an eternity, and as he ran, her door seemed to move farther away from him. He reached it, breathless, and was prepared to pick the lock, but to his dismay, the handle turned easily.

He crept inside, noting the darkened interior. Isla hated the dark. She always left at least one Tesla lamp burning, even though she knew she'd be unconscious. He navigated through the sitting room to the bedroom and switched on a Tesla lamp. He stared at her empty bed for an agonized moment, and his chest squeezed painfully.

"Isla," he whispered and darted across the room to the washroom, hoping, praying, she had fallen asleep in there. The room was empty, and he leaned against the doorframe for support.

He returned to the bedroom and saw a small object

beside the bed, something with fur and a tail. "Oh, Monkey." He picked up the little creature, relieved to see it was still warm and breathing. A crumpled handkerchief lay on the floor, and he picked it up, sniffing and then wincing.

Lewis ran through the door and stopped short, breathing heavily. "Crowe's gone." His eyes widened. "He killed Monkey? Where is Isla?"

Daniel shook his head. "Chloroformed the monkey. He's still breathing, at least. And I'm assuming Crowe waited until Isla was asleep and then took her. All this time, he knew about the spell." Bile rose in his throat, and he coughed. "I'll kill him. He must be taking her to his mother."

Lewis nodded slowly. "That was why he was so insistent we quit the birthday celebration when he noticed the time. He was almost frantic to get her back to the ship. I thought he wanted to get her away from us before we shifted." He frowned. "I don't think he would hurt her. He seemed concerned for her that night."

Daniel cursed and handed Monkey to Lewis. "He didn't hurt her then because he needed to deliver her to his mother." Daniel telescribed a quick message to the local constabulary and asked that a representative be dispatched immediately to the hotel. "Why take her now?"

Lewis frowned. "It makes no sense to me. She was on that flight intending to locate his mother, which he apparently knew all along. Or it didn't take him long once he was aboard. If his purpose is ensuring Malette gets her hands on Isla, all he needs to do is let Isla follow her course."

Daniel rubbed his forehead in frustration. "I can't think. All I know is that she isn't here!"

Lewis watched him quietly. "You're not thinking because you love her. Trust my instincts—I am more clearheaded than you in this."

Daniel sighed. "What are you saying?" He looked at her empty bed. There were no visible signs of struggle. Someone had entered and simply carried her away. His gut clenched, and he felt sick.

"I am saying that you should take a deep breath. I do not believe Crowe means to harm her."

"Then why abduct her?"

"Assuming it is him"—Lewis paused when Daniel glared at him—"which it probably is, perhaps he is trying to keep her away from Malette."

Daniel shook his head. "She must find Malette or the curse becomes permanent. Twenty-four hours a day, every day, for the rest of her life."

Lewis looked at Monkey thoughtfully. "The other possibility is that he is seeking his mother's approval. Gladstone always had it, and Crowe never did."

"True." Daniel paced the perimeter of the room, looking for any detail, no matter how small, that might lend insight.

Lewis shifted Monkey's small body in his hands. "Then why not kill this thing? Why bother using only enough chloroform to render it unconscious? He knows she loves it; he could just as easily have done any number of things to solve the problem." Lewis paused. "He mentioned using chloroform on the monkey when we were in the carriage, do you remember?" Lewis exhaled slowly. "He has been planning this."

Chapter 28

Isla woke before she opened her eyes and sensed that something was wrong. The pillow beneath her head smelled clean, but musty, as though it had been in storage for some time. The bed was not as soft as the one she'd fallen asleep in, and it was significantly smaller. She slowly moved her hand to the edge and wondered if it were more of a cot than a bed.

She breathed deeply, her heart picking up speed as it usually did every morning, but now with an added element of panic. She cracked open her eyes and took in her surroundings. She was in a small room, tidy, but it had the look of a rustic cabin or gardener's cottage. She ran her tongue over dry lips and pushed herself upright, desperately wanting a drink of water, and desperately afraid.

A fire crackled in a small fireplace and cast partial illumination on a figure she recognized. Her heart sank, wondering if she'd misjudged him after all. "Nigel?"

He moved a chair closer to the bed. "I'm not going to hurt you," he said, slowly lowering himself into the seat. "You must forgive the rather barbaric methods I've employed for this. Believe it or not, abduction is not something with which I am familiar."

She swallowed and rubbed a shaking hand across her forehead.

He jumped up from the chair and retrieved a glass of water from a small kitchen at the far end of the room.

She took the drink from him gratefully and wished her brain would function at full capacity. Her thoughts spun, and her limbs were still weak and tingly. Even if she could think clearly, her body probably wouldn't have obeyed her commands. She sipped the water and exhaled slowly.

"Nigel, what on earth," she managed. She held the glass in her lap and shook her other hand, trying to speed circulation.

Don't panic. Do not panic . . .

"I cannot allow you to continue on this path. It will get you killed." He sat down again, bracing his elbows on his knees. "I knew if I tried to talk to you, it wouldn't make a difference."

She stared at him. "What do you know about my 'path'?"

"I know you're looking for a cure for your sister's curse."

She swallowed. "How do you know this?"

"Because Malette was the one who introduced Mr. Brixton into Melody's life. She paid him to charm her and court her, to subtly plant the suggestion that you were stifling her, that she would never be free to make her own choices because of your interference. He told her he knew of a woman who could provide a spell. He took her to Malette, and she gave Malette a lock of your hair."

Isla felt a shaft of cold shoot through her limbs. She hadn't known Melody had gone to such lengths for the curse or that it had been customized especially for Isla. It was no wonder she was still under it all these months later.

Nigel smiled ruefully. "It is how Malette operates. And once she had your hair and a means of delivering the spell that satisfied her desire for poetic justice, Malette set it in motion with your sister none the wiser."

Her heart pounded in alarm, and she absently shook her hand again, and then switched the glass to shake the other. Her legs were restless and tingled, and she wanted to walk around, but she was vulnerable, exposed, wearing only her nightdress. And she had no weapons.

She fought to keep her voice steady. "Nigel, please tell me how you know this."

He looked at her and then studied his hands. "Malette is my mother. She is my and Gladstone's mother."

She opened her mouth, but no words came out. She felt as if large tumblers in her brain clicked into place and opened a lock she'd not realized was there. She pressed her fingers to her eyes, stunned enough to cry but determined not to. There was no time.

"Of course." She was nauseous. "And I was responsible for your brother's death." She looked at Nigel. "They were close, then? Your mother and Gladstone?"

Again, his half-smile was nowhere near happy. He was bitter, she realized. Pained. "Yes. They were close. He was blond and fair and perfect, and his father was the one man Malette loved. She used my father because she needed his Romany blood to extend the reach of her talents." He rubbed his forefinger along the side of his hand as if it itched, or hurt. "My father's people are deeply steeped in magick, spiritualism. I never knew him; he died before I was born. I suspect when she realized she carried me, she no longer had use for him."

Isla squinted at him, horrified. "Do you mean to tell me she used you for spells? Your blood?"

He nodded, still studying his hand. "Blood, hair, saliva, tears." He straightened and cleared his throat. "She will kill you if you go to her. That's why I brought you here."

She swallowed. "Nigel, I can't . . . I cannot stay away. I must try to talk with your mother. The curse will be permanent soon. It is more than an inconvenience if I desire to stay out late. It threatens not only my career but also my life. I may possibly go to sleep and never awaken."

"Not possibly. Assuredly. By my best guess, you have mere weeks until the curse becomes permanent. But if you go to Malette, she will either lock you away until the time passes, or she will kill you outright."

"Well, then—"

"I will find what we need to break the curse," he interrupted sharply, "but you must stay away from her. I am explaining this to you because I know you'll confront her directly if I don't, but my patience is running thin." He sat back in his seat, running a hand through his hair, his other clenched in a fist on his thigh. "She hates you, Isla, with a passion unlike anything I've ever seen. When you arrested my brother, she installed me on the PSRC. My role was to sway the tribunal behind the scenes, to secure his release."

Isla exhaled quietly. "And that did not happen."

"No, it did not."

She spoke quietly. "Your brother was horrible, Nigel. I have never been so relieved to see someone arrested in my life. The fact that he was a shifter was beside the point; the crimes he committed as a human were worse because he was entirely possessed of his rational faculties at the time." She swallowed past a lump in her throat. "You were not the only one whose life he destroyed."

Nigel nodded. "I know. And I am not about to watch my mother destroy yours."

She frowned. "Why did you remain on the Committee? Why remain in London at all? You seem to hate it; I don't think I've ever seen you smile. Not from happiness, anyway."

He looked away, and a muscle worked in his jaw. "Malette left the country in a rush. There were too many variables that could cause trouble for her, including Brixton and your sister, who went looking for Malette when she realized she'd been horribly manipulated and you were in trouble. Even the mighty Malette realized she was not invincible, that she needed to leave the country, at least for a time. Had she picked a fight with an average citizen of little consequence, she might have bullied her way through." He cleared his throat roughly. "But you are not average nor of little consequence."

Isla was glad she hadn't known Melody went looking for Malette, although even if she had known, she'd still not have realized the danger her sister was facing at the time. It seemed that as much as she'd tried to shield Melody from the world, she'd gone out into it anyway.

"I couldn't leave London," Nigel continued. "My task

was to see that the curse was working, that you were suffering appropriately. And yet, oddly enough, I was to ensure nothing befell you that would interfere with that suffering." He shook his head. "I was to be certain you were unable to work at night, especially hunting, and that you would live to see the one-year anniversary. Malette knew you would search for answers and would eventually learn the curse's permanence was eminent. I believe she assumed you would come by the information as a natural course of general investigation— any novice witch has that information to impart. But even Malette couldn't have realized a young witch with exceptional talent would be so precise in her research."

"Hazel."

He nodded. "I watched Miss Hughes uncover information without people even realizing she'd done it. She peeled back details and facts like layers of an onion, and Malette is not an easy one to track. Miss Hughes is smart, and thorough." He paused. "It is my assumption that she is fully aware the curse becomes not only permanent, but effective twenty-four hours a day, not merely six."

Isla swallowed. "Why would she not have told me?"

"Would it have changed your approach? You were determined to find a cure."

"Yes, but—"

"Telling you would not have motivated you more, and it might have made you reckless. In my opinion, Miss Hughes's judgment is sound. It is probably better Malette knows nothing about her, and to Miss Hughes's benefit that she is unassuming. If she were flashier, more competitive . . ." He met Isla's gaze evenly. "Malette does not care for competition."

Isla swallowed.

"So, as the year continued, I was to watch and wait, protect you while you suffered, and then inform her when you were permanently . . . asleep."

Isla folded her arms around herself and rubbed briskly. She was so cold.

Nigel met her eyes. "And then you boarded that airship. I panicked."

"You've been following me for a year." Details flooded and overflowed her until she was numb.

"My apologies," he mumbled.

"It explains why you've been so annoyingly underfoot. And hateful!"

He had the grace to look chagrined.

"And you despise shifters so desperately because you despised Gladstone."

"I don't despise shifters. I hated my brother, and I work for Bryce Randolph, who hates shifters more than anything else on earth. I was obliged to play a role."

"Bryce Randolph was nowhere near the airship, and you were still cruel to Quince, Bonadea, and Lewis."

He rolled his eyes. "I couldn't suddenly pretend indifference. You would have known immediately something was wrong. We all knew those three men were predatory shifters that Pickett was smuggling out of the country." He stood and paced to the wall and back. "Truthfully, there is no love lost in my heart for anyone or anything. I could not care less about the plight of the shifters. I kept working on the Committee because Randolph is easily manipulated, and the rhetoric is easy to spew. And the position kept me in logical proximity to you, which is what my mother wanted."

"Then why the change?" Isla felt circulation returning to her hands and feet. She thought briefly of Daniel warming her hands and realized he would probably be frantic. She was going to have to think carefully. "Why are you suddenly helping me?" *Or attempting to help me*, she thought but didn't say aloud. He was a person who always seemed to be in complete control of himself, but his plan, or lack thereof, spoke of someone on uncertain ground.

He sighed and massaged his forehead; he looked weary. Discontent, confusion, and sadness rolled from him. "I watched you on that airship and knew I could never turn you over to Malette. And then you knocked on my door and invited me to join you and the others on the island. You invited me to be part of something, and that has never happened. Quince, Bonadea, and Lewis must have despised me, yet they were civil to me. They tried to be, well, perhaps not friendly, but decent. Even Pickett lessened his hostility." His dark eyes were nearly fathomless black. She didn't know when she'd ever seen another person so vulnerable or in pain. "I am trying to find an alternate course of action because you are a good person," he murmured, "and you use your talents in the service of others. I will not see Malette destroy you."

The admission could not have come easily, and he looked uncomfortable.

"Thank you," she said. The words were inadequate, but it would have to do for now. She swung her legs out from under the blanket and instinctively folded her arms across her chest.

Nigel opened a satchel on the table and withdrew her

thin cotton robe. "It was the only thing within reach, and I was pressed for time."

She accepted the robe gratefully, and shook her head as she thrust her arms through the sleeves and secured the fastenings. "How on earth did you get me out of there?"

Again, he averted his gaze. "Threw you over my shoulder," he admitted gruffly. "Took you down the back stairs where I had a vehicle waiting."

"Where are we?"

He shook his head. "Better that you don't know."

"Surely I'd have been better off at the inn. Safer."

He laughed. "I got you out of there with no one the wiser. Besides, you were vulnerable there as soon as you started asking questions about magick, local legends, and sorcery . . ."

"You cannot expect me to stay here and do nothing."

"That is exactly what you must do. Isla, you do not understand the nature of this woman."

She frowned, thinking. "She left England immediately after giving Melody the curse to use on me."

He nodded.

"Why did you not break free from her then? It would have been the perfect time for you to disappear, to begin fresh."

His mouth tightened. "She tethers me to her."

Isla stared. "How?"

"A blood spell between the two of us. She can locate me anywhere in the world. She knew I was on that airship, so once in telescribing range, I told her you were searching for her and I was trailing you. I decided the fewer lies I told, the better."

"She'll know we're here, then. Please tell me you brought at least one of my weapons."

"She can't track you, only me. I telescribed that you're still at the inn. She believes I'm staying here because I prefer it to the manor house."

Isla stood and transferred her weight from foot to foot. "Why did you not just tell the others to keep me at the inn, take all of us into your confidence?"

He snorted. "Those four men bow at your feet. You could talk them into anything in a matter of minutes. I couldn't possibly leave you with them. Even Pickett, who seems the most vested in your welfare, would do whatever you said."

She detected an undercurrent of tension, but his expression was unreadable. His eyes showed the only spark of emotion, and she realized that what she'd once read as coldness actually blazed.

"Nigel, you told me you were an artist. You'd carved out a life for yourself before all the business with the Committee. There must be a way to break free from your mother."

"There is a way." He smiled, self-deprecating. "When she is dead, I will be free. Though a condition of our blood connection is that neither of us can kill the other."

She raised a brow. "You would kill her?"

His lips pursed, the familiar cynicism returning. "Of course I would. I had hoped that once she finished her obsession with you, she might leave me alone, find someone else to torment."

"Yet she is your mother."

"That means nothing to me."

"You never envied Gladstone's connection with her?"

He eyed her flatly. "When I was six, she began taking vials of my blood even though I cried and begged her to stop. She would look at me with a smile that held nothing in it. My comfort and contentment were inconsequential to her. I began hating her then."

Isla moved closer to the fire and extended her hands. "How can I possibly be cold in this climate?" she mumbled.

"Malette held nothing in reserve with this curse. You are as close as a person can get to death every night."

She swallowed. "Well, that does explain it."

Silence grew between them, and he finally broke it. "I am sorry. For everything." He met her eyes and then looked down, scratching his neck.

"Thank you for helping me. I have a request."

He shoved his hands in his pockets. "I cannot promise to meet it."

"Telescribe Daniel and tell him I'm safe. He will be concerned. I fear they all will."

"I'm certain they will be. You gather an entourage wherever you go." It wasn't a compliment, but a cynical observation.

"You are jaded, sir."

He smirked. "You haven't the least idea."

"Where are we?" She looked out the window and saw nothing but dense foliage. He was silent, and she turned her attention to him. "At least tell me that much. How far can I go dressed like this and without shoes, anyway?"

He sighed. "My family property. A few miles from the main house."

"And she is not aware I am here?"

"She will be, eventually. Which is why I must get to her first."

"Please tell the others where I am."

"No."

She sighed. "Why?"

"They must remain in town. I'll not have their deaths on what little is left of my conscience."

"You are assuming there will be deaths! We are an accomplished group of people, Nigel, and it may well be that none of us will die!"

"My mother is a shifter."

She blinked. "Very well, I do know a thing or two about that."

"Not this." He turned and grabbed a ring of keys from a nail by the door.

"Wait! Please, wait. I can defend myself, you know I can, especially if you've been trailing me all year. What kind of shifter is she?"

He looked at her. "You wouldn't believe me if I told you. Stay here, Isla. You'll hear from me in an hour or two."

Before she could blink, he was gone, locking the door behind him.

Chapter 29

Isla looked in the cabin's lone cupboard for the third time, wondering what she hoped to find that hadn't been there before. The cabin consisted of the one room and an attached, tiny bathing room, which was little more than an outhouse. The only windows in the whole place were small and chest-high to her and had been crudely barred from the outside with wide pieces of lumber. Shimmying her way out of the small openings might have been a difficult feat, but she couldn't even try. The boards had been nailed securely in place. The door was a solid affair, and the bolt locking it too big to be either picked or kicked loose. She was tempted to try climbing up the fireplace.

Nothing in the cupboard, nothing in the outhouse, nothing under the bed, nothing in the small kitchen dry sink. There was a tiny closet that contained a pair of men's breeches that looked as though they'd been sitting on the shelf for a century, but nothing else.

As soon as Nigel had left, she pawed through the satchel where he'd retrieved her robe and found bread, which she ate, a canteen, which she filled with water from the pitcher, and a length of rope. She grimaced. Had he considered tying her up with it? The satchel also contained a small blanket, a bottle of liquid she identified as chloroform, and a leather-bound journal and pen.

She resisted opening the notebook for quite some time, but as the hours crept by and afternoon arrived, she decided there might be something useful in it. She unwound the leather strap and opened the cover, feeling an enormous twinge of guilt. As she began fanning through the pages, guilt gave way to shock.

There was little by way of written word; the bulk of the contents were drawings. They were exquisite in detail, and accurate to an amazing degree. He had drawn buildings and street scenes in London, images of a pastoral countryside, and people. The definition would not have been clearer on a daguerreotype or photograph. There was a picture of Gladstone, capturing every cruel angle and plane of his face, even the dead look in his eyes. There was a woman, cold and beautiful, who resembled Gladstone, and Isla assumed it was Malette.

There were rough sketches of some of London's government elite, incomplete versions as though he had simply needed to do something with the pen in his hand and didn't care to finish. She turned the page and saw a drawing of her street, then one of her house. She swallowed. Her heart thumped harder as she saw page after page of pictures of herself in various settings. Toward the end of the notebook were beautiful pictures of the airship, portraits of Daniel, Quince, Bonadea, and Lewis. And several more of Isla—standing at the railing, dressed in breeches and corset, down to the dagger at her waist and the one around her thigh.

There was a picture of her on the beach, long, tangled hair blowing in the breeze along with her skirt. Her hand shielded her eyes as she looked over the water. Her eyes burned with tears as she flipped through the last few pages: drawings of the ship's passengers sitting around the fire, their faces depicted in gentler lines than his first renderings. He'd even sketched Samson and Monkey.

Monkey! What had he done with Monkey when he'd taken her? Possibly nothing at all. The little fellow could have screeched until the cows came home, and Isla would never have heard it. Everybody else in the inn would have, however. She bit her lip. If Nigel had used the chloroform on Monkey, she hoped he'd been conservative with the amount.

She flipped to the last page on which he'd written a line of text: *Life's but a walking shadow . . .*

Her heart thumped. Why that quote? Why could he not have written "All's well that ends well"? Or even "bubble, bubble, toil and trouble"? "Life's but a walking shadow" didn't bode well.

She could only assume he'd gone to confront his mother, but he had been gone for hours, and she felt uneasy. His plan, well-intentioned though it was, was far from sound. If Malette had incapacitated him, not only would Isla be none the wiser, she'd be trapped in this little cabin. Nobody knew where she was.

She closed the notebook, wrapped the fastenings, and placed it carefully back into the satchel. She'd intruded on something personal, but blast it all, he hadn't given her much choice. He'd taken all of her choices away, in fact, and she was restless and frustrated. She could not remain in the little room much longer. He'd said the cabin was roughly a few miles away from the main house, although she knew nothing about the area or the terrain. If she could find her way to the mansion, she might then locate Nigel and gain use of his tele-scriber before midnight. Hiking a few miles typically meant nothing to her. True, she was usually armed and had shoes, but she was strong, well-conditioned.

She chewed on her lip for a moment and made a deci-sion. She withdrew the breeches from the closet and shook off the dust. They were too long, and too big around the waist, but she slipped them on, rolled up the cuffs past her ankles, and used the sash on her robe for a belt. The robe itself was shorter than the nightdress, reaching only to her knees. She ripped the seams and ruffles of her nightdress until it was roughly the same length as the robe, allowing her much better freedom of movement. "Apologies, Mama," she mut-tered. The nightgown ensemble was worth a small fortune at Castles'.

The lack of shoes was a problem, but there was no help for that. She glanced at the boarded windows and hefted one of two small logs from next to the fireplace. The glass was thin and easily broken, and she then went to work on the crossed boards. She heaved with all her might, using the log as a battering ram until her arms screamed in protest. She stopped, breathless, and then began again. Finally, the outer-most board gave a fraction of an inch, and the tiny progress strengthened her resolve.

Ten long minutes later, sweat dripping down her face and

her hands raw from the log, the boards fell free of the window and swung down to one side, hanging by a large bolt. She used the rope in Nigel's bag for a harness that she attached to the canteen, and then threaded her head and one arm through the rope.

She wrapped the log in the torn fabric from her nightgown, cleared away the remaining shards of glass from the window, and surveyed her work. It would be a tight fit, but she could manage it. She climbed onto the chair and used it to hoist herself up. Head and then shoulders, twisting this way and that, finally emerged, and she angled the rest of her body and hips through the splintered opening.

The exit wasn't as graceful as she might have hoped, but she used the boards hanging by the side of the window as a brace and clumsily lowered herself to the ground. Her hands and ankles were red and cut, but she was out of the cabin. She dusted off her hands and took in her surroundings, feeling horribly exposed but unwilling to stay locked up any longer. She didn't know where Daniel and the others were, or if they'd even be able to track her, but her aim from the beginning had been to confront Malette, and she would do it or die trying. She couldn't live in limbo, and her time was nearly up. There had to be something the woman would want. Everybody had a price.

The sun had dropped lower in the sky than she'd realized, but it was still late afternoon. She had hours yet, and if midnight approached before she'd located Malette, she would find a place to hide. The thought was unsettling, but she didn't have many options. She looked carefully at the lay of the land outside the cabin and noted soft impressions in the dirt. Nigel's boots. She followed the footprints into the undergrowth and thick vegetation, which led to a walking path that had seen many years of travel.

Nigel had said the cabin was some distance away from the main house, and she hoped that she was headed in the right direction. She could be heading away from the manor with each step, but she had no way to orient herself, no point of reference to anything familiar.

She stepped as carefully as possible but before long her bare feet were a mass of scrapes and bruises. She didn't much care for spiders or large insects—she'd rather face a large predator any day—and prayed she wouldn't step on anything that creeped or crawled or could inject her with venom. The light in the thick forest dimmed the farther she walked, and the sense of foreboding she always felt when the dark crept in was heightened by danger.

She looked around at the trees, shrubs, rocks, ferns, and low-lying ground cover. It blended together in her mind's eye, and where she was usually adept at noting landmarks and distinctive features, she was utterly at a loss. Her only saving grace was that the narrow footpath continued to wind throughout the vegetation that was thick enough in places she was forced to duck down and pause to untangle her hair from branches and needles.

"Curse you, Melody, to the moon and back," she muttered. "And you as well, Nigel Crowe."

Life would be so much simpler if Melody had simply listened to Isla and did exactly as she said. Except, she had to admit, it was Isla's heavy hand that had driven Melody to Mr. Brixton in the first place. If she'd only trusted her little sister to make even small decisions for herself, might Isla right now be at home in England, preparing for a normal sleep?

It was neither here nor there, and Isla did not like to dwell on the past or opportunities ignored or avoided. She would, however, change her approach to Melody when she returned home. If she returned home. The sun continued to dip lower in the sky, and her heart sank with it. She moved steadily forward, her feet aching with each step.

"No weapons, no boots, no telescriber, nothing," she muttered. She paused when she heard something in the forest singing a different tune and recognized it as water. She kept moving forward and eventually came to a river cloaked in greens and grays, the shadows playing on the water as it tumbled over rocks. Spanish moss spilled over tree limbs and hung in delicate, yet thick bundles that touched the water or littered the ground. The humid air felt heavy in her lungs.

Wonderful. Nigel, I am adding you to my complaint list, second only to Melody.

She walked the riverbank, first one direction and then the other, and looked as far ahead through the vegetation as she could before it disappeared in darkness. There was no hope for it. She would have to cross the river by foot, and no one location seemed better than another.

She rolled the trousers to her knees and bunched the fabric of her makeshift tunic in her hand. Taking a deep breath, she stepped into the river. It was much colder than she would have guessed, given the hot climate, but the sun did not shine brightly in this section of forest. The water was slow, which felt like the first stroke of good luck she'd had all day. Her feet stung from the nicks and cuts, but she shoved the pain aside when she began stepping on unknown elements with a slimy texture. Speed was to her benefit, she decided, and she gritted her teeth against the pain as she moved forward as quickly as she could.

At its deepest point, the river reached her thighs, and slimy things continued to shift under her feet. "Ooh, Melody, there are no words!" The sound of her own voice was an odd sense of comfort. She felt isolated, as if she were the only person on a strange planet with no hope of escape.

The water level decreased as she neared the opposite shore, and she detected a faint odor of rotting vegetation. She held her breath to avoid gagging and rushed the last ten feet to the muddy bank.

She coughed and gagged, and took a moment to imagine she was back on her little island, safe and serene. She noticed an odd, light pressure on her legs and looked down to see herself covered in large, black leeches.

She sucked in a huge, horrified breath, but when she tried to scream, nothing came out but a squeak. She'd never fainted in her life, but she felt light-headed and swayed in place.

I am a fierce hunter. I handle sharp weapons, she told herself, but she stared, transfixed, at the slimy bodies that pulsed infinitesimally on her skin.

Sweet mercy, I am going to vomit.

She lost the small amount of bread she'd eaten from Nigel's bag, coughing and spitting on the ground next to her feet.

"I am Isla Cooper. I am *Dr.* Isla Cooper." She chanted the refrain softly in a voice that sounded on the verge of madness. "For the love of heaven, pull yourself together!" The command sounded as though it came from a small child, but she forced herself to bend over without whimpering.

She pulled the leeches from her legs one at a time and threw them into the water with as much force as she could muster. Her actions were more frenzied than efficient, however, and some of the leeches wound up in the trees behind her. The sight of blood on her skin made her dizzy again, and she fell over, narrowly avoiding the vomit puddle.

She felt the sobs rising, then, and was incapable of stopping them. She cried as she hadn't for years, releasing all the pain, anger, and frustration that had been building and had now reached volcanic levels. She fought criminal werewolves, she calmed confused young predators who had only just begun shifting, she conversed with people from all walks of life and had proven herself time and again in school and in her career.

But leeches?

It was the final straw, the last piece of trauma she could stand, and she pulled her knees to her chest. "Melody, if I ever make it home I am going to slap you silly, do you hear me?" Her cries echoed through the trees and mingled with the crickets, which heralded evening's approach with an increase in volume.

Isla stood and stumbled away from the riverbank, searching for another footpath. She traveled upriver through dense undergrowth for a time before spotting a narrow clearing in the trees, almost as though someone had tunneled through the forest and left an opening behind.

Darkness descended by alarmingly quick degrees, and her heart sank. She took a deep, shaky breath and stood still, slapping at buzzing insects that pinched every bit of exposed skin. She was still sunburned from the island, and the sting that accompanied her slaps fueled a slow-burning anger that was much more welcome than panic. Anger was useful. It was productive. It was an active emotion.

She took a sip from the canteen and moved forward on the path strictly by sound and touch. Her eyes eventually adjusted to the deepening darkness, but she was unable to see more than a few feet around herself. The nothing was suffocating, surrounding her on all sides. Fighting to stay angry, she shoved forward, focusing instead on the animals she couldn't see but knew were there.

"Little creatures," she muttered, "take pity on a stupid human." She stumbled and smashed her foot against a rock, cursing with a creativity that would have impressed a sailor. Without meaning to, she thought of Daniel, and her eyes stung.

"Oh, no. No more of that." But she wished more than anything he were there. She missed the confidence he exuded even when she knew he was concerned or stressed. She wanted to kiss him and burrow close for warmth. She wanted him to carry her on his back to save her aching feet. More than anything, she wanted him to find her a deep bathtub. She was no stranger to scrapes, bruises, and dirtied clothing, but her work as an empath felt different. She smelled like swampy water and was a filthy, bloodied mess from head to toe.

She breathed deeply and closed her eyes, searching outside herself for some sense of direction. She moved her feet forward slowly following what *felt* right. Perhaps the birds overhead or the tree frogs she had reached with her empath skills had taken pity on her, but she wound her way unerringly along a path she could not see.

She was tired, and knew she probably should have reached the manor house by now if she were headed in the right direction. She could be right atop it, though, and not realize it. She kept her thoughts fixed on the island, her happy island, whenever the darkness threatened to send her into a panic. It was only dark, after all. She'd not been afraid of the dark as a child. Only in the last year had it become her nemesis, and it made her feel ridiculous.

Isla lost track of time, and her pace slowed. She needed to find a place to sleep, and she decided it wouldn't make a difference one way or another if she simply dropped where she stood on the path. It wasn't as though she was fighting heavy foot traffic, after all. She saw a large, smooth stone to her right at the base of a tree with gnarled, exposed roots. She examined the ground next to the tree and beyond the stone where the raised tree roots created a canopy. She dug out dirt, needles, and fronds, and pulled a small plant or two by the roots with a muttered apology to Quince.

If she burrowed down just right, she'd fit snugly in the small cocoon the tree roots provided. She'd be partially hidden and protected, but if something crawled under there with her, she'd have a devil of a time getting away quickly.

She wearily rubbed the back of her hand on her forehead, which was wet with humidity and sweat. She would be sleeping like the dead before long anyway, so it didn't matter. On a sigh and a prayer, she burrowed down, feet first, beneath the gnarled roots, settling in as well as possible.

Mosquitoes buzzed in her ears and flew around her face

and arms, so she scooped a handful of earth and smeared it along her exposed skin. Mud would have been better, but she'd rationed her water carefully and didn't want to use the only fresh water she had left to avoid bug bites.

Now that she was still, she had time to think. *What am I doing? What was I thinking? I am worse off now than if I'd stayed in the blasted cabin.*

Perhaps that was true, but she knew something was wrong. Nigel should have returned for her, and she'd waited in the cabin for hours. It was possible Malette had detained him; just because she couldn't kill him didn't mean she couldn't make him suffer. If Nigel had taken Isla somewhere in the city, she could have found her way back to the inn, but she'd done the best with what she had. Which was little more than nothing. However, Isla knew herself well enough to admit that waiting with no information or insight concerning her own future wasn't an option she could entertain under any circumstances. She would find Malette or die trying, and she would go down fighting to her last breath.

Chapter 30

I t was dark by the time Daniel spotted the black stone mansion that rested on the island's peninsula, butted up against the edge of a thick jungle threatening to overtake it. He cut the small steamboat's engines and listened, taking in the sounds of insects at night, the occasional splash of fish in the brackish water, the ripple across the surface as a creature left the shore.

There was no light in the house at all, and he could see it only because the clouds had cleared enough for the moon to shine down. He stood behind the wheel with Lewis, Bonadea, and Quince nearby. They all peered through the darkness; nobody broke the silence.

"If Malette is at home, she's not currently receiving," Daniel murmured.

"How would you like to proceed?" Bonadea asked.

"We are at a disadvantage in the dark," Lewis observed, "but perhaps that could work to our benefit. We might investigate the house without being seen."

"She's a witch," Quince added quietly. "She will know her home has been breached."

Daniel craned his head to see the crumbling turrets and widow's walk that looked as though they might topple in a stiff wind. "We would be obliged to use Tesla torches, which would be visible from out here."

"Our only option then is to wait until daylight." Lewis frowned. "If Isla is inside, would you prefer to mount a rescue with her unconscious or awake?

"We don't know what condition she's in. It may be better to take her out asleep." Daniel's jaw clenched, and he tried but failed to shove an image of a wounded Isla out of his head.

"We can do that and still have the benefit of light." Lewis checked his pocket watch. "By five o'clock, we might have enough sunrise to work with, and Isla will still be unconscious. That would be four hours from now."

Daniel nodded, hating to wait but seeing the wisdom in it.

Bonadea pointed to the far side of the house. "Take us around that way so we see the other side."

Daniel idled the motor and slowly trawled alongside the bank until they had a view of the opposite side of the house. Lewis whistled under his breath, and Daniel cut the engine again and followed his friend's gaze.

The house looked as though a giant claw had scooped away a third of the ceiling and a portion of the walls. Jagged pieces stabbed upward while other parts of it had crumbled away like an ancient ruin.

"You're certain she lives here?" Quince whispered. "That does not look habitable."

Daniel shrugged. "According to the map, it's the only building on the family property, aside from"—he paused, squinting into the dark—"two outbuildings that way and a cabin five miles north, right through the heart of that mess." He pointed into the jungle.

"Perhaps she lives there and not here," Bonadea said, eying the pile of stones dubiously. "I mean, she is human, we assume?"

A shadow flickered across the manor's exterior, and Daniel looked up at the moon. He thought he saw something—a cloud? He blinked, wondering if he was so tired he was hallucinating.

Lewis had also looked up and then back at the house with a frown. A sound from high above—the beating of wings—broke the stillness but softly. "Bats?" Lewis mused.

Daniel exhaled. "That would be an incredibly large bat." He tapped his fingers on the wheel, knowing he needed to make a decision. "We'll return in four hours, find a good point of entrance, and see who's inside."

"We could try to find this cabin in the meantime," Bonadea suggested. "Show me the map again." He took it from Daniel and perused it, angling it in the moonlight. "Looks as though it's close to the water along here, and if this is a tributary going to the interior, we might see it without too much bushwhacking through the jungle."

Daniel looked where he pointed, and nodded. "Certainly worth a try." With a backward glance at the mansion, he turned the steamboat and followed the shoreline as dictated by the map. In theory, it ought to have taken twenty minutes to find the cabin, but the water branched into the peninsula in multiple locations, and nearly two hours passed before they came upon a moderate clearing that looked to be a possible candidate for human habitation.

"Through there." Daniel pointed. He guided the boat in carefully, having navigated the terrain enough through the years to know the dangers of a swamp.

Lewis nodded. "I'll go first. We don't all need to go tromping ashore." He gestured to where Quince slumped, asleep. "Wish he would have let us leave him at the inn."

Bonadea chuckled. "He is not about to be excluded from anything, especially where it concerns the doctor. I'll come along, Lewis."

Lewis retrieved a rifle from a trunk at their feet and, with a shrug and a salute, left the boat with Bonadea on his heels, slogging through ankle-deep swamp water.

Daniel readied his own pistol and trained a Tesla torch downward to alert them of anything that might either bite or swallow a person. He breathed a sigh of relief when they made it to relatively solid ground.

He leaned against the captain's seat and listened to the quiet, feeling solitude for the first time since he and Lewis had begun their mad dash to find Isla. He was exhausted. His eyes were gritty and his head ached with a slow, insistent throb. Beneath his physical discomfort ran a wave of fear that he wouldn't find Isla, or by the time he did, it would be too late.

Never one for dedicated prayer, he still sent out a plea to a God who may or may not be listening. *Please, please, please . . .*

"If I have learned one thing about our doctor, it is that

she is resourceful." Quince smiled wearily at Daniel. "Try not to imagine the worst."

Daniel's mouth turned up in a smile. "I thought you were sleeping soundly, Mr. Quince."

"I was! But then there was no noise from the motor and no rumble of voices. I believe the stillness is to blame."

"We shall finish here, and then I'm returning you immediately to the inn."

"Are you suggesting I am too old for adventure?"

"I would never dare suggest such a thing. I, however, am exhausted. The swamp is not the most comfortable of places to spend a night."

Quince yawned. "I wouldn't say that. There's a certain charm about it, no?"

Daniel cocked a brow. "If one finds charm in extreme humidity, multitudinous insects, poisonous reptiles . . ."

"It smells good."

"I suppose right here in this spot it does. There are pockets where it is less . . . so."

Daniel heard a rustle in the foliage and straightened, training the light on the shoreline. Lewis and Bonadea appeared, and Daniel gave each a hand up into the boat. The two shifters exchanged a glance, and Daniel's heart clenched.

"What is it?" He almost preferred ignorance.

"Don't know if it's a good sign or not, but Isla was definitely here. We found the cabin, and Nigel's satchel." Lewis slapped at something on his neck.

"It looks like he locked her in but she broke out a window," Bonadea said. "So we can either be grateful she escaped him or concerned because she's not there anymore."

Daniel's heart pounded. "She's in the jungle." He stared at the spot where the two men had emerged. "She is out there right now, unconscious, in this horrible place." A cold tremor shot through his limbs. When he considered the sheer size of the landmass between their location and the mansion, he felt nauseous. And that was presuming she was headed to the mansion, which she undoubtedly would be if she'd uncovered even the slightest bit of information from Crowe. If she had taken to slogging in the opposite direction for Port Lucy . . . His heart sank. She had twice as far to travel before seeing civilization.

Daniel released a shaky sigh. "Her clothing and shoes were still in her room at the inn. Surely she wouldn't tromp through the jungle barefoot and in her nightclothes." He pinched the bridge of his nose. "Would she?"

Bonadea cleared his throat. "It behooves us to remember she is a strong animal empath. While she undoubtedly faces danger, I would wager she will encounter little hostility from the fauna here."

"I hope you're right," Daniel mumbled.

"Perhaps there is another cabin between here and the mansion, and she has been able to find shelter," Quince said.

"Would she return here for any reason?" Lewis posed the question to the group.

Daniel lifted a shoulder. "I suppose anything is possible."

Bonadea nodded. "Someone should remain here in case she does return. I'm happy to volunteer."

"I'll stay with you." Quince nodded decisively.

"There is a cot in the cabin where you can rest for a few hours," Bonadea told him.

Daniel looked at Lewis, who shrugged. "Two hours remain of our original plan. What should we do?"

Daniel set his jaw. "We go to the mansion. I'm tired of waiting."

Chapter 31

D aniel and Lewis left the steamboat some distance away from the mansion and maneuvered their way on foot through the jungle that bordered the house. Each man had a machete and a pistol, and by the time they neared the big house, both were soaked in sweat and covered with dirt. Clearing a path through the thick undergrowth had been especially cumbersome with limited light—Daniel was leery of announcing their presence so they used the torches sparingly—and he felt the stress of the situation begin to take its toll.

Finally, they stood at the edge of the property where the house overlooked the water. The house was utterly dark, sucking in all the life around it. The air felt heavier, and he forced himself to focus on nothing but the most concrete of details.

"In areas where there are fewer windows, we can use the torches," he whispered to Lewis, who nodded. "We'll begin on the lower level and work our way through each floor."

"Keep an eye out for the witch's spell book," Lewis said.

He glanced at Lewis. "You're certain she'll have one?"

"Every practitioner of any kind of magick has their own spell book. Usually bound, but sometimes they just have individual pages. If that's the case, the pages will be kept in the same portfolio."

Daniel inched his way to the right and looked up at the building, taking in the missing chunk of brick and stone that once formed walls and a ceiling. "Is that an unwritten rule or something? Suppose I decide to practice magick, but I don't want to write down my methods or spells?"

"You're burned at the stake."

Daniel rolled his eyes. "I am genuinely curious."

"Or dunked in water repeatedly. If you drown, it means you're not a witch so you're not required to keep a spell book."

Daniel glanced at his friend with a smile, appreciating the humor.

"Truly, though, it does seem to be an unwritten rule—witches write everything down. My mother is meticulous about keeping records. We have scores of volumes at home—collections from relatives dating back five generations."

Daniel gripped his Tesla torch tightly, his machete in the other hand, and motioned with his head. "We locate Isla first, if she's here, and the spell book second, and then we leave."

Lewis nodded, all traces of humor fading. "We must be prepared to return, though. It may be that we'll need something personal of Malette's, or an ingredient that only she might have access to."

"Very well." He nodded toward the back door and, inhaling quietly, snuck from the shelter of the jungle to the house. He was prepared to pick the lock, but the door handle turned easily. The door swung open, and Daniel didn't know if that meant their task would be simpler than expected, or if they were walking into a trap.

Once inside, they quietly made their way down a narrow hallway, proceeding slowly to avoid shining their torches near the windows. As dark as the house appeared from the outside, Daniel didn't delude himself into believing they would be entirely invisible, but his efforts made him feel better.

The house was clammy and still as a tomb. They wound their way through what was once likely a grand home: large kitchens caked in dust, an enormous formal dining room with tattered drapes that hung in shreds, and a wooden table that had rotted through. Formal parlors, a ballroom, and a grand front entrance completed the first floor. They took a large stone staircase to the second floor.

Here they found sitting rooms and bedroom suites, all in various states of disrepair and disarray. At one end of a hallway, they came to a locked door, and upon picking it, saw the first room of the entire house that had been maintained. It was a large bedroom; there were no cobwebs, no layers of dust or broken furniture. It was neatly kept, but as cold and dark as the rest of the house. There were symbols inscribed along the massive bedframe, and Lewis eyed them before beckoning to Daniel.

"We should leave. I don't know the exact nature of those symbols, but I suspect they are meant to ward off her enemies."

Daniel frowned, but followed Lewis to the door. "Suppose her spell book is in here? It's where I would keep something I wouldn't want in another's hands."

"It could be in there," Lewis agreed as he closed the door. "It could also be in her library or sanctum where she practices magick."

At the center of the second floor were double doors, and Daniel opened them to reveal an enormous area that was open to the sky, which was beginning to lighten.

"This would be the gaping hole then," he said to Lewis, and stepped inside.

To his left was a partial wall, dividing the area. The majority of the third floor remained intact, providing a ceiling for the area to the left which proved to be a library. Along one wall were a row of spices and jars containing various animal parts and a few things Daniel could not identify. Pieces of furniture were scattered throughout in states of disrepair and neglect, and Lewis cursed as he backed into the spindle of a broken spinning wheel that had been discarded in a dark corner. He nudged the contraption with his foot, and the wood knocked against itself as a few spokes dislodged from the wheel.

They crept through the dark room quietly, and Lewis swept his torch beam across large built-in shelves that covered the back wall. "I believe we may be close to finding what we need." He ran his fingertips across several worn, leather-bound volumes.

Daniel frowned. "Where is she?"

Lewis began pulling books from the shelf. "Isla?"

"Malette. If she isn't here, then where is she?" Isla didn't appear to be here either, which meant she was probably outside with an hour before awakening.

He returned to the open area and looked upward. The

sun was rising, but the sky was overcast, and he feared a good storm. His stomach twisted in knots.

A thick sense of foreboding settled on him as the first few drops of rain begin to fall. A circular stone staircase wound its way upward along the far wall and ended on a jagged, crumbling platform that was once part of the third floor. The more the sky lightened, the more the room took on a dark green hue, casting the space in cold shades of black, green, and grey.

A subtle sound echoed through the air and filtered down into the mansion, a rumble he felt in his chest.

Daniel returned quickly to the library. "Lewis, we must go. Or hide."

Lewis frowned. "I haven't found her book yet. Not the right one, anyway."

"I believe she is returning. She cannot find us exposed this way or we're done for."

Lewis shoved a book back onto the shelf and followed Daniel to the open area and back out the second-floor double doors. "There was one cabinet I couldn't open," he said as they ran down the stairs to the main floor, around back, and out the door.

"Locked?"

"Or spell protected."

The sound reverberated again, louder, closer, and they ran for the jungle's thick, concealing cover. A flash of something caught Daniel's eye, and he retraced his steps to see a pair of small buildings mostly hidden by encroaching vegetation. He motioned to Lewis, and they headed toward them as a loud crack of thunder sounded.

Rain pattered around them, quickly gathering in intensity, before they reached the first of the two buildings. It looked to have been recently accessed while the other was covered with unbroken ivy and vines.

"A smokehouse," Lewis panted as they reached the door. "Appears to be, anyway. No windows . . ."

Daniel turned the handle, the door opening with a protesting squeak of rusty hinges. A form slumped in the corner was the only thing in the room, and he swallowed his disappointment when he realized it was Crowe, not Isla.

They ran to his side, and Lewis put his fingers to the man's neck. "Unconscious but alive." He turned Crowe slightly, revealing a mass of cuts and bruises along his face and arms. "Someone beat him soundly."

Daniel's eyes narrowed. "A pity I didn't reach him first. Let's get him away from here. I have questions."

Crowe's hands and feet had been bound, and Lewis quickly cut the ropes. Daniel hoisted the unconscious man over his shoulder and nodded to Lewis, who took both machetes and led the way back into the jungle.

Daniel was exhausted by the time they reached the docked boat, and he gratefully dumped his heavy load onto one of the berths below deck. "See what you can do to awaken him," he told Lewis grimly.

Daniel climbed topside and checked the equipment. He flipped a switch, and the mechanical gears of the rain shelter clicked, grinding until the waterproof covering snapped into place and sheltered the seats and the helm, creating a makeshift room.

"Need the medical kit down here . . ." he heard Lewis call

from below. Daniel retrieved Lewis's medical bag and delivered it to him, and then waited as Lewis opened a jar of salts and waved it under Crowe's nose.

Eventually, Crowe moaned and winced, and rolled onto his side, shielding his torso. His normally olive-skinned complexion was pale beneath a multitude of bruises, and one eye was swollen shut.

He coughed and struggled to rise, and Lewis propped a pillow behind his back and leaned him against the hull. He winced again and hissed in pain as he shifted on the bed.

Lewis gave him a canteen, and Daniel watched impassively as Crowe drank as though he were dying of thirst.

"I suppose it would be too much to hope Isla did that damage to your face," Daniel said, working to maintain an even tone.

Crowe smiled crookedly. "No, she did not. But I fear by now she will dearly wish she had. I left her locked in a cabin."

"She's not there now."

He sobered instantly. "She must be. She was completely safe, I swear. I secured the windows, bolted the door—she doesn't even have shoes!"

"I know." Daniel's lips tightened. "I suggest you explain yourself, or Lewis and I will finish off whatever your enemies have left undone."

Crowe bent his knee and rested his elbow on it. He put his face in his hand and was silent. When he finally spoke, his tone was flat. He rendered an emotionless accounting of his activities over the prior forty-eight hours and explained what his involvement with Isla had been all along. Daniel suspected he left out several details, but under the circumstances, he let it alone.

"After leaving Isla in the cabin, you came here and approached Malette?"

"Yes. I tried to bribe her to release Isla from the curse."

"What did you use as the bribe?" Lewis asked.

Crowe shook his head. "Doesn't make a difference now. She refused and worked me over with her staff."

"Her servants?" Daniel asked.

He shook his head. "A literal staff—long, with a small crystal ball atop. Her favorite plaything." He rolled his eyes and then appeared to regret it, because he kept them closed. He spanned his forehead with thumb and fingertips, rubbing at his temples. "She turned her back on me long enough that I could put a temporary spell on the ball, at least. She won't be able to use it to track Isla. The only way she'll find her is if she sees her with her own eyes."

He sighed. "The whole thing has been unforgivably stupid of me. I've observed Isla long enough to know how she would react when contained. We cannot allow her to get anywhere close to Malette." Crowe's jaw tightened, and he looked away. "I've brought about the one thing I'd hoped to avoid. I thought I was the only one with the grit to actually lock her up to keep her safe. I knew none of the rest of you would."

"You're right about that," Daniel told him flatly. "We were working on a plan together as a group."

Crowe turned to him, dark eyes blazing. "And as a group, *none* of you have any idea what my mother is like. You haven't the least idea!"

"Then you ought to have told us!"

"I do not tell anyone anything!" Crowe touched his fingertip to the corner of his mouth where a trickle of blood had begun to flow. "I have never relied on anyone. I don't share. I do not confide. I have never cared about anyone in my life until—" He closed his mouth and shook his head. "Until that woman. And now she is on a collision course with the most evil person I have ever known."

Daniel studied the man in silence. He didn't know if Crowe loved Isla, but his distress was genuine.

"I cannot . . . We cannot allow her to go anywhere near my mother," he said quietly, his voice hoarse. "We must find the instructions for the cure ourselves, because the only thing Malette ever loved is dead. There is no leverage—I tried."

Daniel released a slow breath. "Do you know if the curse and cure are written down?"

"Of course they are."

Lewis looked at Daniel over his shoulder with one arched brow.

"She logs the spells she deems most important in her personal book. I've never paid much attention to it, but I'm sure it will be locked in the library."

Lewis nodded. "I figured as much. How is it unlocked? She will have guarded it, I imagine."

"Yes." He smiled humorlessly. "But I know most of her tricks. I'll write it for you so if something happens to me, you can still access it."

"Nothing will happen to you, because you're not going to simply walk in the front door again to chat with her," Daniel said. "We do this together, in agreement on one plan. Chaos erupts when people go off on their own."

Crowe looked at him flatly but refrained from comment.

"Sit up," Lewis said and motioned at Crowe. "Is anything broken?" He took Crowe's arm and examined it, probing with his fingertips.

Crowe raised a battered eyebrow. "You're a doctor, now?"

Lewis reached for the other arm and paused when Crowe winced. "I have put together more than one man on a battle-field with shells exploding all around and ray guns firing in every direction. Fairly certain I can handle one man whose mother has slapped him about."

Crowe's lips twitched. "Apologies."

Lewis examined Crowe's torso. "Is your mother a shifter?"

Crowe nodded, eyeing him warily.

"Predatory?"

Crowe laughed but touched his tongue to the blood at the corner of his mouth. "As predatory as they come."

"What kind?" Daniel asked.

Crowe shook his head. "You won't believe me."

"Give it a go."

"She's a dragon."

Daniel squinted at Crowe, and then Lewis. "One too many hits to the head, I'm thinking."

"Do not say I never warned you."

A dragon. Naturally. Daniel sighed, rubbed his eyes, and checked his pocket watch. It was nearly six o'clock. He pulled out his telescriber. "I'll inform the Port Lucy constable that we have a missing person in the jungle near the peninsula. He has several capable deputies who can meet with Bonadea at the cabin and begin their search. Lewis, you and I will return to the manor and find Malette's spell book, and some sort of"—he waved his hand in the air—"body part one would use in a spell. A hair, dragon scale, I don't know."

Lewis snorted, but nodded. "We can be in and out quickly, then help the others find Isla. When we're safely away from Malette, we combine the necessary ingredients and mix up the cure."

"It will not be that simple. Nothing is ever simple with her." Crowe shifted and winced, wrapping his arm around his ribs.

"Have you a better idea?" Lewis asked him.

"No. But do not underestimate her, and do not delude yourselves into thinking she's unaware we're here." He shook his head. "You didn't see her in the house because she didn't want to be seen. She is watching. Waiting. And with any luck, Isla has broken a bone and cannot walk." He rubbed his hand over his hair, muttering, "I should have known she would find a way out of the cabin, but I also assumed she'd be more circumspect wearing only nightclothes and no shoes."

Daniel shot him a glance and then looked out the port-hole at the gathering clouds. "I've known the woman for a handful of weeks, and I could have told you she would walk into a swamp wearing nothing but fig leaves if it meant secur-ing her goal."

"She asked what kind of shifter my mother is, and I didn't tell her. I told her she wouldn't believe me, and if she makes it to the house ignorant of what she's facing . . ." He sighed. "I ought to have told her."

Daniel's telescriber dinged, and he read aloud the message

from the constable. "Son, I have traveled these rivers and swamps all my life, and I would wager my boat that a woman can't find her way through the jungle to that mansion from the coordinates you sent me."

The three men looked at each other, and Daniel decided it would have been funny if he'd not been so concerned. "He's never met this one. She blackmailed her way onto my ship."

Crowe shook his head. "She made my life on the Committee a living hell."

"She's been nothing but wonderful to me," Lewis said with a light shrug.

Daniel and Crowe both turned to him in silence, and Lewis had the temerity to smile. "We should be going," he said. "I'll telescribe Bonadea the details of the plan."

Daniel turned to Crowe. "I realize it would make more sense for you to return to the house with us, but frankly, I don't think you're in a condition to run if need be, or to fight."

"I know how her mind works." Crowe smiled, again without warmth. "I cannot run, but I'll be more use to you as a distraction anyway. You'll need me there."

Daniel studied him. The man could barely stand without support. "She will kill you."

He chuckled, but winced and touched his finger to his mouth again. "She cannot. Part of our loving mother-and-son bond. We cannot kill one another."

"Can she not create a situation where you could be killed secondarily? Caught in cross fire, bring the house down on your head?"

He shrugged, his eyelids heavy as he looked at Daniel.

"She cannot cause my death. At this point, however, it doesn't matter much to me anymore. As long as she's alive, I am chained. If she can never be brought down, I would rather be caught in the cross fire. This is no life."

Daniel was silent before nodding. "We'll take you with us. But you needn't fall on your own sword. Nothing is as fatalistic or set in stone as all that. We go in there today with the intention of coming back out. That includes you." He paused. "What did you offer as your bribe in exchange for Isla's cure?"

Crowe released a quiet sigh. "Myself. I promised to stay here, to be her lackey, her spy. I vowed to stop interfering in her magick by blocking her progress. Between age and maturity, I've become a thorn in her side."

"You can do all of that, and yet she still managed to do this damage to you? Why do you not use your skills against her?"

"She is often a step ahead of me. The older I get, however, the faster I've become. I told her I would stay away from her affairs forever, but it wasn't enough, and frankly I am stunned. She's used me for her own ends from my first breath, but I never have made it easy for her."

"She hates Isla more than she wants cooperation from you."

Crowe nodded. "Now that she has lost Gladstone, she has nothing left but vengeance."

Chapter 32

I sla ineffectually shielded her eyes from the blinding rain and stared at the huge old house. She'd spied it on the other side of a wide river a scant thirty minutes after shoving herself out of her tree root nest.

The river was more of a bay, a body of water that created a horseshoe-shaped configuration of land, one end holding the mansion, and the other end holding Isla. The distance across the water was shorter than the distance around to the house on land, but she didn't think she had the strength to swim. She thought she'd heard the faint noise of a boat when she'd awoken, but there was nobody in sight now.

She looked up at the sound of wings overhead, but the rain hindered her vision. She rubbed her sore and tired eyes. What kind of bird flew in torrential rain? And how big must it have been that she heard it over the sounds of rain on the leaves and the near-constant rumble of thunder?

A sense of foreboding had crept over her when she'd spied the house for the first time that morning, and it had grown by degrees as she'd neared the structure. Nigel had lived in this place? Had been raised here as a small child? Everything about the mansion was sinister, and worlds away from her tidy home in England, from Castles', from everything she enjoyed that was good and true.

At least the driving rain was cleansing, and Isla welcomed the rivulets that ran down her face and diluted the red bloodstains on her tattered clothing. Her hair was drenched through, and while she was still cold from her early morning, awaken-from-death routine, the rain was oddly healing. It was worth the occasional shuddering spasms that shook her frame.

She neared the manor, each step a new lesson in pain. She left a trail of blood in her wake—that alone ought to have made her a prime target for any animal stalking her—and she prayed for numbness in her feet, a prayer that regrettably went unanswered. Her skin displayed dozens of welts left by mosquitoes that must have been as large as blue jays from the size of the bites they left behind. She slapped at them to avoid compulsive scratching, both actions irritated her sunburn, and she decided she was destined to be miserable no matter what she did.

She would keep the pain, though, as opposed to the opposite, which would be to feel nothing. To be stuck in the nothing. Pain and discomfort meant she was still alive, still there. The alternative frightened her beyond words and that thought alone pushed her forward.

I am Isla Cooper, and I have done hard things. The words brought comfort, but not much. She missed her family, her home, the students she taught to hone their empath skills and help those who hurt. She missed Daniel with a longing that ached inside her chest. She missed her new friends from the voyage. She even missed Nigel. She thought of Monkey and sniffled.

She crept from tree to shrub along the shoreline until she neared a small clearing around the house. The jungle marched nearly up to the side of the structure, which was ideal. She paused under the enormous fronds of a tree to wipe her face and rub her mosquito-bitten eyelids and wring her hair out. Once inside the structure, she would likely leave a bloody trail, but she saw no other alternative.

She took one deep breath, then two, cast a prayer heavenward, and ran from the safety of the trees. She had nearly reached a small side door when an enormous *whoosh* sounded above her and knives drove into her shoulders. She was lifted from the ground with terrifying speed and flown out over the water, unable to breathe for the rush of wind.

She managed to turn her head upward and gasped to see an enormous black body with an impressive wingspan, but she was unable to see the creature's head. She sputtered and coughed, crying out in pain as the movement wrenched her shoulders that were pierced by enormous black claws.

She caught her breath when the thing changed directions, flew back over land, and circled above the crumbling house. The pain in her shoulders caused spots to form before her eyes, and she fought to stay conscious. She swung like a rag doll.

The giant bird continued to circle the house but eventually descended, darting with terrifying speed to the roof, half of which had crumbled clear down to the second floor. They flew into the opening with a huge rush of beating wings, and the claws released Isla high enough from the floor that when she hit it, she slipped on mossy, rain-soaked stone, and pain jolted through her knee as it twisted beneath her. Her head hit the floor, and her vision dimmed, slowly darkening the image of beating wings, claws that dripped with her blood, and enormous teeth in a head as terrifying as a monster in a child's fairy tale.

Isla heard a strange sound as though it echoed from far away, down a long tunnel. It pierced her eardrums and cleaved her head in two. She struggled to open her eyes, conscious only of pain and the steady thrum of rain. Her shoulders were on fire, and her leg collapsed under her when she tried to push herself up from a cold, hard surface. Her knee was twisted at an odd angle, and a knot formed on the side of her head. That was where she had hit her head on Daniel's ship, wasn't it? It felt so long ago—a lifetime ago. Logic surged and retreated as she tried to distinguish fact from fantasy.

Fantasy was an enormous bird with a head and teeth that resembled a dragon. A *dragon*. Not unlike the kind she'd read about when she was small. But the fact was there was no such thing as a dragon. She must be so exhausted and overwhelmed with everything her life had become in the past year that she could no longer differentiate between truth and fiction.

The piercing sound echoed again through the room, and she squinted through the rain, her vision blurry. She tried to focus and caught sight of a figure dressed in black, holding a long staff with a small crystal ball at the top. The person moved closer, and Isla shoved herself upright against her protesting shoulders and bit back a cry of pain when she shifted her leg.

Finally, the figure stood before her, and Isla recognized her from Nigel's drawing in his notebook. "Malette," she whispered.

The woman was stunningly beautiful—long, black hair, tall and stately frame with long legs encased in sleek black breeches and boots. Her cloak flowed around her and gathered in puddles and ripples on the floor as she crouched next to Isla, her hand sliding down the staff.

"Dr. Cooper," she murmured. "I have been forced to deal with you from afar. What a pleasure it is to find you've come all this way to meet me."

"What do you want in exchange for a cure?" Isla shoved herself against the stone wall at her back, squeezing herself beneath a narrow portion of the ceiling that remained intact, protecting her from the driving rain.

Malette smiled, her white teeth perfectly aligned and the bicuspids sharp. "Direct and to the point. I respect that." She watched Isla with unnervingly cold eyes the color of green ice.

"I cannot bring back your son, and I am sorry for your pain." Isla fought to keep her voice even and centered herself with a deep breath. She reached outward, hoping to tap into the witch's emotions. If she were a shifter—a giant bird, certainly not a dragon—then Isla might be able to connect.

"*Do not* do that," Malette snapped, and the eyes were no

longer ice but fire. "Stay out of my head, or I will kill you this instant." She stood, towering over Isla.

Isla nearly laughed. "Your amusement would come to a premature end, and I've clearly not suffered enough for your satisfaction."

Malette studied her, her face hard. "You took my joy. You destroyed my son."

Isla closed her eyes and leaned her aching head against the wall. "Your son destroyed himself. And you had another who would have benefitted from a mother's affection."

She laughed. "So, Nigel Crowe has made a friend. I don't believe he's ever had one of those."

Isla realized she wasn't about to coerce Malette into anything. When she'd embarked on her journey, she'd imagined meeting a witch who dabbled in the dark arts but could be as greedy as anyone else. Isla had been prepared to pay her well, but her heart sank with the knowledge that Malette was an entity well beyond anything she'd encountered. Her only hope left was that Malette would keep her in the house until the curse became permanent. She might have a chance to find the spell book, escape, lose herself back into the jungle, and eventually find a way to Port Lucy.

One thing at a time, she told herself to avoid panic and paralysis. *One foot in front of the other.* Her sudden burst of laughter echoed off the walls. She couldn't help herself. She couldn't even manage one foot in front of the other.

She squinted, looking around, taking stock of the crumbling structure. "That's why it's so green in here," she said. "The humidity and lack of a ceiling has spread moss everywhere." She looked at Malette. "Or mold, I guess. That seems more fitting."

Malette arched a beautifully shaped brow. "Playful, now? Feeling snippy?"

Please just lock me up in your dungeon so I can think for a moment . . . "You are going to do with me whatever it is you will." Isla lifted her hand and let it fall back into her lap. "I do not delude myself into believing anything I can say will convince you to tell me the cure, how to reverse the curse. You cannot be bought, and I have nothing that interests you."

Malette's eyes narrowed. "Your sister, perhaps."

Isla's heart thudded. "What do you want with my sister?" She kept her voice even.

"You've spent your life trying to shape hers. Perhaps you might know a fraction of my pain if you see your sister hanged."

Isla sighed. "My sister has brought me nothing but headaches for years. And she has utterly ruined this last year of my life. She cares nothing for what I say, she defies me at every turn, and at the first possible opportunity, she visited a Dark Magick witch in the sorcery quarter *to buy a spell that rendered me nearly dead.*" Her voice rose on the last, and she hoped she was convincing enough. "So you can threaten me all you like with my sister, my family, everyone in my life who supposedly loved and supported me yet left me to handle the responsibility of raising a sibling when I was no more than a child myself." She allowed her fear to pose as anger. "Do you know what my mother believes? She thinks I've traveled to Port Lucy for research. She has no idea I die every night!"

She maneuvered her strong leg beneath her, and shoved

her back upward along the slick surface of the stone wall behind her. She pushed with every ounce of strength she had so she could stand and face the woman who had ruined her life because her own son had reaped the consequences he deserved.

"Do your worst," she spat at Malette, who watched her with eyebrows raised. "I welcome it!"

"Stubborn, ridiculously so," Malette murmured. "Hmm." She tapped the bottom of her staff against the floor, creating the echoing, high-pitched clacking sound that had awoken Isla.

"I am aware of your conflicting feelings for your family, Dr. Cooper." She smiled. "Would you like to know the best part of the curse that afflicts you?"

Dread settled around Isla's heart and squeezed.

"When you arrested my son and ensured his execution, you took from me the one person on earth I loved." Her face remained pleasant, which was somehow worse than her anger. "Gladstone was all I had left of his father. I loved him purely and without reservation as only a mother can. And he loved me." She paced a small path in front of Isla. "You love your family, surely, but without reservation? Without frustration?"

Isla swallowed. "Everyone is frustrated with loved ones at some point or other. It is a normal part of life."

"Not mine!" Malette slammed the staff against the floor, and as much as Isla wished to appear unaffected, she winced and put a hand to her head.

"I would have done anything for my son, and he for me! Your mother—would she drop everything she adores in life to see to you? Your *sister*? Your cousin, the rabble-rouser?"

Malette relaxed, and her lips curved in a gentle smile. "So, you see, your curse can only be broken by true love's kiss. From one who loves you deeply, and for whom your love is equally given. You have no husband or child, but, as you said, only a sister who would rather poison you than bow to your dictates and a mother obsessed with her precious boutique." She lifted a brow in triumph. "*That* is not true love. From your end, undoubtedly. From theirs? Likely a shadow of your affection for them."

The silence between them stretched, and Isla held herself upright by sheer force of will. A single tear escaped and trickled down her face. Isla had always known her weaknesses, had studied her own frustrations and doubts as her education as a therapist had evolved. Malette knew the heart of Isla's discontent, her fear, and had called her bluff then aimed it back at her with a deadly degree of accuracy.

Malette moved closer and brushed Isla's tear away with her fingertip. "When we peel away every defense, every last layer, nothing remains but the pain."

Isla bit her lip, furious that both eyes now burned and filled with tears. She sniffed as they fell, but maintained eye contact with Malette.

"You have spent your young life building up the positive feelings of others," Malette murmured. "But you can see how much more effective it is to find the one fatal flaw."

"That all depends on the ultimate goal," Isla said. "If the aim is to destroy, your method meets with success."

"And I have broken you." Malette's eyes glittered in triumph.

Isla ground her teeth together until her jaw ached. "And

yet, I remain standing. Success is measured by one's definition of it."

Malette's expression hardened, stilled. A sound to Isla's left drew their attention, and Isla looked to see Nigel standing in the doorway, slowly applauding.

"Oh, good," Malette said, her voice bright. "The spawn returns!"

"Oh, Nigel," Isla whispered. He looked to be in worse shape than she was—battered, bruised, and swollen.

Malette glanced at her with a laugh. "You pity him? My, you are nothing but heart. Do you hear that, Nigel? You have a friend, a champion. Dreams really do come true!"

Nigel slowly entered the room, deceptively casual in his stance, hands comfortably in his pockets. "How is the crystal ball working, Mother? Giving you fits, is it?"

"I told you never to call me that!" Malette glanced at the opaque ball atop her staff, and her eyes transformed again from ice to fire. "You will reverse the spell."

"I will fix the ball when you release her."

Isla closed her eyes. "Nigel," she murmured. Malette would cripple him, hurt him in ways that were worse than death.

"You will reverse the spell," Malette said, "or I will destroy her in front of you."

Isla knew he was trading his life for hers, and she would never be able to live with that. "He cast a spell on your magick ball, and you are unable to fix it yourself?"

Malette's eyes swung back to Isla, and Nigel cursed under his breath.

"Isla," he warned.

"He must be more powerful than I realized." Isla glanced at him speculatively. "What a fool you were for doting on the wrong son all those years."

Malette's hand shot to Isla's throat and pinned her to the wall, choking her so completely she was unable to make a sound. In her periphery, Isla saw Nigel move toward Malette, but she pointed her staff in his direction; he flew against the far wall and crumpled to a heap.

Isla's vision dimmed and blurred as she clawed at Malette's hand, which was as cold and hard as granite. She would die without telling her family one last time that she did, indeed, love them beyond words. She would never say those words to Daniel. She would die, and he would never know.

Chapter 33

Isla was freezing. She lay on a cold, hard surface and wondered if this time she was finally dead. She had tried to be a good person, but wherever she was did not feel like heaven. "So, it's hell for me, then," she croaked, her voice raspy. She coughed and put her hand to her neck where Malette's fingers had left bruises. The cold seeped into her bones, and she shivered. How many times could a person awaken from oblivion in one day? Perhaps she had gone mad.

When she was able to focus beyond the blinding pain in her head, she realized she was in a cellar, a jail, with three stone walls and a row of iron bars along the fourth. A manacle circled her ankle, and as she moved to examine it, she cried out involuntarily in pain.

"Find the anger, Isla!" Her hoarse sob bounced crazily off the walls, and her breath stuck in her throat as she sat upright. She coughed again, clutching her head, and considered the potential value in running into the wall with her face. Oblivion might be preferable to the pain. Everything hurt.

A heap in the corner caught her eye, and her heart

thumped when she recognized Nigel's inert form. A manacle on his wrist connected him to the wall.

"Nigel! Oh, no, no, no . . ." She scooted forward as far as the chain would allow, but she was still shy of reaching him by a foot or two. "Nigel, wake up!" She slapped the floor with her open palm. "Wake up!"

She looked up at the room's single barred window; the storm still raged outside. She couldn't tell if the dark sky was because of the storm gathering in intensity or because several hours had passed. She didn't know if Nigel had tried to contact Daniel and the others, she didn't know whether help was on the horizon, she didn't know how she'd escape from a locked dungeon. She didn't know anything.

She slapped the floor again. "Nigel, wake up! I don't even have a hairpin with me to pick this blasted lock, which is entirely your fault because you abducted me in my nightgown! You had better hope you've got something useful on your person because if not, I will . . . I will . . ." Her voice faded on a pathetic whimper, and she almost wished for midnight.

"You'll what?" Nigel's voice was low, weak, and he still hadn't moved.

She felt a surge of hope. "I will flay you with angry words, because I have no weapons, and I am fairly certain at least three bones are broken."

His shoulders shook the littlest bit, and he turned his head. He was laughing, and her relief was overwhelming.

"You're not paralyzed. And you're speaking."

"You're celebrating prematurely," he groaned and caught his breath. "I haven't tried to move my legs, and I'm not sure I remember my name."

"How many fingers do you see me holding up?"

"One, and that's not very polite, Dr. Cooper."

She laughed despite herself. "Why could you not have been this pleasant at home? We might have gotten along famously."

"Enjoy it while it lasts," he grunted and slowly stretched his neck. "If we cannot get out of here, I suspect I shall not be good company for long."

"Can you feel your legs? Do you have sensation below the waist?"

He looked at her flatly. "In some places, yes. Less so in other areas."

She scowled at him. "Can you pick a lock?"

He pushed himself upright. "I can pick a lock. I do not know that I have anything on me that will suffice."

She was still sprawled on the cold floor and for the moment didn't want to move. The pain exploded volcanically whenever she moved. She rested her head on her arm. "Tiepin?"

"Not presently wearing a tie."

"Metal toothpick?"

"No."

"Are any of your limbs constructed with synthetic materials?"

"No!"

"Telescriber?" she asked hopefully.

"My mother took it," he muttered.

She snorted laughter, unable to help herself. "Your mother took your telescriber? Were you breaking the rules, contacting friends after bedtime?"

"It's all fun and games until we never get out of here, and then nobody is laughing anymore."

"At least your mother took yours. Mine never cared one way or another. Apparently, nobody in my life loves me."

"Enough of that. Pity does not become you, and furthermore, you should realize that Malette is nothing but a bundle of lies from beginning to end. She takes ambiguity and twists it until it suits her and is just a shade shy of truth." Nigel's chain rattled as he stood, bracing a hand on the wall. "I suspect we are only a few hours away from evening, and I don't relish the thought of being locked in here with a dead woman."

"That is harsh."

"But honest." He patted his pockets and ran a hand over his shirt. He was dressed in shirtsleeves and trousers only. Goosebumps covered his skin, and she realized he was undoubtedly as cold and uncomfortable as she.

"Your boots!" she said and shoved herself upright with an agonized gasp.

"What of them?"

"Are there nails in the soles?

He lifted the corner of his mouth in reluctant admiration. He sat back down on the floor and muscled the boot off, and then examined the sole and heel of the boot. "Even if there are," he muttered as he turned it this way and that, "they may be too short to be of use."

"Certainly worth the effort. And at least you have boots."

He looked up at her and then at her feet. "I apologize. For everything. I thought I was doing what was best and in reality, I do not think I could have bungled it more if I'd tried." He shook his head. "I had thought that by leaving you without shoes, you would stay put in the cabin." He glared at her, and she frowned.

She sniffed. "Apology accepted. And I forgive you, as you do not know me very well."

"You're the second person today to tell me that," he muttered, trying to find leverage on the boot heel with his fingers.

"Who was the first?"

"Your besotted airship captain."

She gaped. "You've seen Daniel? Today?"

He nodded and smacked the boot on the floor. "He's here. So is Lewis."

"Nigel!" She stumbled pathetically to the bars, grasping two of them and trying to peer out into the hallway. "You might have said something!"

"Figured you knew. How do you think I escaped?"

She turned back to him, still holding the iron bars. "She locked you up before?"

"Well, yes," he said, his exasperation clear. "How do you suppose this happened?" He gestured to the bruises on his face. "I left you in the cabin, came here, mixed a spell in the library to confound her blasted crystal ball, and was in the process of gathering ingredients for your cure when she caught me."

Isla turned and leaned against the bars. "You located the cure?"

"It's in her spell book, which we have yet to locate, but I know enough of the basics she would have used that I decided to at least gather those as a start."

She sighed. "I am sorry you've done all this for my sake. You wouldn't even be here, if . . ."

"If what?" His cynical smile returned. "If I hadn't agreed to spy on you for my mother to ensure that a nasty sleeping spell would mature and then put you into an eternal coma?" He shook his head. "Do not absolve me of anything. A good thrashing is the least I deserve."

"How did the others know you were here?"

"They spoke with Port Lucy's oldest resident gossip. Found the house and then me in one of the storage buildings." He pulled the heel loose, revealing a U-shaped row of spikes protruding from the bottom of the boot. "These on the ends may be long enough." He made quick work of pulling out five nails, and using one of them, began working on the manacle at his wrist.

"How odd that this was your home," she observed as he worked. "And how bizarre it must be to find yourself locked in the dungeon."

"This isn't the first time," he said and frowned at the manacle. "Spent half of my childhood in here."

"*What?*"

"Well, perhaps not half."

"Even a quarter, an eighth, is too much! Once is too much! She is truly an evil person. And she is so beautiful, it's disarming."

He laughed. "Yes. I learned quite early to mistrust beauty."

"Learned to mistrust many things, I suspect," she observed quietly.

"Stay out of my head, Dr. Cooper. There are places in

there best left alone." He paused. "There!" Metal clanked as the manacle dropped from his wrist.

"Why does she not lock these with charms?"

He grinned. "I can disarm those. She figures there's always a chance I can't pick a plain lock."

"How long do you suppose we've been in here?" she asked as he began working on her shackle.

"If I had to guess, an hour, maybe more."

"Then why haven't Daniel and Lewis found us yet?" The thought swam uncomfortably in her head. "She may have caught them."

"She may," he acknowledged. "But this room is hidden behind the kitchen on the first floor. They wouldn't think to look here. My guess is they may be hiding, waiting for her to either leave or turn her back. There are two places where she would have hidden the spell book. I disarmed the protective spell outside her bedroom so they could examine her cabinets in there, while I went to the library in case there were more protective spells there. That's where I was when Malette swooped in with you."

"Is there a definitive escape plan?"

"Before we entered the house, Pickett telescribed Samson to be ready with the airship, but not to hover within sight of the house. It was a loosely formed plan, but the best we could manage at the time."

"So they know I am here?"

"Not yet. None of us knew for sure. We thought you were somewhere in the swamp. Bonadea and the Port Lucy constable are searching for you as we speak." He shook his head. "I tried to scribe Daniel from the library when I heard you in the other room with Malette, but my charge had gone out." He shook the chain attached to her manacle. "Sit, will you please?"

She slowly lowered herself to the ground and bit her lip to keep from crying out as she stretched the leg she'd twisted earlier. He was able to turn her other foot for easier access to the locking mechanism, and as cold as his skin was, the warmth of his hand on her foot was a welcome relief. She closed her eyes and leaned against the bars, breathing deeply. He stilled, and she opened her eyes to see his battered face tensely drawn.

"I am sorry. I am so sorry." He held her foot in both hands. "I'm never sorry about anything, Isla, never bothered to see the aftermath of my actions." He shook his head as if warding off discomfort. "You are an absolute mess, and it's my fault."

She laughed, her voice still raw. "We shall review your lessons on how to best express criticism to a woman."

He smirked. "Do you believe Malette ever bothered with such lessons? There is no 'review' involved."

"Do not trouble yourself about it, Nigel. The fact that you have a conscience, that you mean well, that you feel remorse—those are good things. Things that prove you are nothing like your mother. And once we get our hands on that spell book of hers, we're going to scour it until we find a way to untether you from her."

"Mmm," he said noncommittally as he resumed work on her manacle lock. "I'm not certain there is such a spell."

"Of course there is. By now I've realized that if there is

a spell, there is a counter for it somewhere." She frowned. "Unless it involves death, I suppose."

"Even that is reversible, if you consider Resurrectionists." He grinned and twisted the nail around the locking mechanism.

"Ugh. Nasty business. Even the good ones can raise only an approximation of the original person. A shadow of a soul is still just a shadow." She shuddered.

The manacle clicked, and he opened it with a smile of satisfaction.

"Nicely done, sir." She moved to stand.

"Wait." He held up a hand and removed his other boot, and then both socks. Before she could protest, he put the socks on her feet. "Not the prettiest, perhaps, but they're warmer than what you have on your feet now."

She swallowed past the sudden lump in her throat, reveling in the temporary physical comfort. "Thank you."

He held up the boots. "I would offer these as well, but they're substantially larger than your feet."

She shook her head. "This is wonderful. Thank you."

He reattached the heel of his destroyed boot with the nails that remained, slipped both boots back on, and, grabbing a fresh nail, made his way to the lock on the iron bars. "It is past time to leave this place. When this business is finished, I shall burn it to the ground."

Chapter 34

Daniel peered around the far corner of the library where he stood with Lewis. They had lost all contact with Nigel, had been unable to locate Isla, and had drawn the fiery focus of the home's owner. A blast of fire shot toward him, and he retreated. He telescribed Samson to move in closer with the airship, uncertain where the most ideal spot for extraction would be.

"The roof?" Lewis suggested, reading the message over his shoulder.

"I don't know. We need to find Crowe before then, and as he's not answering his scribes, I'm assuming Malette has done something to him." Daniel and Lewis had arrived in the library over an hour ago, and he'd been nowhere to be found. The one positive light in the past ten minutes was Lewis had finally found the right spell book.

Lewis nodded toward the open area beyond the library. "He said she can't kill him, but she can certainly scorch him with that."

Daniel nodded, grim. "So, there are dragons," he

muttered. "I owe him an apology." They were safe in their corner only because the dragon was too large to enter the room. They had been disabling charms and searching multiple-locked cabinets when the enormous whoosh he'd heard outside the night before had sounded in the outer room. Daniel had looked around the corner and then grabbed Lewis, making a run for cover.

"Not a bat, then," Lewis had commented breathlessly.

The dragon stayed just out of reach, but close enough to heat the area like a blast furnace with the fire that she shot from her mouth.

"Once I gather the ingredients, we can leave," Lewis said. "I am not familiar with all of them, but I saw many of them on her shelves. This may be our only chance at locating some of the more rare items." He paused. "What shall we do about Crowe?"

Daniel rubbed his eyes. "I am not decided. We can't leave him here indefinitely, but we may need to return with reinforcements. Have you deciphered all of the spell?"

"Getting to the last of it now." Lewis winced at the creature's deafening shriek and the blast of fire that followed.

Daniel rested his head against the wall and closed his eyes. He didn't know if Isla was even still alive. She could be dead in the swamp from an insect sting or snakebite. She could have been attacked by a predator in the dark. She could . . .

"Blast," Lewis muttered.

Daniel opened his eyes. "What is it?"

Lewis rubbed his forehead. "We need a drop of the witch's blood, a drop of Isla's blood, and a drop of blood belonging to the one who can break the curse."

Daniel frowned and peered around the corner again. "Who can break the curse?"

"One with whom the victim 'shares equally true love.'" Lewis scratched his head and angled the book toward a window in the alcove. "I don't even know what that means." He traced his finger along the words. "Three drops combined . . . traced along the forehead . . . a kiss from the beloved . . ."

Daniel swallowed. "Very well, we need Malette's blood. I'll nick her with my blade, and we'll collect the drops in a vial." He nodded toward shelves on the library's far wall that contained ingredients and supplies.

Lewis eyed him and turned back to the spell book. "How are you going to get close enough to nick her and collect the blood?"

"We only need her to bleed, yes? I'll throw my dagger at her, if enough blood drips onto the floor, we can use that. If it's spilled while she's still alive, that qualifies, I should think."

Lewis nodded, and then frowned. He raised his voice to be heard over the constant roar of both the dragon and the raging storm. "You won't be able to simply throw it at her. It says the same implement must be used on all three people to draw the blood."

"Blast. Why is nothing ever simple?" Daniel created a mental list.

Distract the dragon so Lewis can grab the supplies from the shelves.

Draw Malette's blood, drip it into a vial, and retrieve the knife for future blood-letting pertinent to the spell.

Find Crowe.

Get out of the manor.

Meet up with Samson and the airship—assuming the dragon hasn't blasted it out of the sky already.

Find Isla.

Administer the cure.

Suddenly the roar stopped. A fluttering of giant wings echoed in the room, and the dragon's shadow, visible from the alcove, shrunk down into the form of a person.

"So," Malette's voice echoed, "you've escaped the dungeon."

Daniel frowned. Who was she talking to? He ventured a quick look around the corner, and his heart stuttered. Isla stood with Nigel, and she was battered and ragged from head to toe. Lightning forked across the sky, illuminating the grim scene with a garishly bright flash. Daniel's fingers curled into a tight fist, and he forced them to relax and grasp his dagger at a sheath at his side.

"Quite industrious, really. Impressive to see you both upright." Malette slowly advanced on the pair. "Your wits are clearly dulled, however. Did you truly think to sneak in here and I wouldn't realize it?"

Lewis joined him at the corner. "There's an empty burlap sack on the floor," he whispered. "Behind the spinning wheel. I'll grab it and sweep the lot on the shelves into the bag. Everything."

"Suppose something breaks?" He glanced at Lewis before turning his attention back to the witch. He couldn't allow himself to look at Isla, not until they were somewhere safe.

"Have to chance it."

Daniel nodded. "I'll distract her, hit her with the dagger, you sweep the shelves. Do not forget that spell book."

He nodded at the worn, leather-bound volume they'd risked everything to obtain.

Lewis nodded.

"Right, then. On my mark," Daniel said, but stopped when Nigel leaped at Malette, clearly catching her by surprise and taking her to the ground. "Go!" Daniel told Lewis then ran from the library and into the open room as Nigel rolled away from Malette, grasping her staff.

Malette shrieked in outrage and transformed, rising and stretching, becoming a dragon while they watched.

Nigel broke the staff in half over his leg, and when Malette blasted an explosive flame in his direction, he tossed the two pieces directly into the fire. Lewis ran for the shelves in the far corner of the library and grabbed the empty sack. Isla dodged beneath the dragon and slipped her way across the rain-slicked floor, where she collapsed in Daniel's outstretched arms.

He hauled her up against him and backed into the library.

"No," she wheezed, looking back at the dragon. "We must help Nigel. Daniel, he saved my life."

He squeezed his eyes shut and kissed her forehead. "I'll help him. You stay here with Lewis."

"What is he doing?" She squinted at the far corner of the room, clutching Daniel's shoulders.

"Gathering things—"

A deafening roar split the air, and Isla winced. She shoved herself away from Daniel. "Go. I'll help Lewis." Her voice was so hoarse he wouldn't have understood had he not read her lips.

Before he could respond, she pushed at him again and limped across the room. She favored one leg, and his heart caught in his throat when she stumbled and fell to the hard stone floor. He was poised to run to her when Lewis beat him to it. He motioned to Daniel and pulled Isla upright.

Sick with worry, he turned his attention to the dragon, who had Nigel cornered. The man was in a bad way—he'd needed good medical attention before they'd returned with him, let alone now. Daniel yelled at the monster as she tracked Nigel with her eyes, and when she turned to him, Daniel ventured closer and threw his dagger with all his strength. It lodged in the creature's shoulder, well above where he'd aimed.

Malette roared and tossed her head, and Daniel ran as she inhaled. A wall of heat erupted behind him, and he dove toward Nigel as she took flight, screeching loudly enough to drown out the thunder from the storm.

"Hurry!" Daniel pulled the injured man to his feet and hauled him to the relative safety of the library while the dragon bellowed and circled the crumbling house.

Lewis hefted the burlap sack full of items from the shelves with one hand and supported Isla with the other. They made their way to Daniel and Nigel at the doorway, and he looked up at the dragon. "Is she wounded?" he shouted.

Daniel nodded. "My dagger. It's in her shoulder."

Another fiery blast drowned Lewis's response, and all Daniel deciphered was " . . . retrieve that dagger. We need it for the cure."

Isla looked up at Malette. "Does anyone have another knife? A sword? Anything?"

"Not here," Nigel shouted and coughed, flecks of blood catching on his shirtfront. He clutched his side, still leaning heavily on Daniel. "Upstairs in storage, maybe," he managed.

Daniel turned, hoping Malette would fall from the sky. "No time," he shouted to Nigel. "And if she leaves now, we may not have another chance." He glanced at Isla, whose days were numbered. They couldn't afford the luxury of waiting while Malette took herself off somewhere to heal and re-group. "We must keep her here."

Nigel nodded as Daniel eased away from him. Lewis said something to Isla, then handed her the bag and ran back to the corner of the room. He pulled the spinning wheel apart and clutched the spindle, still attached to a length of string.

Malette shrieked, and fire poured down through the open roof as she circled high in the air, but her flight became erratic, less smooth and controlled.

Lewis lifted the spinning wheel and hurled it back down again, smashing apart the main components.

The dragon dove at the room, and Nigel picked up a candlestick from a dusty shelf. He stumbled out of the library and hurled his improvised weapon at her with a furious shout, grazing the end of the dagger that still protruded from the dark green scales. Daniel rushed to a shelf and grabbed a few books and debris, following Nigel's lead and striking the creature in the back and wings to distract it. Perhaps they could wound it enough to bring it down.

He risked a glance at Lewis and Isla, who now stood at the library entrance. Lewis grasped the spinning wheel's spindle and tugged the attached string. He handed the spindle to Isla and said something Daniel couldn't hear.

She grasped the spindle tight. Lewis clasped her hand with his and, with his other hand, wove a series of small circles in the air over the item. He then pulled the end of the string and began unwinding it, letting it out as one might when flying a kite. Daniel saw the purpose behind Lewis's actions and hoped desperately that it would work.

Nigel struck the dragon in the side of the head with a rock, and she spun, swinging her tail in a wild arc and slamming into Lewis and Isla. Daniel ran for them, diving to shield Isla, who still maintained her grip on the spindle even as she fell. Lewis crawled toward them, visibly stunned.

"If I can pierce her with this, I can pull it back," Isla said in Daniel's ear, her hoarse voice nearly spent.

He nodded. "I'll do it."

She was about to relinquish the spindle to him when Lewis reached them, shaking his head frantically. "She must be the one to throw it since she held it when I wove the spell."

Spell? He meant the circles in the air he wove above Isla's hand while she held the spindle.

Isla struggled to stand, and Daniel rose with her, wrapping his arm around her waist as she gathered the length of string in one hand and the spindle in the other. She exhaled and focused her gaze on the dragon. Its erratic movement slowed. It swung its enormous head away from Nigel and locked on her with its eerie green eyes. The dragon gradually turned its enormous body toward her.

"Isla, no," Daniel murmured. "Please—"

"Get me closer," Isla whispered to Daniel, and to his horror, blood trickled from her nose. She was hypnotically calming the creature.

He cursed under his breath but lifted her weight against his side and slowly moved her closer to the beast.

Isla hefted the weight of the spindle in her hand and let out a length of the string. She blinked, and faltered, leaning on him completely for support.

"Isla," he whispered.

She pulled her arm back, then hurled the spindle with an anguished cry, striking the dragon in the heart. The beast opened her mouth, spewing forth a final blast of flame, and Daniel took Isla to the ground as fire shot over their heads.

He squinted through the air, which rippled in the heat, and began pulling the singed and fraying string attached to the spindle, afraid it would sever before he could retrieve it.

The dragon staggered, transforming back into Malette. The enormous body twisted and shrunk, and she slumped, human, to the ground, her black hair fanned around her. The spindle fell from her body with a clang against the stone floor.

Isla coughed and spit blood, but clutched the spindle when Daniel had pulled it into her reach. She looked over her shoulder at Lewis, who scrambled to them with an empty jar large enough to hold the bloody spindle.

The silence seemed to roar as loudly as the fire and chaos had. Small flames flickered randomly across the room as books burned and debris crackled. Slowly, Daniel registered the sound of labored breathing; Malette was still alive.

Her malevolent glare found Isla, who stared back at her with blood dripping from her nose. "I told you to stay out of my head," the witch murmured. "Now you've pushed yourself too far."

Isla shook her head. "This won't kill me." She smiled. "You've lost."

Malette coughed and choked. Her breath rattled, but she met Isla's gaze with a final smile of her own, blood trickling from the side of her mouth. "You're too late. Even with the spell book, my blood, the cure must be administered tonight." She laughed, the sound soft and chilling. "Not one year to the day from when you ingested it, but one year to the day when I finished mixing it. You do not have another week. You do not even have another day. Perhaps best of all," she continued, her voice dropping, thin as a thread, "you'll never find the most crucial ingredient because for you, Dr. Cooper, it doesn't exist. *You've* lost, and my son is avenged." She gasped a final, hideous sound, and then was still, her eyes locked on Isla as she breathed her last.

Isla sucked in a shuddering breath. She stared at the still form through tears that blurred the image into a solid mass of black and red.

"What on earth?" Lewis whispered.

Malette's body shimmered, flickering into her dragon form. Before Isla could form a coherent thought, the dragon burst into flame. She stared at the sight, blinking at the heat and searing brightness. As quickly as the fire started, it vanished, leaving a pile of ash in its place.

Rain continued to fall, and gusts of wind swirled around the remains, scattering the ashes into the dark night.

Chapter 35

ever make it in time . . . It had been her fear from
the beginning, and it now pounded through her
head in an awful refrain. She had run out of time.
Malette had won. At least she could tell herself that she had
gone down swinging, that she hadn't given up, had fought to
the bitter end.

Nigel sank onto the floor next to the ashes. "She's dead."
He exhaled quietly.

Isla's brain spun in a million different directions and then
seemed unable to grasp even the simplest of things. Her head
ached in a pounding she was afraid would never subside.

"Isla?" Daniel touched her arm gently.

The deep wounds in her shoulders where the dragon's
claws had dug throbbed, and her feet ached from her tromp
through the jungle.

Isla looked up at the storm-darkened sky. Even without
seeing the moon rise, she could feel how fast midnight was
approaching. She thought back to the night before when

she'd been sleeping under tree roots. So much had transpired in twenty-four hours; it had felt like an eternity.

Lewis turned a page in Malette's spell book and ran his finger over the words. "Perhaps not all is lost. Malette's instructions here at the end say that once the curse has put you to sleep one last time, you must receive a drop of blood and a kiss from 'one who loves you equally.' If we can reach a loved one, perhaps?" He looked up, a note of hope in his voice.

Isla stared at remaining ash and dust, but in her mind, she still saw Malette's eyes, which seemed to laugh at her from beyond the grave. "That's what she meant," she mumbled, numb. "I'll never find the last ingredient because it doesn't exist. Not for me."

"I'll telescribe Samson," Daniel said, fumbling in his pockets. "Tell him to bring the *Briar Rose* airship closer. We'll leave immediately. The engine—perhaps I can find an extra accelerant of some sort to use. The propellers are already turning at their maximum speed, and we'd have to fly around the storm—hope to catch a better wind—but we're much faster in the air than on the ocean . . . If I push her to her limits, we could make it to England in—"

"Weeks," Isla said softly.

The four of them fell silent.

Isla looked at Daniel. Tears pooled and spilled over, and she cried softly, fearing her heart would break. Malette was still in her head, insisting nobody loved her enough to break the curse, and fate was wretched beyond all measure because she'd fallen in love with Daniel Pickett and he was too kind. She'd thought when Malette was going to kill her that she should have told him she loved him, but now she realized it was an unfair burden to place upon him. He would try to break the curse for her and because his feelings weren't the same as hers, it wouldn't work. He'd never forgive himself.

A clock in the library sounded midnight's first chime. It echoed throughout the dark hall, mingling with the steady thrum of rain. Her physical pain was so thorough and familiar by now she'd grown accustomed to it. She didn't even feel the cold anymore.

The chiming continued, like a death knell.

Lewis shook his head, riffling through the diary pages. "Something, there must be something . . ." he murmured.

Isla released a shuddering sob, unwilling to admit defeat, and yet she felt the lethargy stealing upon her even as stood there.

Daniel gathered her close. "Isla, you're safe," he whispered and wiped her tears. "I'll stay here with you, nothing will happen to you. I promise."

She turned her face into his neck. There was so much in her heart and so little time to express it. "Daniel," she said, "I cannot tell you how much . . ." Her voice broke, and she shuddered. "It is too late," she whispered.

Daniel's expression hardened. "No," he said. "We will find a way. I will not quit. I will never stop." He cradled her head with his hand and rocked back and forth.

The chiming clock continued, and as the darkness encroached, she clutched a fistful of his shirt. She didn't want to miss a moment with him, and the nothing was taking her again.

"No!" She cried despite her resolve to be strong. There were too many things she wanted to say, too much left to do.

"No . . ." Her voice faltered, and she registered the familiar heaviness in her arms and legs.

Daniel's embrace tightened. "We will find a way," he whispered in her ear. "I will save you, Isla. I will never, ever stop."

Chapter 36

Isla succumbed to the darkness, and Daniel let his own tears gather.

His worry for her over the past two days had consumed him even as he'd tried to remain rational. He had done everything he could think of to help her retrieve what she needed and get her to safety. For the bulk of those hours he hadn't been certain she was even still alive, and when he'd seen her in Malette's lair, his relief at seeing her was eclipsed only by his fear he would witness her death.

By dragon.

He had yet to fully absorb the reality surrounding him. He had helped Isla slay the dragon, only to have her fall into darkness. A darkness that, according to Malette, would be permanent. He held Isla close. Her breathing and pulse slowed, as it always did at midnight, and as always, his own pulse increased with panic as he waited for her to breathe again.

He waited. And waited.

Finally, a full minute later, Isla's chest rose and fell in a shallow breath. He swallowed, relieved that she was still alive, and hoping perhaps he'd have until six o'clock to find another solution, another way to save her.

He would drive himself mad if he stayed there, waiting for her to breathe, so he eased himself away from her side and stood over her for a moment.

Daniel ran a hand through his hair, bunching it in his fist and scrunching his eyes closed. "She did it," he muttered. "The witch found a way even from the grave . . ." He swallowed reflexively, feeling ill. All the work, all the tears and sweat and effort and agony—to come to this? He shook his head. "There must be something . . ."

Lewis pushed himself to his feet with a groan. He wiped his arm across his forehead and paged through the diary. "We'll find a way, Daniel. Let me do some digging in the library." He glanced at Crowe. "Are there lanterns somewhere? We need light."

Crowe nodded and stiffly shoved himself to his feet. "Upstairs in storage. Should be kerosene there as well. I'll help you look."

Lewis swept his eyes over Crowe's battered body. "You stay here with Daniel. I can find the lamps."

Crowe nodded. "Let me see the spell book."

Lewis handed the book to him and then made his way to the doors. He shoved them open, and the resulting creak sounded loud in the room.

Daniel stepped out onto the broken edge of the floor. Open to the sky, he let the wind and the rain lash at him, willing himself to feel something—anything—besides the encroaching numbness.

Isla is gone.

The idea would not leave him. He dug his hand into his hair and looked out over land and air. There was nothing but marshland and river water beneath him, and the sky was equally dark.

Isla is gone.

And he loved her so much, it hurt. He heard footsteps and glanced over his shoulder as Nigel approached him.

Daniel had seen the extent of the damage Malette had done to her son—the bruises and cuts were plentiful—but the man had held himself together, and Daniel had yet to hear him complain even once about the physical pain.

Crowe remained silent, squinting against occasional gusts of wind.

"I refuse to accept this," Daniel finally bit out, fury building. He hated Malette so much it physically burned. "Why, *why?*"

"Because she was evil. She was evil incarnate, there was not a decent bone in her body." Nigel cursed and rubbed his face.

"There has to be something." Daniel's thoughts spun, grasping and discarding the tiniest of possibilities. "Something . . . anything . . ."

"There is." Nigel looked at him with clouded eyes.

"What?" It took Daniel a moment before he realized that Crowe held Malette's spell book by his side. His finger holding a place near the back of the book.

Nigel flipped open the book to the page he had marked. "She made some personal notes here." He pointed to something Daniel couldn't read. "It's in Romanian. She kept all of her personal notes in either French or Romanian."

Daniel felt a shiver of anxiety run through the numbness in his chest. "What does it say?"

"The kiss—the actual kiss?"

Daniel waited, not daring to allow even a moment of hope to rise up in him.

"It must occur after the first strike of midnight but before the last."

Daniel barked out a laugh. "Midnight has come and gone. The clock has chimed its last." He shook his head. "Isla was right. We are too late."

Nigel shook his head. "I don't believe that is what Malette meant. I believe she meant the *end* of the midnight hour—before the last minute when midnight changes to one o'clock. I believe we have an hour before the curse becomes permanent."

Daniel couldn't make sense of it. He looked at Nigel, feeling faint, numb. An hour? Could it be possible?

Nigel snapped the book shut. "We have Malette's blood. We have Isla's. We simply need to mingle it with the blood from a loved one's finger, and trace it onto her forehead. And then the kiss."

"But her family—"

"—is not here," Nigel finished. "Even if they were, I'm not sure they could break the curse."

"What do you mean?"

Nigel offered him a ghost of a smile. "You're either modest or stupid, I'm not sure which."

Daniel studied the man carefully.

"You love her," Nigel said wearily. "It's obvious to everyone—except, perhaps, the two of you."

Daniel shook his head, his lips tightening. "I do not wish to discuss it."

"You have to do it."

"No! We have exactly one drop of Malette's blood extracted from the spindle. Once used, it is gone. If I were to attempt it and meet with failure—"

"Fool!" Crowe's eyes looked blacker and fiercer than ever. "Do you love her or not?"

"Of course I do! I love her more than my own life!"

"Then prove it!"

Daniel looked at the darkness around him and shook his head, feeling perilously close to tears. "I have no more claim to her than anyone else," he said. "There have been no declarations of love, no discussions about building a life together. It won't work."

"Never in my life have I ever watched *anyone* the way you two look at each other."

Daniel thought back to his interaction with Isla before reaching Port Lucy, of the times she'd whispered in his ear, her lips lightly grazing him. Of the way she leaned subtly back into his hand when he escorted her through a door before him, or up a flight of stairs. He'd registered the details on a deeper level where there was no conscious thought—it was those signals and more that had driven him half mad with desire for her, for everything about her, everything he wanted with her.

It might work . . . He allowed himself to hope, even as he realized how dangerous that was. Malette was vicious and cruel. If she'd built in any other surprises to her blasted curse, they would never know, and time was against them. *Still.*

What was it he'd heard Lia say even as a young girl? Work and luck. Faith and hope in good things.

Could he truly walk away before he'd tried every possible option? Quince, Bonadea, Lewis—they had cared for her and loved her. Even Nigel, who had been one of her harshest critics, a thorn in her side, had saved her more than once.

Could he do any less?

Lewis returned with two glowing lanterns and motioned with his head. "Crowe, help me in the library. We must mix the concoction for Isla to drink."

Daniel looked at him dubiously. "She's unconscious."

"Then we shall sit her upright and open her mouth. As for the kiss from a loved one—we'll think on it."

"Problem already solved," Nigel said, glaring at Daniel. He shuffled forward, wincing as he made his way to the library with Lewis.

"How so?" Lewis asked before they disappeared around the corner and their conversation was muted.

Daniel returned to the main room, away from the wind and rain, and sat next to Isla's prostrate form, noting the blue that had already stolen across her features. He lifted her from the cold floor and pulled her to him, wrapping his arms tightly around her and tucking her head under his chin.

He rocked her slowly, back and forth, for what felt like an eternity. He whispered all the things they were going to experience together once she awoke, He had to clear his throat more than once as his eyes burned with unshed tears. He hoped he was telling her the truth, that he wouldn't have to return to London with her in a state resembling death.

He occasionally heard Lewis's and Nigel's murmured

conversation coming from the library. Feeling desperate to do something, *anything*, he retrieved his telescriber from his pocket and sent a message to Samson. He was determined to get them all away from the cursed manor house and the evil that had brought about so much pain and loss. Before long, he heard the whir of the airship and, through the ruins, saw the familiar sight of the *Briar Rose* as Samson maneuvered her close to the building.

Daniel stood, cramped and stiff, but still holding Isla close, and made his way into the library where Lewis and Nigel worked side-by-side, reading from the spell book and combining ingredients from Malette's stash.

Lewis glanced up from his work. "Is that the airship?"

Daniel nodded. "I'm taking her aboard. As soon as you're finished, we can go."

Nigel frowned as he measured out a spice and added it to the small bowl on the table. "This will take a bit longer," he said, glancing at Daniel. "We're nearly finished mixing, but it needs to steep."

Daniel looked at the clock on the wall. "How much time?"

Lewis ran a finger down the page. "Fifteen minutes."

Daniel's heart thumped. "So, at most, we'll have a window of five minutes." He paused, thinking. "Can it steep aboard the airship?"

Nigel nodded and stirred the contents of the bowl with a small, wooden spoon. He looked at Lewis. "We have everything?"

Lewis consulted the book again and nodded. "Done."

Nigel grabbed the bag containing the spindle, and Lewis carefully lifted the bowl and spell book. As they left the library and made their way through the outer room to the collapsed wall, Daniel glanced at Nigel. "I'm sorry, Crowe."

Nigel shook his head and cast one last, unreadable look at the floor where his mother had died. "There is nothing for me here. Never has been. I'm better off."

Samson docked the *Briar Rose* and helped them aboard. The 'ton gently took Isla from Daniel and carried her to the wheelhouse. The three men followed: Daniel, anxious and unsettled; Nigel, winded and slow, and Lewis, carefully carrying the cure.

In the wheelhouse, Samson lay Isla on the settee near the windows, and Daniel mentally reviewed the past hour. They had done everything they possibly could. It had to be enough.

Please, let it be enough.

Lewis explained everything to Samson while both Daniel and Nigel watched the clock. The minutes ticked closer to the one o'clock hour, and for the first time in his life, Daniel felt faint.

Nigel finally lifted the bowl and swirled the contents. He gestured toward Isla. "Lift her up."

Daniel propped Isla against his arm and pulled her chin down with his thumb. Nigel slowly poured a small amount into her open mouth and, when it trickled down her throat without choking her, added more.

Daniel laid her back down and glanced at the clock over his shoulder. Seconds passed. He briefly closed his eyes, hoping Nigel's supposition about the time was right.

Lewis held out the small vial containing Malette's blood and the spindle, sharp and deadly and still stained red from piercing the witch's heart.

Without a word, Nigel took the spindle from Lewis and knelt next to Isla. Daniel knelt on her other side.

Nigel carefully lifted Isla's hand and stabbed the sharp end of it into her finger. Daniel extended his own finger, and Nigel did the same to him.

Daniel touched the blood welling on his fingertip to Isla's. Nigel unstopped the vial of Malette's blood and carefully poured out the single drop onto Daniel's and Isla's joined fingertips.

"Quickly now," Nigel said.

Daniel moved his hand to Isla's forehead and smeared the mass of dark red onto her smooth skin. He sucked in a deep breath, hoping the blood from Malette was enough, that all contributions were mixed in well enough, that somehow it would work.

Framing her face with his hands, he slowly bent over Isla and kissed her unresponsive lips. He closed his eyes against the tears that burned hot. He kept them tightly closed and remained connected to her, still, unmoving, for the space of a minute—then two.

The room was silent.

Her lips were still. She did not return his kiss.

Daniel felt a sob build in his throat, and his tears fell onto her closed eyelids. He clasped her close, hauling her into his arms and squeezing her so tightly he felt her ribs against his fingertips. He rocked slowly back and forth, her dead weight heavy against his arms.

The only sound in the room was his ragged breathing. It hadn't worked.

Chapter 37

Isla was swimming. She was deep beneath the surface of the nothing, the dark, but something was different. She surged upward with a speed she didn't recognize, had never felt. Her thoughts, fuzzy at first, sharpened to a razor point, and she was aware of herself, of her soul, in the darkness. Was this it, then? She was awake, yet not, soaring through the nothing. Was she under the curse forever? Was this to be her fate? Her mind echoed with Malette's final words.

You've lost. My son is avenged . . .

Still she flew upward, feeling wind that wasn't there against her face. Noise sounded from far away and drew closer, she flew ever faster, so fast she couldn't breathe.

She couldn't breathe!

She battled and clawed with everything she possessed to draw in a gasping breath, finally bursting free of the surface and into the light. She sucked in as much air as she could, lifting her arms to shove at the vise that gripped her so painfully she saw stars floating above her in the black night sky.

She sobbed, fighting to pull in one more breath, just one more . . .

"Isla!" Hands grabbed her head, and the tremendous pressure on her lungs eased. "Isla!" Daniel's face was inches from her own, his face soaked in tears, his expression a combination of pain and something else. Hope.

Her eyes widened. The wheelhouse. She was awake in the airship, and it was so very dark outside.

Daniel shook, his big, strong frame trembling with his sobs. He pulled her closer to his chest, and she put her arms around his head and neck. This was heaven, her heaven. If she was dead, she wasn't going to complain. Confusion continued to bounce around in her brain, and she looked again at the black sky outside, and then at the clock on the wall.

The clock that clearly showed the time at 1:00.

It was past midnight, and she was awake.

"What happened?" she managed.

Daniel drew in a ragged breath, and she wondered if he was experiencing a war memory. She rubbed his hair with a hand that wasn't tingly, wasn't heavy. She felt strong.

"Shh, Daniel, it is fine. Everything is fine. Do you know where you are?"

"Do I . . . ?" He gradually stilled and slowly pulled back.

"Oh, Daniel! Dear man, what happened?" His face was ravaged in grief and shock. There was something she needed to remember. Something Malette said about the curse . . .

She moved her hand from Daniel's tear-stained face to her forehead. She was so confused. She felt something sticky on her fingers and looked, noting red.

Blood.

The clock.

The dark night sky.

Her finger throbbed and she lifted her left hand. Blood smeared down her forefinger and onto her wrist.

She looked at Daniel, shock settling in. Her heart beat faster, and her finger throbbed in time.

A kiss from one who loves you equally . . .

"Who kissed me?"

"I did," Daniel whispered. He wiped his face, smearing red along his cheek from his pierced finger. "I didn't know what else to do."

Nigel stood up and shook his head. "Lackwit wouldn't admit he loves you. We might have avoided all of this horrible mess if you'd both just said something!"

Isla felt herself blush. "I didn't want to tell you because you would have felt awful for not returning the feeling, and I couldn't have you live your life believing you failed me. You're a good man who rescues the strays, and I knew you would take it all on yourself . . ." She trailed off, lifting her shoulder in a helpless shrug.

Daniel laughed and pulled her close, planting a quick kiss on her lips. "Thank all things holy that Nigel and Lewis were here. I don't think I could have done this alone."

Isla felt her eyes burn again with tears, and this time one escaped.

Nigel cleared his throat and glanced away.

Isla was surprised to see Daniel touch a fingertip to his own eye. "Thank you," he murmured. "Were it not for you, Nigel, none of this could have happened." He shrugged and swallowed. "Isla would be sleeping," he whispered, "and I would be bereft. I am not a man with many friends," he continued, "but I am honored to count you three among them."

Daniel returned his gaze to Isla and smiled sheepishly. "I almost didn't kiss you in time."

"But you did."

His smile faded. "I suppose I thought you'd awaken immediately. It took several minutes, and I thought . . . I thought . . ."

"I know. I had to swim through the darkness, and then I couldn't breathe. I fear you were crushing my lungs."

"I was distraught." Daniel heaved a long, slow sigh and wrapped his arms carefully around her.

"I love you," she whispered.

He nodded and kissed her neck. "And I love you."

"Why did you not say anything to me?" She pulled back and looked at him. "You had to have known how I felt about you. Don't you have experience with these romantic imbroglios?"

Daniel coughed in embarrassment. "I wonder if you would retrieve a few fresh bandages, please, Lewis? Nigel was a bit aggressive with the finger-piercing."

Isla laughed, and she lifted her finger, which still throbbed like the devil. "I think of all the injuries I've sustained over the past few weeks, this one hurts the worst!" She wrapped herself closer to Daniel. "And the one I am most happy to have endured."

Chapter 38

Daniel instructed Samson to head directly for the cabin in the swamp where Quince and Bonadea had waited.

"Oh, my dear," Quince said as soon as they had all gathered in the wheelhouse later that night. He took Isla's hand and led her to the sofa. "You look much improved."

She smiled, exhausted but happy. "Thank you, Mr. Quince. I feel refreshed." She looked at the rest. "I am so grateful for all of you. You've saved me, and that is a debt I can never repay though I will spend the rest of my life trying. And Nigel—" She paused, tears gathering. "I am so sorry about everything. I am sorry for my part in anything that has caused you unhappiness."

Nigel shook his head. "I am the one who must apologize." He cleared his throat and addressed the small group. "I wish to clear the air between us."

"I wasn't aware it was muddled," Daniel said with a smile.

Nigel nodded but his face remained solemn. "I sabotaged

our flight to Port Lucy to delay Isla's arrival, as I'm sure you all suspected."

Daniel exhaled slowly. "I did, though I had no inkling of the motivation behind it."

"My mother is—was—unpredictable, often left home on a whim. She tracked me with her staff and globe, and she always knew my location to the tiniest degree, while I had only a vague sense of where she was at any particular time. When we left England, I knew she was at the mansion, but I needed time. I was at a loss in deciding how to keep Isla away from her but still obtain the things she would need for the cure."

"So you sabotaged the ship to buy time?" Lewis clarified.

He nodded. "It was a risk, but then I also knew that you would be forced to put the ship down somewhere for the others to shift over the Full Moon Phase. Malette knew I was approaching, of course, but her talents weren't limitless—she didn't know Isla was on board. I figured she may search me out and demand to know why I'd abandoned my post, but I was desperate. The closer we flew to Port Lucy, the sicker I felt. I'd been trailing Isla for nearly a year, had come to know her character from afar. She did not deserve the curse that had been placed upon her."

He looked at Isla. "Somewhere in the middle of my family mess was a smart woman who did the right thing for everyone all the time. I thought she was ridiculous at first. I couldn't believe someone with a kind heart, a genuinely kind heart, actually existed."

Crowe lifted his shoulder, and a muscle moved in his jaw. "And Isla was flying straight to my mother. At the time, I felt

I had no allies, could rely only on my own judgment, which was little more than panic."

He shook his head with a half-laugh. "Isla found her way, barefoot and weaponless, through a forested jungle that has taken more than one victim to his death. Of all women in the world, I could not have intentionally chosen a worse candidate for abduction and a lecture about what she ought to do. I should have given her information about Malette months ago. I should have included all of you in my speculations concerning my mother's possible reaction."

"So your vitriol about shifters really was just a performance," Quince said.

Nigel nodded. "An effective cover. And when I needed to 'perform,' I envisioned my brother." He smiled, jaded, then cleared his throat and addressed the three shifters. "I wish you all the best of everything, and I am better for knowing you. I thank you for your friendship despite my churlish behavior."

Quince, Bonadea, and Lewis each shook hands with him.

As Isla thought back on their rushed departure from London and the odd mix of personalities aboard, she would never have predicted such an outcome in a million years.

"I, again, offer my thanks to you all," she said, looking around the room at each of her friends. "And Nigel, thank you for the socks and for breaking me out of the dungeon." She smiled at him, thinking of the things she'd learned about him the last few days. "I used to believe you were quite odious."

He laughed, a genuine sound of mirth, one she'd never heard from him. "I am quite odious. But then, you've met my mother so it stands to reason, no?"

Daniel shook his head. "You are not your mother."

Isla agreed. "Definitely not."

Their journey back to England was filled with card games, conversation, and even hours of comfortable silence. Isla found the companionship comforting. Nigel was returning to England with Isla and Daniel, and though she missed Quince, Lewis, and Bonadea, she was happy they were settled into their new lives.

She made notes on her experiences with Lewis and his reaction to the deep hypnotherapy, as well as notes about her tie to Malette as she was dying. She made new lists, detailing such things as "Islands to Visit for Future Holidays," "Ten Reasons Why Melody Is Not the World's Worst Sister," and "Ten Ways Isla Will Be a Better Sister."

Nigel drew anything and everything in his sketchbook. When he reluctantly showed her and Daniel his drawings, Isla pretended amazement as though she was seeing them for the first time. As Nigel grew more comfortable in their company, Isla realized how funny he was. His sense of humor before had always lent itself to . . . well, nothing like humor. Now the cutting jabs and jaded remarks had a softer edge— there was no malice behind it, just a delightfully dry wit.

Daniel caught up on business matters—paperwork and details he'd neglected on the voyage to Port Lucy—and more often than not, the group gathered together in the wheelhouse to visit. The sunny hours were bright, and cloudy hours were cozy.

Isla loved to sit in the comfortable window seats high above the rest of the ship, watching Daniel monitor the weather and fly the ship. She would often daydream about shoving him against the wall and kissing him senseless as he'd done to her all those weeks ago.

They were only a few days away from arriving in England when Daniel made a surprise announcement one evening after lunch.

"I think it is time that we had a dance on deck under the stars tonight."

Isla smiled in surprise. Nigel and Samson stared.

Daniel shrugged. "We were supposed to have a ball on the beach for your birthday, remember? And I ruined it. So I've decided to make it up to you. Please meet on deck this evening at six o'clock for dinner."

Isla looked at Samson. "Is this your idea?"

Samson shook his head, eyebrows raised. "Amazingly, no."

Daniel checked the Victrola on the deck, making certain it wouldn't fall over if the ship caught a burst of wind. He straightened his sleeves, secured his cuff links, and snapped his formal captain's jacket firmly into place.

Nigel appeared on deck in his finery, his nostrils already flaring with irritation. "I've never danced a day in my life. I'll man the Victrola."

"Nonsense. You just sway around; there's nothing to it." Daniel slapped his shoulder.

He turned to see Isla emerge from the stairwell, poised but uncertain on the top step. She wore the blue skirt and white blouse he remembered from their vacation on the island, but she'd also added an outer corset—one from Port Lucy, he noted, not one with pockets for throwing stars—that accentuated her assets to perfection.

As he approached, her eyes widened. "My goodness," she said, "I'd forgotten how commanding you look in your finery!"

He was silently relieved by her approval. They had all become informal in the days since leaving Port Lucy, and he remembered her first reaction to him in his shirtsleeves and breeches. That she approved of his entire formal ensemble appealed to the masculine sense of pride he usually pretended he didn't have.

"And you are a vision of loveliness." He kissed her hand with a flourish. "As you have enjoyed lamentably limited time dancing and flirting, I thought it appropriate for you to refresh your skills before we return home."

"Because I will suddenly be spending so much more time at balls and soirees?" She raised a brow, smiling. "I am on the shelf, or have you not heard?"

"Fine wine is never ideal when first bottled."

She laughed out loud. "It is good that I didn't know you as a younger girl. I would have been unable to string two words together."

He bowed and led her out onto the deck. She spied Nigel, and her eyes sparkled.

"Mr. Crowe, how mysterious and dashing you are, with just a hint of danger! You do turn out nicely when not manacled to a wall." She winked, and he chuckled.

He took her fingers and placed a kiss on her hand. He paused, seeming to search for words and coming up short. "You are beautiful, Dr. Cooper," he finally murmured. "And kind. And a very good friend."

She blinked and quietly exhaled. "Likewise, Mr. Crowe."

Samson appeared on deck from the galley, a waiter's linen draped over his arm. "Honored guests, your meal awaits."

Isla fairly glowed as she threaded one hand around each gentleman's arm. From the moment they sat at the table together and Samson served them a limited meal of white fish and potatoes, Daniel observed her with new eyes. He paid attention to every movement, every glance, the smallest of gestures toward him. She placed her hand on his when teasing. She blushed, repeatedly, when he plied her with compliments or murmured an innuendo in an undertone. She sought out Nigel's contributions during the course of polite conversation but simultaneously leaned closer to Daniel.

She joked about the smallest of details from stories he'd shared and even after a conversation with Crowe or Samson, her eyes found their way back to him. There was a familiarity about her behavior with him that should have taken months to achieve. He could only attribute it to the inordinate amount of pressure they'd been under from the first moment she caught his arm and demanded passage. She'd eased him back from the brink of madness when he'd gone mentally back to the war. She'd trusted him to comfort her through her most vulnerable times, honored him by allowing him to stand guard over her.

He blinked when she asked him something. "I'm sorry?"

"I believe I was promised a dance," she said.

"It would be my greatest pleasure." He pulled her chair out as she stood and escorted her from the meal.

Samson hurried over to the Victrola and spun the crank. He lifted the needle and strains of a waltz sounded from the large horn.

Daniel bowed, Isla curtsied, and with her hand in his and his arm around her back, he stepped into the familiar movements, surprised—and yet not—at the ease of it. She was physically adept, even while still recovering from the awful injuries Malette had inflicted, comfortable in her skin and accustomed to efficiency of movement in her work and training. They moved together without a stumble, without a single misstep.

The night took on a surreal feel—Samson had strung the beach lights across the deck, and the stars blinked through clouds. The sensation was flight, untethered by anything.

The waltz ended, and though Daniel slowed their movements, he didn't fully stop.

She met his eyes and lightly arched a brow. "Are you going to kiss me tonight, Captain Pickett? Perhaps steal one from me behind a potted palm?"

His lips quirked. "A pity there are no potted palms on deck."

She shrugged airily. "Yes. A pity indeed. But perhaps we don't need one. We seem to be quite alone."

He glanced around the deck and realized Crowe and Samson were indeed absent. He could only imagine Crowe had suggested it to the 'ton, and Daniel vowed to thank the man later.

He stilled, one arm around her, and placed his hand alongside her cheek. He lowered his mouth to hers, slowly, wanting the moment to last forever. He touched her lips with his and closed his eyes, his heart thumping at her sigh. She wound her arms around his neck, and he pulled her close, devouring her like one starved, and yet realizing he could never get enough.

She gripped his hair and met his ardor, and he smiled against her lips. "All you needed was to ask, Dr. Cooper."

"I would never want to seem too forward, Captain Pickett," she said, slightly winded.

"Am I hurting you?" He ran his hand gently over her shoulder where the dragon had sunk her claws in deep.

She shook her head, her lips looking delightfully kiss-swollen in the soft light. "Do you know how badly I would have to be hurting right now to protest?"

He laughed softly and bent down to lift her into his arms. He carried her to a nearby deck chair and settled onto it, holding her. She laid her head on his shoulder, and he tipped his head back. The sky flew by overhead, and now that they were still, he noticed the chill. He sat up and maneuvered out of his jacket, smiling at her laughter as he nearly dumped her onto the deck. They settled back into the chair, and he draped his coat over her.

"We'll stay out here until you're too cold," he murmured.

"This is perfect. We'll stay here until your legs are asleep." She turned her face to his neck, nuzzling with her nose and placing a soft kiss above his collar.

He lost track of the time. They looked at the stars, he told her about the origins of his love of airships and sailing, and she told him about the first flight she'd ever taken—which had been on a Pickett airship.

"Little did I know," she whispered.

"Little did you know." He kissed her forehead.

She tilted her head back and reached up, pulling his mouth to hers.

He was lost, completely and utterly, until he heard a rough throat-clearing. At the far end of the deck, Nigel Crowe climbed the stairs to the wheelhouse with Samson on his heels.

Isla lifted her head and looked at the other two, and then back at him. She bit her lip, but then smiled, and he was sure he'd have seen a blush if the light had been bright enough.

She touched her forehead to his. "Thank you, Daniel Pickett, for taking such good care of me. I would have you know it has meant the world to me. You mean the world to me."

His throat burned, and he captured her lips one more time. "And you to me, Isla Cooper. I cherish the day you bullied your way into my life."

She closed her eyes and smiled. She wound her arms around his broad shoulders and squeezed gently. "Smartest thing I've ever done in my life was threaten you with exposure of your nefarious deeds."

"Smartest thing I've ever done was capitulating to you." He lifted his head and winked. "Besides, you were wearing all that weaponry. I could hardly resist."

Her lips twitched at the corners. "You removed my weaponry, if I recall."

"And if I recall, I missed some. You held out."

"I had to! Leaving a girl utterly defenseless like that . . ."

"You clawed your way barefoot through a tropical jungle and then faced down an entity of true evil, all without a single weapon." He shook his head. "I've experienced enough extreme emotion in the last two months to last an eternity. Please do not ever leave me."

"Never."

"Will you marry me? You must."

She smiled. "Of course I will. And not just because you saved me from the dark."

"Good. Tonight, then."

She blinked. "Tonight? You want to marry tonight?"

"Yes. We'll use Crowe. As an agent of the Crown, he's authorized."

She was flabbergasted. "Daniel—"

"We managed to bring you back from the brink of oblivion and have waited long enough; we are sleeping in the same bed tonight. I'll not be the one to tarnish your good name, so we will marry, and then not only will people not disapprove of us sharing a suite, they will wish us well."

She gave him a faux pout. "You know how fussy I am about important society events. I cannot believe you will not be even a bit sensitive to my socialite proclivities."

"Mm-hm. Also, I don't care what you wear as long as you include the thigh dagger."

She laughed, tipping her head back and genuine joy rippled through her entire frame. She was strong, whole, and free. And very much in love. "For you, Captain Pickett, I'll even include the throwing stars."

"Yes, please." He smiled and lowered his lips to hers.

"One more," she murmured.

"One more."

Acknowledgments

As always, my heartfelt thanks to my family, my writing partners, Jennifer Moore and Josi Kilpack, and to the wonderful people at Shadow Mountain: Chris, Heidi, Lisa, Richard, Heather, Malina, Sarah, and Jill. A million thanks also to my agents, Bob DiForio and Pam Victorio, for their work on my behalf.

A special and tender acknowledgement goes to the wonderful readers who have been so supportive of this steampunk venture, who loved *Beauty and the Clockwork Beast*, and who couldn't wait to hear Daniel's story. To fans of Disney's animated *Sleeping Beauty*, I hope you find the gems sprinkled throughout this book that are my nod to the classic cartoon.

A special thanks also goes to my daughter, Nina, for helping me with plot snags and brainstorming. It was her idea that the dragon could just combust at the end. ("I mean, she's a dragon, right?")

Discussion Questions

1. The origins of the "Sleeping Beauty" fairy tale date back to 1697. Why does this particular story have such lasting appeal? What elements of the fairy tale are present in *Kiss of the Spindle*? Where do the two stories diverge?

2. Steampunk is a specific genre that blends a classic setting with steam-powered or gear-powered technology. What other steampunk novels have you read? In what ways did the steampunk elements in the story help establish the setting, develop the characters, or advance the plot? What was your favorite steampunk invention?

3. Isla and Nigel have an antagonistic working relationship at the beginning of the novel, though by the end, they have found more common ground. Have you ever worked with someone who was hard to get along with? How were you able to resolve your differences?

4. Family relationships play an important role in the story. Discuss Isla's relationship with her mother and sister as it compares to Nigel's relationship with his mother and

brother. Are they healthy relationships? How do our relationships with our family help shape our character?

5. Daniel's experience in the war left him suffering the effects of PTSD. Isla's ability as an empath allow her to help him during an difficult time. Do you know anyone who is still suffering from a traumatic event? In what ways have you been able to help that person?

6. The characters are able to celebrate Isla's birthday on a lovely tropical island. Where has been your favorite place to go on a vacation? What made it memorable? What is your favorite birthday memory?

7. The three shifters—Quince, Bonadea, and Lewis—are all taking a risk traveling to Port Lucy on Daniel's airship, yet they willingly do so in order to protect their families. Have you ever been asked to make a sacrifice to protect someone you love?

8. Isla, Daniel, Lewis, and Nigel literally slay a dragon at the end of the story. What kinds of dragons have you had to slay in your life?

About the Author

NANCY CAMPBELL ALLEN is the author of fifteen published novels and numerous novellas, which span genres from contemporary romantic suspense to historical fiction. In 2005, her work won the Utah Best of State award, and she received a Whitney Award for *My Fair Gentleman*. She has presented at numerous writing conferences and events since her first book was released in 1999. Nancy received a BS in Elementary Education from Weber State University. She loves to read, write, travel, and research, and enjoys spending time laughing with family and friends. She is married and the mother of three children. Visit her at nancycampbellallen.com.